PENGUIN CLASSICS

THE PENGUIN BOOK OF DEMONS

SCOTT G. BRUCE is a professor of history at Fordham University. He is the editor of *The Penguin Book of the Undead*, *The Penguin Book of Hell*, and *The Penguin Book of Dragons*, and has written four books about the abbey of Cluny. He has lectured throughout the United States, Canada, and Europe, and has held visiting research appointments at the Technische Universität Dresden, in Germany; the Universiteit Gent, in Belgium; Emmanuel College, University of Cambridge, in the United Kingdom; and the École des hautes études en sciences sociales, in France. He worked his way through college as a grave digger.

For Philip Pullman,
who stole our daemons back

Hell is empty,
And all the devils are here

—William Shakespeare, *The Tempest*, Act 1, Scene 2

Devils are depicted with bats' wings and good angels with birds' wings not because anyone holds that moral deterioration would be likely to turn feathers into membrane, but because most men like birds better than bats.

—C. S. Lewis, *The Screwtape Letters* (postscript)

Contents

THE PENGUIN BOOK OF DEMONS

LEGENDS OF THE FALL:
REBEL ANGELS IN ANCIENT JUDAISM

I AM LEGION:
DEMONS IN ANCIENT CHRISTIAN THOUGHT

APES OF GOD:
DEMONS IN EARLY MODERN EUROPE

SERPENT KINGS AND ANIMAL SPIRITS:
DEMONS OF THE EAST

THE ALLURE OF THE INCUBUS:
DEMON LOVERS THROUGH THE AGES

Creeping Horrors:
Malevolent Spirits in the
Modern Imagination

Introduction

Evil spirits are ubiquitous in world literature as the invisible agents of all kinds of human maladies. This volume sets out to gather the most formative and influential stories about their origins and activities, primarily in the western tradition, but with frequent reference to the rich repositories of uncanny anecdotes preserved in Middle Eastern, Asian, and Native American religions and folklore.

The English word "demon" is Greek in origin; its Latin cognate informed the same word in many European vernaculars (*le demon, der Dämon, il demone, el demonio*). In Greco-Roman antiquity, demons were not malevolent. Pagan poets and philosophers from Hesiod to Plato to Apuleius praised the activities of these incorporeal spirits as trustworthy guides of human decisions and as intermediaries who carried messages between mortals and the gods they worshipped. In ancient Judaism, however, questions about the origin of evil led to answers that implicated demons as nefarious actors in a cosmology informed by legends about a revolt against God in Heaven, disobedient angels who lusted after human women, and a great king named Solomon who mastered diabolical forces through the power of a magic ring. Whether they were understood as rebel spirits loyal to Satan or as the ghosts of the Nephilim, the illicit offspring of divine and mortal intercourse whom God destroyed with a global deluge, demons acquired a negative association far removed from their benign pagan origins. Demoted from their role as voices of conscience and couriers of prayer, they betrayed their sacred trusts, demeaned their divine status, and manufactured maladies to the detriment of humankind.

These traditions, both pagan and Jewish, informed the writings of the earliest Christians. Apostolic authors did not dispute the power of Satan and his minions, but struggled to overcome them in a world saturated by their evil influence. Christ's denial of the Devil's temptations in the desert provided a template for his followers to resist demonic forces at every turn and thereby earn their place as legitimate successors of his earthly mission. There was no systematic demonology in ancient Christian thought, but the Hebrew scriptures provided guiding principles for the early apologists. "For all the gods of the Gentiles are devils" (Psalm 95:5) was a rallying cry for Christian writers, who blackened the reputation of pagan gods with the claim that they were malevolent entities in disguise. Magic and idolatry were nothing more than deceptions that led the devotees of these gods to perdition. Augustine and other church fathers laid the foundations of medieval demonology in their refutation of the last generations of pagan philosophers, who clung tenaciously to their positive estimation of these aerial spirits. Adapting the legend of the rebel angels from ancient Judaism, Christian authors asserted that Satan and his minions were not evil in nature but fell from grace because of their own free will. Likewise, the influence of demons over mortals depended entirely on human consent, but their supernatural abilities gave them the upper hand in this contest of wills.

The late ancient world was a battleground between the soldiers of Christ and the armies of Satan. Spiritual combat was the primary motif in the hagiographical literature that extolled the virtues of desert saints like Antony and his western emulators like Martin and Guthlac. While diabolical influences dominated ordinary Christians, often through the possession of their bodies, the sign of the cross was the saint's riposte that wrested control away from the demons and reaffirmed Christ's victory over them. Early medieval authorities populated their edifying stories with garrulous devils in many shapes and sizes. These spirits of the air flitted easily between our world, where they lured the living into temptations, and their infernal homeland, where they tormented sinful souls in Hell. As Christianity made advances into the pagan countryside of western Europe, preachers extolled the protecting power of baptism against demonic incursions and warned their parishioners that the ancient gods were evil frauds, who were nothing less than malevolent spirits claiming the names of legendary villains and demanding worship due only to God.

After the turn of the first millennium, the currency of demons as tools for teaching the faithful remained undiminished. Founded on the authority of the New Testament and the church fathers, medieval demonology developed hand in hand with the valorization of the cults of powerful intercessory saints, especially the Virgin Mary. After the Fourth Lateran Council (1215) decreed a renewed responsibility among all Christians to make confession and celebrate the mass regularly, stories about demons increasingly called attention to the personal accountability of foolhardy people who initiated contact with them, notably necromancers and magicians, and the horrible fate that awaited them. Pacts with demons to achieve some worldly end bound hapless humans to diabolical masters. The manuals of late medieval inquisitors were replete with cautionary tales drawn from the testimony of condemned witches about the sexual demands that such contracts could entail. The question whether divine and mortal beings could mate and produce offspring was an old one, but it persisted in stories and songs about the allure of demon lovers, the preternatural powers of their children, and the dangerous costs of such unnatural congress.

While the appearance and activities of premodern European demons have dominated the western imagination for centuries, other cultures across the globe have nurtured stories about capricious spirits that play comparable roles in their respective societies. The unpredictable jinn of the Arabian Peninsula probably predated the advent of Islam in the seventh century, but they survived as a literary motif in renowned story cycles crafted by Muslim authors, in which King Solomon also played a prominent role. The Greek culture of medieval Byzantium feared a female child-eating demon known as the Gellou above all others. The legend of her depredations began on the island of Lesbos and have persisted in rural Greece down to the present day. Across Asia, stories about indigenous demons circulated long before the grip of great religious systems took hold. These tales traveled freely along the trade routes that connected the coast of the Mediterranean with the grasslands of eastern China and beyond. North America was also replete with oral traditions about malevolent spirits, many of which did not appear in writing until European settlers recorded them. In their manifold arts of depredation, all of these demons gave voice to the fears and anxieties of the cultures that created them.

While Protestants once cast aspersions on Catholic demonology as the aggregate of medieval superstition in the age of the Reformation, many Christian denominations in the present day still embrace habits of belief about the reality of demons that would have been legible to premodern Europeans. Popular preachers like the Evangelical televangelist Oral Roberts (1918–2009) and Southern Baptist minister Billy Graham (1918–2018) repeatedly evoked Christ's mandate to the apostles to "cast out devils" (Matthew 10:8) during their ministries. It is not surprising that the practice of exorcism remains popular in modern Adventist and Pentecostal traditions throughout the world. The popularity of the film *The Exorcist* (dir. William Friedkin, 1973) heightened the fear of demonic possession and increased the demand for this ritual, especially among Evangelical Christians. It also left its mark on popular culture. To take one example, a musical collaboration between Brian Eno and David Byrne in 1981 (*My Life in the Bush of Ghosts*) included a song called "The Jezebel Spirit," which featured a vocal sample of a rite of exorcism performed in contemporary New York City played over looping rhythms influenced by African and Middle Eastern traditions. The industry of modern exorcists reminds us that many people throughout the world still blame their physical and spiritual maladies on the schemes of demons; the Devil's work is never done.

Thriving on lies and false promises, demons have become even more insidious in an age when social media facilitates the rapid diffusion of misinformation. Accusing religious and political rivals of participation in diabolical plots is currently the most popular iteration of demonic activity in contemporary discourse. This strategy of defamation succeeds in two ways. It discredits one's enemies as the nefarious agents in an indisputably harmful agenda, while simultaneously reducing complex problems in need of reasoned debate to an unequivocal judgment about an opponent's moral standing. In their retreat from modern rationalism, demons have found a haven in the private thoughts of troubled minds. The belief in "inner demons"—invisible entities that whisper frenzied and destructive ideas in our heads—is the last vestige of the centuries-old traditions collected in this book about the form and function of evil spirits in human societies.

SCOTT G. BRUCE

Suggestions for Further Reading

Chang, Chun-shu, and Shelley Hsueh-lun Chang. *Redefining History: Ghosts, Spirits, and Human Society in P'u Sung-ling's World, 1640–1715*. Ann Arbor: University of Michigan Press, 1998.

Clark, Stuart. *Thinking with Demons: The Idea of Witchcraft in Early Modern Europe*. Oxford: Clarendon Press, 1997.

Harkins, Angela Kim, Kelley Coblentz Bautch, and John C. Endres, eds. *The Watchers in Jewish and Christian Traditions*. Minneapolis: Fortress Press, 2014.

Harte, Jeremy. *Cloven Country: The Devil and the English Landscape*. London: Reaktion Books, 2022.

Kiessling, Nicolas. *The Incubus in English Literature: Provenance and Progeny*. Seattle: Washington State University Press, 1977.

Proctor, Travis W. *Demonic Bodies and the Dark Ecologies of Early Christian Culture*. Oxford: Oxford University Press, 2022.

Rampton, Martha. *Trafficking with Demons: Magic, Ritual, and Gender from Late Antiquity to 1000*. Ithaca, NY: Cornell University Press, 2021.

Ruys, Juanita Feros. *Demons in the Middle Ages*. Kalamazoo, MI: ARC Humanities Press, 2017.

Simon, Ed. *Devil's Contract: A History of the Faustian Bargain*. New York: Melville House, 2024.

White, David Gordon. *Daemons Are Forever: Contacts and Exchanges in the Eurasian Pandemonium*. Chicago: University of Chicago Press, 2021.

Acknowledgments

The idea for *The Penguin Book of Demons* belongs to my editor, John Siciliano, who has been a supportive collaborator in my writing for Penguin Classics for the past decade. Professor Paul Cobb (University of Pennsylvania) curated chapter 5 on the Islamic jinn, and Professor Richard P. H. Greenfield (Queens University) wrote the introductions and rendered the translations in chapter 6 on the Byzantine Gellou. I am grateful to them both for their expertise. Three PhD candidates in history at Fordham University provided assistance as well. Benjamin A. Bertrand and W. Tanner Smoot translated some of the medieval Latin texts. They also proofread the manuscript with great care alongside Amanda Racine. I appreciate their help and camaraderie. Anne, Mira, and Vivienne heard many of these stories about demons at the dinner table. Their patience with my infernal pursuits has been nothing less than heroic.

The Penguin Book
of Demons

LEGENDS OF THE FALL

Rebel Angels in Ancient Judaism

The wastelands of the ancient Near East teemed with dangerous supernatural beings. The Egyptian Book of the Dead *warned of tomb guardians who lay in wait for anyone presumptuous enough to intrude upon their sacred space without knowledge of the proper rites or evidence of the ritual purity required to enter. In Mesopotamia, incantations intoned with trembling lips and amulets clutched with anxious hands warded off the invisible spirits that roamed the desert steppe and protected against the lethal sting of snake and scorpion that they caused. The ancient Israelites shared this belief that malevolent, semidivine creatures lurked in the darkness beyond their settlements, like the night hag Lilith (Isaiah 34:14) and the "hairy ones" who danced in the ruins of cities forsaken by God (Isaiah 13:21). Chief among them was Azazel, the desert demon to whom they sent the scapegoat ritually laden with their iniquities and driven into the wastes bound for destruction on the Day of Atonement (Leviticus 16:7–10 and 20–22). God could command these superhuman beings to do his bidding, like the "Destroyer" sent to slay the firstborn sons of Egypt to compel Pharoah to free the Israelites from bondage (Exodus 12:21–36) and the "Adversary" known as Satan, who tormented Job to test his faith (Job 2:1–10). The Hebrew scriptures hinted darkly that these spirits were the product of the illicit union between "sons of God" and human women (Genesis 6:1–4), but it was only centuries later in the Second Temple period (516 BCE–70*

CE) *that Jews wove a tapestry of stories to explain the origin of demons. These tales implicated rebel angels who had seduced mortals and spawned a race of terrible giants, the Nephilim, whose malicious spirits caused ruin for humankind.*

THE MYSTERY
OF THE NEPHILIM[1]

Attributed to the Jewish patriarch Moses, the Book of Genesis (composed in the sixth or fifth century BCE) commenced the Hebrew scriptures with the story of God's creation of the universe, the world, and humankind. Tricked by the serpent, Adam and Eve committed the first sin, for which God expelled them from the Garden of Eden. The wickedness of their descendants so disappointed God that he decided to wipe out his creations with a great deluge. He spared only Noah, whom he instructed to build an ark to preserve himself, his family, and two of every bird and beast to replenish the earth after it had been washed clean by forty days and nights of rain. The role of the Nephilim in this tradition is ambiguous and mysterious. Before the flood, the Book of Genesis hinted that members of God's heavenly court ("sons of God") had intermingled with mortal women to produce a race of creatures called "the Nephilim," a Hebrew word that later Greek and Latin translators rendered as "giants." These translators took their cue from the Book of Numbers, which related how Moses had sent spies into the land of Canaan, who returned with an ominous report that it was inhabited by the Nephilim: "The land which we have viewed, devoureth its inhabitants: the people, that we beheld, are of a tall stature. There we saw certain monsters of the sons of Enac, of the giant kind: in comparison of whom, we seemed like locusts" (Numbers 13:32–33). The Book of Genesis implied that the sexual commerce between angels and humans that produced the Nephilim was such a terrible transgression

that it moved God to sadness and prompted his decision to
destroy the world with the great flood.

And after humankind had begun to multiply upon the earth
and had produced daughters, the sons of God, seeing that
these daughters were beautiful, took wives for themselves
from whomever they chose, and God said, "My spirit will not
remain in humankind forever, for he is flesh and his days will
be one hundred and twenty years." There were, however, giants on the earth in those days. Indeed, afterwards the sons of
God joined with the daughters of men and they bore children.
These were the mighty men of old, men of renown. Seeing
that there was much wickedness of humankind on the earth
and that every thought of their heart turned toward evil all the
time, God regretted that he had made humankind on the earth
and, moved within by the sadness of his heart, he said, "I will
wipe out humankind, whom I have created, from the face of
the earth, from human beings even to the animals, from the
reptile even to the birds of the sky, for I am sorry that I have
made them."

THE PRISON OF
THE FALLEN[1]

The seduction of mortal women by divine angels and the fate of their offspring, the Nephilim, captured the imagination of Jewish writers in the Second Temple period (516 BCE–70 CE). Chief among them was the author of the Book of Enoch, an apocalyptic text allegedly written by the great-grandfather of Noah, but actually a composite work composed between 300 and 100 BCE. The first section of the text, known as the Book of the Watchers, dealt with the origin of evil in God's creation. It described how a group of angels violated the natural order by lusting after human women, how these unions produced monstrous children who wreaked havoc upon the earth, and how they shared knowledge of metallurgy, cosmetics, enchantments, astrology, and other hidden arts with humankind, much to their detriment. Appalled by the corruption of his creation, God instructed Enoch, "the scribe of righteousness," to announce his judgment of punishment to the rebel angels. Enoch returned with the angels' petition for mercy, which God refused. The prophet then received a vision of the terrible wasteland beyond Heaven where the angels would be imprisoned until the Day of Judgment. The fate of the Nephilim was also grim. After the destruction of their physical bodies, their incorporeal spirits were doomed to linger on the earth to cause hardship to humankind. Later authors interpreted the punishment of the Nephilim as the origin of demonkind.

And it came to pass when the children of men had multiplied that in those days beautiful and attractive daughters were born to them. And the angels, the children of heaven, saw them and lusted after them, and they said to one another: "Come, let us choose for ourselves wives from among the children of men and let us have children with them." And Semyaz, who was their leader, said to them: "I fear that perhaps you will not agree to do this deed, and I alone will have to pay the penalty for this great sin." And they all answered him, saying: "Let us all swear an oath and bind ourselves by mutual promises not to abandon this plan, but to do it." Then they all swore together and bound themselves by oaths upon it. There were altogether two hundred angels who descended in the days of Jared onto the summit of Mount Hermon.[2] And these are the names of their leaders, their chiefs of ten: Semyaz, Arakeb, Rame'el, Tam'el, Ram'el, Dan'el, Ezeqel, Baraqyal, As'el, Armaros, Batar'el, Anan'el, Zaqe'el, Sasomaspe'el, Kestar'el, Tur'el, Yamayol, and Arazyal.[3]

And they all took wives for themselves, and they began to go among them and to defile themselves with them, and they taught them charms, incantations, the cutting of roots, and the properties of plants. And the women became pregnant, and they gave birth to great giants, whose height was three thousand cubits.[4] These giants consumed all the resources of the people. And when the people could no longer sustain them, the giants turned against them and devoured them. And they began to sin against birds, wild beasts, reptiles, and fish, and to devour one another's flesh, and drink each other's blood. Then the earth made its accusation against the lawless ones.

And Azaz'el taught the people how to make swords and knives and shields and breastplates and made known to them the metals of the earth and the art of fashioning them into bracelets and ornaments, and the art of cosmetics involving all kinds of costly stones and colorful tinctures. And there arose much godlessness, and they committed adultery and were led astray and became corrupt in all their ways. Amasras taught incantations and the knowledge of herbs; and Armaros, the casting of enchantments; and Baraqyal, astrology; and Kokarer'el, the constellations; and Tam'el, the knowledge of the stars; and Asder'el, the course of the moon. And as the people perished, they cried out, and their cry went up to heaven.

Then the archangels Michael, Raphael, and Gabriel looked down from heaven and saw how much blood was shed upon the earth and how much lawlessness was wrought there. And they said one to another: "The earth cries with a voice of the utmost lament up to the gates of heaven. And now to you, O holy ones of heaven, the souls of people make their case, saying, 'Bring our cause before the Most High.'" And they said to the Lord of the ages: "Lord of lords, God of gods, king of kings, and God of the ages, the throne of your glory endures for all the generations of the ages, and your name is holy and glorious and blessed for all the ages! You have made all things, and you have power over all things and all things are naked and open in your sight, and you see all things, and nothing can hide itself from you. You see what Azaz'el has done, who has taught all forms of unrighteousness on the earth and revealed the eternal secrets that were preserved in heaven, which people were striving to learn. They have gone to the daughters of the people upon the earth, and have slept with the women, and have defiled themselves, and revealed to them all kinds of sins. And the women have borne giants, and the whole earth has been filled with blood and unrighteousness. And now, behold, the souls of those who have died are crying and making their case to the gates of heaven, and their lamentations have ascended and cannot cease because of the lawless deeds done on the earth. And you know all things before they come to pass, and you see these things and you suffer them, and yet you do not tell us what we should do about it."

Then the Most High, the Holy and Great One, spoke and sent Asuryal to the son of Lamech and said to him: "Go to Noah and tell him in my name 'Hide yourself!' and reveal to him the end that is approaching, that the whole earth will be destroyed, for a deluge is about to cover the land. And then instruct him how to escape, so that his seed may be preserved for all the generations of the world." And then the Lord said to Raphael: "Bind Azaz'el hand and foot, and cast him into the darkness and make an opening in the desert, which is in Duda'el, and cast him therein.[5] And place upon him rough and jagged rocks and cover him with darkness and let him abide there forever and cover his face, so that he may not see the light. And on the day of the great judgment, he will be cast into the fire. And heal the earth which the angels have corrupted and proclaim the healing of the earth, so that all the children of men may not perish because of all the secret things that the watchers have disclosed and have taught to their sons. The whole earth has been corrupted through the works that were taught by Azaz'el. To him ascribe all sin." And to Gabriel the Lord said: "Proceed against the bastards and the reprobates and against the children of adultery and destroy the children of the watchers. Send them against one another, so that they destroy each other in battle, for they will not have any length of days. And no request that they make of you will be granted to their fathers on their behalf, for they had hoped to live an eternal life, but each one of them will only live for five hundred years." And the Lord said to Michael: "Go, bind Semyaz and his companions, who fornicated with the women and defiled themselves with them in all their uncleanliness. And when their sons have slain one another and they have seen the destruction of their beloved ones, bind them fast for seventy generations underneath the valleys of the earth, until the judgment that lasts forever and ever is concluded. In those days, they will be led to the abyss of fire and to the torment and the prison, where they will be confined forever. And whoever will be condemned and destroyed will be bound together with them to the end of all generations. And destroy all the souls of pleasure and the children of the watchers because they have wronged mankind. Destroy all wrong from the face of the earth and let every evil work come to an end and let the plant of righteousness and truth appear and it will prove to be a blessing. The works of righteousness and truth will be planted in truth and joy forevermore.

And then shall all the righteous escape,
And they shall live until they produce thousands of children
And all the days of their youth and their old age
Shall they complete in peace.

"And then the whole earth will be tilled in righteousness and planted with trees and full of blessing. And pleasant trees will be planted on it, and they will plant vines on it and the vine that they plant there will yield wine in abundance and each measure of seed sown on it will produce a thousandfold and each measure of olives will yield ten presses of oil. And all the children of men will become righteous and all nations will offer adoration and will praise me and everyone will worship me. And the earth will be cleansed from all defilement and from all sin and from all punishment and from all torment. And in those days, I will open the store chambers of blessing that are in heaven to send them down upon the earth over the work and labor of the children of men. And truth and peace will be joined together throughout all the days of the world and throughout all the generations of men."

Before these things happened, Enoch was hidden and none of the children of the people knew where he was hidden and where he abided and what had become of him, but his activities had to do with the watchers and his days were with the holy ones.[6] And I, Enoch, was blessing the Lord of majesty and the King of the ages, and lo! God called upon me—Enoch the scribe—and said to me: "Enoch, you scribe of righteousness, go, and declare to the watchers who have left the high heaven, the holy eternal place, and have defiled themselves with women, and have done as the children of earth do, and have taken for themselves wives: 'You have caused great destruction on the earth. And you will have no peace nor forgiveness of sin and because you delight in your children, you will witness the murder of your beloved ones, and you will lament over the destruction of your children, and you will make supplication for eternity, but mercy and peace you will not attain.'"

And Enoch went and said to Azaz'el, "You will have no peace. A severe sentence has gone forth against you to put you in chains. And you will not have mercy nor any request granted to you, because of the unrighteousness that you have taught, and because of all the works of godlessness and unrighteousness and sin that you have shown to the people." Then I went and spoke to the watchers all together, and they were all afraid, and fear and trembling seized them. And they asked me to draw up a petition for them, so that they might find forgiveness, and to read their petition in the presence of the Lord of Heaven. For from that time forward they could not speak with him nor lift up their eyes to heaven because they were ashamed of their sins, for which they had been condemned. Then I wrote out their petition, and the prayer in regard to their spirits and their deeds individually and in regard to their requests that they should have forgiveness. And I went off and sat down at the waters of Dan, in the land of Dan, to the southwest of Hermon, where I read their petition until I fell asleep.[7] And behold a dream came to me, and visions fell down upon me, and I saw visions of punishment, and a voice came bidding me to tell it to the sons of heaven, and reprimand them. And when I woke up, I came to them, and they were all sitting together, weeping in Lesya'el, which is between Lebanon and Sanser, with their faces covered.[8] And I recounted to them all the visions that I had seen while I slept, and I began to speak the words of righteousness, and to reprimand the heavenly watchers.

I saw in my sleep what I will now say with a tongue of flesh and with the breath of my mouth, which the Great One has given to man to converse with and to understand with the heart. As He has created and given to the people the power of understanding the word of wisdom, so has He also created me and given to me the power of reprimanding the watchers, the children of heaven: "I wrote out your petition, and in my vision, it appeared in this way, that your petition will not be granted to you throughout all the days of eternity, and that judgment has been passed on you. Yes, your petition will not be granted to you. And from now on, you will not ascend into heaven for all eternity, and the decree has gone forth to bind you for all the days of the world. And you will see the destruction of your beloved sons and you will have no pleasure in them, but they will fall before you by the sword. And your petition on their behalf will not be granted, nor on your own behalf, even though you weep and pray and speak all the words contained in the document that I have written. And this vision was shown to me. Behold, in the vision, clouds invited me and a mist summoned me, and the course of the stars and the lightning sped and hastened me, and the winds in the vision caused me to fly and lifted me upward, and bore me into heaven. And I approached until I drew close to a wall that was built of crystals and surrounded by tongues of fire and it began to frighten me. And I went into the tongues of fire and drew close to a great house that was built of white marble and the walls of the house were like a mosaic made of white marble, and the floor was made of crystal. Its ceiling was like the path of the stars and the lightning, and between them were fiery cherubim and their heaven was as clear as water.[9] A wreath of fire surrounded the walls, and its portals blazed with flames. And I entered that house, and it was as hot as fire and as cold as ice. There were no delights of life there. Fear covered me and trembling gripped me. And as I quaked and trembled, I fell upon my face and I beheld a vision. And lo! there was a second house, greater than the first, and the portal stood open before me, and it was built of towering flames. And in every respect, it so exceeded the former house in splendor and magnificence and size that I cannot describe it. And its floor was composed of fire, and above it was lightning and the path of the stars, and its ceiling was also made of fire. And I looked and saw there a lofty throne. It looked like it was made of crystal, and it had wheels like the shining sun, and I heard the voice of the cherubim. And from underneath the throne came streams of flaming fire, so that I could not look upon it. And the Great Glory sat upon it and His raiment shone more brightly than the sun and was whiter than any snow. None of the angels could enter and look upon His face because of His magnificence and glory, and no flesh could behold Him. A curtain of flames was all around Him, and a great fire stood before Him, and none around Him could draw close to Him. Ten thousand times ten thousand stood before Him, yet he needed no counselor. And the most holy ones who were near to Him did not leave by night nor depart from Him. And up to that point, I was flat on my face, trembling, and the Lord called me with His own mouth, and said to me: 'Come here, Enoch, and hear my word.' And one of the holy ones came to me and roused me and made me rise up and approach the door and I bowed with my face downwards.

"And He answered and spoke to me, and I heard His voice: 'Fear not, Enoch, you righteous man and scribe of righteousness. Approach and hear my voice. And go, say to the watchers of heaven, who have sent you to intercede for them: "You should intercede for the people and not them for you. Why have you left the high, holy, and eternal heaven and lain down with women and defiled yourselves with the daughters of men and taken for yourselves wives and acted like the children of earth, and produced giants as your sons? And although you were holy, spiritual, and eternal, you have defiled yourselves with the blood of women and have produced children with the blood of flesh, and, like the children of men, you have lusted after flesh and blood just like those who die and perish. For this reason, I have given them wives, so that they can produce children with them, so that nothing might be wanting to them on earth. But you were once creatures of spirit, endowed with eternal life, and immortal for all generations of the world. And therefore, I did not appoint wives for you, for your dwelling was in heaven. And now, the giants, who are produced from the union of spirit and flesh, will be called evil spirits and their dwelling will be on the earth. Evil spirits have proceeded from their bodies because they are born from men, yet their primal origin is from the holy watchers. They will persist as evil spirits on earth. And the spirits of the giants will afflict, oppress, destroy, attack, do battle, and work destruction on the earth. They will take no food, but nevertheless they will hunger and thirst and cause offences. And these spirits will revolt against the children of men and against the women who produced them. After the slaughter and destruction and death of the giants, their spirits will go forth and destroy without incurring judgment. In this way, they will wreak havoc until the day of the great judgment, when the present age will be consummated.

"And now regarding the watchers who have sent you to intercede for them, who had once been in heaven, say to them: 'You have been in heaven, but all the mysteries had not yet been revealed to you, and you knew worthless ones, and these in the hardness of your hearts you have made known to the women, and through these mysteries women and men work much evil on earth.' Say to them, therefore: 'You will have no peace.'"

I saw the treasuries of all the winds. I saw how He had furnished with them the whole creation and the firm foundations of the earth. And I saw the cornerstone of the earth. I saw the four winds that bear the earth and the firmament of the heaven. And I saw how the winds stretch out the vaults of heaven and have their station between heaven and earth. These are the pillars of the heaven. I saw the winds of heaven that turn the circumference of the sun and all the stars to their setting. I saw the winds on the earth carrying the clouds. I saw the paths of the angels. I saw at the end of the earth the firmament of the heaven above. And I approached and saw a place that burns day and night, where there are seven mountains of magnificent stones, three towards the east and three towards the south. And those towards the east were made of colored stone, one of pearl and one of jacinth, and those towards the south were made of red stone. But the middle one was made of alabaster and reached to heaven like the throne of God, and the summit of the throne was made of sapphire. And I saw a flaming fire. And beyond these mountains is the end of the great earth. There the heavens were completed. And I saw a deep abyss with columns of heavenly fire, and among them I saw pillars of falling flame, which were beyond measure in height and depth. And beyond that abyss I saw a place that had no firmament of the heaven above, and no firmly founded earth beneath it. There was no water upon it and no birds; it was a wasteland and a horrible place. I saw there seven stars like great burning mountains, and when I asked about them, the angel said to me: "This place is the end of heaven and earth. This has become a prison for the stars and the host of heaven. And the stars that roll over the fire are those who have transgressed the commandment of the Lord in the beginning of their rising, because they did not come forth at their appointed times. And He was angry with them and bound them until the time when their guilt should be consummated in ten thousand years."

And Uriel said to me: "Here will stand the angels who have joined themselves with women, whose spirits assumed many different forms to defile mankind and led them astray by sacrificing to demons as though to gods. Here will they stand until the day of the great judgment, in which they will be judged. And the women of the angels, who likewise went astray, will become sirens." And I, Enoch, alone saw the vision, the ends of all things, and no man will witness what I have witnessed.

And these are the names of the holy angels who watch. Suru'el, one of the holy angels, who watches over the world and over Tartarus. Raphael, one of the holy angels, who watches over the spirits of men. Raguel, one of the holy angels, who takes vengeance on the world of the luminaries. Michael, one of the holy angels, who watches over the best part of mankind and over chaos. Saraqa'el, one of the holy angels, who watches over the spirits of mankind, who sin in the spirit. Gabriel, one of the holy angels, who watches over Paradise and the serpents and the cherubim.

And I proceeded into the chaos. And I saw there something horrible. I saw neither a heaven above nor a firmly founded earth, but a place both chaotic and terrible. And there I saw seven stars of heaven bound together, like great mountains and burning with fire. Then I said: "For what sin are they bound, and for what reason have they been cast here?" Then Uriel, one of the holy angels who was with me, said: "Enoch, why do you ask, and why are you eager for the truth? These are the stars of heaven, which have transgressed the commandment of the Lord, and have been bound here for ten thousand years, the time demanded by their sins." And from there I went to another place, which was still more horrible than the first, and I saw a terrible thing: a great fire there that burned and blazed, and the place was cleft as far as the abyss and full of great descending columns of fire. I could neither see nor guess its length or magnitude. Then I said: "How fearful is this place and how terrible to look upon!" Then Uriel, one of the holy angels who was with me, answered and said to me: "Enoch, why do you have such fear and fright?" And I answered: "Because of this fearful place, and because of the spectacle of pain." And he said to me: "This place is the prison of the angels, and here they will be imprisoned forever."

AGAINST THE GIANTS[1]

The Book of Jubilees presented itself as a divine revelation received by Moses during his time on Mount Sinai (Exodus 24:12). Composed in the second century BCE, it was, in fact, a commentary on the Book of Genesis and the early chapters of the Book of Exodus, with its chronology of events organized in jubilees (increments of forty-nine years). Like the Book of Enoch, the Book of Jubilees amplified the story of the rebel angels and their lust for human women by introducing new features to the legend. As related by one of the archangels, it narrated how the rebellion of the Watchers took place not in Heaven, but after their arrival on earth, where God had sent them to instruct humankind. Once they had been corrupted by desire, their forbidden unions produced not only the Nephilim but many races of giants, who waged war against one another. After their slaughter, the malignant spirits of these giants afflicted the grandchildren of Moses as demonic forces responsible for disease and death. Moses petitioned God to condemn the demons to a place of otherworldly punishment, but their leader, Mastema, lobbied successfully to keep a tenth of his followers on earth to fulfill their role as punishers of human wickedness. In response, God instructed the archangels to share with his chosen people knowledge of herbal remedies that would protect them from the maladies caused by demonic powers.

And in the second week of the tenth jubilee, Mahalalel took as his wife Dinah, the daughter of Baraki'el, the daughter of his father's brother, and she bore him a son in the third week in the sixth year, and he named him Jared, for in his days the

angels of the Lord descended to the earth, those who are called
the watchers, to instruct the children of men to act with judgment and righteousness on the earth.[2] And in the eleventh
jubilee, Jared took a wife, and her name was Baraka, the
daughter of Rasujal, a daughter of his father's brother, in the
fourth week of this jubilee, and she bore him a son in the fifth
week, in the fourth year of the jubilee, and he named him
Enoch. And he was the first among men born on earth who
learned writing and knowledge and wisdom, and who wrote
down the signs of heaven according to the order of their
months in a book, so that men would know the seasons of the
years according to the order of their separate months. And he
was the first to write a testimony, and he testified to the sons
of men among the generations of the earth, and recounted the
weeks of the jubilees, and made known to them the days of the
years, and set in order the months and recounted the Sabbaths
of the years as we made them, as they were known to him.
And what was and what will happen he saw in a vision while
asleep, just as it will happen to the children of men throughout
their generations until the day of judgment. He saw and understood everything, and wrote his testimony, and placed the
testimony on earth for all the children of men and for their
generations.[3] And in the twelfth jubilee, in the seventh week
there, he took a wife, and her name was Edni, the daughter of
Danel, the daughter of his father's brother, and in the sixth
year in this week she bore him a son and he called his name
Methuselah. And, moreover, he was with the angels of God
these six jubilees of years, and they showed him everything
that is on earth and in the heavens, the rule of the sun, and he
wrote down everything. And he testified to the watchers, who
had sinned with the daughters of men, for they had begun to
unite themselves, so as to be defiled, with the daughters of
men, and Enoch testified against them all. And he was taken
from among the children of men, and we conducted him into
the Garden of Eden in majesty and honor, and behold, there
he writes down the condemnation and judgment of the world,
and all the wickedness of the children of men. And on account
of his testimony, God brought the waters of the flood upon all

the land of Eden, for there he was sent as a sign and that he should testify against all the children of men, that he should recount all the deeds of the generations until the day of condemnation . . .

And it came to pass when the children of men began to multiply on the face of the earth and daughters were born to them that the angels of God saw them on a certain year of this jubilee and found them beautiful to look upon and they chose wives among them for themselves, and they bore sons and these sons were giants. And lawlessness increased on the earth and all flesh was corrupted, men and cattle and beasts and birds and everything that walks on the earth—all of them were corrupted and they began to devour each other, and lawlessness increased on the earth and the thoughts of all men dwelt on evil continually. And God looked upon the earth, and behold, it was corrupt, and all flesh had been corrupted, and everyone upon the earth committed all manner of evil before his eyes. And God said that he would destroy humankind and all flesh upon the face of the earth that he had created. But Noah found grace before the eyes of the Lord. And God was exceedingly angry with the angels whom he had sent to the earth, and he gave the command to root them out of all their dominion, and he ordered us [the archangels] to bind them in the depths of the earth, and behold, they are bound there and kept separate. And against their sons—the giants—went forth a command from him that they should be smitten with the sword, and removed from under heaven. And he said, "My spirit will not always abide with man, for they are flesh and their days will be one hundred and twenty years." And he sent his sword into their midst, so that each person slew his neighbor, and they began to slay each other until they all fell by the sword and were destroyed from the earth. And their fathers [the watchers] witnessed their destruction, and after this they were bound in the depths of the earth forever, until the day of the great condemnation, when judgment is made on all those who have corrupted their ways and their works before the Lord.

[GOD SENDS THE FLOOD TO DESTROY HIS CREATION, BUT INSTRUCTS NOAH TO BUILD AN ARK]

And in the twenty-eighth jubilee Noah enjoined upon his sons' sons all of the commandments and judgments that he knew, and he exhorted his sons to observe righteousness, and to cover the shame of their flesh, and to bless their creator, and honor father and mother, and love their neighbor, and guard their souls from fornication and uncleanness and all iniquity. For owing to these three things came the flood upon the earth, namely, owing to the fornication by which the watchers against the natural order had sex with the daughters of men, and chose for themselves wives, and thereby made the beginning of uncleanness. And they produced sons, the Nephilim, and they were all different from one another and they devoured one another: the giants slew the Nephil, and the Nephil slew the Eljo, and the Eljo slew humankind, and one man slew another. And everyone committed iniquity and shed much blood, and the earth was filled with iniquity. And after this they sinned against the beasts and birds, and all that moves and walks on the earth and much blood was shed on the earth, and every thought and desire of men imagined vanity and evil continually.

And the Lord destroyed everything from the face of the earth, because of the wickedness of their deeds. And Noah said, "And we were left, you and I, my sons, and everything that entered with us into the ark, and behold, I see from your works before me that you do not walk in righteousness, for you have begun to walk in the path of destruction, and you are parting one from another, and you are envious of one another, and so it follows that you are not in harmony, my sons, each with his brother. For I see and behold that the demons have begun their seductions against you and against your children, and now I fear on your behalf that after my death you will shed the blood of humankind upon the earth, and that you, too, will be destroyed from the face of the earth." . . . And in the third week of this jubilee the unclean demons began to lead astray the children of the sons of Noah, and to cause them to commit errors, and to destroy themselves. And the sons of Noah came to Noah their father, and they told him about the demons that were leading them astray and blinding and slaying his sons' sons. And he prayed before the Lord his God, and said:

"God of the spirits of all flesh, who has shown mercy to me
And has saved me and my sons from the waters of the flood,
And has not caused me to perish as you did the sons of
    perdition;
For your grace has been great towards me,
And great has been your mercy to my soul;
Let your grace be lifted up upon my sons,
And let not wicked spirits rule over them
Lest they should destroy them from the earth.
But bless me and my sons,
So that we may increase and multiply and replenish the earth.
For you know how your watchers,
The fathers of these wicked spirits, acted in my day,
And as for these spirits that persist in living,
Imprison them and hold them fast in the place of
    condemnation,
And let them not bring destruction on the sons of your
    servant, my God.
For they are malignant and exist only to destroy.
And let them not rule over the spirits of the living,
For you alone can exercise dominion over them.
And let them not have power over the sons of the righteous
    from now on and for evermore."

And the Lord, our God, bid us [the archangels] to bind them all. And the chief of the wicked spirits, Mastema, came and said: "Lord, creator, let some of the spirits remain with me, and let them heed my voice, and do all that I command, for if some of them are not left to me, I will not be able to execute the power of my will on the sons of men, for great is the wickedness of the sons of men." And God said: "Let the tenth part of them remain before him, and let nine parts descend into the place of condemnation." And he commanded one of us [the archangels] to teach Noah all of the remedies, for God knew that they would not walk in uprightness nor strive in righteousness. And we did this according to all his words. All the evil spirits we bound in the place of condemnation and a tenth part of them we left, so that they might be subjects of Satan on the earth. And we explained to Noah all the remedies to treat the diseases of the demons, together with their seductions, and how he might heal them with herbs of the earth. And Noah wrote down all of these things in a book as we instructed him concerning every kind of medicine. Thus, the evil spirits were prevented from hurting the sons of Noah.

A REMEDY AGAINST
DEMONIC ATTACKS[1]

According to the Book of Jubilees, the archangels taught the ancient Israelites knowledge of herbal remedies to protect them against the physical maladies caused by demons. This tradition endured into the early Christian era, when the Roman Jewish historian Flavius Josephus (ca. 37/38–100 CE) mentioned it in The Judean War, *his account of the ill-fated rebellion of the Jews against Rome (66–73 CE). The identity of the ambient root that he called* baaras *is unknown, but its name likely derived from the Hebrew word* ba'ar *("to burn") because it was flame-colored. The novel way of extracting this dangerous root by having a dog pull it out persisted in the European Middle Ages as the method for uprooting yet another perilous plant with medicinal properties: the mandrake, whose shrieks were lethal to human ears.*

The valley that surrounds Jerusalem on the north side is a place called *baaras*, where a root by the same name grows. It has a color similar to a flame and in the evening, it flashes like lightning. It does not make it easy for those who approach and wish to pull it out, for it retreats for a long time and does not remain still unless someone pours a woman's urine or menstrual blood upon it. And moreover, if you touch it, death is certain, unless by chance you carry the root dangling from your hand. It can also be harvested by another method without danger, as follows. Dig in a circle around the whole root, so that only a small part of it is still covered by the earth. Then, tie a dog to it. When that dog tries to follow the person who tied it, the root pulls up easily. The dog dies immediately, handed over as though in the place of the person by whom the herb should have been pulled. Nor indeed is there any fear afterwards for those who pick the root up. Despite such great dangers, it is valuable to harvest because of the single power that it possesses. For if it is only administered to the sick, it quickly drives away those beings which are called demons, the spirits of the worst kind of men, who plunge into the living and kill those for whom there is no help.

I AM LEGION

Demons in Ancient Christian Thought

The earliest Christians inherited rich yet contradictory traditions about the origins and activities of demons from Greco-Roman poetry and philosophy as well as from the Hebrew scriptures and Jewish apocryphal literature. New Testament authors depicted Satan and his minions as the adversaries of Christ and the enemies of humankind, but they did not offer a comprehensive guide to their character or nature. Early Christian apologists drew inspiration from Israel's demonization of the gods of their enemies to blacken all pagan deities as lesser, malevolent forces who worked against the saving mission of Jesus. In the same breath, they refuted the Neoplatonic interpretation of demons as helpful intermediaries between mortals and the divine. Featured in almost every genre of early Christian literature from the earliest visionary tours of Hell, where "angels of Tartarus" tortured sinful souls, to apocryphal stories about the apostles, in which magicians aped their God-given powers with diabolical assistance, demons emerged as unambiguously hostile entities in Christian articulations of a new worldview in which "the god of this world," Satan, "has blinded the minds of the unbelievers to keep them from seeing the light of the gospel of the glory of Christ" (2 Corinthians 4:4).

INTIMATE ADVERSARIES

In New Testament literature, the primary opponent of Jesus was Satan, "the prince of the power of this air" (Ephesians 2:2), whose dominion over this world necessitated Christ's incarnation. Always acting with evil intent, Satan and his demonic minions had deceived the pagans who worshipped them as gods (1 Corinthians 10:19–22) and worked through them to thwart the saving mission of the Christians. The exorcism of demons from possessed individuals by Jesus and his followers not only affirmed their spiritual authority on earth but also demonstrated the reality of the cosmic war between Jesus and Satan and provided proof that Jesus would win in the end. The ability of those afflicted by demons to recognize Jesus as the son of God suggests that they were once angels who had inhabited Heaven with Christ and knew his true identity before their rebellion against God.

(A) THE TEMPTER IN THE DESERT[1]

Then Jesus was led into the desert by the spirit to be tempted by the devil. And when he had fasted for forty days and forty nights, thereafter he was hungry. And the tempter approached and said to him, "If you are the son of God, say the word to turn these stones into bread." Jesus said in response, "It is written, 'Man does not live on bread alone, but in every word that proceeds from the mouth of God.'" Then the devil took him up into the holy city and set him upon the pinnacle of the temple and said to him, "If you are the son of God, cast yourself down, for it is written, 'He will hand you over to his angels and they will bear you in their hands lest perhaps you strike your foot against a stone.'" Jesus said to him, "Again it is written, 'You will not tempt the Lord, your God.'" Again, the devil took him up onto a very high mountain and showed to him all the kingdoms of the world and their glory and said to him, "I will give to you all of these, if you fall down and adore me." Then Jesus said to him, "Begone, Satan! For it is written, 'You will adore the Lord, your God, and you will serve him alone.'" Then the devil left him and behold angels came and ministered to him.

(B) THE DWELLER IN THE TOMBS[2]

And they came across the channel of the sea into the region of the Gerasenes. And as Jesus disembarked from the boat, immediately a man with an unclean spirit rushed to him from the tombs. He had a small dwelling among the tombs and no one could bind him, not even with chains. For he had been bound often with shackles and chains and always tore them apart and broke them into pieces and no one could tame him. And night and day he was among the tombs and in the mountains, shouting and cutting himself with stones. Seeing Jesus from afar, he came running up and worshipped him. And crying with a loud voice, he said, "What do you have to do with me, Jesus, son of the highest God? I adjure you by God not to torment me!" Jesus said to him, "Go forth from this man, unclean spirit!" And he asked him, "What is your name?" And the man said to Jesus, "My name is Legion, for we are many." And he pleaded with Jesus much not to drive him out of the region. And at the foot of the mountain there was a large herd of foraging swine. And the spirits pleaded with him, saying, "Send us into the swine, so that we may enter into them." And Jesus immediately granted this to them. And going forth from the man, the unclean spirits entered into the swine and the herd, numbering about two thousand, rushed with great speed down into the sea, and were drowned in the water. And those who fed them fled and spread word in the city and in the fields and the people came out to see what had happened. And they came to Jesus and saw the man who had been troubled by the demon sitting clothed and with a clear mind and they were afraid. And those who had witnessed what had happened told them how he had treated the demon and also concerning the swine. And they asked him to depart from their shores. And when Jesus boarded the ship, the man who had been troubled by the demon asked if he could come with him. Jesus did not allow it, but said to him, "Go home to your friends and tell them how much the Lord has done for you and how he has had mercy upon you." And the man went forth and began to make it known in Decapolis how much Jesus had done for him and everyone marveled.

(C) A GARRULOUS DEMON[3]

And it happened that, as we went to prayer, a certain girl in the grip of a spirit of divination met us. She earned a large profit for her owners by telling the future. Following Paul and us, this girl cried out, saying, "These men are servants of the highest God, who announce to you the way of salvation." She did this for many days until Paul grew annoyed, turned to the spirit and said, "I command you in the name of Jesus Christ to leave her." And the spirit went forth from her that same hour. But her owners, seeing that their hope of profit had vanished, grabbed hold of Paul and Silas and led them to the rulers in the marketplace.

IN THE GUISE OF GODS[1]

Justin Martyr (ca. 100–ca. 165 CE) was an early defender of the Christian religion who was put to death for his faith. At a time when pagans regarded Christianity as an irrational superstition, Justin argued that polytheism was nothing more than an empty façade erected by demons to deceive humankind and hinder the saving message of Christ. The Hebrew scriptures had foretold this in no uncertain terms: "They sacrificed to devils and not to God, to gods whom they knew not" (Deuteronomy 32:17). In a letter written in defense of Christianity to the Roman Senate sometime between 155 and 160 CE, Justin explained that demons in the guise of gods had enslaved the human race by means of magic, war, and immoral behavior. Appropriating the story of the Watchers from Jewish apocryphal traditions to explain the origin of demonkind, Justin described how these evil spirits masqueraded as gods and used their fraudulent authority to compel Roman magistrates to persecute innocent Christians.

When God made the whole world and subjected earthly things to humankind and arranged the heavenly bodies for the increase of fruits and the rotation of the seasons, and appointed all of this by divine law . . . He also committed the care of humankind and of all things under heaven to his angels, whom He appointed over them. But the angels violated their responsibilities because they were captivated by the love of women and had children with them who are called demons. Moreover, the fallen angels and their offspring afterwards subdued the human race to themselves, partly by means of magical writings, partly by fears they instilled in them and punishments they inflicted on them, and partly by teaching them to offer sacrifices and incense and libations, which the fallen angels needed after they were enslaved by lustful passions. And among humankind they sowed murders, wars, adulteries, discord, and all manner of wickedness. Thus it was that the poets and writers of legends, not knowing that it was the fallen angels and those demons who had been produced by them that did these things to men and women and cities and nations, ascribed them to Jupiter himself and to those whom they thought were his children and to the children of those who were called his brothers—Neptune and Pluto—and to the children of their children. For they called them by whatever name each of the fallen angels had given to himself and his children.

THEIR WORK IS THE RUIN
OF HUMANKIND

Active in the city of Carthage in Roman North Africa, the theologian Tertullian (ca. 155–ca. 220 CE) was the first Latin author to examine the infiltration of demons into all aspects of Roman culture. In his treatise On the Spectacles, *he warned his Christian readers that participation in popular Roman pastimes, like chariot races, gladiatorial battles, athletic competitions, and the theater, made them vulnerable to demonic attacks because of the pagan rites associated with these games. Only the rite of baptism and the cultivation of Christian practices separate from Roman spectacles could ensure the safety of their souls. For, as Tertullian explained, the subtle and insubstantial nature of demons allowed them to infiltrate human bodies unde-tected to attack the soul directly, causing sickness and death.*

(A) THE PERILS OF
MURDEROUS PLEASURE[1]

May God avert from His people any such passionate eagerness for murderous pleasure! For how monstrous it is to go from God's church to the devil's—from the sky to the stye, as they say; to raise your hands to God, and then to weary them in the applause of an actor; out of the mouth, from which you have uttered "Amen" over the sacrament, to cheer for a gladiator; to cry "for ever and ever" to anyone else but to God and Christ!

What is to save such people from possession by evil spirits? We have the case of a woman—the Lord himself is witness—

who went to the theater and returned possessed. During the exorcism, when the unclean spirit was scolded for having dared to attack a believer, it answered firmly: "And in truth I did it most righteously, for I found her in my own domain."

(B) BRINGERS OF MALADY[2]

And we affirm indeed the existence of certain spiritual entities, nor is their name unfamiliar. The philosophers acknowledge that there are demons; Socrates himself waiting on a demon's will. Why not? Since it is said an evil spirit attached itself specially to him even from his childhood, turning his mind no doubt from what was good. The poets are all acquainted with demons, too; even the ignorant common people make frequent use of them in cursing. In fact, they call upon Satan, the demon-chief, in their curses, as though with some instinctive knowledge from their soul . . . We are instructed, moreover, by our sacred books how from certain angels, who fell of their own free will, there sprang a more wicked demon-brood, condemned by God along with the leaders of their race and that chief we have mentioned. It will, for the time being, suffice to give an account of their activities. Their work is the ruin of humankind. From the beginning, spiritual wickedness sought our destruction. They inflict upon our bodies diseases and other grievous calamities, while by violent assaults they inflict on the soul sudden and extraordinary excesses. Their marvelous subtlety and slenderness give them access to both parts of our nature. As spirits, they can do no harm; for, invisible and intangible, we are not cognizant of their action except by its effects, as when some inexplicable, unseen poison in the breeze blights the apples and the grain while in the flower or kills them in the bud or destroys them when they have reached maturity; as though by the tainted atmosphere in some unknown way spreading abroad its pestilential exhalations. So, too, by an influence equally obscure, demons and angels breathe into the soul, and rouse up its corruptions with furious passions and vile excesses or with cruel lusts accompanied by every kind of delusion. And of all delusions attributed to them, the greatest involves recommending themselves as gods to the deceived and deluded minds of men. What is daintier food to the spirit of evil than turning men's minds away from the true God by the illusions of a false deception? And here I will explain these deceptions and how the demons manage them.

Every spirit has wings. This is a common property of both angels and demons. So they are everywhere in a single moment; the world is as one place to them; all that is done over the whole extent of it, it is as easy for them to know as to report. Their swiftness of motion passes for divinity, because their nature is unknown. Thus they wish to appear as the authors of the things which they announce; and sometimes, no doubt, the bad things are their doing, never the good . . . From dwelling in the air, and their nearness to the stars, and their commerce with the clouds, they have means of knowing the preparatory processes going on in these upper regions, and thus can give promise of the rains which they already feel. Likewise, they are deceptive with regard to the treatment of diseases. For, first of all, they make you ill; then, to get a miracle out of it, they command the application of remedies either altogether new or contrary to those in use, and immediately withdrawing their hurtful influence, they appear to be healers . . . They do it all so that men will believe that stones are gods and not seek after the one true God.

ORIGEN'S FOLLY[1]

Christian thinkers did not always construct their notions about the nature of demons on the foundation of pagan thought. In the early third century, a biblical scholar named Origen of Alexandria (ca. 185–ca. 255) wrote a treatise entitled On First Principles, *in which he offered the lineaments of a Christian cosmology based on reason and revelation. For Origen, rational souls existed with God since creation, but over time the cooling of their love for their creator caused them to recede from his presence. Some became angels, while others became human beings. Those who receded furthest from God became demons. Origen believed that all souls would eventually return to their creator, but the process of return, which involved a fiery purification after death, could take many lifetimes across multiple worlds. In the end, though, even the Devil would be saved. Origen faced criticism for these speculations during his lifetime and thereafter, which culminated in his condemnation as a heretic in the sixth century. One of his most outspoken critics was Jerome of Stridon (ca. 346–420). Around 410, a Roman Christian named Avitus obtained a Latin translation of* On First Principles. *Alarmed by what he had read, he wrote to Jerome to ask for an explanation of Origen's meaning. Jerome's response was a severe rebuke of the folly of the Alexandrian's radical cosmology, especially the notion that humans could become demons and vice versa as their souls struggled to migrate back to God.*

Take then what you have asked for, but know that there are countless things in this book to be abhorred and that, as the Lord says, you will have to walk among scorpions and serpents . . . When he comes to deal with rational creatures and to describe their fall into earthly bodies as due to their own negligence . . . he maintains that after every end a fresh beginning springs forth and an end from each beginning, and that a complete transformation is possible, so that one who is now a human being may in another world become a demon, while one who due to his negligence is now a demon may hereafter be placed in a more material body and thus become a human being. So far does he carry this transforming process that according to his theory an archangel may become the devil and the devil in turn could be changed back into an archangel . . . moreover, the very demons and rulers of darkness in any world or worlds, if they are willing to turn to better things, may become human beings and so come back to their first beginnings. That is to say, after they have endured the discipline of punishment and torture for a longer or a shorter time in human bodies, they may again reach the angelic heights from which they have fallen. From this, it may be shown that we human beings may change into any other rational being and that not once only but time after time. We and the angels will become demons if we neglect our duty, and demons may attain to the ranks of angels, if they cultivate sufficient virtue . . . In the second book he maintains a plurality of worlds; not, however, as Epicurus taught, many similar worlds existing at the same time, but a new one beginning each time that the old comes to an end.[2] There was a world before this world of ours, and after it there will be first one and then another and so on in regular succession. He is in doubt whether one world shall be so completely similar to another as to leave no room for any difference between them or whether one world shall never wholly be indistinguishable from another . . . For he evidently maintains that all bodies will perish and that we will be incorporeal, as according to him we were before we received our present bodies. Again, he argues for a variety of worlds and maintains that angels will become demons, demons either angels or men, and men in their turn demons; in a word, everything will be turned into something else . . . And after a lengthy discussion, he argues that all corporeal creatures must exchange their material form for subtle and spiritual bodies and that all substance must become one pure and inconceivably bright body, of which the human mind can at present form no conception.

DELIVERED FROM
FILTHY TYRANNY[1]

In his towering treatise entitled Concerning the City of
God Against the Pagans, *Bishop Augustine of Hippo (354–
430) responded to pagan criticism that the adoption of
Christianity as the official religion in the Roman Empire
under Emperor Theodosius the Great (d. 395) heralded a
new age of calamity. Polytheists claimed that the abandon-
ment of the old gods had resulted in the sack of the city of
Rome by the Visigoths in 410 and the political turmoil in
its wake. Augustine answered with a lengthy critique of
Roman religion, including a pointed refutation of Platonist
theology. He took aim at a treatise entitled* On the God
of Socrates *by the Neoplatonic philosopher Apuleius
(ca. 124–ca. 170), who claimed that demons deserved worship as the mediators between mortals and the gods. The
bishop focused his criticism on the pagan's assertion that
demons had unruly passions like human beings and concluded that they were not worthy of devotion. Although
they were immortal, demons always strived to seduce mortals into misery and deprive them of eternal life. For Augustine, Jesus Christ was the only mediator necessary for
Christians, because he understood the wretchedness of
their mortal condition through his incarnation, while re-
taining the blessedness of his divine nature. The bishop's
unrivaled authority as a theologian ensured that his discussion of demons in this treatise became a cornerstone of
Christian teaching in the western tradition.*

There is, they say, a threefold division of all beings possessed of a rational soul; there are gods, men, and demons. The gods occupy the most exalted situation; mankind has the most lowly; and demons are in between. For the gods have their abode in heaven; mankind lives on earth; demons dwell in the air. And their natures are graded to correspond to their different elevations. The gods are superior to men and demons, while men are set below gods and demons in respect of difference of merit as well as in the order of the physical elements. The demons are in the middle position; they are inferior to the gods and dwell below them, but superior to men, having their abode above them. In common with the gods, they have immortality of body; in common with men, they have passions of the soul. Therefore it is not remarkable, the Platonists tell us, that they delight in the obscenities of the shows and the fantasies of the poets, seeing that they are subject to human desires, which are remote from the gods, and altogether alien to them. It follows then that in his detestation of poetry and his prohibition of poetical fictions, it is not the gods, who are all of them good and sublime, that Plato has deprived of the pleasures of stage shows; it is the demons.

These ideas can be found in many writers; but the Platonist Apuleius of Madaura has devoted a whole book to the subject, under the title *The God of Socrates*. In this book he discusses and explains to what class of divinities that power belonged which was attached to Socrates in a kind of friendly companionship. The story is that he constantly received warnings from this divinity to abandon some line of action when the contemplated enterprise was not destined to be successful. Apuleius says quite frankly that this power was not a god but a demon and supports his contention with a wealth of argument, in the course of which he takes the statement of Plato about the sublime situation of the gods, the lowly state of man and the intermediate position of the demons, and subjects it a thorough examination . . . In fact he was prepared to give his book the title *The God of Socrates*, whereas in line with his own discussion, in which he makes a carefully and copiously argued distinction between gods and demons, he ought to have called it *The Demon of Socrates*. However, he has preferred to make this point in the actual discussion rather than in its title. The fact is that as a result of the healthy doctrine which has shone upon the world of men, mankind in general has conceived a horror of the very name of demon, so that anyone reading the title *The Demon of Socrates*, before studying the discussion in which Apuleius seeks to establish the excellence of demons, would conclude that Socrates was by no means a normal human being.

But what is it that Apuleius himself has found to praise in demons, apart from the subtlety and stability of their bodies and the elevation of their abode? As for their morality, in the general remarks he makes about demons as a whole, he has nothing good to say of them but a great deal of ill. In fact, when one has read the book, one can no longer be astonished that these demons wished the obscenities of the stage to have a place among divine ceremonies, and that while eager to be accounted gods, they could find pleasure in the scandals of the deities, and that everything in the sacred rites which arouses laughter or disgust by reason of its celebration of obscenity or its degraded barbarity is very much to their taste.

Apuleius the Platonist also treats of the character of the demons, and says that they are liable to the same emotional disturbances as human beings. They resent injury, they are mollified by flattery and by gifts, they delight in receiving honours, they enjoy all kinds of rites and ceremonies and they are annoyed at any negligence about these. Among their functions he mentions divination by means of auguries, haruspication, clairvoyance, and dreams; and he ascribes to them the remarkable feats of magicians. He gives this brief definition of demons: species, animal; soul, subject to passions; mind, rational; body, composed of air; life-span, eternal.

Putting aside all other points, I want to limit my consideration to the matter of the passions of the soul which, according to Apuleius, the demons share with us. If the four elements are full of the living beings, which belong to each of them, fire and air filled with immortal beings, water and earth with mortals, I would like to know why the souls of the demons are disturbed by the storms and tempests of the passions. For "disturbance" represents the Greek *pathos* [passion] and that is what Apuleius means by calling the demons "subject to passions" [*passiva*], since the word "passion" [*pathos* in Greek] signifies an irrational movement of the soul . . . What folly it is then, or rather what madness, for us to subject ourselves to demons by any kind of worship, when the true religion sets us free from the vicious tendencies in which we resemble them! Apuleius is very tender toward the demons—he even pronounces them worthy of divine honours; and yet he is forced to admit that the demons are prompted by anger. But we, on the contrary, are bidden by the true religion not to be influenced in any way by such things. The demons hate some men and love others—not as a result of a calmly considered decision, but because their soul, in the phrase of Apuleius, is "subject to passions"; as for us, we have the instruction of the true religion that we should love even our enemies. Lastly, the true religion bids us adjure all those movements of the heart, all those agitations of the mind, all those storms and tempests of the soul which in the demons make a raging sea of passion. It is nothing but folly, nothing but pitiable aberration, to humble yourself before a being whom you would hate to resemble in the conduct of your life and to worship one whom you would refuse to imitate. For surely the supremely important thing in religion is to model oneself on the objects of one's worship.

In spite of that, the demons clearly hold sway over many men, who are unworthy to participate in the true religion, and they treat them as prisoners and subjects; and they have persuaded the greater part of them to accept the demons as gods, by means of impressive but deceitful miracles, whether miracles of action or of prediction. But there are others who have observed the viciousness of these demons with rather more careful attention. The demons have failed to persuade them of their divinity; and so they have pretended that they are intermediaries between gods and men, securing for mankind the benefits of the gods. And yet when men have decided that not even this honourable position is to be accorded to the demons, because, seeing their wickedness, they did not believe them to be gods (since they would have it that all gods are good), even so men could not bring themselves to declare that demons were altogether unworthy of any divine honour, especially because they were afraid of shocking the general public. For they saw that people in general were enslaved to those demons by the superstitious beliefs to which they were inured, thanks to all those ceremonies, and all those temples.

Thus it is necessary that the mediator between God and man should have a transient mortality, and a permanent blessedness, so that through that which is transient he might be conformed to the condition of those who are doomed to die, and might bring them back from the dead to that which is permanent. So it is that good angels cannot mediate between wretched mortals and blessed immortals, because they also are both blessed and immortal. On the other hand, bad angels could mediate, because they are immortals, like the gods, and wretched, like men. Utterly different from them is the good Mediator who, in contrast with the immortality and misery of the bad angels, was willing to be mortal for a time, and was able to remain in blessedness for eternity. Those immortals, in their pride, those wretches, in their wickedness, sought to seduce men into misery by their boast of immortality; to prevent this, the good Mediator by the humility of his death and the kindness of his blessedness has destroyed their power over those whose hearts he has purified, through their faith, and delivered from the filthy tyranny of those demons.

So here is man, in his mortality and misery, so far removed from the immortals in their felicity. What kind of mediation is he to choose to unite him to immortality and felicity? What he could find to delight him in the immortality of the demons is in fact nothing but misery; what he might have recoiled from in the mortality of Christ no longer exists. With the demons, everlasting misery is to be dreaded; with Christ, death is not to be feared, for death could not be everlasting, and the felicity which is to be welcomed is everlasting. For the being who is immortal and wretched intervenes simply to prevent one passing to a blessed immortality, since the obstacle that stands in the way, that is, the misery itself, always persists. But the one who is mortal and blessed interposed in order to make an end of mortality, and give immortality to those who were dead— as he showed by his resurrection—and to give to the wretched the happiness from which he himself had never departed.

THE ANGELS OF TARTARUS[1]

Inspired by the apostle Paul's cryptic claim to have been "caught up to the third heaven" where he heard things that cannot be told (2 Corinthians 12:1–4), an anonymous Christian author writing between 250 and 400 CE confected a story about the apostle's journey to the otherworld, where he witnessed the glories awaiting the saints in Heaven and the horrors in store for sinners in Hell. The Apocalypse of Paul *portrayed for Christian readers a terrifying tableau of torments, where the souls of false Christians and impious clergy suffered punishments befitting their crimes. While demons held sway over the earth in the early Christian imagination, they were not yet inhabitants of Hell. The tormentors who tortured the damned in the* Apocalypse of Paul *were "angels of Tartarus," an allusion to the fallen angels of Satan's retinue fated to join him in the lake of fire after the final judgment (Revelation 20:10).*

When the angel had ceased speaking to me, he led me outside beyond the city through the midst of trees and back from the places of the land of good things, and he set me at the river of milk and honey. And after that, he led me to the ocean that bears the foundation of heaven. The angel responded and said to me, "Do you know that you are departing this place?" And I said, "Yes, Lord." And he said to me, "Come and follow me, and I will show you the souls of the impious and the sinners, so that you may know what kind of place they have." And I went with the angel and he took me toward the setting of the sun and I saw the beginning of heaven built upon a great river of water, and I asked, "What is this river of water?" And the angel said to me, "This is the ocean that surrounds the entire earth." And when I was at the furthest reaches of the ocean, I looked and there was no light in that place, but only shadows and sadness and sorrow, and I sighed.

And I saw to the north a place of various and diverse torments full of men and women, and the river of fire flowed upon them. I looked and I saw pits great in depth and in them were many souls together and the depth of the pit was about three thousand cubits and I saw the souls groaning and crying and saying, "Have mercy upon us, Lord" and yet, no one had mercy upon them. And I asked the angel and said, "Who are they, Lord?" And in response, the angel said to me, "These are the ones who placed no hope in the Lord as a helper." And I asked and said, "Lord, if these souls remain like this, piled one upon the other for thirty or forty generations, unless they are cast deeper down, I do not believe that the pits will hold them all." And he said to me, "The abyss has no end, for beyond this follows what lies beneath it. And it is such that if someone hurled a stone with great strength and aimed it into a very deep pit and it took many hours for it to hit the bottom, this abyss is like that too. Indeed, when souls are cast in there, they barely reach the bottom after forty years have passed." Truly, when I heard this, I mourned and groaned for the human race. In response, the angel said to me, "Why do you mourn? Are you more merciful than God? Indeed, since God is good and he knows that there are punishments, he treats the human race with patience, allowing each person to do their own will during the time that he or she dwells upon the earth."

Yet I looked back at the river of fire and I saw there a man seized by the throat by angels of Tartarus, holding in their hands an iron implement with three hooks, with which they were piercing the entrails of this old man. And I asked the angel and said, "Lord, who is this old man who suffers such torments?" In response, the angel said to me, "The man whom you see was a presbyter, who did not fulfill his ministry well. When he was eating and drinking and fornicating, he was also offering Lord's sacrifice at his holy altar."

And I saw not far off another old man, whom four evil angels were leading, running with great haste, and they submerged him up to his knees in the river of fire and they struck him with stones and wounded his face like a storm and they did not allow him to say, "Have mercy on me." And I asked the angel, and he said to me, "This one whom you see was a bishop, and he did not fulfill his duties well. Indeed, he received a great title, but he did not enter into the holiness of the one who gave the name to him for his entire life, because he made no just judgment and he had no pity for widows and orphans. But now it is paid back to him according to his iniquity and his works."

―――――――――

And I looked and saw at his side another man, whom they brought out in haste and they cast him into the river of fire, and he was sunk up to his knees. And an angel in charge of his torments arrived with a long flaming knife, with which he sliced the lips of this man and his tongue as well. And with sighs, I wept and asked, "Who is that man, Lord?" And he said to me, "That one whom you see was a lector and he read to the people, but he did not follow God's commandments, so now he suffers this particular torment."

―――――――――

And I saw there girls draped in black garments and four terrifying angels holding in their hands flaming chains, which they put on the necks of the girls and led them into the darkness. And again with tears I asked the angel, "Who are these ones, Lord?" And he said to me, "These are girls who had been virgins, but had lost their virginity without their parents' knowledge. For this reason they suffer these particular torments forever more."

―――――――――

And I looked and saw other men and women upon a flaming spit, and beasts were tearing at them, and they were not allowed to say, "Have mercy upon me, Lord." And I saw the angel of torments subjecting them to the worst torture and saying, "Recognize the son of God. For it was preached to you, but you did not listen when the holy scriptures were read to you. Because of this, the judgment of God is just. Your own evil actions have seized you and led you into these torments." But with sighs and tears, I asked, "Who are these men and women who are strangled in this fire and suffer these torments?" And he responded to me, "These are women who defiled the creation of God when they aborted infants from the womb, and those are the men who lay with them." Indeed, the infants of these women addressed the Lord God and the angels in charge of the torments, saying, "Protect us from our parents, for they have defiled the creation of God. They possessed the name of God, but did not follow his commandments. They abandoned us to be eaten by dogs and trampled by pigs. Others they cast into the river." But these infants were delivered to the angels of Tartarus in charge of the torments, who led them to a spacious place of mercy. But their fathers and mothers were tortured in everlasting torment.

And after this, I saw men and women wrapped in clothing full of pitch and burning sulfur and there were dragons coiled around their necks and shoulders and feet, and angels with fiery horns grasped them and struck them and blocked up their nostrils, saying to them, "Why did you not know the time when it was right for you to repent and serve God and you did nothing?" And I asked, "Who are these ones, Lord?" And he said to me, "These are people who seemed to make a renunciation to the Lord [during baptism], wearing our habit, but the hindrances of the world made them miserable and unable to show love. They had no pity on widows and orphans, received no stranger or pilgrim, made no offering, and had no pity on their neighbor. Their prayer did not ascend pure to the Lord God even one day, but the many hindrances of the world held them back and they could not do right in the sight of God, and the angels surrounded them in the place of torments."

THE FALL OF
SIMON MAGUS[1]

Early Christian authors were suspicious of magic, because they believed that demons were instrumental in its practice. One of the earliest adversaries of the apostles was a magician named Simon Magus, who offered Peter and Paul a sum of money in exchange for the ability to perform their God-given powers (Acts 8:9–24).[2] Legends sprang up around Simon in late antiquity, including a story about a duel between the apostles and the magician in the presence of Emperor Nero. As retold in the thirteenth century by Jacobus de Voragine (ca. 1230–98), this tale demonstrated once and for all that the power of the apostles derived from God, while the tricks of magicians, including their ability to fly, were demonic in origin.

Peter and Paul went to Nero and began to expose all Simon's sham wizardry; and Peter added that just as there are in Christ two substances, namely the divine and the human, so there were two substances in this sorcerer, the human and the diabolical. Simon's reply . . . was: "I cannot tolerate the slanders of this man any longer. I shall order my angels to avenge me on him." "I do not fear your angels," Peter told him. "Rather it is they who fear me." . . . Unable to bear the shame of this public humiliation, Simon vanished from view for the space of a year, and Marcellus, after witnessing these miracles, became a disciple of St. Peter. In time Simon came out of hiding and Nero welcomed him back as his friend. According to Leo, Simon then called the people together and told them that he had been deeply offended by the Galileans; and for that reason he was intending to abandon the city whose protector he had been, and to name the day on which he would ascend to heaven, because he did not deign to live on earth any longer. On the appointed day he climbed to the top of a lofty tower, or, according to Linus, to the top of the Capitol, and wearing a crown of laurel on his head, leapt off and began to fly. Paul said to Peter: "Leave me to pray: you take command!" Nero said: "Simon spoke the truth. You two are charlatans." Peter said to Paul: "Look up and see!" Paul looked up and saw Simon flying, and asked Peter: "What are you waiting for? Finish what you have begun, for the Lord is already calling us!" Then Peter said: "You angels of Satan, you who keep Simon aloft in the air, I adjure you in the name of our Lord Jesus Christ, carry him no more! Let him fall!" At once Simon was released; he dropped to the ground, his neck was broken and he died. When Nero saw this, he was deeply distressed at the loss of such a man and said to the apostles: "You have grieved me deeply. I shall have you put to death, and make a terrible example of you!"

MASTERED BY MAGIC

Demons in the King Solomon Tradition

The unrivaled opponent of demons in the Judeo-Christian tradition was Solomon (d. ca. 930 BCE), the son of David and his successor as the king of Israel. Renowned for his wealth and wisdom, Solomon built the massive First Temple in Jerusalem to house the Ark of the Covenant. He was by all accounts a successful monarch around whom many legends circulated. His reputation as the author of numerous biblical books, including the Book of Proverbs, the Song of Songs, and Ecclesiastes, contributed to the notion that he also composed incantations and books of magic. Early Christian authors praised Solomon not only as a wise king but also as a potent magician, whose name appeared on innumerable amulets and talismans that offered protection from evil influences. Christian and Islamic folklore amplified Jewish traditions about this ancient ruler and the power of his ring's seal, often depicted in the form of a pentagram, against malevolent spirits. Solomon remained synonymous with magical knowledge and the subjugation of demons well into the early modern period, when numerous spell books and grimoires borrowed his name to lend authority to the incantations inscribed therein.

FROM SAGE TO MAGE

Solomon's reputation for wisdom and learning preceded his reputation as a magician and an exorcist. The author of the Book of Kings (composed in the mid-sixth century BCE) exalted the king of Israel both as a prolific author of proverbs and songs and as an expert on natural lore. A few centuries later, the Roman Jewish historian Flavius Josephus (ca. 37/38–100 CE) amplified this tradition in his An-tiquities of the Jews, a sprawling history of the Jewish people from creation to the First Jewish-Roman War (66–73 CE). In this work, Josephus credited the ancient mon-arch with a God-given power over evil spirits and related a story about a Jewish exorcist who expelled a demon not only with knowledge of herbs and incantations passed down from Solomon but also by the invocation of the great king's name.

(A) THE WISDOM OF SOLOMON[1]

And God also gave wisdom to Solomon and understanding beyond measure and a capacity of heart like the sand on the sea shore. And Solomon's wisdom surpassed the wisdom of the people of the east and of the Egyptians. And he was wiser than all men, wiser even than Ethan the Ezrahite and Heman and Chalcol and Dorda, the sons of Mahol, and he was re-nowned in all nations thereabouts. Solomon also uttered three thousand proverbs and his songs numbered one thousand and five. And he spoke about trees from the cedar that is in Leba-non to the hyssop that grows from the wall, and he discussed animals and birds and reptiles and fish. And they came from all peoples to hear Solomon's wisdom and from all the kings of the earth, who heard his wisdom.

(B) SOLOMON'S POWER OVER DEMONS[2]

Now the prudence and wisdom which God had bestowed on Solomon was so great, that he surpassed the ancients, insomuch that he was no way inferior to the Egyptians, who are said to have been beyond all men in understanding; nay, indeed, it is evident that their wisdom was very much inferior to that of the king's. He also excelled and distinguished himself in wisdom above those who were most eminent among the Hebrews at that time for prudence; those I mean were Ethan, and Heman, and Chalcol, and Darda, the sons of Mahol. He also composed one thousand and five books of proverbs and songs, and three thousand books of parables and similitudes. For he spoke a parable about every kind of tree, from the hyssop to the cedar; and likewise, also about beasts, about all sorts of living creatures, whether upon the earth, or in the seas, or in the air. For he was not unacquainted with any of their natures, nor did he pass over any inquiries about them, but he described them all like a philosopher, and demonstrated his exquisite knowledge of their several properties. God also granted him the skill of expelling demons, which is a body of knowledge both useful and beneficial to humankind. He also composed incantations to relieve illnesses. And he left behind him the ways of using exorcisms, by which demons can be expelled, so that they never return and this method of curing remains in force down to the present day. For I have seen a certain man of my own country, whose name was Eleazar, releasing people possessed by demons in the presence of Emperor Vespasian, and his sons, and his captains, and the great number of his soldiers.[3] The manner of the cure was this. He held up to the nose of the possessed man a ring that had [under its seal] a piece of a root prescribed by Solomon and thereby drew out the demon through his nostrils. And when the man immediately fell down, Eleazar abjured the demon never to return into him, evoking

Solomon by name and reciting the incantations which he had composed. And then to persuade the spectators and to demonstrate to them that he had such a power, Eleazar placed a cup or basin full of water a little way off, and commanded the demon to overturn it as it fled the body, and thereby to let the spectators know that he had left the man. And when this was done, the skill and wisdom of Solomon were shown very clearly.

ENSLAVED BY
SOLOMON'S RING[1]

*Set during the reign of Solomon in the tenth century BCE
and narrated in the voice of the king himself, the* Testament
of Solomon *presented an elaborate legend relating how the
biblical monarch employed a magical ring given to him by
the archangel Michael to command a host of demons to
construct the First Temple, the sacred building that housed
the Ark of the Covenant. A parade of demons appeared before his throne, each forced by the ring's power to reveal its
name, purpose, and weakness. In the end, Solomon's
power did not last; having succumbed to lust and idolatry,
he subsequently lost his power over the demonic host.
Most likely written by a Christian author between the first
and third centuries CE, the* Testament of Solomon *is the
richest narrative about demon lore to survive from antiquity. The anonymous author drew on traditions about malevolent spirits from cultures around the Mediterranean
rim. Originally written in Greek, this legend percolated
for centuries in many forms and languages in Jewish,
Christian, and Muslim literary traditions.*

The Greek title

Testament of Solomon, Son of David, who reigned in Jerusalem, and subdued all the spirits of the air, of the earth, and
under the earth; through [them] he also accomplished all the
magnificent works of the Temple; [this tells] what their authorities are against men, and by what angels these demons are
thwarted.

Prologue: Solomon's praise

Blessed are you, Lord God, who has given this authority to Solomon. Glory and power to you forever. Amen.

Ornias the demon tries to interfere with the boy who helps Solomon build the Temple

Once upon a time, when the Temple of the city of Jerusalem was being built and the artisans were working on it, Ornias the demon came as the sun was setting and took half the wages and provisions of the master workman's little boy. Also, each day (the demon) was sucking the thumb of [the boy's] right hand. So the little boy, who was much loved by me, grew thin.

Solomon interrogates the boy

But I, Solomon, interrogated the boy one day and said to him, "Have I not loved you more than all the other artisans working in the Temple of God, and have I not been paying you double wages and provisions? Why then are you growing thinner every day?"

The boy said, "I beg you, King, listen to what is happening to me. After we are dismissed from work on the Temple of God, when the sun has set and I am resting, an evil spirit comes and makes off with half my pay and half my provisions. Also he grabs my right hand and sucks my thumb. You can see that when my soul is in distress, my body grows thinner every day."

Through the archangel Michael the Lord God grants Solomon the magical ring which gives Solomon power over demons

When I, Solomon, heard these things, I went into the Temple of God and, praising him day and night, begged with all my soul that the demon might be delivered into my hands and that

I might have authority over him. Then it happened that while I was praying to the God of heaven and earth, there was granted me from the Lord Sabaoth through the archangel Michael a ring which had a seal engraved on precious stone. He said to me, "Solomon, Son of David, take the gift which the Lord God, the highest Sabaoth, has sent to you; [with it] you shall imprison all demons, both female and male, and with their help you shall build Jerusalem when you bear this seal of God."

According to Solomon's instructions, the boy brings back the demon with the aid of the magical ring

Now I became so joyful that I continually sang hymns of praise to the God of heaven and earth and glorified him. The next day, I ordered the child to come to me and I gave the seal to him. Then I said to him, "At the moment the demon appears to you, fling this ring into his chest and say to him, 'Come! Solomon summons you!' and come running back to me as fast as you can before he says anything that would frighten you."

Now it happened that at the usual time the pesky demon Ornias came like a flaming fire to take the little boy's pay, as was his custom. According to Solomon's instructions to him, the little boy flung the ring into the chest of the demon and said to him, "Come! Solomon summons you!" and started to take off running to Solomon as fast as he could go. But the demon screamed and said to the little boy, "Why have you done this? Remove the ring and give it back to Solomon, and I shall give you all the silver and gold of the earth."

But the little boy replied, "As the Lord God of Israel lives, I will never withstand you if I do not deliver you to Solomon." Then the little boy went and spoke to Solomon, "King Solomon, I brought the demon to you just as you commanded me; observe how he is standing bound in front of the gates outside, crying out with a great voice to give me all the silver and gold of the earth so that I would not deliver him to you."

Solomon interrogates the demon, learns his name
and his activity, and by the power of the seal
ring commands him to work on the Temple

When I heard these things, I, Solomon, got up from my throne and saw the demon shuddering and trembling with fear. I said to him, "Who are you? What is your name?" The demon replied, "I am called Ornias."

I said to him, "Tell me, in which signs of the zodiac do you reside?" The demon replied, "In Aquarius. I strangle those who reside in Aquarius because of their passion for women whose zodiacal sign is Virgo. Moreover, while in a trance I undergo three transformations. Sometimes I am a man who craves the bodies of effeminate boys and when I touch them, they suffer great pain. Sometimes I become a creature with wings [flying] up to the heavenly regions. Finally I assume the appearance of a lion. In addition, I am descended from an archangel of the power of God, but I am thwarted by Ouriel, the archangel."

When I, Solomon, heard the archangel's name mentioned, I honored and glorified the God of heaven and earth. After I sealed [the demon] with my seal, I ordered him into the stone quarry to cut for the Temple stones which had been transported by way of the Arabian Sea and dumped upon the seashore. But being terrified to touch iron, he said to me, "I beg you, King Solomon, let me have a measure of freedom, and I shall bring up all the demons."[2] Since he did not want to be subject to me, I prayed that the archangel Ouriel would come to help me. Immediately I saw the archangel Ouriel descending to me from heaven.

The archangel Ouriel aids Solomon
in overcoming Ornias

The angel commanded sea monsters to arise out of the sea and he withered up their species and cast his fate to the ground. In this same way he also subjected the great demon Ornias to cut stones and to bring to completion the construction of the

Temple which I, Solomon, was in the process of building. Again, I glorified the God of heaven and earth and I commanded Ornias to come near according to his fate. Then I gave him the seal and said, "Go and bring here to me the Prince of Demons."

Ornias the demon brings Beelzeboul, the Prince of Demons, to Solomon with the help of the magical ring

So Ornias took the ring and went to Beelzeboul, and said to him, "Come! Solomon summons you!" But Beelzeboul said to him, "Tell me, who is the Solomon of whom you speak?" Then Ornias flung the ring into the chest of Beelzeboul and replied, "Solomon the king summons you!" Beelzeboul cried out like [one who is burned] from a great burning flame of fire, and when he had gotten up, he followed [Ornias] under coercion and came to me. When I saw the Prince of Demons approaching, I glorified God and said, "Blessed are you, Lord God Almighty, who has granted to your servant Solomon wisdom, the attendant to your thrones, and who has placed in subjection all the power of the demons."

Solomon interrogates Beelzeboul

Then I interrogated him and said, "Tell me, who are you?" The demon said, "I am Beelzeboul, the ruler of the demons." I demanded that without interruption he sit next to me and explain the manifestations of the demons. Then he promised to bring to me all the unclean spirits bound. Again, I glorified the God of heaven and earth, continually giving thanks to him.

Solomon interrogates Onoskelis and learns of her activity

I now asked the demon if there were any female demons. When he replied that there were, [I said that] I wanted to see [one]. Beelzeboul went off and showed me Onoskelis, who had a very beautiful form. Her body was that of a woman with a fair complexion, but her legs were those of a mule.

When she came to me, I said to her, "Tell me who you are." She responded, "My name is Onoskelis. I am a spirit which has been made into a body. I recline in a den on the earth. I make my home in caves. However, I have a many-sided character. Sometimes I strangle men; sometimes I pervert them from their true natures. Most of the time, my habitats are cliffs, caves, and ravines. Frequently, I also associate with men who think of me as a woman, especially with those whose skin is honey-colored, for we are of the same constellation. It is also true that they worship my star secretly and openly. They do not know that they deceive themselves and excite me to be an evildoer all the more. For they want to obtain gold by remembering [me], but I grant little to those who seriously worship me."

Next I asked her how she came into being. She said, "I was generated from an unexpected voice which is called a voice of the echo of the black heaven, emitted in matter."

I said to her, "By what heavenly body do you travel?" She replied, "By the full moon, because by the moon I pass over more things." Then I said, "What angel thwarts you?" She responded, "One that is also in *you*, King!" Now because I thought these [remarks were meant] in ridicule, I commanded a soldier to strike her. But she cried out in a loud voice and said, "I say to you, King, by God's wisdom I have been entrusted to your power."

Onoskelis compelled to spin hemp for the construction of ropes

So I uttered the name of the Holy One of Israel and commanded her to spin the hemp for the ropes used in the construction of the Temple of God. She was sealed and bound in such a way that she was made powerless, so that she had to stand day and night to spin the hemp.

Solomon interrogates Asmodeus
and learns of his activity

I commanded another demon be brought to me; and he [Beel-zeboul] brought me the evil demon Asmodeus, bound. I asked him, "Who are you?" He scowled at me and said, "And who are *you*?" I said to him, "You [dare to] answer [so arrogantly] when you have been punished like this?" He continued to give forth the same look and said to me, "How *should* I answer you? You are the son of a man, but although I was born of a human mother, I [am the son] of an angel; it is impossible for one of heavenly origin [to speak] an arrogant word to one of earthly origin. My constellation [is like an animal which] re-clines in its den in heaven; some men call it the Great Bear, but others the Offspring of a Dragon. Moreover, a smaller constel-lation accompanies my constellation, for the high position and throne of my father is always in the sky. So do not ask me so many things, Solomon, for eventually your kingdom will be divided. This glory of yours is temporary. You have us to tor-ture for a little while; then we shall disperse among human beings again with the result that we shall be worshiped as gods because men do not know the names of the angels who rule over us."

When I, Solomon, heard these things, I bound him with greater care. Then I ordered him to be flogged with a rod and to defend himself by stating his name and [reporting] his activ-ity. The demon stated, "I am the renowned Asmodeus; I cause the wickedness of men to spread throughout the world. I am always hatching plots against newlyweds; I mar the beauty of virgins and cause their hearts to grow cold."

I said to him, "Is this all that you do?" He spoke again, "I spread madness about women through the stars and I have often committed a rash of murders."

Asmodeus thwarted by the angel Raphael, as well as a smoking liver and a gall of a fish

Then I abjured him by the name of the Lord Sabaoth, "Asmodeus, fear God, and tell me by which angel you are thwarted." The demon said, "Raphael, the one who stands before God; but also a liver and a gall of a fish smoking on coals of charcoal drives me away." I asked him again, saying, "Do not hide anything from me, for I am Solomon, Son of David. Tell me the name of the fish you fear." He replied, "It is called the sheatfish. It is found in the rivers of Assyria and it is hatched only there; I am also found in those parts."

Asmodeus required to mold clay for the vessels of the Temple

I said to him, "Is there not something else about you, Asmodeus?" He said to me, "The power of God which binds me with unbreakable bonds by his seal knows that what I have related to you is true. I beg you, King Solomon, do not condemn me to water." But I smiled and replied, "As the Lord, the God of my fathers, lives, you shall have irons to wear and you shall mold clay for all the vessels of the Temple, eliminating the cost of the mold." Then I ordered ten water jars to be made available and [I commanded] him to be encircled by them. Though he complained bitterly, the demon carried out the things which he had been commanded. Asmodeus did this because he also had knowledge of the future. So I, Solomon, glorified God, who gave me this authority; then, taking the liver and the gall of the fish, along with a branch of storax, I lit a fire under Asmodeus because he was powerful, and his voice was thwarted, as well as a tooth full of venom.[3]

Solomon interrogates Beelzeboul again and learns his activities

Then I summoned Beelzeboul to appear before me again. When he was seated, I thought it appropriate to ask him, "Why are you alone Prince of the Demons?" He replied, "Because I am the only one left of the heavenly angels [who fell]. I was the highest-ranking angel in heaven, the one called Beelzeboul. There also accompanied me another ungodly [angel] whom God cut off and now, imprisoned here, he holds in his power the race of those bound by me in Tartarus. He is being nurtured in the Red Sea; when he is ready, he will come in triumph."

I said to him, "What are your activities?" He replied, "I bring destruction by means of tyrants; I cause the demons to be worshiped alongside men; and I arouse desire in holy men and select priests. I bring about jealousies and murders in a country and I instigate wars."

Then I said to him, "Bring to me the one you said is being nurtured in the Red Sea." He retorted, "I will bring no one back to you. But there will come a certain demon whose name is Ephippas who will bind him and bring him up out of the abyss." I responded, "Tell me why he is in the abyss of the Red Sea and what his name is." He, however, said, "Do not ask me; you are not able to learn that from me. He will come to you because I, too, am with you." So I said to him, "Tell me in which star you reside." "The one called by men the Evening Star," he said.

Beelzeboul thwarted by "the Almighty God"

Then I said, "Tell me which angel thwarts you." "The Almighty God," he replied. "He is called by the Hebrews Patike, the one who descends from the heights; he is [called] by the Greeks Emmanouel. I am always afraid of him, and trembling. If anyone adjures me with the oath [called] 'the Elo-i,' a great name for his power, I disappear."[4]

Beelzeboul compelled to cut marble for the Temple

Now when I, Solomon, heard these things, I commanded him to cut blocks of Theban marble. As he was beginning to cut, all the demons cried out with a loud voice because [he was their] king, Beelzeboul.

Beelzeboul required to inform Solomon about heavenly things

Nevertheless, I, Solomon, persisted in interrogating him, saying, "If you wish to obtain a release, inform me about heavenly things." Beelzeboul replied, "Listen, King, if you burn oil of myrrh, frankincense, and bulbs of the sea along with spikenard and saffron, and light seven lamps during an earthquake, you will strengthen [your] house. And if, being ritually clean, you light [them] at the crack of dawn, just before the sun comes up, you will see the heavenly dragons and the way they wriggle along and pull the chariot of the sun." When I, Solomon, heard these things, I rebuked him and said, "Be silent and continue cutting marble just as I ordered you."

Solomon interrogates Lix Tetrax, the demon of the wind

After I praised God, I, Solomon, requested the presence of another demon and he appeared before me. He was bearing his face on the air high above and the remaining part of his body was crawling along like a little snail. Suddenly, he broke through a large contingent of soldiers, raised up a blustering cloud of dust from the earth, transported it upward, and hurled it against me many times [while I watched] in amazement. I exclaimed, "What do we have here?" [But this continued] for a long time. When I stood up, I spat on the ground at that spot and I sealed [him] with the ring of God. As a result, the moving air stopped. Then I asked him, saying, "Who are you?" After he had stirred up another cloud of dust, he answered me, "What do you want, King Solomon?" I answered him, "Tell me what you are called; also, I want to interrogate you." Thus, I give thanks to God who instructs me as to how to respond to their evil plots.

So the demon said to me, "I am called Lix Tetrax." "What is your activity?" I queried. He responded, "I create divisions among men, I make whirlwinds, I start fires, I set fields on fire, and I make households non-functional. Usually, I carry on my activity in the summertime. If I get the chance, I slither in under the corners of houses during the night or day. I am the direct offspring of the Great One." I asked him, "In which constellation do you reside?" He replied, "Toward the very tip of the horn of the moon when it is found in the South—there is my star. Therefore, I was assigned to draw out the fever which strikes for a day and a half. As a result, many men, when they see [this], pray about the day-and-a-half fever, [invoking] these three names, 'Baltala, Thallal, Melchal,' and I heal them." Then I, Solomon, said to him, "But when you wish to do evil, who grants you the power?" He replied, "The angel by whom also the day-and-a-half fever is stopped."

The demon Lix Tetrax, thwarted by the archangel Azael, is compelled to help raise stones for the Temple workmen

Finally, I asked him, "By what name are you thwarted?" He responded, "The name of the archangel Azael." Then I placed my seal on the demon and commanded him to pick up stones and hurl them up to the heights of the Temple for the workmen; compelled, the demon complied with his orders.

Solomon interrogates the seven heavenly bodies of this world of darkness, and learns of their activities and thwarting angels

Again, I glorified God, who gave me this authority, and I commanded another demon to appear before me. There came seven spirits bound up together hand and foot, fair of form and graceful. When I, Solomon, saw them, I was amazed and asked them, "Who are you?" They replied, "We are heavenly bodies, rulers of this world of darkness." The first said, "I am Deception." The second said, "I am Strife." The third said, "I am Fate." The fourth said, "I am Distress." The fifth said, "I am Error." The sixth said, "I am Power." The seventh said, "I am The Worst. Our stars in heaven look small, but we are named like gods. We change our position together and we live together, sometimes in Lydia, sometimes in Olympus, sometimes on the great mountain."

Then I, Solomon, continued questioning them, beginning with the first. "Tell me what you do." He responded, "I am Deception. I plot deception and I devise the most evil heresies. But there is one who thwarts me, the angel Lamechiel."

The second said, "I am Strife. I cause strife by making available clubs, pellets, and swords, my implements of war. But I have an angel who thwarts me, Baruchiel."

Likewise, the third said, "I am called Fate. I cause every man to fight in battle rather than make peace honorably with those who are winning. But why am I talking so much? There is an angel who thwarts me, Marmaroth."

The fourth [, Distress,] said, "I cause men to lack moderation; I divide them into factions; I keep them separated. Since Strife follows in my footsteps, I set men against each other and do many other similar things to them. But why am I talking so much? There is an angel who thwarts me, the great Balthioul."

The fifth said, "I am Error, King Solomon, and I am leading you into error, and I led you into error when I made you kill your brothers.[5] I lead people into error by hunting for graves and I teach them [how] to dig them up. I lead [men's] minds to stray away from religion, and I do many other bad things. However, there is an angel who thwarts me, Ouriel."

Likewise, the sixth said, "I am Power. I raise up tyrants, I depose kings, and I grant power to all those who are enemies. There is an angel who thwarts me, Asteraoth."

Similarly, the seventh said, "I am The Worst, and you, King, I shall harm when I order [you to be bound] with the bonds of Artemis. Because these things affect you, you have desire like a beloved one, but to me [that is] a desire which corresponds to myself [which is] wisdom. For if anyone is wise, he will not follow in my steps."

But I, Solomon, when I heard these things, sealed them with the ring of God and commanded them to dig the foundation of the Temple. It stretched out 250 cubits in length. So all the things which were commanded them were accomplished.

Solomon interrogates the headless demon called Murder and learns of his activity and what thwarts him

Again, I asked that other demons visit me in succession and there was brought to me a demon, a man [who had] all his limbs, but no head. I said to him, "Tell me who you are and what you are called." The demon replied, "I am called Murder; for I devour heads, wishing to get a head for myself, but I do not consume enough. I long for a head to do exactly what you do, King."

When I heard these things, I stretched out my hand against his chest and put my seal on him. Then the demon jumped up, tore himself loose, and muttered, saying, "Woe is me! How did I fall in with a traitor, Ornias? I do not see." So I said to him, "How is it possible for you to see?" He replied, "Through my breasts!" When I, Solomon, heard the delight in his voice, I wished to learn more. So I asked him, "How is it possible for you to speak?" He responded, "My voice has taken over voices from many men; for I have closed up the heads of those among men who are called dumb. When infants are ten days old, and if one cries during the night, I become a spirit and I rush in and attack [the infant] through his voice. What is more, my visit to premature [infants] is harmful. My strength happens to reside in my hands, that is, like [that which takes place] at an executioner's block, I grab hold of heads, cut [them] off, and attach [them] to myself; then, by the fire which is continually [burning] in me, I consume [them] through my neck. I am the one who inflames the limbs, inflicts the feet, and produces festering sores. It is by a fiery flash of lightning that I am thwarted." I ordered him to stay with Beelzeboul until the time when a friend might arrive.

Solomon interrogates the doglike demon, Scepter

Then I ordered another demon to make his presence before me. He became before me in the form of a gigantic dog, and he spoke to me in a loud voice, "Hail, O King Solomon!" I was astounded and said to him, "Who are you, dog?" He said, "You suppose that I am a dog; but before your time, King, I was a man. I accomplished many unlawful deeds in the world and I was so extremely strong that I restrained the stars of heaven and now I am preparing more evil works. Consequently, I deceive men who follow my star closely and I lead [them] into stupidity; I also subdue the hearts of men through their throats and in this way I destroy [them]."

The demon Scepter helps Solomon to obtain an emerald stone for the Temple and Solomon learns of Scepter's thwarting angel

I said to him, "What is your name?" he replied, "Scepter." Then I said to him, "What is your activity and why do you seem to me to be so prosperous?" The demon said, "Turn over your manservant to me and I shall spirit him off to a place in the mountains where I shall show him an emerald stone shaken loose from its foundation. With it, you will adorn the Temple of God."

When I heard these things, I immediately ordered my household servant to accompany him and to take the ring bearing God's seal with him. I told him, "Go with him and whoever shows you the emerald stone, seal him with the ring, observe the place in detail, and bring the ring back to me." So when [the demon] went out and showed him the emerald stone, [the household servant] sealed him with the ring of God, and brought the emerald stone back to me. I then decided to have the two demons, the headless one and the dog, bound, and [to request that] the stone be carried about day and night like, as it were, a light for the working artisans.

Next I extracted from that moving stone 200 shekels for the supports of the altar, for the stone was shaped like a leek. Then I, Solomon, when I had glorified the Lord God, locked up the treasure chest containing the stone and commanded the demons to cut marble for the construction of the Temple. Also, I asked the dog in private, "By which angel are you thwarted?" he replied, "By the great Briathos."

Solomon interrogates the Lion-Shaped Demon

I commanded another demon to come before me. He came roaring like a stately lion and he took his place and questioned me by word: "King Solomon, I have this particular form [and am] a spirit which can never be bound. I am one who sneaks in and watches over all who are lying ill with a disease and I make it impossible for man to recover from his taint. I have another activity. I involve the legions of demons subject to me for I am at the places [where they are] when the sun is setting. The name for all demons which are under me is legion."[6] Then I asked him, "What is your name?" He replied, "The Lion-Shaped Demon, an Arab by descent." So I said to him, "How are you and your demon thwarted, that is, who is your angel?" The demon said, "If I tell you his name, I place not only myself in chains, but also the legion of demons under me."

So I said to him, "I adjure you by the name of the great God Most High: By what name are you and your demons thwarted?" The demon said, "By the name of the one who at one time submitted to suffer many things [at the hands] of men, whose name is Emmanouel, but now he has bound us and will come to torture us [by driving us] into the water at the cliff. As he moves about, he is conjured up by means of three letters."

So I sentenced his legion to carry wood from the grove [of trees. Then I sentenced] the Lion-Shaped One to saw it up as kindling with his claws and to throw it under the perpetually burning kiln.

Solomon interrogates the three-headed dragon spirit, Head of the Dragons, and learns that he is thwarted by the angel of the Wonderful Counselor who ascended at the "Place of the Skull"

Now when I had worshiped the God of Israel I ordered another demon to come forward. This time a three-headed dragon with an awful skin appeared before me. I asked him, "Who are you?" He said, "I am a three-pronged spirit, one who overpowers by means of three deeds. In the wombs of women, I blind children. I also turn their ears around backwards and make them dumb and deaf. Finally, I strike men against the body and I make [them] fall down, foam [at the mouth], and grind their teeth. But there is a way by which I am thwarted [, namely,] by [the site] which is marked 'Place of the Skull,' for there an angel of the Wonderful Counselor foresaw that I would suffer, and he will dwell publicly on the cross. He is the one who will thwart me, being the one among [the angels] to whom I am subject.

"But at the place at which he ascended, King Solomon, he will erect a dark pillar formed on the air after Ephippas has brought gifts from the Red Sea, from inside Arabia. In the foundation of the Temple which you have begun to build, King Solomon, there is hidden away much gold. Dig it up and confiscate it." So I, Solomon, sent my servant and found [that it was] just as the demon told me. After I sealed [him with] the ring, I praised God.

Next I said to him, "Tell me what you are called." The demon replied, "Head of the Dragons." So I ordered him to make bricks for the Temple of God.

Solomon interrogates Obyzouth, the female demon with disheveled hair, and learns of her activity

Then I ordered another demon to appear before me. There came before me one who had the shape of a woman but she possessed as one of her traits the form of one with disheveled hair. I said to her, "Who are you?" She replied, "And who are you? Or what need is there for you to inquire about the sort of deeds I do? But if you want to inquire, go to the royal chambers and, after you have washed your hands, sit again on your throne and ask me and then you will learn, King, who I am."

When I had done this and had sat on my throne, I, Solomon, asked her and said, "Who are you?" She replied, "Obyzouth. I do not rest at night, but travel around all the world visiting women and, divining the hour [when they give birth], I search [for them] and strangle their newborn infants. I do not go through a single night without success. You are not able to give me orders. I even make the rounds [and go] into the remotest areas. Otherwise, my work is limited to killing newborn infants, injuring eyes, condemning mouths, destroying minds, and making bodies feel pain."

Obyzouth, thwarted by the angel Raphael and by writing her name on a piece of papyrus, is hung by her hair in front of the Temple

When I, Solomon, heard these things, I was amazed. I did not look at her shape, for her body was darkness and her hair savage. I, Solomon, said to her, "Tell me, evil spirit, by what angel are you thwarted?" She said to me, "By the angel Raphael; and when women give birth, write my name of a piece of papyrus and I shall flee from them to the other world." When I heard these things I ordered her to be bound by the hair and to be hung up in front of the Temple in order that all those sons of Israel who pass through and see might glorify the God of Israel who has given me this authority.

Solomon interrogates the Winged Dragon and learns of his activities

I again ordered another demon to appear before me; and there came to me one who was in the form of a wallowing dragon, having the limbs of a dragon and wings on its back, but the face and feet of a man. When I saw him, and became amazed, I said to him, "Who are you and from where have you come?"

The spirit said to me, "This is the first time I have stood before you, King Solomon, a spirit made a god among men, but thwarted by the seal which was given to you by God. Well, I am the so-called Winged Dragon. I do not copulate with many women, but with only a few who have beautiful bodies, who possess a name of Touxylou of this star. I rendezvous with them in the form of a winged spirit, copulating [with them] through their buttocks. One woman I attacked is bearing [a child] and that which is born from her becomes Eros. Because it could not be tolerated by men, that woman perished. This is my activity. Suppose, then, that I alone am content while the rest of the demons troubled by you, being downcast, should speak the whole truth; they will cause the stack of wood about to be gathered by you for construction of the Temple to be consumed by fire."

As the demon was saying these things, suddenly the breath coming out of his mouth set the forest of Lebanon on fire and burned up all the wood which I was going to put into the Temple of God. Now I, Solomon, saw what the spirit had done and I was amazed.

After I glorified God I asked the dragon-shaped demon, saying, "Tell me by what angel you are thwarted." He replied, "By the great angel who is seated in the second heaven, who is called in Hebrew Bazazath." When I, Solomon, heard these things and invoked his angel, I condemned him to cut marble for construction of the Temple of God.

Solomon interrogates Enepsigos, the female demon with two heads, and learns of her activities and her thwarting angel, Rathanael

Then I praised God and commanded another demon to come before me. Again there came before me a spirit who had the shape of a woman, but on her shoulders were two separate heads with arms. I asked her, "Tell me who you are." She answered, "I am Enepsigos, but I am called by countless names." Then I said to her, "By what angel are you thwarted?" She responded to me, "What are you after? What do you want? I can change my appearance, first being taken for a goddess, and then becoming one who has some other shape. In this regard, do not expect to know all things about me, but because you are here in my presence, listen to this: I hover near the moon and because of this I assume three forms. At times, I am conjured up as Kronos by the wise men. At other times, I descend around those who bring me down and appear in another form. The capacity of a heavenly body is invincible, incalculable, and impossible to thwart. At any rate, changing into three different forms, I also descend and become like what you see. I am thwarted by the angel Rathanael, who takes his seat in the third heaven. On account of this, therefore, I say to you, this Temple cannot contain me."

The demon Enepsigos,
sealed with a triple-link chain, prophesies

Accordingly, when I, Solomon, had prayed to my God and invoked the angel Rathanael about whom she spoke, I made use of the seal and sealed her down with a triple-link chain; and as I bound her down, I made use of the seal of God. Then the [evil] spirit prophesied to me, saying, "You are doing these things to us now, King Solomon, but after a period of time your kingdom shall be divided. At still a later time this Temple shall be destroyed and all Jerusalem shall be demolished by the king[s] of the Persians and Medes and Chaldeans. Also, the implements of the Temple which you are making shall serve other gods. Along with these [events], also all the vessels in which you have entrapped us shall be broken in pieces by the hands of men. Then we shall come forth with much power and we shall be scattered here and there throughout the world. We will lead astray all the inhabited world for a long time until the Son of God is stretched upon the cross.[7] For there has not yet arisen a king like him, one who thwarts all of us, whose mother shall not have sexual intercourse with a man. Who holds such authority over the spirits except that one? The one whom the first devil shall seek to tempt, but shall not be able to overcome, the letters of whose name add up to six hundred forty-four—he is Emmanouel. Because of this, King Solomon, your time is evil, your years are short, and your kingdom shall be given to your servant."

Solomon explains why he wrote the testament

When I, Solomon, heard these things, I glorified God. Though I was amazed at the defense of the demons, I distrusted them and did not believe the things which were said by them until they occurred. But when they happened, then I understood, and at my death I wrote this testament to the sons of Israel and I gave [it] to them so that [they] might know the powers of the demons and their forms, as well as the names of the angels by which they are thwarted. When I had glorified the God of Israel, I commanded the spirit to be bound up with unbreakable bonds.

Solomon interrogates Kunopegos, the cruel sea-horse demon

When I had praised God, I commanded another spirit to appear before me. There came before me another demon who had the form of a horse in front and a fish in back. He said in a great voice, "King Solomon, I am a cruel spirit of the sea. I rise up and come on the open seas with the sea and I trip up the greater number of men [who sail] on it. I raise myself up like a wave and, being transformed, I come in against the ships, for this is my activity: to receive beneath the sea treasures and men. For I raise myself up, take men, and hurl them under the sea. So I am always lusting after [their] bodies, but until now I have been casting [the treasures] out of the sea. However, since Beelzeboul, the ruler of the spirits of the air and the earth and beneath the earth gives advice about the activities with respect to each one of us, I therefore came up out of the sea to have some consultation with him.

"But I also have another reputation and activity: I change myself into waves, come up from the sea, and show myself to men. They call me Kunopegos because I change myself into a man. The name is true to me. Moreover, I cause a type of seasickness when I pass into men. So when I came for a consultation with the ruler Beelzeboul, he bound me up and delivered me into your hands. Now I am standing before you and, because of not having water for two or three days, my spirit is ceasing from speaking to you."

The demon Kunopegos, thwarted by the angel Iameth, is sealed in a bowl and stored away in the Temple of God

So I said to him, "Tell me by what angel you are thwarted." He replied, "By Iameth." Then I ordered him to be cast into a broad, flat bowl, and ten receptacles of seawater to be poured over [it]. I fortified the top side all around with marble and I unfolded and spread asphalt, pitch, and hemp rope around over the mouth of the vessel. When I had sealed it with the ring, I ordered [it] to be stored away in the Temple of God.

Solomon interrogates a lecherous spirit and learns his activity and that he will be thwarted by the Savior or by the Savior's mark on the forehead

I ordered another spirit to appear before me. There came a spirit having the shadowy form of a man and gleaming eyes. I asked him, saying, "Who are you?" He replied, "I am the lecherous spirit of a giant man who died in a massacre in the age of giants." So I said to him, "Tell me what you accomplish on earth and where you make your dwelling."

He replied, "My home is in inaccessible places. My activity is this: I seat myself near dead men in the tombs and at midnight I assume the form of the dead; if I seize anyone, I immediately kill him with a sword. If I should not be able to kill him, I cause him to be possessed by a demon and to gnaw his own flesh to pieces and the saliva of his jowls to flow down." So I said to him, "Fear the God of heaven and earth and tell me by what angel you are thwarted." He replied, "He who is about to return [as] Savior thwarts me. If his mark is written on [one's] forehead, it thwarts me, and because I am afraid of it, I quickly turn and flee from him. This is the sign of the cross." When I heard these things, I, Solomon, locked up the demon just like the other demons.

Solomon interrogates the thirty-six heavenly bodies and learns of their activities and what thwarts them

Then I commanded another demon to appear before me. There came to me thirty-six heavenly bodies, their heads like formless dogs. But there were among them [those who were] in the form of humans, or of bulls, or of dragons, with faces like the birds, or the beasts, or the sphinx. When I, Solomon, saw these beings, I asked them, saying, "Well, who are you?" All at once, with one voice, they said, "We are thirty-six heavenly bodies, the world rulers of the darkness of this age. But you, King, are not able to harm us or to lock us up; but since God gave you authority over all the spirits of the air, the earth, and [the regions] beneath the earth, we have also taken our place before you like the other spirits."

Then I, Solomon, summoned the first spirit and said to him, "Who are you?" He replied, "I am the first decan of the zodiac [and] I am called Ruax. I cause heads of men to suffer pain and I cause their temples to throb. Should I hear only, 'Michael, imprison Ruax,' I retreat immediately."

The second said, "I am called Barsafael. I cause men who reside in my time period to have pains on the sides of their heads. Should I hear, 'Gabriel, imprison Barsafael,' I retreat immediately."

The third said, "I am called Artosael. I do much damage to the eyes. Should I hear, 'Ouriel, imprison Artosael,' I retreat immediately."

The fourth said, "I am called Oropel. I attack throats, [resulting in] sore throats and mucus. Should I hear, 'Raphael, imprison Oropel,' I retreat immediately."

The fifth said, "I am called Kairoxanondalon. I cause ears to have obstructions. If I hear, 'Ourouel, imprison Kairoxanondalon,' I retreat immediately."

The sixth said, "I am called Sphendonael. I produce tumors of the parotid gland and tetanic recurvation. If I hear, 'Sabael, imprison Sphendonael,' I retreat immediately."

The seventh said, "I am called Sphandor. I weaken the strength of the shoulders and deaden the nerves of the hand,

and I make limbs paralyzed. If I hear, 'Arael, imprison Sphandor,' I retreat immediately."

The eighth said, "I am called Belbel. I pervert the hearts and minds of men [. . .] If I hear, 'Karael, imprison Belbel,' I retreat immediately."

The ninth said, "I am called Kourtael. I call forth colics into the bowels. If I hear, 'Iaoth, imprison Kourtael,' I retreat immediately."

The tenth said, "I am called Metathiax. I cause pains in the kidneys. If I hear, 'Adonael, imprison Metathiax,' I retreat immediately."

The eleventh said, "I am called Katanikotael. I unleash fights and feuds in homes. If anyone wishes to make peace, let him write on seven laurel leaves the names of those who thwart me: 'Angel, Eae, Ieo, Sabaoth, imprison Katanikotael,' and when he has soaked the laurel leaves [in water], let him sprinkle his house with the water and I retreat immediately."

The twelfth said, "I am called Saphthorael. I put dissensions into the minds of men and I delight when I cause them to stumble. If anyone writes down these words, 'Iae, Ieo, sons of Sabaoth,' and wears them around his neck, I retreat immediately."

The thirteenth said, "I am called Phobothel. I cause loosening of the tendons. If I hear, 'Adonai,' I retreat immediately."

The fourteenth said, "I am called Leroel. I bring on chill[s] and shivering and sore throat. If I hear, 'Iax, do not stand fast, do not be fervent, because Solomon is fairer than eleven fathers,' I retreat immediately."

The fifteenth said, "I am called Soubelti. I unleash shivering and numbness. If I hear only, 'Rizoel, imprison Soubelti,' I retreat immediately."

The sixteenth said, "I am called Katrax. I inflict incurable diseases on men. If anyone wants to regain health, let him pulverize coriander and rub it on his lips, saying 'I adjure you by Zeus, retreat from the image of God,' and I retreat immediately."

The seventeenth said, "I am called Ieropa. I sit on the stomach of a man and cause convulsions in the bath; and on the street I find the man and make [him] fall to the ground. Whoever says into the right ear of the afflicted for the third time, 'Iouda Zizabou,' you see, makes me retreat."

The eighteenth said, "I am called Modebel. I separate wives from husbands. If anyone writes the names of the eight fathers and places them in the doorways, I retreat immediately."

The nineteenth said, "I am called Mardero. I inflict incurable fevers; write my name in some such way in the house, and I retreat immediately."

The twentieth said, "I am called Rhyx Nathotho. I locate myself in the knees of men. If anyone writes on a piece of papyrus 'Phounebiel,' I retreat immediately."

The twenty-first said, "I am called Rhyx Alath. I produce the croup in infants. If anyone writes, 'Rarideris,' and carries it, I retreat immediately."

The twenty-second said, "I am called Rhyx Audameoth. I inflict heart pain. If anyone writes, 'Raiouoth,' I retreat immediately."

The twenty-third said, "I am called Rhyx Manthado. I cause the kidneys to suffer pain. If anyone writes, 'Iaoth, Ouriel,' I retreat immediately."

The twenty-fourth said, "I am called Rhyx Aktonme. I cause the ribs to suffer pain. If anyone writes on a piece of wood from a ship which has run aground, 'Marmaraoth of mist,' I retreat immediately."

The twenty-fifth said, "I am called Rhyx Anatreth. I send gas and burning up into the bowels. If I hear 'Arara, Arare,' I retreat immediately."

The twenty-sixth said, "I am called Rhyx, the Enautha. I make off with minds and alter hearts. If anyone writes, 'Kalazael,' I retreat immediately."

The twenty-seventh said, "I am called Rhyx Axesbuth. I cause men to suffer from diarrhea and hemorrhoids. If anyone adjures me in pure wine and gives it to the one who is suffering, I retreat immediately."

The twenty-eighth said, "I am called Rhyx Hapax. I unleash insomnia. If anyone writes, 'Kok; Phedismos,' and wears it down from the temples, I retreat immediately."

The twenty-ninth said, "I am called Rhyx Anoster. I unleash

hysteria and cause pains in the bladder. If anyone mashes up the seeds of laurel into pure oil and massages [the body with it], saying 'I adjure you by Marmaraoth,' I retreat immediately."

The thirtieth said, "I am called Rhyx Physikoreth. I bring on long-term illnesses. If anyone puts salt into [olive] oil and massages his sickly [body with it] saying 'Cherubim, seraphim, help [me],' I retreat immediately."

The thirty-first said, "I am called Rhyx Aleureth. [In the case of] swallowing fish bones, if anyone puts a bone from his fish into the breasts of the one who is suffering, I retreat immediately."

The thirty-second said, "I am called Rhyx Ichthuon. I detach tendons. If I hear, 'Adonai, malthē,' I retreat immediately."

The thirty-third said, "I am called Rhyx Achoneōth. I cause sore throat and tonsillitis. If anyone writes on ivy leaves, 'Leikourgos,' heaping them up in a pile, I retreat immediately."

The thirty-fourth said, "I am called Rhyx Autoth. I cause jealousies and squabbles between those who love each other. But the letters Alpha and Beta, written down, thwart me."

The thirty-fifth said, "I am called Rhyx Phtheneoth. I cast the evil eye on every man. But the much-suffering eye, when inscribed, thwarts me."

The thirty-sixth said, "And I am called Rhyx Mianeth. I hold a grudge against the body; I demolish houses; I cause the flesh to rot. If anyone writes on the front entrance of his house as follows, 'Melto Ardad Anaath,' I flee from that place."

When I, Solomon, heard these things, I glorified the God of heaven and earth and I ordered them to bear water. Then I prayed to God that the thirty-six demons who continually plague humanity go to the Temple of God.

I condemned some of the demons to do the heavy work of the construction of the Temple of God. Some I locked up in prisons. Others I ordered to battle the fire in [the production of] gold and silver, and to sit down beside lead and cinerary urns, and for the rest of the demons to prepare places in which they ought to be locked up.

Riches are given to Solomon by all the kings
of the earth, including Sheeba, the Queen of the South,
who was a witch

Then I, Solomon, was honored by all men under heaven, for I was building the Temple of God and my kingdom was running well. All the kings were coming to me to observe the Temple of God that I was building, and they supplied me with gold and silver, and brought in bronze, iron, lead, and wood for the Temple furnishings.

Among them Sheeba, Queen of the South, who was a witch, came with much arrogance and bowed down before me.

Solomon hears the conflict between
an old man and his son

Now it happened that one of the artisans, a dignified man, threw himself down before me, saying, "King Solomon, Son of David, have mercy on me, an elderly man." I said to him, "Tell me, old man, what you want." He replied, "I beg you, King, I have a son, my only son, and every day he does terribly violent things to me, striking me in the face and head and threatening to send me to a terrible death. Because he did this, I came forward [to request] a favor—that you will avenge me."

When I heard these things I commanded his son to be brought before me. When he came I said to him, "Do you admit to this?" He replied, "I did not become so filled with rage, King, that I struck my father with my hand. Be kind to me, O King, for it is not right to pay attention to such a story and [to his] distress." Therefore, when I, Solomon, heard the young man, I summoned the elderly man to come and reconsider. But he did not want [to come] and said, "Let him be put to death."

The demon Ornias prophesies that the son will die

Then, noticing that the demon Ornias was laughing, I became very angry that he would laugh in my presence. Dismissing the young man, I ordered Ornias to come out and I said to him, "Cursed one, did you laugh at me?" He replied, "I beg you, King; I did not laugh because of you, but because of the wretched old man and the miserable young man, his son, because after three days he will die. See, the old man has the intent of doing away with him in an evil manner."

I said, "Does he really have such an intent?" The demon said, "Yes, King." Then I commanded the demon to go away and the old man and his son to come back, and I ordered them to become friends. Then I said to the elderly man, "In three days bring your son back to me." When they had prostrated themselves before me, they departed.

Ornias is compelled to explain how he knows God's plan for the future

Then I ordered Ornias to be brought to me again and I said to him, "Tell me how you know that the young man will die in three days." He responded, "We demons go up to the firmament of heaven, fly around among the stars, and hear the decisions which issue from God concerning the lives of men. The rest of the time we come and, being transformed, cause destruction, whether by domination, or by fire, or by sword, or by chance."

I asked him, "Tell me, then, how you, being demons, are able to ascend into heaven." He replied, "Whatever things are accomplished in heaven [are accomplished] in the same way also on earth; for the principalities and authorities and powers above fly around and are considered worthy of entering heaven. But we who are demons are exhausted from not having a way station from which to ascend or which to rest; so we fall down like leaves from the trees and the men who are watching think that stars are falling from heaven. That is not true, King; rather, we fall because of our weakness and, since there is nothing on which to hold, we are dropped like flashes of lightning to the earth. We burn cities down and set fields on fire. But the stars in heaven have their foundation laid in the firmament."

The prophecy of Ornias the demon is fulfilled

When I, Solomon, heard these things, I commanded the demon to be kept under guard for five days. After five days I summoned the old man but he did not want to come. Then when he did come, I saw that he was depressed and mourning. I said to him, "Where is your son, old man?" He replied, "I have become childless, O King, and without hope I keep watch at the grave of my son." Upon hearing these things and knowing that the things which were spoken to me by the demon were true, I glorified the God of heaven and earth.

Sheeba, the Queen of the South, tours the Temple

Now when Sheeba, the Queen of the South, saw the Temple I was building, she thought it was marvelous and contributed ten thousand copper shekels.[8] She entered the inner part of the Temple and saw the altar, the cherubim and seraphim overshadowing the mercy seat, the two hundred gems glittering from the various ornaments of the lamps, and lamps also decorated with emeralds, hyacinth, and lapis lazuli. She also saw the silver, bronze, and gold vessels and the bases of the pillars entwined with bronze wrought in the pattern of a chain. Finally, she saw the Bronze Sea, which was supported by thirty-six bulls. And all were busy working in the Temple [. . .] of pay amounting to one gold talent apart from the demons.

A letter from Adarkes, king of Arabia, requesting Solomon's help against the wind demon

The king of Arabia, Adarkes, sent a letter containing the following:

"King of Arabia, Adarkes, to King Solomon, greetings. I have heard about the wisdom which has been granted to you and that, being a man from the Lord, there has been given to you understanding about all the spirits of the air, the earth, and beneath the earth. There still exists a spirit in Arabia. Early in the morning a fresh gust of wind blows until the third hour. Its terrible blast even kills man and beast and no [counter-] blast is ever able to withstand the demon. I beg you, therefore, since this spirit is like the wind, do something wise according to the wisdom which has been given to you by the Lord your God and decide to send out a man who is able to bring it under control. Then we shall belong to you, King Solomon, I and all my people and all my land; and all Arabia will be at peace if you carry out this act of vengeance for us. Consequently, we implore you, do not ignore our prayer and do become our lord for all time. Farewell my lord, as ever."

The immovable cornerstone

After I, Solomon, read this letter, I folded it, gave it to my servant, and said to him, "After seven days, remind me of this letter." So Jerusalem was being built and the Temple was moving toward completion. Now there was a gigantic cornerstone which I wished to place at the head of the corner to complete the Temple of God. All the artisans and all the demons who were helping came to the same [location] to bring the stone and mount it at the end of the Temple, but they were not strong enough to budge it.

Solomon's servant boy entraps the Arabian wind demon in a leather flask with the aid of the ring

When seven days had passed and I remembered the letter of the king of Arabia, I summoned my servant boy and said to him, "Load up your camel, take a leather flask and this seal, and go off to Arabia to the place where the spirit is blowing. Then take hold of the wineskin and [place] the ring in front of the neck of the flask [against the wind]. As the flask is being filled with air, you will discover that it is the demon who is filling it up. Carefully then, tie up the flask tightly and when you have sealed [it] with the ring, load up the camel and come back here. Be off, now, with blessings."

Then the boy obeyed the orders and went to Arabia. Now the men from the region doubted whether it was possible to bring the evil spirit under control. Nonetheless, before dawn the house servant got up and confronted the spirit of the wind. He put the flask on the ground and placed the ring on [its mouth]. [The demon] entered the flask and inflated it. Yet the boy stood firm. He bound up the mouth of the flask in the name of the Lord Sabaoth and the demon stayed inside the flask. To prove that the demon had been overcome, the boy remained three days and, [when] the spirit did not blow any longer, the Arabs concluded that he had really trapped the spirit.

The Arabian wind demon, named Ephippas, is brought to the Temple, where it is interrogated by Solomon and puts the immovable cornerstone in place

Then he loaded the flask on the camel. The Arabs sent the boy on his way with gifts and honors, shouting praises to God, for they were left in peace. Then the boy brought in the spirit and put it in the foremost part of the Temple. The following day I, Solomon, went into the Temple [for] I was very worried about the cornerstone. [Suddenly,] the flask got up, walked for seven steps, and fell down on its mouth before me. I was amazed that [even though the demon was entrapped in] the flask, he had the power to walk around, and I ordered him to get up. Panting, the flask arose and stood up. Then I asked him, saying, "Who are you?" From the inside the spirit said, "I am a demon called Ephippas [and I live] in Arabia."

I said to him, "By what angel are you thwarted?" He said, "By the one who is going to be born from a virgin and be crucified by the Jews."

Then I said to him, "What can you do for me?" He responded, "I am able to move mountains, to carry houses from one place to another, and to overthrow kings." I said to him, "If you have the power, lift this stone into the beginning of the corner of the Temple." But he responded, "I will raise not only this stone, King; but, with [the aid of] the demon who lives in the Red Sea, [I will] also [lift up] the pillar of air [which is] in the Red Sea and you shall set it up where you wish."

When he had said these things, he went in underneath the

stone, lifted it up, went up the flight of steps carrying in the stone, and inserted it into the end of the entrance of the Temple. I, Solomon, being excited, exclaimed, "Truly the Scripture which says, *It was the stone rejected by the builders that became the keystone*, has now been fulfilled," and so forth.[9]

The demon Ephippas and the demon of the Red Sea bring back the pillar and lift it up in the air

Again, I said to him, "Go, bring me the one you said [would help lift up the] pillar [which is] in the Red Sea. So Ephippas went off and brought forth the demon and both transported the pillar from Arabia. However, having outwitted [them] because these two demons could have upset the whole world with one tip of the scales, I sealed [them] around on one side and the other, and said, "Keep watch [on them] carefully." Thus, they have remained holding up the pillar in the air until this very day as a proof of the wisdom granted to me. The enormous pillar was suspended through the air, lifted up by the spirits, and thus from below the spirits appeared just like air lifting [it] up. When we looked intently, the lower part of the pillar became somewhat oblique, and so it is to this day.

Solomon interrogates the demon from the Red Sea [named Abezethibou], learns of his history and activity, and adjures him to hold up the pillar

Then I interrogated the other spirit, the one who came up out of the sea with the pillar. "Who are you, what are you called, and what is your activity? For I have heard many things about you." But the demon said, "I, King Solomon, am called Abezethibou; and once I sat in the first heaven whose name is Amelouth. Therefore, I am a hostile, winged demon with one wing, plotting against every wind under the heavens. I was present at the time when Moses appeared before Pharaoh, king of Egypt, hardening his heart. I am the one whom Jannes and Jambres, those who opposed Moses in Egypt, called to their aid. I am the adversary of Moses in [performing] wonders and signs."[10]

I therefore said to him, "How is it that you are found in the Red Sea?" He responded, "During the time of the Exodus of the sons of Israel, I gave Pharaoh pangs of anxiety and hardened the heart of him, as well as of his subordinates. I caused them to pursue closely after the sons of Israel, and Pharaoh followed with [me] and [so did] all the Egyptians. I was there at that time and we followed together. We all approached the Red Sea. Then it happened that at the time when the sons of Israel crossed over, the water turned back upon us and covered over the company of Egyptians. I was [to be] found there. I, too, was engulfed by the water, and I remained in the sea, being held down there by the pillar until Ephippas arrived."

Next I, Solomon, adjured him to hold up the pillar until the End. Then, under [the direction of] God, I adorned the Temple of God in total beauty. And I was rejoicing and praising God.

Solomon falls madly in love with a beautiful Shummanite woman and sacrifices to Jebusite gods to obtain her

I now took countless wives from every land and kingdom. I also took a journey to the kingdom of the Jebusites and saw a woman in their kingdom, and I fell madly in love with her and wanted her to be a wife in my harem. So I said to their priests, "Give me this Shummanite because I am madly in love with her." They replied, "If you love our daughter, fall down before our gods, the great Raphan and Moloch, and take her." However, I did not want to worship [their gods], so I said to them, "I worship no foreign god."

But they threatened violence against the maiden, saying, "If you have the opportunity to go to the kingdom of Solomon, say to him, 'I will not go to bed with you unless you become like my people and take five locusts and sacrifice them in the name of Raphan and Molech.'" So because I loved the girl—she was in full bloom and I was out of my senses—I accepted as nothing the custom [of sacrificing] the blood of the locusts. I took them in my hands and sacrificed in the name of Raphan and Molech to idols, and I took the maiden to the palace of my kingdom.

The glory of God departs from Solomon and he writes this testament

So the spirit of God departed from me and from that day on my words became as idle talk. She convinced me to build temples of idols.

As a result I, wretched man that I am, carried out her advice and the glory of God completely departed from me; my spirit was darkened and I became a laughingstock to the idols and demons. For this reason I have written out this, my testament, in order that those who hear might pray about, and pay attention to, the last things and not to the first things, in order that they may finally find grace forever. Amen.

DWELLERS IN THE WASTELAND

WASTELAND

Demons in Dark Age Europe

In late antiquity, demons dwelled in the empty places on the outskirts of the Christian imagination, especially in the vastness of the desert. There they confronted an ever-increasing influx of hermits and other "athletes of God" who invaded their domain in pursuit of solitude and an escape from the social obligations of urban life. Some authors in this period thought about demons abstractly as personifications of the sins that diverted monks from their holy purpose, like the socalled noonday demon who caused listlessness and distraction. For others, however, these agents of the Devil were real threats to solitary monks. Visiting their remote cells by night, demons not only appeared in alluring forms to arouse their passions but also struggled physically with the saints in ways that left them bruised and bleeding in the morning. As the literature of the desert spread to western Europe, so too did the range of demonic activity. From the sixth century onward, demons appeared increasingly outside of their desert habitat, but their power was diminished. While dangerous to ordinary people, they were depicted as paper tigers easily vanquished by the saints. They remained formidable adversaries in the otherworld, however. In the early Middle Ages, stories about visions experienced by monks on the verge of death portrayed demons as predatory in their pursuit of sinful souls, which they snatched greedily from the helping hands of angels and carried off to the depths of Hell.

THE DESERT,
A BATTLEFIELD[1]

*Antony (ca. 251–356) was the first of the "desert fathers."
Inspired by the Gospel message to give everything he
had to the poor and follow Christ (Matthew 19:21–24),
Antony and others like him sold all of their belongings, cut
their social ties, and retreated into the wilderness, where
they adopted lives of extreme deprivation. Despite his
longing for solitude, Antony's reputation for virtue at-
tracted onlookers and admirers as well as political and religious leaders in need of his guidance. An account of his
holy life written in Greek around 360 by Archbishop Athanasius of Alexandria became a bestseller in western Europe owing to a Latin translation made in the early 370s by
Evagrius of Antioch. Demons figured strongly in Antony's
trials as a hermit. Just as the Devil had tempted Christ in
the desert (see pp. 31–32), so too did legions of demons
strive to distract Antony by enticing him with the allure of
food and sex and by frightening him into losing heart and
faltering in his commitment to God. Sometimes they attacked him physically, leaving him weak with wounds and
pain. The outcome of these contests was never in doubt;
prayers and the sign of the cross were the hermit's best de-
fenses against these violent onslaughts. This account of
Christian heroism in the face of demonic attacks provided
a template for writing hagiography throughout the Middle
Ages.*

While Antony was busy with all of these things that caused
everyone to love him, the devil, an enemy of the word Christian,

could not bear to see such outstanding virtues in a young man and so he attacked him with his old wiles. First of all he tried to see whether he could drag Antony away from the form of life to which he had committed himself: he made him remember his possessions, his sister's protection, his family's high status. He tried to awaken in him a desire for material things or for the fleeting honours of this world, for the pleasures of different kinds of food and all the other attractions which belong to a life of indulgence. Finally he reminded Antony of how difficult it is to attain the goal of virtue and the very hard work involved in achieving it; he also reminded him of the weakness of the body and the length of time needed. In short he created the greatest confusion in Antony's thoughts, hoping to call him back from his proper intention . . . but when, as a result of Antony's prayers to God, the devil realized that he had been driven out by Antony's faith in Christ's sufferings, he seized the weapons with which he normally attacks all young people, using seductive dreams to disturb him at night. First he tried to unsettle him at night by means of hostile hordes and terrifying sounds, and then he attacked him by day with weapons that were so obviously his that no one could doubt that it was against the devil that Antony was fighting. For the devil tried to implant dirty thoughts but Antony pushed them away by means of constant prayer. The devil tried to titillate his senses by means of natural carnal desires but Antony defended his whole body by faith, by praying at night and by fasting. At night the devil would turn himself into the attractive form of a beautiful woman, omitting no detail that might provoke lascivious thoughts, but Antony called to mind the fiery punishment of hell and the torment inflicted by worms: in this way he resisted the onslaught of lust.

———————

Then the holy Antony, considering that a servant of God ought to take as his model the way of life of the great Elijah and to use it as a mirror to organize his own life, moved away to some tombs situated not far from his settlement. He asked one of his friends to bring him food at regular intervals. And when this brother had shut him up in one of the tombs, Antony remained there alone. But the devil was afraid that, as time went on, Antony might cause the desert to become inhabited, so he gathered together his minions and tortured Antony by beating him all over. The intensity of the pain deprived Antony of his ability both to move and to speak, and later he himself would often tell how his injuries had been so serious that they were worse than all the tortures devised by men . . . Then there was a sudden noise which caused the place to shake violently: holes appeared in the walls and a horde of different kinds of demons poured out. They took on the shapes of wild animals and snakes and instantly filled the whole place with spectres in the form of lions, bulls, wolves, vipers, serpents, scorpions and even leopards and bears, too. They all made noises according to their individual nature: the lion roared, eager for the kill; the bull bellowed and made menacing movements with his horns; the serpent hissed; the wolves leaped forward to attack; the spotted leopard demonstrated all of the different wiles of the one who controlled him. The face of each of them bore a savage expression and the sound of their fierce voices was terrifying. Antony, beaten and mauled, experienced even more atrocious pains in his body but he remained unafraid, his mind alert . . . Jesus did not fail to notice his servant's struggle but came to protect him. When at last Antony raised his eyes, he saw the roof opening above him and, as the darkness was dispelled, a ray of light poured in on him. As soon as this bright light appeared, all of the demons vanished and the pain in Antony's body suddenly ceased.

―――――――――

[At the request of his followers, Antony preached the guidelines for his way of life, including a warning about the threat of demons.] "The demons are hostile to all Christians, but they especially hate those who are monks and virgins of Christ. They set traps along their paths and strive to undermine their commitment by means of irreverent and obscene thoughts, but let them not strike terror into you. For the prayers and fasting of those who have faith in the Lord cause the demons to collapse immediately, but even if they are driven back a little way, do not think that you have gained complete victory. For they have a tendency, when wounded, to rise up with even greater violence and to change their method of attack: when they have no success with dirty thoughts, they use fears to terrify, transforming themselves into women one moment, wild animals the next moment and then serpents as well as huge bodies with a head reaching to the roof of the house, and finally turning into troops of soldiers and an infinite number of different shapes. All these vanish as soon as the sign of the cross is made . . . Now I will reveal to you other means of deception practiced by the demons. They often come at night, pretending to be angels of God and praising the monks' dedication, admiring their perseverance and promising future rewards. When you see them, protect yourselves and your dwellings with the sign of the cross and immediately they will dissolve into nothing for they fear the sign of victory by which the Saviour, depriving them of their powers of the air, has shown them up. They also often leap around, twisting their limbs in various contortions and impudently present themselves to us so as to fill our minds with terror and make our bodies shudder in horror. But in this case, too, a firm faith in God will put them to flight as if they were merely feeble jokes."

A few days later another struggle took place with the same enemy. While Antony was busy (for he was always working so that he could present his visitors with some small gift in repayment for the things they brought him), someone pulled the plait or reed of the basket he was weaving. This movement made Antony stand up and he saw a creature with a human form down to the groin but whose lower body was in the shape of an ass. Seeing this, Antony made the sign of the cross on his own forehead and just said, "I am a servant of Christ: if you have been sent to me, I shall not run away." There was not a moment's delay: at once the hideous monster fled with its attendant evil spirits, more swiftly than you could relate it, and as it rushed in headlong flight it was destroyed. The death of the monster which had been scared off and killed marked the destruction of all the demons who despite all their efforts were unable to drive Antony from the desert.

TAMING A HELL-BEAST[1]

The exorcism of demons was a common feature of Christian hagiography because it displayed Christ's power over the Devil and the authority of his saints to act in his name. In the later fourth century, Jerome of Stridon (ca. 346–420) included several stories of exorcisms in his accounts of the careers of three desert hermits who modeled their lives on the example of Antony: Paul, Malchus, and Hilarion. Perhaps taking his cue from the possessed swine in the story of Christ's exorcism of the Gerasene demoniac (see pp. 32–33), Jerome tailored a vignette unique in the tradition of Christian saints' lives, in which Hilarion subdued a murderous camel driven into a frenzy by demonic influence.

It is not enough to mention only humans: every day brute animals that had gone wild were brought to him. One of these was a Bactrian camel of enormous size which had already trampled many people to death. Restrained by very thick ropes, it was brought to Hilarion by thirty or more men making a great noise. Its eyes were bloodshot, it foamed at the mouth, its rolling tongue was swollen, and above every other source of terror there resounded its loud roar. The old man ordered it to be untied. At once those who had brought the animal and those who were with the old man all ran away, without exception. Hilarion went up to it by himself and said in Syriac, "You do not frighten me, devil, with your huge body. You are exactly the same in a fox as in a camel." While he was speaking he stood with outstretched hand. The beast came up to him, raging wildly and looking as if it was going to eat him, but immediately it knelt down, bending its head right to the ground to the amazement of all those present, suddenly displaying as much gentleness as it had previously shown ferocity. But the old man explained to them that in order to harm people the devil also enters into animals; he is inflamed with such great hatred of men that he is very keen to destroy not only them, but also their possessions.

FRENZIED POSSESSIONS[1]

The appeal of the ascetic life of the desert saints spread quickly to Europe, in no small part thanks to the inspiration ignited by the Latin translation of Athanasius's Life of Antony. *Among his earliest emulators in the west was Martin of Tours (ca. 316/336–397). Originally from Pannonia (modern Hungary), Martin enlisted in the Roman army as a young man, but refused to fight because he was a "soldier of Christ." He spent several years as a wandering hermit before settling in Poitiers (modern France), where he preached against pagan practices in the countryside. Elected bishop of Tours in 371, he established a monastic retreat in nearby Marmoutier, where he and his brethren lived in caves. Shortly before Martin's death in 397, his friend Sulpicius Severus wrote down many of the miracles performed by the saint during his lifetime, including the resurrection of the dead. The exorcism of demons featured prominently in Sulpicius's* Life of Martin, *both as a demonstration of his God-given power and as a tool to convert pagans to Christianity.*

At the same period, the slave of a man called Taetradius, who was of proconsular rank, was possessed by a demon tormenting him to death with great pain. When Martin was asked to lay his hand on him, he ordered that the man should be brought to him. But it was utterly impossible for the evil spirit to be brought out from the cell where it was, so fiercely did it attack those who tried to enter with its rabid bites. Then Taetradius threw himself at the blessed man's feet, begging him to come along to the house where the possessed man was being held. But Martin said that he was unable to enter a house that belonged to a pagan, an adherent of a false religion. For at that time Taetradius was still entangled in the error of paganism. So he promised that if the demon was driven out of the boy, he would become a Christian. Then Martin laid his hand on the boy and cast forth the unclean spirit from him. When he saw this, Taetradius believed in the Lord Jesus and was immediately made a catechumen; not long afterwards he was baptized and continued always to have an extraordinary affection for Martin as the person responsible for his salvation.

During this same period and in the same town, as Martin was entering a house belonging to the head of some family, he stopped on the very threshold, explaining that he could see a horrifying demon in the entrance hall to the house. When he ordered it to depart, the demon seized the owner's cook, who was in the inner part of the building. The wretched thing began to tear him with its teeth and to maul anyone it came across. The house was thrown into confusion, the household members panicked, and the people turned and ran. Martin stood in the way of this raving creature and first ordered it to stop. But when it raged and showed its teeth and, with mouth wide open, threatened to bite him, Martin put his fingers in its mouth and said, "If you have any power, eat these." But then, as if it had received white-hot metal in its jaws, it withdrew its teeth a long way, refusing to touch the holy man's fingers. Forced by these punishments and torments to flee from the body of the man who was possessed, it was not allowed to leave through his mouth but was expelled in a flow of diarrhea, leaving behind it foul traces.

Then when a sudden rumour concerning barbarian movements and attacks had thrown the city into a panic, Martin gave the order that a man possessed of a demon should be brought before him. He commanded it to state publicly whether this news was true. It then confessed that it was accompanied by ten demons who had spread this rumour throughout the population so that this fear, if nothing else, might drive Martin from the town; it admitted that the barbarians were not planning an attack at all. And so, as soon as the unclean spirit had confessed these things in the middle of the church, the city was freed from the fear and confusion rife at that time.

THE ANCIENT GODS
ARE FRAUDS[1]

The extirpation of pagan beliefs in the countryside re-
mained a pressing concern among Christian prelates
throughout the early Middle Ages. In the sixth century, a
bishop in Portugal named Martin of Braga (ca. 520–80)
wrote a letter to a neighboring church official in which he
lamented the stupidity of sinful countryfolk who venerated
demons in the guise of pagan gods. In this letter, Martin
explained the origin of the rebel angels, the fall of human-
kind, and the deception of the demons, who adopted the
names of ancient criminals and enticed foolish people to
worship them as though they were divine. Even worse,
many of those who directed their devotion to the demons
were already Christians, who recklessly forsook the sign of
the cross for the signs of the Devil.

After God in the beginning had made heaven and earth, he
made spiritual creatures, the angels, to stand in God's sight
and praise him in that heavenly home. One of them, made to
be an archangel surpassing all others, saw himself radiating
such glory that he did not give the honour to his Creator but
claimed to be like him. Because of this pride—along with
many other angels who supported him—he was thrown out of
that heavenly place into this air of ours, which is beneath the
heavens. An archangel at first, he then lost his glorious light
and became the Devil, dark and horrifying. It was the same
with those other angels who had agreed with him and were
also thrown out of heaven, losing their own brightness: they
were made into demons . . .

After this fall of the angels, it pleased God to shape man from the mud of the earth . . . Then, once the Devil saw that man was made to inherit the place in God's kingdom from which he had fallen, envy led him to persuade man to transgress God's commandments, and for that offence man was driven out of Paradise into exile in this world of ours, to bear much labour and grief . . . Humans, once again forgetting the God who had created the world, forsook their Creator to worship creatures. Some adored the sun, some the moon and stars, some fire, some the deep water or water from springs, believing them all not to be made by God for man's use but to be gods who had come forth on their own.

Then the Devil and his servants, the demons, began showing themselves to humans in various forms, talking to people and trying to get them to offer sacrifices to them high in the mountains and deep in the woods, worshipping them as gods. And they used the names of people who were criminals, people who had spent their lives in all sorts of criminality and law-breaking.

So one demon would claim to be Jupiter, who had been a magus so sunk in incestuous adultery that he took his own sister—whose name was Juno—as his wife, seduced his daughters, Minerva and Venus, and also committed the most disgusting incest with his grandchildren and all his relatives. But another demon named himself Mars, the instigator of discord and conflict. Then another demon, the deceitful deviser of all theft and fraud, decided to call himself Mercury: people who lust as much for profit as this god sacrifice to him when they pass through a crossroads by making mounds of rocks and throwing stones at them. Also, another demon took the name of Saturn for himself: since cruelty was his whole existence, he even ate his own children as they were being born. Another pretended to be Venus, a woman who was a whore and had whored herself not only in countless adulteries but also with Jupiter, her father, and her brother Mars.

See how lost people were in those days when ignorant peasants honoured the demons—sinning grievously—with devices of their own, and then for their own purposes the demons used the language invented by such people, so that they would worship them as gods, offer them sacrifices and imitate the evil deeds of the demons whose names they invoked . . . The damage that peasants do now, however, does not happen without God's permission because they have made God angry and do not believe wholeheartedly in the faith of Christ. So fickle are they that they name each day of the week with the name of a demon, saying "the day of Mars," "of Mercury," "Jupiter," "Venus" and "Saturn," though no day was made by those demons—just by sinners and criminals of the Greek people . . .

Such is the madness that a person baptized in the faith of Christ does not keep the "Lord's day," saying instead that he keeps "Jupiter's day" and the days "of Venus" and "Saturn," to whom no day belongs, though in their own countries they were adulterers, magicians, the wicked and the unquiet dead. As I have said, however, stupid people show honour and veneration to the demons under the guise of these names of ours! . . .

As you can see, all this happens *after* renouncing the Devil, after you have been baptized. Going back to worshipping demons and evil acts of idolatry, you have betrayed your faith and broken the pact that you had made with God. You have abandoned the sign of the cross that you took in baptism, and you look to different Devil's signs made with little birds, sneezes and many other things . . . Likewise, a person who stays with the different spells devised by magicians and sorcerers has discarded the spell of the Holy Creed and the Lord's Prayer and has trampled upon the faith of Christ because it is not possible to worship God and the Devil together.

LURKING ON THE THRESHOLD

By the sixth century, demons were no longer a serious threat in hagiographical literature. To be sure, they remained on the center stage as the primary adversaries of the saints, but they were largely defanged. Whether encountered lurking in monastic gardens or holding clandestine meetings in abandoned pagan temples, a word of authority or the sign of the cross was enough to banish them. In many stories, their banter with the saints and among themselves was entertaining and almost comical. Widely read by medieval monks, the Dialogues *of Pope Gregory the Great (ca. 540–604) featured several verbose demons whose discourse lent color and texture to his anecdotes about the intervention of the saints. There were advantages to this kind of storytelling. While Gregory's* Dialogues *were didactic in character, they were also amusing and therefore memorable to their monastic audience.*

(A) THE DEMON IN THE GARDEN[1]

One day, a nun went into the garden and saw a lettuce that appealed to her. Forgetting to bless it with the sign of the cross, she ate it greedily. Immediately after this, the nun was possessed by a demon. She fell down to the ground and was tormented without mercy. News of this soon reached Bishop Equitius, who hastened to visit the afflicted woman and help her with his prayers. As soon as he came into the garden, the demon spoke with the nun's voice to justify himself, saying, "What have I done? What have I done? I was sitting there on the lettuce, and she came and ate me!" But the man of God commanded him with great zeal to depart and not to linger any longer in the servant of almighty God. The demon did so at once and presumed to trouble her no more.

(B) THE CABAL IN THE TEMPLE[2]

As I narrate the acts of holy men, there comes to my mind what God in his great mercy did for Bishop Andrew of Fondi. I want everyone to read this story as a warning. Those who have dedicated themselves to celibacy should not dwell among women, lest their souls perish by having at hand that which they unlawfully desire. This story is neither doubtful nor uncertain, for there are almost as many witnesses to justify the truth of the tale, as there are inhabitants in that city.

When this venerable man Andrew was leading a virtuous life with diligent care, answerable to his priestly function and acting with self-control, there lived in his residence a holy woman, who had served him in the past before he was bishop. Andrew assured himself of his own intentions and had no doubt of hers, so he was content to allow her to remain in his house. The devil took his decision as an occasion to assault him with temptation. He began to present before the eyes of the bishop's mind the form of that woman, so that by such allurements ungodly thoughts might possess his whole heart.

In the meantime, it happened that a Jew was traveling from Campania to Rome. As he approached the city of Fondi, night was falling. Unable to find lodging, he took shelter in a temple dedicated to Apollo not far from the city. He intended to find rest there, but he was so afraid to reside in such a wicked and sacrilegious place that he signed himself with the cross, even though he was not a Christian.

Around midnight, as he lay awake out of fear of that forlorn and deserted temple, he looked about and spied a troop of wicked spirits marching before a demon of greater authority. The master demon took up his place and sat down in the middle of the temple, where he began diligently to ask his servants how they had spent their time and what wickedness they had done in the world. And when each one told what he had done against God's servants, one of the demons stepped forward and proclaimed that he had put into the mind of Bishop Andrew a temptation of the flesh concerning that holy woman who lived in his residence. The master demon listened attentively; what a boon it would be to corrupt the soul of so holy a man! The servant demon went on with his tale and related that the previous evening he had assaulted the bishop so mightily that the man had been compelled to touch the woman on her back. Hearing this joyful news, the wicked serpent and old enemy of humankind urged his servant with winsome words to labor diligently in the task he had already begun, in order to complete the spiritual ruin of that virtuous prelate and thereby earn a reward greater than that of his fellow demons.

The Jew lay awake all the while and heard everything the demons said, but he was very afraid. At length, the master demon sent some of his companions to see who he was and how he had presumed to lodge in their temple. When they approached and eyed him sharply, they found that he had marked himself with the sign of the cross. They marveled at this and said, "Alas, alas, here is an empty vessel, but yet it carries the sign!" Upon hearing this news, the entire pack of demons fled straightaway.

Having heard what had passed between them, the Jew rose up and hastened to the bishop, whom he found in the church. Taking the prelate aside, he demanded to know what temptation troubled him, but shame prevailed and he would not confess the truth. Then the Jew replied and told Andrew that he was guilty of casting his eyes wickedly on one of God's handmaidens, but the bishop did not acknowledge the truth. "Why do you deny it?" asked the Jew. "For is it not true that yesterday evening you advanced so far in sinful temptation that you presumed to touch her on the back?" When the bishop realized from hearing these details that the truth was known, he humbly confessed what he had so obstinately denied. Then the Jew, moved with compassion, told him how he learned about this and what the assembly of wicked spirits had said about the bishop. Hearing this, Andrew fell face down upon the earth and prayed. Then he immediately dismissed from his house not only the holy woman, but also all of the women who attended to her. And not long thereafter, he converted the temple of Apollo into an oratory dedicated to the blessed apostle Andrew. He was never again troubled by temptations of the flesh.

For his part, the Jew who had rescued the bishop found everlasting salvation, for Andrew baptized him and made him a member of the holy church. Thus, by God's providence, the Jew who had cared for the spiritual health of the Christian attained for himself the singular benefit of the Christian faith. And almighty God by the same means brought one man to embrace piety and virtue and preserved another in a holy and godly way of life.

INHABITANTS OF HELL[1]

The demeanor of demons in early medieval visionary liter-
ature was more intimidating than their conduct in the lives
of the saints. These narratives followed a specific pattern.
A devout individual, usually a monk, died and then re-
turned to life to narrate to friends and family a vision that
he had received of the afterlife. In the company of an angel,
the man's soul had made the journey to the outskirts of
Hell to witness the terrifying torments of the damned. This
kind of literature had a moral agenda; it was intended as a
warning for readers to cultivate virtue in this life in order
to avoid punishment in the world to come. In this story
told by Bede in his Ecclesiastical History of the English
People *(completed in 731), demons near the lip of Hell*
were dangerous and daunting as they intimidated the soul
of Dryhthelm, who was especially vulnerable in the ab-
sence of his angelic guardian.

Around that time, a remarkable miracle occurred in Britain
similar to those that happened long ago. For in order to arouse
the living from the death of the soul, a certain man who was
already dead returned to life and he recounted many things
worthy of remembering that he had seen. I think that it is
worth gathering some of them together briefly in this work.
There was a man, the father of a family in the region of North-
umbria called Cunningham, who was leading a religious life
with the rest of his household. Laid low by a bodily illness and
brought to death's door as it grew worse day by day, he died in
the early hours of the evening. When the sun rose, however, he
returned to life and immediately sat up. Everyone who had
been sitting around his body in mourning was struck with a

great fear and turned in flight. Only his wife remained, for she loved him very much, though she trembled with fright. He consoled her by saying: "Do not fear, for truly I have now risen from the death by which I was held and I have been permitted to live among humankind once more. Nevertheless, from this time forward I must conduct my life very differently than I had before." He immediately got up and went to the oratory in the village, where he prayed well into the day. Soon thereafter he divided everything that he possessed into three separate portions. He gave one portion to his wife and another to his sons, but the third he retained for his own good by giving it directly to the poor. Not long thereafter he abandoned the cares of this world by entering the monastery at Melrose, which is enclosed almost entirely by a bend in the river Tweed. Once he had received his tonsure, he entered his own secluded cell, which the abbot had provided for him. There until the day of his death he lived a life of great repentance of mind and body, so that even if his tongue was silent, his life would have revealed that this man had seen many things either dreadful or desired that have been concealed from other men.

He told us what he had seen with the following words: "A man with a luminous appearance and bright clothing was my guide. We went forth without speaking in what seemed to me to be the direction of the rising of the sun at the solstice. As we walked, we arrived at a valley that was very broad and deep and seemed to stretch on forever to our left. One side of the valley was very terrifying with raging flames; the other was equally intolerable owing to fierce hail and cold blasts of snow gusting and blowing away everything in sight. Both sides were teeming with the souls of men, which seemed to be thrown back and forth, as though by the onslaught of a storm. When those poor souls could no longer endure the intensity of the immense heat, they leapt into the midst of the deadly cold. And when they could find no respite there, they leapt back to the other side to burn in the midst of those unquenchable flames. Since a countless number of misshapen souls was subject to the torture of this alternating misery far and wide as far as I could see without any hope of respite, I began to think that perhaps this was Hell, for I had often heard stories about the agonizing torments there. My guide, who walked ahead of me, answered my thought: 'Do not believe this, for this is not the Hell you are thinking of.'

"But when he led me a little way further on, completely shaken by this terrifying scene, suddenly I noticed that the places before us began to grow gloomier and covered in darkness. As we entered this place, the shadows became so thick that I could see nothing else except for the outline and garment of my guide. As we progressed 'through the shadows in the lonely night,' behold suddenly there appeared before us thick masses of noisome flames spouting up into the air as though from a great pit before falling back into it again. When we arrived in this place, my guide suddenly disappeared and abandoned me alone in the midst of the shadows and this terrifying scene. As the masses of flames spouted to the heights and plunged to the depths of the pit over and over again, I saw that the tips of the rising flames were full of human souls, which like sparks ascending with smoke shot up to the heights and then, when the flames withdrew, fell back into the depths once again. Moreover, an incomparable stench poured forth with these flames and filled this entire realm of shadows. And after I had stood there for a long time, unsure what I should do or which way to turn or what fate awaited me, suddenly I heard behind me the sound of a great and most wretched wailing and at the same time raucous laughter as though some illiterate rabble was hurling insults at enemies they had captured. And as the noise became louder and finally reached me, I saw a crowd of evil spirits cheering and laughing as they dragged the souls of five people crying and wailing into the midst of the shadows. I could discern among these people one tonsured like a priest, a layman, and a woman. Dragging the souls with them, the evil spirits descended into the midst of the burning pit, and it happened that, as they went further down into the pit, I could not clearly distinguish the wailing of the people and the laughter of the demons, for the sound was confused in my ears. In the meantime, insubstantial spirits rose up out of that flame-spitting abyss and rushing forward, they surrounded me. With flaming eyes and blowing a putrid flame from their mouths and nostrils, they tormented me. They also threatened to grab me with the fiery tongs that they held in their hands, but although they terrified me, they never dared to touch me. Surrounded on every side by enemies and blinded by the shadows, I cast my eyes this way and that way to see if by chance the help that I needed might arrive from somewhere. Back on the road along which we had come there appeared something like the brightness of a star shining among the shadows, which grew little by little as it hastened quickly towards me. When the light approached, all of the vile spirits who were trying to seize me with their tongs scattered and fled. It was in fact my guide whose arrival put the spirits to flight. Presently he turned to the right and began to lead me in the direction of the rising sun in wintertime. Without delay he led me out of the shadows and into gentle breezes of serene light."

ENTRUSTED
TO TORMENT YOU[1]

Stories about the desert hermits inspired Christian ascetics in northern Europe to seek refuge from the world and its temptations in remote places. Precipitous mountainsides and fetid swamps replaced the arid wastelands of early Christian hagiography, but the struggles of the saints against their demonic adversaries remained the same. In the mid-eighth century, a monk named Felix composed an account of the pious life of Saint Guthlac (ca. 674–714). Modeled on Athanasius's Life of Antony *but set in the fenlands of East Anglia, the story of Guthlac featured a terrifying invasion of the saint's hermitage by a horde of demons, who beat him and carried him aloft to frightening heights before threatening to hurl him into the depths of Hell. The timely arrival of Saint Bartholomew caused the demonic host to retreat, thereby permitting an escort of angels to return Guthlac to the solitude of his cell in the swamp.*

Around that same time, in the intervening course of a few days, when the man of blessed memory, Guthlac, was keeping vigil in uninterrupted prayer at the darkest time of a certain night—as was his accustomed manner—he suddenly saw his entire little cell filled with a loathsome crowd of impure spirits. For the door was opened for them as they were approaching from all sides; thus, with them entering through the floor and wattle-walls, neither the joints of the doors, nor the apertures of the walls denied entrance to them; but, erupting from the sky and the earth, they covered the entire space with clouds of dark air. They were truly wild in appearance, horrible in shape, with large heads, long necks, a lean face, a pale expression, a rough beard, prickly ears, a grim brow, wild eyes, stinking mouths, equine teeth, a flaming throat, crooked jaws, broad lips, horrid-sounding voices, burnt hair, plump cheeks, a large chest, mangy thighs, knotted knees, curved legs, a swollen heel, rear-facing soles, a gaping mouth, and hoarse shouts. Indeed, they were said to shudder in their immeasurable wailing, such that they nearly filled the entire space from heaven down to earth with loud bellows. And without delay, attacking and intruding his home and castle, quicker than a word, they led the man of God outside his cell with bound limbs and threw him into the muddy waters of the dark swamp. Then, transporting that man through the harshest places of the swamp, they pulled him among the densest branches of briars, so that the joints of his limbs were torn to shreds. When they had passed a great part of the shadowy night in those afflictions, they made Guthlac stand for a brief period, commanding him to withdraw from his hermitage. That man, however, responding with a stable mind, sang as if with prophetic speech: "The Lord is at my right hand, that I may not be moved."[2] Then, taking up their tortures once again, they began to scourge him with whips as though made from iron. When, after innumerable kinds of torments, after lashes of iron whips, they saw Guthlac persist with an unshaken mind, a firm faith in what he had begun, they began to carry him among the cloudy spaces of the icy air to the horrid buzzing of their wings. Thus, when he had come to the lofty summit of the air—horrible to say!—behold, the zone of the northern sky seemed to darken with the dim vapor of dark clouds. For you could see innumerable forces of impure spirits coming henceforth to meet them. Therefore, with the throng joined as one, making their way in the thin air with an immense clamor, they brought the servant of God, Guthlac, all the way to the heinous entrance of hell. Truly, that man, gazing upon the smoking caverns of that infernal burning realm, forgot all the torments which he had previously endured by the malign spirits, as if he himself had not suffered them. For not only could you see the burning whirlpools of surging flames swelling there, but also sulfurous vortices mixed with frozen hail seemed nearly to reach the stars with spherical whirlwinds; hence, malign spirits, roaming among the gloomy caverns of the smoking abyss, were tormenting the souls of the impious—in their wretched fate—with diverse kinds of tortures. Therefore, when the man of God, Guthlac, trembled at the innumerable displays of tortures, the throng of guards—as if with one voice—said to him: "Behold, power was given to us to thrust you into these punishments, and it was entrusted to us to torment you there with various tortures among the torments of this most dreadful hell. Look at the fire, which you have inflamed in your failings, it is prepared to consume you; look, the smoldering doors of Erebus open for you with a gaping cleft; now the bowels of the Styx prefer to devour you, just as the whirlpools of the Acheron gape with horrendous jaws." With this and many other similar things having been said by them, the man of God, despising their threats and responding with unshaken senses, with a steadfast soul and a sober mind, said: "Woe to you, sons of darkness, seed of Cain, ember of ashes. If it is in your power to betray me to these punishments, see that I am ready; so why do you bring forth vain threats from lying hearts?"

Truly, as those demons were girding themselves in order to thrust Guthlac into Gehenna's waiting torments, behold! St. Bartholomew, with an immense sheen of heavenly light, breaking through the middle of the darkness of that gloomy night by an outpoured brightness, presented himself before them veiled in a golden splendor from the ethereal abode of shining Olympus. Thus, the malign spirits, not enduring the brightness of heavenly splendor, began to gnash their teeth, to grumble, to flee, to tremble, and to fear. Truly, St. Guthlac, perceiving the approach of his most faithful helper rejoiced, restored with spiritual joy.

Then, St. Bartholomew commanded the band of guards to lead that man back to his place with great tranquility, without any trouble of offense. Without delay, complying with the apostolic precepts, they performed the command quicker than a word. For they flew up, carrying that man back with great gentleness, as if on the most tranquil fittings of their wings, so that he could be led more moderately in neither chariot nor ship. Truly, when they had come to the spaces of midair, the sound of singing psalms was appropriately heard, saying: "The saints shall go from strength to strength" and so on.[3] Therefore, with dawn imminent, when the sun had turned away the nocturnal shadows from the sky, the athlete of Christ, with a triumph acquired from his enemies, stood in the same place from which he was first carried, giving thanks to Christ. Then, when, in his accustomed way, he was devoting morning praises to Lord Jesus, diverting his eyes a little, he saw standing to his left two of the attendant spirits, known to him above all the rest; when he asked them why they wept, they responded: "We bewail our power, everywhere broken by you, and we lament our feebleness against your might; for we do not dare to touch or approach you." Saying this, they vanished from his sight like smoke.

SPIRITS OF FIRE AND AIR

The Riddle of the Jinn

The jinn (also known as djinn or genies) were mythological creatures in Islamic folklore. An especially powerful or malevolent jinni was also known as an 'ifrit. Although they were distinct from demons in the Judeo-Christian tradition, they shared many of the same characteristics. Composed of fire and air, the jinn boasted supernatural powers. They could make themselves invisible, transform their shape and size, and fly rapidly from place to place. While they were morally neutral, many popular stories featured vengeful jinn who had rebelled against their servitude under King Solomon and suffered imprisonment in containers sealed with his magic ring. Unlike Judeo-Christian demons, the jinn were not innately malevolent nor exiles from Heaven; rather, they were a race of creatures who inhabited the earth before the creation of Adam and Eve. Their relationship with human beings was sometimes problematic, especially when people mistook them for deities due to their unearthly powers and misdirected to them the reverence owed to God alone. Jinn could also be devout. Some listened attentively to the preaching of Jesus and Mohammad and adopted monotheism as their religion. Others were fickle, self-serving, and dangerous, especially when released from their resented captivity.

QURANIC DEMONOLOGY[1]

*According to Muslim tradition, God revealed his teachings
to the prophet Mohammad (ca. 570–632) through the
archangel Gabriel. Recited in Arabic, these revelations circulated orally at first, but shortly after Mohammad's death,
his followers compiled and preserved them in writing. The
Qur'an ("the recitations") became the fundamental religious text of Islam. Several chapters of the Qur'an make
reference to the jinn, but often in such a way that presumed
knowledge of them among listeners and readers. Influenced by the legend of King Solomon (see pp. 62–94), the
Qur'an confirmed the ancient king's dominion over these
supernatural creatures, who served him as builders. While
the jinn were distinctive from human beings in their nature
and abilities, both races of creatures received God's revelation through Mohammad. Upon hearing the prophet recite
the Qur'an, some jinn called upon their brethren to become Muslims, but only the righteous ones heeded Mohammad's message.*

To Solomon We subjected the wind, travelling a month's journey morning and evening. We gave him a spring flowing with
molten brass, and jinn who served him by leave of his Lord.
Those of them who did not do Our bidding We shall chasten
with the torment of the Fire. They made for him whatever he
pleased: shrines and statues, basins as large as watering-
troughs, and built-in cauldrons. We said: "Give thanks, House
of David." Yet few of My servants are truly thankful.

And when We had decreed his death, they did not know
that he was dead until they saw a worm eating away his staff.
And when his corpse fell down, the jinn realized that had they

had knowledge of the unknown, they would not have remained in shameful bondage.

Tell how We sent to you a band of jinn who, when they came and listened to the Koran, said to each other: "Hush! Hush!" As soon as it was ended they betook themselves to their people to give them warning. "Our people," they said, "we have just been listening to a scripture revealed since the time of Moses, confirming previous scriptures and pointing to the truth and to a straight path. Our people, answer the call of God's summoner and believe in Him! He will forgive you your sins and deliver you from a woeful scourge. Those that pay no heed to God's summoner shall not go unpunished on the earth. There shall be none to protect them besides Him. Surely they are in evident error."

Do they not see that God, who created the heavens and the earth and was not wearied by their creation, has power to raise the dead to life? Yes. He has power over all things.

Say: "It is revealed to me that a band of jinn listened to God's revelations and said: 'We have heard a wondrous Koran giving guidance to the right path. We believed in it and shall henceforth serve none besides our Lord. He (exalted be the glory of our Lord!) has taken no consort, nor has He begotten any children. The Blaspheming One among us has uttered a wanton falsehood against God, although we had supposed no man or jinnee could tell of God what is untrue.'"

(Some men have sought the help of jinn, but they misled them into further error. Like you, they thought that God could never resurrect the dead.)

"'We have made our way to high heaven, and found it filled with mighty wardens and fiery comets. We sat eavesdropping, but eavesdroppers find comets lying in wait for them. We cannot tell if this bodes evil to those who dwell on earth or if their Lord intends to guide them.

"'Some of us are righteous, while others are not; we follow different ways. We know we cannot escape on earth from God, nor can we elude His grasp by flight. When we heard His guidance we believe in Him: he that believes in his Lord shall fear neither dishonesty nor injustice.'"

A SHORT HISTORY
OF THE JINN[1]

The Qur'an's ambiguity about the place of the jinn in the Muslim worldview prompted medieval intellectuals to compose stories to explain their origin and history. In the tenth century, an obscure group of Muslim scholars known as the Brethren of Purity composed dozens of learned epistles on topics ranging from mathematics to the natural sciences to religious opinion. In a treatise couched as an allegorical fable entitled The Case of the Animals versus Man Before the King of the Jinn *(Epistle 22), they addressed the ethics of humankind's dominion over the animal kingdom. A digression in this work narrated a short history of the jinn that explained their place in the cosmos. According to this origin story, the jinn populated the earth before the creation of Adam, but they were corrupt in many ways. Angels sent by God vanquished them and adopted one of their captives, a young jinn named Lucifer, as their own. After the flood, humans and jinn lived together on earth, but their relationship was sometimes fraught. King Solomon controlled the jinn, but some rebelled against him; these he punished with imprisonment. Since then many jinn heeded the message of Jesus and Mohammad and embraced the faith, which accounts for the harmonious relationship between humans and jinn at the present time.*

"In ancient times," the wise jinni said, "before the creation of Adam, forefather of the human race, we jinn were the earth's denizens. It was we who covered the earth, land and sea,

mountain and plain. Our lives were long and filled with blessings in profusion. We had kings, prophets, faith, and law. But
we grew wanton and violent, ignored our prophets' precepts,
and ever worked corruption on earth, until finally the earth
and its denizens joined in crying out against our wrongs.

"When that era was drawing to a close and a new age was
dawning, God sent a host of angels down from heaven to
settle the land, and they scattered the vanquished jinn to the
far corners of the earth. Many they took captive—among
them, the accursed Satan Lucifer, Adam's pharaoh, then still a
callow lad. Raised among the angels, Lucifer acquired their
knowledge. Outwardly he resembled them, and inwardly he
adopted their nature and stamp. As the ages passed he became
a chief among them, and for aeons they followed his commands and bans. But that era too came to an end, and a new
age began. God revealed to those angels that were on earth: 'I
shall place a vice-regent on earth in place of you; and you shall
I raise to the heavens.' The earth angels were loath to leave
their familiar homeland and answered: 'Wilt Thou place there
one who will work corruption there and shed blood,' as did
the race of jinn, 'while we celebrate Thy praises and sanctify
Thee?' God said, 'I know what you know not; for I have sworn
an oath upon Myself that in the end, after the age of Adam
and his seed, I shall leave not one—angel, jinni, human or any
living creature—on the face of the earth.'

"When God created Adam, fashioned him, breathed of His
spirit into him, and from him formed Eve, his mate, He ordered the angels on earth to bow down before the two and
submit to their command. All obeyed except Satan. For he was
haughty and arrogant. A savage, jealous frenzy seized him
when he saw his dominion ending and knew that he must follow and be a leader no more."

————————

"[The race of Adam] procreated and their seed grew numerous, and some of the jinni race mingled with them and taught
them the arts of planting and building, showed them what was
good for them and what was harmful. Befriending mankind,

the jinn won their affection, and for a time they lived together on the best of terms.

"But whenever the race of Adam recalled the enmity of the accursed Satan Lucifer and how he had cozened their forefather, their hearts filled with rage and rancour toward the jinni race. When Cain killed Abel, Abel's progeny blamed the prompting of the jinn and hated them yet more. They sought them everywhere and tried to catch them with every trick of magic, witchcraft, and sorcery they knew. Some they clapped in bottles and tormented with all manner of smoke and foul vapours, nauseating and revolting to the jinni race.

"So things went until God sent the prophet Idrīs.[2] He smoothed relations between men and jinn through community of faith, law, submission, and religion. The jinn returned to the realms of men and lived in concord with them from the time of the Great Flood until the days of Abraham. But when Abraham was cast into the fire, men thought knowledge of the mangonel had come to the tyrant Nimrod from the jinn.[3] And when Joseph's brothers cast him into the pit, this too was laid to the wiles of Satan, who was of jinni race. When God sent Moses, he reconciled the jinn and Israel through religious faith and law, and many of the jinn embraced his faith.

"In Solomon's time, God strengthened his dominion and subjected the demons and jinn to him. Solomon subdued the kings of the earth, and the jinn boasted to mankind that he had achieved this by their help. Without their aid, they said, he would have been just another human king. The jinn led humans to believe that they had knowledge of the unseen. But, when Solomon died, and the jinn, still suffering their humiliating chastisements, knew nothing of his death, mankind realized that had the jinn possessed occult knowledge they would not have remained in such degrading torment.[4]

"Again, when the hoopoe brought his report of Bilqīs, and Solomon said to the throng of jinn and men, 'Which of you will bring me her throne?'[5] The jinn bragged, and one sprite, Ustur son of Māyān of Kaywān, said, '*I'll have it here before you rise from your place*'—that is, before the court recesses.

Solomon said, 'I want it faster!' At that, a man with knowledge of the Book, Āsaf son of Barkhiyya, said, 'I'll have it here in the twinkling of an eye.' And when he saw it already standing steady at his side, he said, 'This is by the grace of my Lord,' and he knelt in prayer.[6] Man had clearly outdone the jinn. The court ended, and the jinn left, hanging their heads, the human rabble at their heels, trampling, gloating, and hooting at them.

"After the events I have mentioned, a band of jinn escaped from Solomon, and one rebelled against him. Solomon sent troops after them and trained them to snare the jinn with spells, incantations, magic words, and revealed verses, using sorcery to confine them. He produced a book for this purpose, found in his treasury after his death. Until he died Solomon kept the rebel jinn at work with arduous tasks.

"When Christ was sent, he called all creatures, men and jinn alike, to God and imbued them with yearning for Him. He showed them the way and taught them to mount to the Kingdom of Heaven. Several jinni bands embraced his faith. Keeping to a monastic path, they did rise up to heaven. There they overheard tidings among the celestial throng and relayed the reports to soothsayers.[7]

"When God sent Muhammad, God bless and keep him, the jinn were barred from eavesdropping and said, 'We do not know whether evil is intended against those on earth or whether their Lord desires them to go right.'[8] Some jinni bands embraced Muhammad's faith and became good Muslims.[9] Ever since then, down to our own days jinni relations with Muslims have been peaceable.

"Assembly of jinn," the jinni scholar concluded, "do not antagonize them and spoil our relations with them. Don't stir up smouldering hatred or revise the ancient bias against us that is ingrained in their nature. For hatred is like the fire latent in stones that appears when they're struck together: it lights the matches that can burn down houses and bazaars. God protect us from the triumph of the wicked and the sway of the iniquitous, which brings ruin and disgrace!"

PRISONS OF THE JINN

No stories have done more to shape the image of the jinn in the western imagination as those found in the One Thousand and One Nights, *a collection of Arabic folktales that grew over time from its origins in the eighth century. The framing conceit of these tales is well-known. Upon the discovery that his wife has been unfaithful to him, a fictional Persian king killed her and married a series of young virgins, only to have each of them put to death the day after the wedding to avoid dishonor and heartbreak. Eventually the king married the daughter of his vizier, the enterprising Scheherazade, who began to tell the king a story every night before going to sleep, but never quite reached the end. The king's curiosity compelled him to keep Scheherazade alive night after night so that he could learn the sequel to each story. After one thousand and one nights had elapsed, the king found that he had fallen in love with Scheherazade and so spared her life. One of the themes in these stories was the fate of the jinn imprisoned by King Solomon and the perilous situation of those who released them unknowingly from their bondage.*

(A) THE RING AND THE LAMP[1]

Young Aladdin accompanies a magician disguised as his lost uncle to a cave full of riches.

When the stone was removed, there appeared a cavity about three to four feet deep, with a small door and steps for descending further. "My son," said the magician to Aladdin, "follow carefully what I am going to tell you to do. Go down into this cave and when you get to the foot of the steps which you see, you will find an open door that will lead you into a vast vaulted chamber divided into three large rooms, adjacent to each other. In each room, you will see, on the right and the left, four very large bronze jars, full of gold and silver—but take care not to touch them. Before you go into the first room, pull up your gown and wrap it tightly around you. Then when you have entered, go straight to the second room and the third room, without stopping. Above all, take great care not to go near the walls, let alone touch them with your gown, for if you do, you will immediately die; that's why I told you to keep it tightly wrapped around you. At the end of the third room there is a gate which leads into a garden planted with beautiful trees laden with fruit. Walk straight ahead and cross this garden by a path which will take you to a staircase with fifty steps leading up to a terrace. When you are on this terrace, you will see in front of you a niche in which there is a lighted lamp. Take the lamp and put it out and when you have thrown away the wick and poured off the liquid, hold it close to your chest and bring it to me. Don't worry about spoiling your clothes— the liquid is not oil and the lamp will be dry as soon as there is no more liquid in it. If you fancy any of the fruits in the garden, pick as many as you want—you are allowed to do so."

When he had finished speaking, the magician pulled a ring from his finger and put it on one of Aladdin's fingers, telling him it would protect him from any harm that might come to him if he followed all his instructions. "Be bold, my child," he then said. "Go down; you and I are both going to be rich for the rest of our lives."

Lightly jumping into the cave, Aladdin went right down to the bottom of the steps. He found the three rooms which the magician had described to him, passing through them with the greatest of care for fear he would die if he failed scrupulously to carry out all he had been told. He crossed the garden without stopping, climbed up to the terrace, took the lamp alight in its niche, threw away the wick and the liquid, and as soon as this had dried up as the magician had told him, he held it to his chest. He went down from the terrace and stopped in the garden to look more closely at the fruits which he had seen only in passing. The trees were all laden with the most extraordinary fruit: each tree bore fruits of different colours—some were white; some shining and transparent like crystals; some pale or dark red; some green; some blue or violet; some light yellow; and there were many other colours. The white fruits were pearls; the shining transparent ones, diamonds; the dark red were rubies, while the lighter red were spinel rubies; the green were emeralds; the blue turquoises; the violet amethysts; the light yellow were pale sapphires; and there were many others, too. All of them were of a size and a perfection the like of which had never before been seen in the world. Aladdin, however, not recognizing either their quality or their worth, was unmoved by the sight of these fruits, which were not to his taste—he would have preferred real figs or grapes, or any of the other excellent fruit common in China. Besides, he was not yet of an age to appreciate their worth, believing them to be but coloured glass and therefore of little value. But the many wonderful shades and the extraordinary size and beauty of each fruit made him want to pick one of every colour. In fact, he picked several of each, filling both pockets as well as two new purses which the magician had bought him at the same time as the new clothes he had given him so that everything he had should be new . . .

Thus weighed down with such, to him, unknown wealth, Aladdin hurriedly retraced his steps through the three rooms so as not to keep the magician waiting too long. After crossing them as cautiously as he had before, he ascended the stairs he had come down and arrived at the entrance of the cave, where the magician was impatiently awaiting him. As soon as he saw him, Aladdin cried out: "Uncle, give me your hand, I beg of you, to help me climb out." "Son," the magician replied, "first, give me the lamp, as it could get in your way." "Forgive me, uncle," Aladdin rejoined, "but it's not in the way; I will give it to you as soon as I get out." But the magician persisted in wanting Aladdin to hand him the lamp before pulling him out of the cave, while Aladdin, weighed down by this lamp and by

the fruits he had stowed about his person, stubbornly refused
to give it to him until he was out of the cave. Then the magician, in despair at the young man's resistance, fell into a terrible fury; throwing a little incense over the fire, which he had
carefully kept alight, he uttered two magic words and immediately the stone which served to block the entrance to the cave
moved back in its place, with the earth above it, just as it had
been when the magician and Aladdin had first arrived there . . .

After all the endearments and the favours his false uncle had
shown him, Aladdin little expected such wickedness and was
left in a state of bewilderment that can be more easily imagined than described in words. Finding himself buried alive, he
called upon his uncle a thousand times, crying out that he was
ready to give him the lamp, but his cries were in vain and could
not possibly be heard by anyone. And so he remained in the
darkness and the gloom . . . For two days, Aladdin remained
in this state, eating and drinking nothing. At last, on the third
day, believing death to be inevitable, he raised his hands in
prayer and, resigning himself completely to God's will, he
cried out: "There is no strength nor power save in Great and
Almighty God!"

However, just as he joined his hands in prayer, Aladdin unknowingly rubbed the ring which the magician had placed on
his finger and of whose power he was as yet unaware. Immediately from the ground beneath him, there rose up before him a
jinni of enormous size and with a terrifying expression, who
continued to grow until his head touched the roof of the chamber and who addressed these words to Aladdin: "What do you
want? Here I am, ready to obey you, your slave and slave of all
those who wear the ring on their finger, a slave like all the
other slaves of the ring."

At any other time and on any other occasion, Aladdin, who
was not used to such visions, would perhaps have been overcome with terror and struck dumb at the sight of such an extraordinary apparition, but now, preoccupied solely with the
danger of the present situation, he replied without hesitation:
"Whoever you are, get me out of this place, if you have the

power to do so." No sooner had he uttered these words than the earth opened up and he found himself outside the cave at the very spot to which the magician had led him.

Aladdin returns home to tell his mother about the magician's deceit.

That night Aladdin, having had no rest in the underground cave where he had been buried and left to die, fell into a deep sleep from which he did not awake until late the following morning. He arose and the first thing he said to his mother was that he needed to eat and that she could not give him a greater pleasure than to offer him breakfast. "Alas, my son," she sighed, "I haven't got so much as a piece of bread to give you—yesterday evening you ate the few provisions there were in the house. But be patient for a little longer and I will soon bring you some food. I have some cotton yarn I have spun. I will sell it to buy you some bread and something else for our dinner." "Mother," said Aladdin, "leave your cotton yarn for some other occasion and give me the lamp I brought yesterday. I will go and sell it and the money I get will help provide us with enough for both breakfast and lunch, and perhaps also for our supper."

Taking the lamp from where she had put it, Aladdin's mother said to her son: "Here it is, but it's very dirty. With a little cleaning I think it would be worth a little more." So she took some water and some fine sand in order to clean it, but no sooner had she begun to rub it than all of a sudden there rose up in front of them a hideous *jinni* of enormous size, who, in a ringing voice, address her thus: "What do you want? Here am I, ready to obey you, your slave and the slave of all those who hold the lamp in their hands, I and the other slaves of the lamp."

But Aladdin's mother was in no state to reply; so great was her terror at the sight of the *jinni*'s hideous and frightening countenance that at the first words he uttered she fell down in a faint. Aladdin, on the other hand, had already witnessed a similar apparition while in the cave, and so, wasting no time and not stopping to think, he promptly seized the lamp. Replying in place of his mother, in a firm voice he said to the *jinni*: "I am hungry, bring me something to eat." The *jinni* disappeared and a moment later returned, bearing on his head a large silver bowl, together with twelve dishes also of silver, piled high with delicious foods and six large loaves as white as snow, and in his hands were two bottles of exquisite wine and two silver cups. He set everything down on the sofa and then disappeared.

Aladdin's mother awakens and they enjoy the meal laid out by the jinni.

Aladdin's mother was greatly astonished by what her son told her and by the appearance of the *jinni*. "But, Aladdin, what do you mean by these *jinn* of yours?" she said. "Never in all my life have I heard of anyone I know ever having seen one. By what chance did that evil *jinni* come and show itself to me? Why did it come to me and not to you, when it had already appeared to you in the treasure cave?"

"Mother," replied Aladdin, "the *jinni* who has just appeared to you is not the same as the one that appeared to me; they look like each other to a certain extent, being both as large as giants, but they are completely different in appearance and dress. Also, they have different masters. If you remember, the one I saw called himself the slave of the ring which I have on my finger, while the one you have just seen called himself the slave of the lamp which you had in your hands. But I don't believe you can have heard him; in fact, I think you fainted as soon as he began to speak."

"What?" cried his mother. "It's your lamp, then, that made this evil *jinni* appear to me rather than to you? Take it out of my sight and put it wherever you like; I don't want ever to touch it again. I would rather have it thrown out or sold than run the risk of dying of fright touching it. If you were to listen to me, you would also get rid of the ring. One should not have anything to do with *jinn*; they are demons and our Prophet had said so."

(B) A BOTTLE FROM THE SEA[2]

[The fisherman] looked up to heaven and said: "O my god, you know that I only cast my net four times a day. I have done this thrice and got nothing, so this time grant me something on which to live." He pronounced the Name of God and cast his net into the sea. He waited until it had settled and then he tried to pull it in, but found that it had snagged on the bottom . . . The fisherman stripped off his clothes and, after diving in, he worked his hardest to drag the net to shore. Then, when he opened it up, he found in it a brass bottle with a lead seal, imprinted with the inscription of our master Solomon, the son of David, on both of whom be peace. The fisherman was delighted to see this, telling himself that it would fetch ten gold dinars if he sold it in the brass market. He shook it and, discovering that it was heavy as well as sealed, he said to himself: "I wonder what is in it? I'll open it up and have a look before selling it." He took out a knife and worked on the lead until he had removed it from the bottle, which he then put down on the ground, shaking it in order to pour out its contents. To his astonishment, at first nothing came out, but then there emerged smoke which towered up into the sky and spread over the surface of the ground. When it had all come out, it collected and solidified; a tremor ran through it and it became an *'ifrit* with his head in the clouds and his feet on the earth. His head was like a dome, his hands were like winnowing forks and his feet like ships' masts. He had a mouth like a cave with teeth like rocks, while his nostrils were like jugs and his eyes like lamps. He was dark and scowling.

When he saw this *'ifrit* the fisherman shuddered; his teeth chattered; his mouth dried up and he could not see where he was going. At the sight of him the *'ifrit* exclaimed: "There is no god but the God of Solomon, His prophet. Prophet of God, do not kill me for I shall never disobey you again in word or in deed." "*'Ifrit*," the fisherman said, "you talk of Solomon, the prophet of God, but Solomon died eighteen hundred years ago and we are living in the last age of the world. What is your story and how did you come to be in this bottle?" To which the *'ifrit* replied: "There is no god but God. I have good news for you, fisherman." "What is that?" the fisherman asked, and the *'ifrit* said: "I am now going to put you to the worst of deaths." "For this good news, leader of the *'ifrits*," exclaimed the fisherman, "you deserve that God's protection be removed from you, you damned creature. Why should you kill me and what have I done to deserve this? It was I who saved you from the bottom of the sea and brought you ashore."

But the *'ifrit* said: "Choose what death you want and how you want me to kill you." "What have I done wrong," asked the fisherman, "and why are you punishing me?" The *'ifrit* replied: "Listen to my story," and the fisherman said: "Tell it, but keep it short as I am at my last gasp." "Know, fisherman," the *'ifrit* told him, "that I was one of the apostate *jinn*, and together with Sakhr, the *jinni*, I rebelled against Solomon, the son of David, on both of whom be peace. Solomon sent his vizier, Asaf, to fetch me to him under duress, and I was forced to go with him in a state of humiliation to stand before Solomon. 'I take refuge with God!' exclaimed Solomon when he saw me, and he then offered me conversion to the Faith and proposed that I enter his service. When I refused, he called for this bottle, in which he imprisoned me, sealing it with lead and imprinting on it the Greatest Name of God. Then, at his command, the *jinn* carried me off and threw me into the middle of the sea.

"For a hundred years I stayed there, promising myself that I would give whoever freed me enough wealth to last him for ever, but the years passed and no one rescued me. For the next hundred years I told myself that I would open up all the treasures of the earth for my rescuer, but still no one rescued me. Four hundred years later, I promised that I would grant three wishes, but when I still remained imprisoned, I became furiously angry and said to myself that I would kill whoever saved me, giving him a choice of how he wanted to die. It is you who are my rescuer, and so I allow you this choice."

When the fisherman heard this, he exclaimed in wonder at his bad luck in freeing the *'ifrit* now, and went on: "Spare me, may God spare you, and do not kill me lest God place you in the power of one who will kill you." "I must kill you," insisted the *'ifrit*, "and so choose how you want to die." Ignoring this, the fisherman made another appeal, calling on the *'ifrit* to show gratitude for his release. "It is only because you freed me that I am going to kill you," repeated the *'ifrit*, at which the fisherman said: "Lord of the *'ifrits*, I have done you good and you are repaying me with evil. The proverbial lines are right where they say:

> "We did them good; they did its opposite,
> And this, by God, is how the shameless act.
> Whoever helps those who deserve no help,
> Will be like one who rescues a hyena."

"Don't go on so long," said the *'ifrit* when he heard this, "for death is coming to you." The fisherman said to himself: "This is a *jinni* and I am a human. God has given me sound intelligence which I can use to find a way of destroying him, whereas he can only use vicious cunning." So he asked: "Are you definitely going to kill me?" and when the *'ifrit* confirmed this, he said: "I conjure you by the Greatest Name inscribed on the seal of Solomon and ask you to give me a truthful answer to a question that I have." "I shall," replied the *'ifrit*, who had been shaken and disturbed by the mention of the Greatest Name, and he went on: "Ask your question but be brief." The fisherman went on: "You say you were in this bottle, but there is not room in it for your hand or your foot, much less the rest of you." "You don't believe that I was in it?" asked the *'ifrit*, to which the fisherman replied: "I shall never believe it until I see it with my own eyes." . . .

[W]hen the fisherman told the *'ifrit* that he would not believe him until he saw this with his own eyes, a shudder ran through the *'ifrit* and he became a cloud of smoke hovering over the sea. Then the smoke coalesced and entered the jar bit by bit until it was all there. Quickly the fisherman picked up the brass stopper with its inscription and put it over the mouth of the bottle. He called out to the *'ifrit*: "Ask me how you want to die. By God, I am going to throw you into the sea and then build myself a house in this place so that I can stop anyone who comes fishing by telling them that there is an 'ifrit here who gives anyone who brings him up a choice of how he wants to be killed."

When the 'ifrit heard this and found himself imprisoned in the bottle, he tried to get out but could not, as he was prevented by Solomon's seal, and he realized that the fisherman had tricked him. "I was only joking," he told the fisherman, who replied: "You are lying, you most despicable, foulest, and most insignificant of 'ifrits," and he took up the bottle. "No, no," called the 'ifrit, but the fisherman said: "Yes, yes," at which the 'ifrit asked him mildly and humbly what he intended to do with him. "I am going to throw you into the sea," the fisherman told him. "You may have been there for eighteen hundred years, but I shall see to it that you stay there until the Last Trump. Didn't I say: 'Spare me, may God spare you, and do not kill me lest God place you in the power of one who will kill you'? But you refused and acted treacherously towards me. Now God has put you in my power and I shall do the same to you . . . so now I am going to destroy you by throwing you into the sea here, imprisoned in this bottle." The 'ifrit cried out: "I implore you, in God's Name, fisherman, don't do this! Spare me and don't punish me for what I did. If I treated you badly, do you for your part treat me well, as the proverb says: 'You who do good to the evil-doer, know that what he has done is punishment enough for him.' . . . This is a time for generosity and I promise you that I shall never act against you again but will help you by making you rich."

At this, the fisherman made the 'ifrit promise that were he freed, far from hurting his rescuer, he would help him. When the fisherman was sure of this and had made the 'ifrit swear by the Greatest Name of God, he opened the bottle and the smoke rose up, until it had all come out and had formed into a hideous shape. The 'ifrit then picked the bottle up and hurled it into the sea, convincing the watching fisherman that he was going to be killed. The man soiled his trousers, crying: "This is not a good sign!" but then his courage came back and he said: "God Almighty has said: 'Fulfill your promise, for your promise will be questioned.'[3] You gave me your word, swearing that you would not act treacherously to me, as otherwise God will do the same to you, for He is a jealous God Who bides His time but does not forget. I say to you what Duban the wise said to King Yunan: 'Spare me and God will spare you.'"

The *'ifrit* laughed and told the fisherman to follow him as he walked ahead. This the fisherman did, scarcely believing that he was safe. The pair of them left the city, climbed a mountain and then went down to a wide plain. There they saw a pool, and after the *'ifrit* had waded into the middle of it, he asked the fisherman to follow him, which he did. When the *'ifrit* stopped, he told the fisherman to cast his net, and the man was astonished to see that the pond contained coloured fish— white, red, blue, and yellow. He took out his net, cast it and when he drew it in he found four fish, each a different colour. He was delighted by this, and the *'ifrit* said: "Present these to the sultan and he will enrich you. Then I ask you in God's Name to excuse me, since at this time I know no other way to help you. I have been in the sea for eighteen hundred years and this is the first time that I have seen the face of the land." After advising the fisherman not to fish the pool more than once a day, he took his leave, speaking words of farewell. Then he stamped his foot on the earth and a crack appeared into which he was swallowed.

(C) THE JINN AT WAR[4]

[Musa] and his men then rode off with 'Abd al-Samad in front, guiding them. They had travelled all that day, then a second day and then a third, when they came in sight of a high hill, on whose crest, as they looked, they could see a rider made of brass carrying a broad-headed spear which gleamed almost blindingly. On this statue there was an inscription that read: "You who come to me, if you do not know the road to the City of Brass, rub the rider's hand. It will turn and you must take whichever direction it points to when it stops; go freely and without fear, for it will lead you to the city." . . . [A]ccordingly the emir rubbed the statue's hand, which turned like lightning and pointed to a different direction from the one that he and his party were taking. So they set off on what turned out to be the right way, and they followed it night and day until they had covered a long distance. Then one day, in the course of their journey, they caught sight of a pillar of black stone in which stood a figure sunk up to its armpits. This had two huge wings and four hands, one pair like those of a man and a second pair with claws like a lion's paws. The hair on its head was like horses' tails; it had two eyes like burning coals and in the middle of its forehead a third eye like that of a lynx, from which flashed sparks of fire. The figure itself was black and tall and crying out: "Praise be to God, Who has decreed that I must endure the great affliction of this painful punishment until the Day of Resurrection." Musa's men were scared out of their wits by this sight and turned back in fright. Musa himself asked 'Abd al-Samad what the figure was and when he said that he didn't know, Musa told him to go up to it and investigate in the hope of finding out more about it. 'Abd al-Samad said that he was afraid, but Musa told him: "There is no need to fear as he cannot reach you or anyone else, placed as he is." So 'Abd al-Samad approached and asked the figure: "What is your name and what are you? What placed you here like this?" It replied: "I am an 'ifrit of the jinn. My name is Dahish, son of al-A'mash, and I am kept confined here by the might and power of God to undergo torment for such time as He pleases."

Musa then told the shaikh to ask him why he was imprisoned in the pillar, and when he did, the 'ifrit said:

"My story is a strange one. One of the children of Iblis had an idol made of red carnelian, which was entrusted to my care and which was worshipped by a great and important sea king, the leader of an army of a million jinn, whose swords were at his disposal and who would answer his summons however difficult matters might be. These jinn, his servants, were under my command and obedient to my orders, and they all rebelled against the authority of Solomon, son of David. As for me, I would enter into the middle of the statue and from it give my commands and prohibitions, and as it happened, the king's daughter loved it, frequently prostrating herself before it and worshipping it wholeheartedly. She was the loveliest lady of her time, beautiful and graceful, and radiantly perfect. Solomon heard about her and sent a message to her father saying: 'Give me your daughter in marriage; smash your idol of carnelian and bear witness that there is no god but God and that Solomon is His prophet. If you do that, we shall share alike in both profits and obligations, but if you refuse, I shall bring against you armies you cannot resist. You will have to prepare to answer to God when you have donned your shroud, for my armies will fill every open space and leave you as a figure of the dead past.'

"When Solomon's messenger arrived, the king showed excessive insolence in his self-esteem and pride. He asked his viziers what they had to say about the message, Solomon's request for the hand of the princess and his demand that the king destroy the carnelian idol and adopt his religion. They answered: 'Great king, how can Solomon attack you when you are in the middle of this great sea? Even if he moves against you, he will not be able to defeat you, as the *marids* fight for you. If you ask for help from the idol that you worship, it will aid you and bring you victory. The best thing to do is to consult your lord'—by which they meant the idol—'and listen to its reply. If it advises you to fight Solomon, then do so, but otherwise, do not fight.' On hearing that, the king went immediately to the idol, offering sacrifices and killing sacrificial victims. He prostrated himself before it, shed tears and recited these lines:

> My Lord, I know your power, but here is Solomon, who wants
> you smashed.
> My Lord, I seek your aid. Command me and I shall obey."

The *'ifrit*, half buried in the pillar, then told 'Abd al-Samad and his listening companions: "In my ignorance and folly, caring nothing for Solomon, I entered the idol and began to recite:

I have no fear of him, I the omniscient.
If he wants to fight me I shall march on him and snatch away
his soul.

When the king heard my answer his confidence was strengthened and he decided to give battle. Solomon's envoy was met
with a painful beating when he arrived, and repulsed ignomin-
iously with a threatening message: 'You are guilty of wishful
thinking. Are you threatening me with vain words? Either
come to me or I shall come to you.'

"When Solomon's messenger returned to tell him everything that had happened, Solomon became furiously angry
and even more determined. He collected armies of *jinn*, men,
beasts, birds and venomous reptiles. He ordered his vizier al-
Dimriyat, the king of the *jinn*, to gather together *marids*, and
al-Dimriyat mustered six hundred thousand devils, while at
his command Asaf ibn Barkhiya collected a force of a million
or more men. He provided equipment and arms, after which
he and the *jinn* and men mounted on his flying carpet with the
birds flying overhead and the beasts following below. When he
reached his destination he encircled the sea king's island, filling the ground with his forces . . . When Solomon surrounded
the island with his armies, he sent a message to the king saying
'I have now come, so either defend yourself against my attack
or enter my service, acknowledging that I am God's messenger, breaking your idol, worshipping the One God, the object
of all worship, and giving me your daughter in lawful wed-
lock. Then you and your people must recite the formula: *I confess that there is no god but God and that Solomon is the
prophet of God*. If you say that, then you are assured of safety,
while if you refuse it will not help you to try to shelter yourself
from my attack on this island. God, the Blessed and Exalted,
has commanded the wind to obey me and to carry me to you
on this carpet. I shall make an example of you and your punishment will be a lesson to others.'

"When Solomon's messenger brought his master's message
to the king, the king replied: 'This demand cannot be met, so

tell him that I am coming out against him.' The messenger went back to Solomon and gave him this reply, after which the king summoned the people of his land and collected a million *jinn* from among those who were subject to him, to whom he added the *marids* and devils from the islands and mountain tops. He equipped his armies, opening his armouries and distributing weapons. As for God's prophet Solomon, he drew up his armies, ordering the wild beasts to divide in two, with one half taking up their station on the right of the men and the other on their left. The birds were to patrol the islands, and when the attack was launched they were to peck out the eyes of their enemies with their beaks and strike at their faces with their wings, while the wild beasts were to savage their horses. 'To hear is to obey,' they all replied, 'for we owe obedience to God and to you, prophet of God.'

"Solomon then set up for himself a marble throne studded with gems and plated with red gold, seating his vizier Asaf ibn Barkhiya on his right, together with the human kings, and his other vizier al-Dimriyat, with the kings of the *jinn*, on his left. In front of him were the beasts, together with the vipers and the other snakes. They then launched a concerted attack on us and fought against us for two days over a wide battlefield. On the third day, disaster overtook us and God's judgement came upon us. I was the first to come out against Solomon with my troops, and I told them to hold their positions while I went out to challenge al-Dimriyat. He came to meet me like a huge mountain with blazing flames and billowing smoke, and as he came, he shot at me with a fiery meteor, and this bolt of his proved stronger than my fire. So loudly did he bellow that it seemed to me that the sky had fallen in on me, and the mountains shook at the sound of his voice. At his command, his force then launched a single charge against us; each side shouted against the other; fire and smoke rose high; hearts were almost splitting and the fight became furious. The birds were attacking us from the air and the beasts were fighting on the ground. I continued my duel with al-Dimriyat until we had tired each other out, but then I weakened and my companions and my troops deserted me as the tribes of my *marids* were routed. At that, Solomon, God's prophet, called out: 'Seize this great tyrant, ill-omened and miserable as he is!' Men attacked men and *jinn* fought *jinn*; our king was defeated, while the spoils fell to Solomon as his troops charged ours, with the wild beasts spreading around us to right and left and the birds overhead tearing out eyes, sometimes with their beak, using their wings to strike at men's faces. The beasts savaged the horses and tore at the men until most of us were stretched on the ground like fallen palm trunks. I myself flew away from al-Dimriyat, but he pursued me over the distance of a three-month journey until I fell into the plight in which you see me."

EATERS OF CHILDREN

The Witch-Demons of Byzantium

Building on the archetypal stories of the New Testament and the early church fathers, an orthodox tradition of demonology emerged from the fourth century in the Greek Christian literature of the Eastern Roman Empire (now commonly known as Byzantium). Here the demons, as fallen angels, preserved aspects of their former nature, such as immortality and incorporeality, but they had many limitations. Having lost their natural luminance and goodness, they had become completely evil, embodying all negative Byzantine cultural values. And they were thought to be dangerous. Lurking invisibly everywhere and possessing no individual identity or shape of their own, demons could transform their appearance at will to tempt or possess their human victims, luring them into actions that would jeopardize the salvation of their souls. At the same time, however, alongside these conceptions, other understandings of demons persisted and evolved in popular thought. Here some sort of physicality was ascribed to them, and a vast array of specific types was identified, based on their particular functions and where they were thought to live. One tradition of this type, which persisted throughout the long span of Byzantine history and continued in Greek folk belief into the modern era, was that of a specifically female demon, known by a variety of names, but perhaps most commonly as the Gellou, who was blamed for the illness and death of newborns and children.

MONKS CONTEMPLATE
THE NATURE OF DEMONS[1]

*Although debate continues as to whether or not the
dialogue* Concerning Demons *was actually written by Michael Psellos (1018–ca. 1075) himself, to whom it is attributed, or was composed by someone else in the following
century, the importance of the glimpse it provides into the
complex traditions concerning the nature of demons is un-
deniable. Where the orthodox tradition largely ignores
questions of how demonic beings could actually do the
things they are said to do in the stories of hagiography (see
pp. 99–103),* Concerning Demons *provides logical answers
to a slew of problems those stories raise. Contemporary
medical and scientific theory plays an important part in
the explanations offered in this work for how demons op-
erate, but there is certainly no sense at all of any doubt in
their existence. Set against a background of Byzantine per-
secution of Bogomil heretics in Thessaly, the central character, Thrax ("the Thracian"), tells his interlocutor, Timothy,
everything he knows about demons, much of which he
claims to have been taught by a monk named Mark, who
was formerly an initiate of a demonic cult. Thanks to a
partial translation into Latin by the Renaissance scholar
Marsilio Ficino (1433–99), the content of this work became a staple source on demonology in western Europe
down to the eighteenth century.*

Timothy: An older brother of mine was married to a woman
who was very sensible, but who experienced great difficulty in
giving birth and was afflicted by all sorts of illnesses. Once,

while she was in labor, she had a bad turn and went completely crazy; she ripped her dress and started shrieking fluently in a foreign language, one that was not recognized by those who were present there. They, of course, all stood around in dismay, not being able to do anything in the face of such an impossibly bad situation, but some women—for their kind is ingenious and very effective when something happens—brought in a foreigner who was bald, extremely old, and with skin that was wrinkled and burnt black. This man drew a sword, stood beside the bed, angrily took hold of the sick woman, and hurled a string of insults at her using his native language—for he was Armenian. And she, for her part, answered back in the same language. At first, she was full of abuse and sat up in bed looking for a fight, but, as the foreigner increased his conjurations and threatened to strike her as though he was in a rage, the woman then shrank away, started to tremble, spoke submissively, and fell asleep. We were astounded, not because she had acted crazily—because we see that happen everywhere—but because she, a woman who had never ever set eyes on any Armenians and who knew nothing but the women's quarters and the weaver's tools, was speaking in their language. When she had come to her senses, I asked her what she had experienced and if she had noticed anything else as a consequence of what had happened. She said that she had seen a demonic apparition, which was shadowy and resembled a woman with windswept hair, coming at her; terrified, she had fallen flat on her bed, but she had no idea what had happened thereafter.

That is what she said and she was set free of the demon. But since then, I have been fascinated by this problem, wondering first how the demon that caused the woman such trouble made itself appear female, for it really is a problem if some of the demons are male and others female, just like animals which are born on earth and die. Second, how it used the language of the Armenians, for that is a very tough one too, if some of the demons speak the languages of the Greeks, others of the Chaldeans, others of the Persians, and others of the Syrians. And lastly, how it shrank back from the sorcerer's threats and was frightened by his raised sword, for what would a demon suffer from a sword when it cannot be cut and is immortal? These questions are troubling and bothering me a lot, and I need a solution to them. I think that you are well placed to provide that since you have a good grasp of the beliefs of the ancients and you have acquired a lot of information.

The Thracian: I would like to provide an answer for the things you are asking about, Timothy, although I am afraid that we may both appear to be going too far, you asking questions about things that no one has studied, and me trying to talk about things that should be kept secret, certainly when bearing in mind that such things are easily misrepresented by ordinary people. But anyhow, since, according to Antigonos, one should trust friends not only with easy things but sometimes also with difficult ones, I will try to resolve your problem, working my way through it on the basis of what I have learned from Mark.[2]

He said that there is no kind of demon that is naturally masculine or feminine, for such properties belong to compound beings, whereas demonic bodies are simple. Since demonic bodies are pliable and flexible, however, they are naturally suited to every kind of appearance. Just as you can see the clouds sometimes take the shape of men or bears or dragons or other things, so it is with the bodies of demons; but, while all these different shapes are taken on by the clouds when they are moved by the winds outside them, with the demons this change of shape happens from their preference for whatever they want for the bodies they are manipulating, and so they sometimes compress them into a smaller volume or sometimes expand them to a very large size, just as we see happening with the bodies of earthworms because of their softness and pliability. And demons can change not only in size, but also in shape and color in various ways—for the demonic body is naturally suited to do both since, being malleable, it can assume the appearance of shapes and, being airy, it can take on all sorts of colors like the air. But while the air is colored by something outside it, the demonic body projects the appearance of colors onto itself by the power of its imagination. For just as when we are frightened "pallor seizes our cheeks" and, when we are embarrassed, redness does the same, our soul, depending on whether it feels this way or that, projects these alterations onto our bodies, and it is in this way we should think of what happens with the demons, for they too are producing the appearance of colors on their own bodies from within.[3] So each demon can make its body assume the appearance it has chosen and imposes on the surface of its body some kind of color. Sometimes it appears as a man, but sometimes it adopts the form of a woman, or it rages like a lion, pounces like a panther, or rushes out like a wild boar; and, if it seems appropriate to it, it can take on the form of a wineskin and even on occasion it can appear as a little whining dog. It changes between all these forms and does not have one that is permanent, for the demonic body does not have enough solidity to keep the appearances it has adopted. But the same thing happens with demons as tends to occur with air and water, where, if you pour color into it or draw a shape on it, it immediately dissolves and breaks up; for in the case of demons as well, their colors and shapes and appearances, whatever they may be, simply slip away.

So that, Timothy, is Mark's explanation, and it seems plausible to me. From now on you must not be bothered by the idea that there is an inherent distinction between male and female in demons, for such things only exist at the level of appearance and nothing of the sort is permanent or stable in them. So, if the demon that caused problems for your sister-in-law when she was giving birth looked like a woman, it was not female in any permanent way, but was only assuming the form of a woman.

Timothy: But, Thrax, why does this kind of demon not sometimes take one form and sometimes another, like the other demons, but always looks like this? For I have heard from many people that all women who are giving birth see it in a female form.

The Thracian: Mark also provided a credible reason for this, for he said that all demons do not possess the same power and will, but there is considerable variation between them even in this respect, for they can be irrational, as is the case with mortal and complex animals. Among those, human beings, since they possess intellectual and mental capacity, have a well-developed imagination which can extend to almost the entire realm of sense perception—what is in heaven, and what is on the earth; but a horse or an ox and animals like them have only a partial imagination which they use on a handful of things that they can imagine, so that they know the others in their herd, their manger, and their owners; while mosquitoes, flies, and worms have a limited and disorganized imagination, so that each one does not know the hole from which it emerged, nor where it is going or needs to go, but it only has imagination for one thing—its food.

And it is the same with the multitude of different kinds of demons. For even if the fiery and aerial ones among them, which possess a complex imagination, change themselves into whatever kind of appearance they choose, the kind that hates light is the opposite to them, for it has a very limited imagination and so it does not change into many shapes since it cannot imagine many different appearances and it does not possess a body which suits this or is easily altered. But the aquatic and terrestrial demons which are in-between those that have been mentioned can change into many shapes, although they remain for the most part in those which they prefer. Those which live in damp places and enjoy a quieter life frequently make themselves into birds and women, and so the Greeks give them feminine names: naiads, nereids, and dryads. Those that inhabit arid places have dry bodies, like the Onoskelis, and give themselves the appearance of men, but sometimes resemble dogs, lions, and other animals which exhibit masculine behavior.[4] It is no wonder then that the demon which attacks women who are giving birth is seen as female in shape, as it is lewd and likes impure moisture and adopts the shape which corresponds to the kind of life it enjoys.

As for the way it spoke Armenian, Mark did not explain that, because I did not ask him about it. But I think the answer is to be found in the fact that there is no language specific to demons, even if one may speak Hebrew or Greek or Syriac or another foreign language. What need do those who speak without speech have of speech, as I said before? But, just as some angels look after some peoples, so too some demons are associated with some peoples, and so they each learn the language of each people. That is why some of them prophesy in hexameters among the Greeks, others have their invocations in the Chaldean language among the Chaldeans, just as among the Egyptians their assistance is asked for with Egyptian speech, and, why then, the demons which live among the Armenians, even if they happen to have gone somewhere else, employ that language as if they themselves were born there.

Timothy: Very good, Thrax, but what are they afraid will happen to them from threats and a sword? What do they think they will suffer from those, so that they cower and retreat?

The Thracian: It is not just you now, Timothy, who is puzzled by this sort of thing; I was puzzled too when I was talking to Mark before, but he completely cured me of my confusion. "Every kind of demon is filled with both arrogance and cowardice," he said, "but the material ones more than the others. For if someone threatens the aerial ones, which possess a lot of sense, they know how to evaluate the person who is threatening them and, unless that person is one of God's saints and invokes the terrible name of the Word of God with divine power, they will not leave the people they are troubling. But as the material demons fear being sent back into the abyss and subterranean places, and they fear even more the angels who have been sent into those places, whenever someone threatens them with being sent back to those places and pronounces the names of the angels who have been appointed to do this, they are frightened and very upset, for they cannot evaluate the person who is threatening them either, because they are stupid. Even if it is some old woman or some arrogant old man who is casually uttering these threats, they often get frightened and go away, as though the people making these threats were actually able to make them work; that is how timid and lacking in common sense they are. Because of this they are easily manipulated by the disgusting race of sorcerers with bodily waste—I mean saliva, nails, and hair—and when these are bound up with lead and wax and thread, they are made to cause tragic outcomes through illicit conjurations."

"So, if that is what they are like," I said, "why do you and many others revere them, when their weakness should be despised?"

"Neither I nor anyone else with even a moderate amount of sense, I think, has anything to do with these vile things, but rather it is sorcerers and other unspeakable people who find them attractive. Those of us who used to distance ourselves from those disgusting activities [of sorcerers related to material demons] would serve the aerial demons in particular and in our sacrifices to them would offer up prayers to prevent a subterranean demon from slipping in. For if it happened that one of those did slink in to scare us, it would also throw stones, because it is typical for subterranean demons to throw stones at those they meet, although with little feeble tosses. And so, we avoid meeting them."

"But what did you gain from your worship of the aerial ones?" I asked.

"Nothing, nothing useful, sir," he replied, "because of their arrogance, conceit, deception, and empty illusion. Flashes of fiery light emanate from them onto their worshippers, like the fading brightness of shooting stars, which fanatics dare to call divine visions, although they contain nothing true, nothing solid, nothing reliable—for what could there be that was light in demons which have become darkened? And these are, in fact, tricks of theirs, like optical illusions or those which people who are called conjurors do to deceive spectators. And I, poor fool that I am, long ago searched for the truth about this and tried to distance myself from this cult but, because I was enchanted, I was prevented from doing so until now and my ruin would have been certain if you had not put me back on the right track, like a beacon shining out at night upon a moonless sea."

As he said this, Mark bathed his cheeks with tears. So as to make him feel better I said, "You can be sad later on, but now it is time to celebrate your salvation and show thanks to God who has set your soul and your mind free from the demons who were destroying them. But I want to know this; tell me if it is possible for demonic bodies to be struck?"

"They can be struck," said Mark, "so that they may even feel pain when something hard contacts their skin."

"But how," I said, "since they are spirits and have no substance? Sensation is something that belongs to things with substance."

Mark said, "I am surprised you do not know that sensation is not felt either by muscles or sinews, but by the spirit that is in them. So, if a sinew is pinched or chilled or feels something else, the pain is sent by its spirit to the spirit. Substance by itself cannot feel pain, but rather the spirit within it, since substance that has been paralyzed or deadened is without sensation, for it has lost its spirit. The demonic spirit, which because of its nature has sensation throughout, sees and hears directly through every part of itself and experiences the feeling of touch and feels pain when it is wounded, just like solid bodies. It differs from them, however, because, while mortals heal with difficulty or not at all when they have been wounded, demons immediately come back together again after they have been wounded, like masses of air or water do when something solid falls into them, except that it feels distress at the moment the wound occurs; so, it also fears and is frightened by iron spikes. Because they know this, those who practice protective rituals set spits and swords upright in places that they do not want the demons to approach and use many other methods either to ward them off with things that they do not like or to attract them with things they do like." Mark explained this about them in a credible way, so it seems to me.

SAINTS IN PURSUIT
OF THE GELLOU

Whatever Byzantine intellectuals made of popular belief in demons, and although orthodox theology firmly asserted that the demons could do nothing without God's permission, it is clear that the activity of these malevolent beings was widely feared. The most tangible evidence of this comes from numerous surviving exemplars of amulets designed to protect their wearers from demonic assault, whether this was thought to be the direct result of the inherent malice of the demons themselves or to stem from the rituals of sorcerers who had sent them to do their evil will. Although some of these amulets are distinctly non-Christian and come from a line of activity that has roots directly in the ancient world, the great majority contain at least some elements drawn from the symbols and rituals of the faith. Particularly interesting, in that they provide an explanation and justification for why the amulet might be thought to work, are a considerable number of written charms from the later medieval and early modern periods designed to counter the nefarious and harmful activities of Gellou through the power of either the legendary saints Sisinnios and Sisinnodoros or the archangel Michael.

(A) ON THE TRAIL OF
THE CHILD-EATER[1]

During the consulate of King Laurentios, there was a woman in the land of the Ausitai, that is, Arabia, called Meletene.[2] She had given birth to seven children and the abominable female demon who is called Gellou had taken each of them. Meletene had again become pregnant and was about to give birth, so she built a tower and secured it with nails and sealed it with lead, inside and outside, and laid up provisions in the tower to last twenty-five years. Meletene took two servant girls with her and went into the tower. The saints of God Sysinnios and Sysinnodoros were brothers of Meletene; they were serving in the military unit of Arabia. One day after they had set up camp, they went off to the tower to see their sister. When they reached the door, they called out to her to open it for them. But Meletene was determined not to open it for them and said to them, "I cannot open it for you because I have given birth to a child and I am afraid to open it." But they were equally determined and said, "Open it for us because we are messengers from God, and we come bearing God's mysteries!" So, she opened it for them and the saints of God went in. But that unclean Gellou turned herself into dirt, laughing as she did so, and went inside on the throat of one of the saints' horses. And so, around midnight, she killed the child. Meletene lamented bitterly and said, "Sysinnios and Sysinnodoros, why did you do this? This is why I did not want to open the door for you." Then the saints of God raised their hands towards heaven and asked to receive authority against the abominable Gellou. After they had prayed for a long time, an angel of God was sent to them, and he said to them, "The Lord God has heard your prayer and has sent me to strengthen you and give you power wherever you may go."

When the brothers left the tower, they mounted on horses with winged bridles and went off in pursuit through the nooks and crannies of the mountains of Lebanon. And when they encountered a pine tree, the saints asked it, "Pine tree, did you see the abominable Gellou pass by?" And the pine tree said to them, "No, I did not see her." Then the saints said to it, "Because you have hidden the abominable one from us, may your shoots be rootless and your seeds withered." Then they encountered an olive tree and said to it, "Olive tree, did you see the abominable Gellou pass by?" And she said to them, "Yes, my lords, here and there towards the sea. Yes, for twenty plants, for eating heads, for children's brains, she's staying there."[3] And the saints said to the olive tree, "Your fruit will be blessed and it will be used in the Lord's church."

Then the saints caught up with the abominable Gellou on the seashore and said to her, "Through us, his unworthy servants, God commands you to be subdued." But the abominable Gellou, when she saw the saints, rushed away towards the sea. The saints held to their course and caught up with her again. Then the abominable Gellou said, "Why are you tormenting me so, Sysinnios and Sysinnodoros?" And Saint Sysinnios answered her and said, "Bring Meletene's seven children back to me and I will not torment you." The abominable one said to him, "If *you* can bring back the mother's milk you sucked, then I will give you Meletene's seven children!" Then God's saint Sysinnios implored God, and said, "Lord, you said that 'With God nothing will be impossible.'[4] Show your goodness in me and let everyone know your name, because you alone are God." And immediately God's saint Sysinnios brought back his mother's milk out of his mouth. And he said to the abominable Gellou, "Look, here's my mother's milk! Now you bring back Meletene's seven children." And immediately she too brought back Meletene's seven children.

Then the abominable Gellou said to the saints, "Saints of God, I beg you not to torment me so. Wherever this phylactery is placed, there I may not enter, and wherever it is read, I may not go into that place.[5] If I see it, I will run a mile. And if someone writes out my twelve names, I will not harm their house nor will I have any power over their home; I will not destroy their animals, nor will I have control over their limbs or brains." Then Saint Sysinnios conjured her, and said, "I conjure you in the name of God, which the rock heard and broke open, that you tell me your twelve names." Then, she said to him in reply, "I am unable to endure this conjuration, so let me tell you: my first name is Gellou; the second, Mothrous; the third, Abizous; the fourth, Maramatotous; the fifth, Marmanilla; the sixth, Seleninous; the seventh, Ariane; the eighth, Salasaleutou; the ninth, Egyptiane; the tenth, Asbletous; the eleventh, Himabibon; and the twelfth Ktarkarischou."

We solemnly swear to you by the cherubim and seraphim who say "Holy, holy, holy, Lord God Sabaoth." May the home of so-and-so, the servant of God, be safe from envy and magical medicine, jealousy, magic, enchantment, malicious talk, hinderance, and retribution, and may this house be preserved from every diabolical wickedness and plot, wherever this phylactery is placed. God of Saint Mamas, Saint Polykarpos, Saint Tarasios, Saint Dometios, the holy martyrs Panteleimon and Ermolaos, the holy martyr Niketas, Saint Babyla, Saint Porphyrios, Saint Blasios, Saint Eulogios, Saint Nicholas, Saint Basil, Saint John Chrysostomos, Saint Leon, Saint Eleutherios, Saint Demetrios, Saint George, Saint Theodoros, Saint Jacob of Persia, Saint John the Baptist, Saint John the Theologian, Saint Eustathios, Saint Orestes, Saint Andrew, the three hundred and eighteen holy fathers, Saints Kosmas and Damianos, Saint Epiphanios, Saint Herinarchos, the holy martyrs Auxentios, Eugenios, and Orestes, Mardarios and Loukas the virgin, and the holy martyrs Pegasios, Aphtonios, Elpidiphoros and Anempodistos, and our most praiseworthy Lady, Theotokos and ever virgin Mary, and all your saints. Amen.

(B) MICHAEL SUBDUES
A DEMON OF STRIFE[6]

As the arch-general Michael was coming down from Mount Sinai, Abyzou met with him, she who has control over human passions and sufferings, and the demons who were thrown out of heaven. When he saw her, the arch-general Michael said to her, "Who are you, and where are you going?" The spirit replied, "I am the one who controls human passions and sufferings, spiritual and physical; I induce impulsive desires and troubles; I enter people's houses by changing my shape to be like a snake, a dragon, a reptile, or a four-footed animal; I make women's milk dry up; I make the babies wake up and cry and be smothered; I make them get out of their beds; I make priests hate each other; I make men and women talk to each other in church; I rouse a pair of bulls to kill each other; I make a river deep enough to destroy sheep and cattle; I send strife at sea to sink ships."

When he heard this, the arch-general Michael said to her, "Tell me your name." The spirit said, "I am called Pataxaro, and by some, Artemis." But the archangel Michael said, "Tell me about yourself before I hand you over to the fire!" Then the spirit said this: "By the throne of God and his renowned eyes and uplifted arm, I am telling you the truth and I am not lying; whoever can write my forty names, I may not harm him nor his house nor will I have power to lead him astray.

"My names are: Gilou, Morphou, Morpheilatou, Rinou, Solomonen the Egyptian woman, Anamardalea, Lydrisei, Pekelazou, Adelarchou, Pastere, Melchesedek, Nebik, Nemetrikes, Phlegymon, Heleso, Amele, Ermokonea, Zerderodios, Endikaios, Pekoureos, Gobphokter, Dadoukime, the twenty-fifth Phyganyn, Phygodotheos, Anophes, Anopheos, Ebdolbaleosi, Sophotate, Remeris, Didiaktikos, Domesak, Tarachou, Tarich, Philarchos, Kaukalas, and Anas. When you lie down say, 'Holy Joel, help me,' and put his name near your head."

THE LADY OF
THE MOUNTAIN[1]

Demons were thought capable not only of giving people an advantage by revealing hidden information, but also of helping the unscrupulous sorcerer or his clients achieve all manner of things they wanted. These were almost always things that had socially undesirable ends. Most were serious matters—freeing someone from charges in the law courts, harming enemies, forcing women or men to have sex—but others were relatively frivolous, such as this example from a Greek medico-magical miscellany written around 1440, which employs a female demon to enhance the performance of a horse.

On the first day of the month of August, put honey and pine nuts in a bowl and different colored silks. Write on paper the words "Linomo Kouoro."[2] Take these and go to a hill that same day and, at midday, put them on a solid rock and hide. Then the Lady of the mountains comes and says, "Who has done this nice thing for me?" And answer, "I did, and I want this and that." And she says, "Go, may it turn out for you as you wish." Make the silk into a ribbon and hang it on your horse's neck. Then write on paper the words "wind blaster" and fasten it to its right hoof; and on the left front hoof "high flying eagle"; and on one of the back ones "victory"; and on the other "power." Make these things into an amulet and hang them just as I have told you, and your horse will run like an eagle.

LEGENDS OF
THE CHILD-EATER[1]

From 1898 to 1900, as a student at Cambridge University, John Cuthbert Lawson (1874–1935) held a coveted Craven Studentship, a fellowship that funded study abroad to facilitate research projects related to the study of the language, literature, history, and archaeology of ancient Greece and Rome. Lawson's project was the investigation of survivals of ancient Greek beliefs in the customs and superstitions of their modern counterparts. During his two years in Greece, he traveled extensively and spoke to hundreds of individuals about local lore, while also scouring information from little-known histories of particular regions and islands. The result of his inquiries was published in 1910 as a book-length study entitled Modern Greek Folklore and Ancient Greek Religion: A Study in Survivals. *Rich in knowledge of ancient and medieval literature and replete with colorful anecdotes from his travels, Lawson's book provides the fullest modern summary of information about the Gellou. According to his research, these child-eating demons originated in a tradition from the island of Lesbos about the vengeful ghost of a young woman who died before marriage and preyed upon the flesh of children whose mothers she envied.*

The surviving pagan deities fall naturally into two classes. There are the solitary and individual figures such as Demeter, and there are the gregarious and generic class to which belong, for example, the Nymphs. An exceptional case may occur in which some originally single personality has been multiplied into a whole class. The Lesbian maiden Gello, who, according to a superstition known to Sappho, in revenge for her untimely death haunted her old abodes preying upon the babes of women whose motherhood she envied, is no longer one but many; the place of a maiden, whom death carried off before she had known the love of husband and children, has been taken by withered witch-like beings who nonetheless bear her name and resemble her in that they alight, like Harpies, upon young children and suck out their bodily fluids.

The individuality of this Gello continued to be recognized to some extent as late as the tenth century; for Ignatius, a deacon of Constantinople, in his life of the Patriarch Tarasius named her as a single demon, though he added that the crime of killing children in the same way was also imputed to a whole class of witches. "Hence," comments Allatius, "it has come about that at the present-day Striges (that is, the witches of whom Ignatius speaks), because they practice evil arts upon infants and by sucking their blood or in other ways cause their death, are called Gellones."[2] In the story also which exhibits the chief qualities of this demon, her name (in the form *Gulou*) appears still as a proper name.

But the multiplication of the single demon into a whole class dates from long before the time of Allatius. John of Damascus in the eighth century used the plural *geloudes* as a popular word, the meaning of which he took to be the same as that of Striges (*striggai*); and Michael Psellos too in the eleventh century evidently regarded these two words as interchangeable designations of a class of beings (whether of demons or of witches, he leaves uncertain); for after an exact account of the Striges and their thirst for children's blood, he says that newborn infants who waste away (as if from the draining of their blood by these Striges) are called *Gillobrota*, "Gello-eaten."

The story of Leo Allatius, which sets forth the chief qualities of Gello, is a legend of which the Saints Sisynios and Synidoros are the heroes. The children of their sister Melitene had been devoured by this demon, and they set themselves to capture her. She, to effect her escape, at once changed her shape, and became first a swallow and then a fish; but, for all her slippery and elusive transformations, they finally caught her in the form of a goat's hair adhering to the king's beard. Then addressing to her the words "Cease, foul Gello, from slaying the babes of Christians," they worked upon her fears until they extorted from her a confession of her twelve and a half names, the knowledge of which was a safeguard against her assaults.

It is this list of names in which the various aspects of her activity appear. The first is *Gulou*, one of the forms of the name *Gello*; the second is *Mora*, the name of a kind of Lamia; the third *Buzou* or "blood-sucker"; the fourth *Marmarou*, probably "stony-hearted"; the fifth *Petasia*, for she can fly as a bird in the air; the sixth *Pelagia*, for she can swim as a fish in the sea; the seventh *Bordona*, probably meaning "stooping like a kite on her prey"; the eighth *Apletou*, "insatiable"; the ninth *Xamodrakaina*, for she can lurk like a snake in the earth; the tenth *Anabardalia*, possibly "soaring like a lark in the air"; the eleventh *Psuxanaspastrai*, "snatcher of souls"; the twelfth *Paidopniktria*, "strangler of children"; and the half-name *Strigla*, a kind of witch.

Whether these names are anywhere still remembered as a mystic incantation, or all the qualities which they imply still imputed to the Gelloudes, I cannot say. But a modern cure for such of the demon's injuries as are not immediately fatal has been recorded from Amorgos: "If a child has been afflicted by it, the mother sends for the priest to curse the demon, and scratches her child with her nails; if these plans do not succeed, she has to go down at sunset to the shore, and select forty round stones brought up by forty different waves; these she must take home and boil in vinegar, and when the cock crows the evil phantom will disappear and leave the child alone."

A THOUSAND ARTS OF INJURY

Demons in the
High Middle Ages

Christianity triumphed over local religious beliefs in the west by the turn of the first millennium, when the monastic chronicler Rodulphus Glaber (985–1047) boasted that "a white mantle of churches" had covered northern Europe. Adorning these churches and cathedrals were monumental sculptures depicting the Last Judgment, which represented the blessings bestowed upon the virtuous and the punishments awaiting the damned at the end of time. Demons played a prominent role in these images. Grinning and leering, these hideous fiends dragged the souls of the damned in chains into a gaping Hellmouth as Christ looked on from his seat of judgment. While demons were active on earth as the tempters of the saints in early medieval literature, writings from the High Middle Ages (ca. 1000–1400) presented them more frequently in their native habitat. Moreover, generic demons of late antique hagiography gave way to idiosyncratic devils with individual names, particular purposes, and specialized torments. The proliferation of narratives describing Hell in this period, from the twelfth-century Vision of Tundale *to the fourteenth-century* Divine Comedy *of Dante Alighieri (ca. 1265–1321), provided terrifying tableaus for the cruel industry of these demons in a subterranean realm where their purpose was clear and their power uncontested.*

A MALICE FORETOLD
IN SCRIPTURE[1]

While high-minded theologians like Thomas Aquinas (1225–74) contemplated the nature of demons in treatises that interrogated the origins of evil for an elite and learned readership, the Cistercian preacher Caesarius of Heisterbach (ca. 1180–1240) laid out the scriptural evidence for their character in his widely read Dialogue on Miracles, *a massive compendium of hundreds of pithy anecdotes designed for use in sermons. Caesarius devoted the fifth book of his* Dialogue *to the topic of demons and the danger that they posed to sinners. He prefaced this book with a succinct discussion of the biblical sources for Satan and his minions written with a clarity that anticipated its reuse by preachers at countless pulpits throughout medieval Europe.*

How demons came to be, how many there are,
how malicious they are, and how hostile
they are toward humankind.

It seems fitting to discuss the tempters after treating the topic of temptation. Demons are referred to by epithet as tempters, because whenever any temptation compels the mind to sin, they are identified as its authors or agents. If the devil tempted the first human being in Paradise and if he presumed to tempt Christ in the desert, which person will he dare not to tempt in this world? Accordingly, two angels have been assigned to every person: a good angel to protect them and a bad angel to test them.

Novice: There is no doubt in my mind about the holy angels and what they are because the writings of the prophets speak often concerning them. What demons truly are, how many there are, how malicious they are, and to what eternal flames they are appointed, I want you to show me from the writings of both the Old and New Testaments.

Monk: The testimonies that offer proof of these things are abundant. Concerning Lucifer, that is, the devil, so named because of the beauty of his creation and his fall, Isaiah said, "How have you fallen, Lucifer, you who rose in the morning?"[2] And after he became the devil and fell from heaven, the savior bore witness, when he said, "I saw Satan falling from heaven like lightning."[3] Concerning the devil, Job said, "On a certain day when the sons of God came to stand before the Lord, Satan was also present among them."[4] And in the psalm where David speaks concerning the traitor Judas, he said, "May the devil stand at his right hand."[5] Habakkuk, too, when speaking of Christ, said, "The devil shall go forth before his feet."[6] And in many other places, the scripture calls to mind the devil. John bears witness in the Apocalypse that he did not act alone and did not fall alone, when he says, "There was a great battle in heaven. Michael and his angels fought with the dragon, and the dragon fought and his angels. And they did not prevail and no place for them was found any more in heaven."[7] Through his own malice, glorious Lucifer turned into a dragon, concerning whose beauty and attractiveness Ezekiel said, "You are the seal of resemblance, full of wisdom, and perfect in beauty. You were amidst the pleasures of the paradise of God. Every precious stone was your covering."[8] It is thought that a tenth part of the angels fell. Because of their multitude, the apostle called them "powers of the air."[9] Indeed, they filled the air when they fell. Concerning their pride, the prophet speaks to Christ in the psalm, "The pride of those who hate you ascends continually."[10] And the Lord in the gospel says to the Jews: "You accomplish the works of your father, the devil. He was a liar from the start and the father of lies."[11] That he is hostile to humankind, Job bears witness, when he says, "He will drink up a river and he will not marvel"—meaning the unbelievers, namely pagans, Jews, and heretics—"and he has faith that the Jordan will flow into his mouth," meaning the baptized faithful.[12] The apostle Peter warns us as well, saying, "Be sober, brothers, and keep watch, because your adversary, the devil, roams about like a roaring lion seeking someone to devour. Resist him, strong in faith."[13] What is said about one is understood concerning the rest because the singular number is often used for the plural. That they are doomed to eternal damnation is held from the words of the Lord, which he will speak to the wicked in judgment, "Go, cursed ones, into the eternal fire, which was prepared for the devil and his angels."[14] And I think that the fifth book of this work is the proper place to discuss demons, because the philosophers refer to the number five as the apostate number, the reason being that when paired with any other odd number and multiplied, it always reveals itself either at the beginning or at the end. In the same way, the devil, withdrawing from the four-sided square of eternal stability, straightaway allies himself with wicked men, as though with uneven numbers. His iniquity is always revealed at the start or the end of any act or speech.

TUNDALE'S TORMENTORS[1]

Composed in the middle of the twelfth century, the Visio
Tnugdali *(Vision of Tundale) was a harrowing account of a
voyage through Hell experienced by a sinful knight named
Tundale. Unlike the subjects of monastic tours of the un-
derworld popular in the early Middle Ages, Tundale's soul
suffered the torments of the damned as his journey progressed ever deeper into Satan's domain. The author's ability to imagine the demonic denizens of Hell in all their
horrifying detail and the cruel torments they inflicted on
sinful souls was unrivaled in medieval literature. Translated from Latin into numerous languages and depicted in
artwork, the grisly images conjured by this text left an in-
delible mark in the hearts and minds of generations of
Christian readers.*

When they had passed through dark and dry places, a house
appeared before them, its doors open. This house that they
saw was huge, as tall as a mountain in its great size, and it was
round like an oven, where loaves are baked. Fire came out of
it, which charred whatever souls it found within a thousand
paces. But Tundale's soul, which had learned a similar torment
from another experience, could not approach any closer. To
the angel who led him, he said, "Poor me, what will I do? Behold we approach the gates of death and who will free me?"
The angel responded, "You will be freed from this flame outside, but you have to enter that house from which it pours
forth." And when they neared the house, they saw execution-
ers with axes and knives and sticks and double-bladed instruments, with pickaxes and bores and very sharp scythes, with
spades and shovels and other equipment. With these tools,

they could flay or decapitate or cleave or hack as they stood before the doors in the midst of the flames and under their hands the multitude of souls endured all of the torments we have already discussed. When Tundale's soul saw that this was much greater than all of the other penalties he had seen before, he said to the angel, "I pray, my lord, please free me from this punishment alone, and I will give myself over to all of the punishments that follow this one." The angel replied, "This punishment is greater than all of the others that you have previously seen. Nevertheless, you will see all kinds of torments even greater than you were able to see or ponder before." He continued, "To administer this punishment, rabid dogs await your arrival inside." Trembling and weak with distress, with whatever prayers he could muster, Tundale asked to avoid this punishment. Nevertheless, he could not accomplish what he wished. When the demons saw that Tundale's soul was giving in, they surrounded him and reproached him with a great outcry. Then they tore him to pieces with their instruments of torture and dragged his mangled soul into the flames. What can I say concerning what happened inside this house of Phristinus? For there was lamenting and sadness, pain and groaning and the gnashing of teeth. A tenacious fire was built outside, a vast conflagration inside. There was always an insatiable desire for food, and yet the excess of gluttony could not be sated. Their genitals were tortured with great wracking pains and corrupted with putrefaction that gushed with worms. These beasts burrowed not only into the genitals of laymen and laywomen, but also—even worse, which I cannot say without grave sorrow!—into the genitals of those abiding under the religious habit. No strength could suffice to endure these exhausting, ubiquitous tortures. No gender and no way of life was spared from these misfortunes. What I fear to relate, love compels me to say, that the monastic habit of men and women was present among those being tormented; and those whose profession seemed more holy were judged worthy of the harsher penalties. After Tundale's soul had endured these and similar unspeakable torments for a long time, he returned to himself and confessed that he was guilty and worthy of such punishments. But when it pleased the divine will, without knowing how, as we said, Tundale realized that his torments were over. Nevertheless, he sat in the darkness and in the shadow of death. After he had sat there for a little while, he saw a light, namely the spirit of life, who had previously served as his guide.

As the angel led the way, they saw a beast very different from all of the other beasts they had previously seen. It had two feet and two wings, a very long neck, and an iron beak. It even had iron claws and from its mouth it vomited a relentless flame. This beast sat in a swamp that was frozen over with ice, where it devoured any souls it could find. While they were in its stomach, these souls were reduced to nothing as their punishment. The beast then regurgitated them onto the surface of the frozen swamp, where their torments were renewed once again. All of the souls that descended into the swamp, men as well as women, were pregnant, and burdened in this way they awaited the time when they would give birth. The offspring that they had conceived stung their entrails like vipers, causing these wretched souls to thrash about in the fetid waves of a sea of death hardened over with ice. When the time came to deliver, they screamed, filling the depths with their cries as they gave birth to serpents. I repeat that not only the women, but also the men gave birth to them, not through those parts that nature made for this function, but through their arms and likewise through their chests, and the serpents came bursting out through all of their limbs. These newly born beasts had heads of burning iron and the sharpest beaks, with which they shredded the bodies from which they emerged. On their tails, they had many spines like twisted fishhooks, with which they pierced those souls that gave birth to them. These beasts sought to leave their hosts, but when they could not extract their tails, they turned their burning iron heads back into the bodies and did not stop consuming them until they were reduced to raw nerves and dry bones. And so, crying out together, the grating of the icy waves and the screaming of the suffering souls and the growling of the emerging beasts reached to the heavens, so much so that the demons, if there were any spark of pity in them, might be rightly moved to feel mercy born of sympathy. For upon all of their limbs and fingers you could see the heads of many beasts that gnawed them down to the very nerves and bones. These beasts had living tongues like vipers, which consumed the roof of the mouth and the windpipe all the way down to the lungs. Likewise, the genitals of the men and the women were like serpents, which eagerly mangled the lower parts of their stomachs and pulled out their guts. Then Tundale said, "Tell me, I ask, what evil deeds have these souls committed, for which this punishment has been prepared, for I believe that it is not comparable to any of the torments I have ever seen." The angel said, "As I told you earlier, because those who are considered to be holier are sentenced to harsher torments if they sin, it follows that they obtain a greater glory, if they do not earn this punishment through any kind of guilt." He continued, "For this is the punishment of the monks, the canons, the nuns, and all other members of ecclesiastical orders, who either through their tonsure or through their habit are known to have lied to God. For this reason, their members are consumed by diverse pains because they acted without constraint. Indeed, they sharpened their tongues like serpents and thus they suffer these flames. Also their genitals, which were not restrained from the forbidden pleasure of sexual intercourse, are either cast away or they produce savage beasts to increase their pain." And the angel added, "We have said enough about this. This punishment is particular to those who called themselves devout and were not; nonetheless, those who stained themselves with unbridled pleasure will also endure these torments. And for this reason, you will not escape this, because while you were in your body, you did not fear to defile yourself with immoderate behavior." After the angel said these things, demons assaulted Tundale, seized his soul, and gave him to the beast to be devoured. Once consumed, his soul suffered either inside the creature or in the fetid swamp, but we should not repeat what we have said earlier. After Tundale experienced the punishment of the birth of the vipers, a spirit of pity appeared and talking softly it consoled him, saying, "Come, my dearest friend, you do not have to suffer this anymore." And with a touch, the spirit healed him and enjoined him to follow him for the rest of the journey. Tundale did not know how far they went, for as we learned before, they had no light except for the brightness of the spirit of light. Indeed, they went through places that were terrible and more dire than what had come before. Their path was very narrow and it went down as though from the peak of the highest mountain into the depths, and the further he descended, the less Tundale hoped to return to life.

Then Tundale said, "Since we have seen so much evil thus far, so that I say what is worse could not be seen or even conceived, where again does this path lead from these so far into the depths?" The angel said in response, "That way leads to death." And Tundale said, "Since this path is so very narrow and difficult and we have seen no one on it besides ourselves, is this what the Gospel referred to when it said, 'Broad and wide is the way that leads to death and many enter through it'?"[2] The angel answered, "The evangelist did not speak about this road, but about the forbidden and shameless life of the world, for it leads through this to that." After they went on further and struggled a great deal, they came into a valley and saw there many foundries of smiths, in which they could hear a loud lamenting. Tundale said, "Do you hear what I hear, my lord?" The angel answered, "I hear it and I understand." And then Tundale asked, "Does this punishment have a name?" "This torturer is called Vulcanus," said the angel, "through whose ingenuity many souls are toppled and tormented by him when they fall." Tundale inquired, "My lord, do I deserve to suffer this punishment?" The angel replied, "You do." And after he said this, the angel walked ahead and Tundale followed in tears. As they approached, torturers rushed toward them with burning tongs and ignoring the angel, they seized the soul that followed him. Holding him tight, they threw him into a forge burning with fire and fanned the flames with bellows. Just as iron is weighed, so too the souls were weighed until the multitude that burned there was reduced to nothing. When they were liquefied in this way, so that nothing appeared to remain except for water, they were pierced with iron pitchforks and placed upon an anvil. There they were struck with hammers until twenty or thirty or a hundred souls were rendered into a single mass. Even so, what is worse, they did not die in this way, even though they longed for death and could not find it. The torturers spoke to each of them, saying, "Is that enough?" And others attending another forge answered, "Throw them to us and let us see if it is enough." When the demons threw them, others caught them with metal tongs before they struck the ground and, as before, dragged them through the flames. And thus, the wretched souls were tossed this way and that way, suffering and burning there until their skin and their flesh, their nerves and their bones were reduced to ash and a flickering flame. After Tundale's soul was tossed in these torments for a long time, his advocate appeared to him and in the usual way took him from the midst of the flame and asked, "How are you doing? Were the delights of the flesh so sweet to you that for them you would endure so many and such awful torments?" Tundale could not respond because after such suffering he did not have the strength to utter a word. When the angel of the Lord saw that he was so sorely afflicted, speaking softly, he consoled Tundale, saying, "Take heart, because the Lord is the one who leads you into the depths and back out again. Therefore, be brave because even though the punishments you have suffered are bad, there are greater punishments from which you will be freed if that is the will of our redeemer. For God does not long for the death of the sinner, but for his conversion and return to life." And after this, the angel said, "Everyone you saw above still awaits the judgment of God, but those who are in the depths below have already been judged, for you have not yet come to the very depths of Hell." And leading him in the usual way, he comforted Tundale and bid him to undertake the rest of the journey.

DUNSTAN'S TONGS[1]

Stories about the victory of the saints over the Devil and his minions remained popular throughout the Middle Ages. One of the most memorable anecdotes of this kind involved a struggle between Saint Dunstan (ca. 909–88) and a demon who tempted him in a smithy. The demon had already contrived Dunstan's downfall while he was a young man at the court of King Æthelstan. Exiled from the king's palace, the saint retired to a small cell at Glastonbury, where the demon visited him once again. The legend of Dunstan's tongs first appeared in the twelfth-century account of his life written by Osbern of Canterbury and thereafter became a popular element of the saint's tradition in art and literature.

But lest the devil seem to pity the poverty of Dunstan, whom he previously did not allow to live in the palace, now he strove to expel him from his shack. Thus, the deceitful demon, covered in the deceitful likeness of a man, sought out the cell of the young Dunstan under a gloomy evening sky, stuck his head through the window of his shack, saw that man occupied in the work of a smith, and asked him to forge some piece of work for him. Dunstan, however, neither noticing his cunning nor acknowledging his rudeness, turned his thoughts to the requested work. Meanwhile, that devil began to produce words in a perverse composition, to introduce the names of women, and to recall lustful thoughts; next he started to show scruples, only to repeat the same things again. Then truly the athlete of Christ, perceiving who this was, set into the fire the tongs with which he held firmly a piece of iron and invoked Christ under his breath. And when he saw that the tips of the tongs were white-hot, driven by a holy rage, he quickly snatched them from the fire, caught the devilish face with the tongs, and, struggling with all his strength, dragged the monster inside. At that moment, Dunstan was applying his strength while holding his ground. As the one who was held escaped from his captor's hand, the wall collapsed and the devil howled with such a savage roar, growling: "O what this bald man has done; O what this bald man has done!" For indeed, Dunstan had thin but beautiful hair, and he cried out such things about the man of God. Moreover, when the morning arrived, not a small multitude of nearby people flocked to him, asking what that clamor could have been, which had frightened them with such vehemence while they were sleeping. "It was that rage of the demon," he said, "which on no occasion suffers me to live, and also attempts to evict me from my cell. Be wary of that demon; because if you could not bear the voice of him enraged, how will you be able to endure the society of the damned?" After this day, Dunstan prepared for war, ready to provoke the devil to a contest in strength, to weaken his own body by fasting, and to fortify his spirit with prayers, knowing that the devil could be overpowered by nothing more than what the Lord said: "in fasting and prayer."[2] With the chastity of his body, he obtained such a cleanliness of the heart that he could just escape whatever the sinister spirit had undertaken.

FROM HOLY HOUND TO
DEVIL DOG[1]

*Despite the triumph of Christianity in cities and towns
across northern Europe, local beliefs remained tenacious
in the countryside. The religious customs of rural people
often combined elements of Christianity with homegrown
traditions, all of which appeared unorthodox in the eyes of
church authorities. Such was the case of the cult of Saint
Guinefort, a holy greyhound renowned as a healer of children. In the early thirteenth century, Guinefort was worshipped as a saint in the region around Lyons, France.
When news of this cult reached the ears of the Dominican
friar Stephen of Bourbon (1180–1261), he investigated the
case. Where the local peasants found a shrine that brought
hope of healing for their children, the friar discovered—
much to his horror—the deceptions of a demonic influence.*

Insulting to God are superstitions that attribute divine honors
to demons or to any other creature, as idolatry does, and as
wretched women do by magic who seek cures by worshipping
elder trees or by making offerings to them, by scorning churches
or the relics of the saints, by carrying their children there or to
ant hills or to other sites to obtain healing. They did so re-
cently in the diocese of Lyons, where, when I was preaching
against magic and hearing confessions, many women confessed that they had brought their children to Saint Guinefort.
And since I believed that this was some legitimate saint, I
asked and at last I heard that he was a certain greyhound, who
died in this way. In the diocese of Lyons, near the town of the
nuns called Villeneuve, in the territory of the lord of Villars,

there was a certain castle, whose lord had a wife and a little boy. When the lord and lady had left the house, and the nurse had done likewise, the boy was left alone in his room. A giant serpent entered the house and made its way to the child's room. Seeing this, the greyhound, who had remained behind, quickly followed the serpent, and pursued it beneath the cradle, which fell over as they fought. The dog bit the serpent, which defended itself likewise by biting the dog, but in the end the dog killed it and flung it far from the cradle of the child. This left the cradle stained with the serpent's blood, as well as the ground and the dog's mouth and head. The dog stood near the crib, badly wounded by the serpent. When the nurse returned and saw the commotion, she believed that the child had been killed and devoured by the dog. She screamed with great lament. Hearing this, the boy's mother likewise rushed in, saw the same scene, came to the same conclusion, and likewise screamed. The knight did the same; arriving there, he believed the same thing, so he drew his sword and killed the dog. Then, coming upon the boy, they found him sleeping peacefully and unharmed. Looking about, they found the serpent disfigured by dog bites and dead. Realizing the truth and grieving that they had unjustly killed the dog that had done them such a useful service, they cast his body into a well that lay before the gate of the castle and they dropped a great pile of stones upon him and planted trees next to it as a memorial of the event.

After the castle had been destroyed by divine will, the estate was abandoned by its owner and deserted. Hearing about the dog's noble deed and how it was killed although innocent for a feat that should have been praised as worthwhile, people from the countryside visited the site, honored the dog as though he was a martyr, and prayed for their illnesses and their necessities. They had been seduced by the devil and deluded in that place again and again, so that through this he could lead them into error. Women especially who had weak or sickly children brought them to the place and in a certain town a few miles away they met an old woman who taught them to perform the rite and to make offerings to demons and to summon them, and she led them to the place. When they arrived, they offered salt and certain other items, and they hung the child's clothes upon bushes all around and they fastened a needle into the wood that had grown over the place. They passed the naked child through an opening that was between the trunks of two trees, the mother standing on one side holding the child and casting him nine times to the old woman who was on the other side. They summoned by the invocation of demons the fauns that lived in the forest of Rimita, so that they might take away the sick and weak boy (whom they said belonged to the demons) and bring back to them their rightful child, plump and fat, alive and well, whom the fauns had previously carried off with them. And, after they had done this, these murderous mothers took the child and placed him naked at the foot of a tree in a cradle with straw. They lit two candles the length of your thumb at both ends, from a fire which they had brought there and fastened them on the trunk overhead. They withdrew a little way away so that the candles could burn down and so that they could not hear or see the wailing child, and thus these burning candles consumed many children with fire and killed them, as we discovered there from some others. Indeed, a certain woman told me that, when they had summoned the fauns and withdrawn, she saw a wolf (or a devil in the form of a wolf) come out of the forest and steal up to the child, whom it would have devoured if she had not been moved by motherly affection to prevent it from doing so. If they returned to the child and found him still alive, they carried him to a nearby river with rapids called Chalaronne and immersed him nine times. Only an especially hardy child would evade death on the spot or immediately thereafter. So we went to that place, summoned the local people, and preached against this practice. We ordered the dead dog to be dug up and the grove to be chopped down and burned together with the bones of the dog. And I placed an edict from the lords of the land concerning the taking or reclamation of the bones by anyone who came to the place for any such purpose.

PREYING ON THE LAITY[1]

According to Caesarius of Heisterbach, demons inflicted a "thousand arts of injury" on unwary people. While many of the anecdotes in his Dialogue on Miracles *related the woeful fates of sinful prelates and monks, laypeople were equally susceptible to the snares of the Devil. Necromancers featured prominently in these stories. These masters of the dark arts summoned demons for a variety of nefarious purposes, often with dangerous consequences for their inquisitive friends and students. Caesarius also implicated women in these stories in two different ways: as demonic disguises to lure young men to their doom; and as figures of vanity around which demons swarmed.*

Concerning a knight who disbelieved in the existence of demons until he saw them with his own eyes with the help of a necromancer.

A certain knight, Henry by name, from the castle of Falkenstein, served as the butler of our fellow monk Caesarius, then abbot of Prüm. And as I heard the story from Caesarius, this knight doubted the reality of demons and whatever he heard or ever had heard concerning them, he dismissed as foolishness. So he summoned a clerk, Philip by name, who had made a name for himself as a necromancer and nagged him to show him some demons. Even when this man responded that demons were terrifying and dangerous to behold and no one should seek them out, the knight did not relent in his request. Philip responded, "If you will guarantee my safety, that no harm will come to me from your relatives or friends if by chance you are deceived or frightened or injured by any demons, then I will do as you ask." And the knight agreed.

At noon hour on a certain day, the reason being that the powers of the demons are greater in the middle of the day, Philip led the knight to a crossroad, traced a circle around him with the tip of a sword, and explained to the man inside the circle the way the circle worked, saying, "If you extend any part of your body outside of the boundary of this circle before my return, you will die, because demons will seize you and that will be the end of you. He also warned the knight to give them nothing that they request, to promise them nothing, and not to make the sign of the cross. And he added, "The demons will tempt and terrify you in many different ways, but they can cause you no harm, if you heed my instructions." Then the necromancer departed.

While the knight was sitting alone in the circle, behold he saw coming toward him swells of water, then he heard the grunting of pigs, the roar of winds, and many other illusions like these, by which the demons tried to frighten him. But because missiles that are foreseen do less harm, he was not disturbed by these apparitions. Last of all, he spied in the neighboring forest something that looked like a loathsome human shadow, taller than the treetops, which hastened toward him. And he knew immediately that this was the devil, as indeed it was. When it reached the circle, it paused and asked the knight what he wanted from him. He looked like a giant man, immensely large and blacker than black, draped in dark clothing, and so hideous that the knight could not bear to look upon him. Henry said to him, "It was good of you to come. I wanted to have a look at you." "For what purpose?" the devil asked. "I have heard many things about you." Henry responded. "Like what?" the devil asked. "Not many good things and a very many bad things," the knight answered. "Human beings often judge me and condemn me without cause," the devil said. "I harm no one and I wound no one unless I am provoked. Your master Philip is a good friend of mine and I return the favor. Ask him if I have ever done him wrong. I do what pleases him and he obliges me in every way. I came to you just now because he summoned me to do so." Then the knight said, "Where were you, when he summoned you?" The demon responded, "I was on the far side of the ocean, the same distance away as we currently are from the sea. And therefore, it seems right that you should recognize my efforts to get here with a gift of some kind." The knight asked, "What do you want?" The demon responded, "I desire and ask that you give me your cloak." When Henry said no, the devil asked for his belt, and then a sheep from his flock. When he was denied these things, he made his last request for a rooster from his courtyard. The knight asked him why he wanted a rooster. The demon answered, "To sing to me." When Henry asked how he planned to take possession of the rooster, the devil said, "Don't you worry about that; you only have to give him to me." Then the knight said, "I will give you nothing at all. Tell me, though, how do you know so much?" The demon responded, "There is no evil in the world that is hidden from me. And so that you know this to be true, behold in such and such a town in such and such a house, you lost your virginity and in such and such a place you committed such and such sins." And the knight could not deny it, because the devil spoke the truth . . . After the demon asked again for I know not what and Henry denied him yet again, he reached out with his hand as though he wanted to seize the knight and drag him away. This terrified Henry so much that he fell backwards and cried aloud. Hearing his voice, Philip came running and upon his arrival, the apparition disappeared. From that time onwards, the knight was always very pale and never recovered his natural complexion. He corrected his ways and was a firm believer in the existence of demons. It was not long ago that he died.

Concerning a clerk of Toledo, who was captured by demons and carried to Hell.

Our fellow monk of blessed memory, Gotteschalk of Valmarstein, related to me something that should not be passed over in silence. One day when Gotteschalk asked the aforesaid Philip to tell him some curious anecdotes concerning the necromantic arts, he responded as follows, "I will tell you about an amazing event that actually happened in Toledo during our time. When many scholars from different places were studying the art of necromancy in that city, certain young men from Swabia and Bavaria heard stupendous and unbelievable stories from their master. Wanting to test whether these stories were true, they said to him, 'Master, we want you to show us with visual proof the skills that you are teaching us, so that we may reap the fruit of our studies.' Even though he rebuffed them, they did not quiet down, the reason being that people from that part of the world are strange, so at the appropriate hour he led them into a field, made a circle around them, warning them under threat of death to stay inside of it, and he ordered them not to give anything to anyone who asks or to receive anything offered.

"Moving a short distance from them, he summoned demons with his incantations. Soon they appeared in the guise of soldiers properly armed and marched in formation around the young men. Sometimes they would pretend to fall, at other times they would point their spears and swords toward the students, trying in every way to lure them outside of the circle. When the demons were unsuccessful at doing so, they transformed themselves into the most beautiful young women and danced in a circle around them, inviting the young men with their enticing movements. One of them, more attractive than the others, singled out one of the students. Every time she danced toward him, she offered up a golden ring, kindling his lust inwardly by suggestion and outwardly by the movement of her body. After she had done this many times, the young man could no longer resist and thrust his finger outside of the circle toward the ring. Immediately she dragged him out by the same finger, and they disappeared.

"With their prey in hand, the evil assembly dissolved in a whirlwind. The master came running when he heard the screaming and crying of his disciples, who complained about the capture of their colleague. He said to them, 'I am not at fault. You compelled me to do this. I told you what would happen. You will not see him again.' They replied to him, 'If you do not restore him to us, we will kill you.' Fearing for his life, because he knew that the Bavarians were filled with rage, he answered, 'I will see if there is any hope for him.' Summoning the leader of the demons, he reminded the demon of his faithful service and told him that his work would be diminished, and he would be killed by his disciples unless the young man was restored. Moved by his plight, the devil responded, 'I will hold a council on your behalf at such and such a place tomorrow. You will be present and if by some means you can get him back through a judgment, then I am fine with that.'

"What more to say? At the command of their leader, the council of evil spirits convened. The master made his complaint regarding the violence done to his disciple. From the adversary came this response: 'Lord,' he said, 'I have done neither harm nor violence to him. He was disobedient to his master because he did not follow the rule of the circle.' While they were arguing in this way, the leader asked a certain demon next to him concerning the judgment, saying, 'Oliver, you always offered sound counsel. You never accepted a person contrary to justice. Settle the question of this case.' This demon responded, 'I judge that the young man should be sent back to his master.' Turning immediately to the adversary, he said, 'Return him, because you were very rude to him.' The assembled demons agreed with this judgment. At the command of the judge, they quickly fetched the student from Hell, returned him to his master, dismissed the council, and returned the relieved master to his disciples with their prize restored. But the young man's face was haggard and deathly pale, the color so transformed that it seemed as though he had just been revived from the grave. He related to his colleagues what he had seen in Hell and showed them more by example than by word how hateful and contrary to God the study of necromancy was. Departing from that place, he entered a monastery of the Cistercian order."

Concerning demons who swarmed upon an overdressed woman in Mainz.

An upright citizen told me this story, asserting that it truly took place in Mainz in our times, if I remember correctly. On a certain Sunday, when a priest was making the rounds in his church and sprinkling the people with holy water, coming to the main door of the building, he saw a woman approaching in a pompous manner. She was adorned with many ornaments like a peacock. In the train of her garments, which trailed a long way behind her, there was a multitude of demons. They were as small as mice and as black as Ethiopians, laughing loudly and clapping their hands and leaping about just like fish caught in a net. For truly the fancy attire of women is the devil's net. When the priest saw this, he made this chariot of demons wait outside, summoned the congregation, and commanded the demons to stay put. The woman tarried in terror, while the priest, who was a good and just man, obtained through prayer that the people would merit to see these visions. Realizing that she had been held up to ridicule by demons because of the pomposity of her dress, the woman returned home, changed her clothes, and that vision became an opportunity for humility, both for her and for the other women present.

THE PSALM-SKIPPER
DEMON[1]

Toward the end of the Middle Ages, preachers warned of de-
mons assigned to keep track of very specific sins. One of
them was Tityvillus, an imp who specialized in collecting
evidence for the negligence of the clergy and laypeople dur-
ing church services. Identified by his sack, which brimmed
with syllables dropped by lazy choir singers, or his sheet of
parchment, on which he wrote the names of daydreamers
and gossips during sermons, Tityvillus carried the proof of
these transgressions back to Hell, where the Devil used
them as evidence against sinners, who would suffer under
the weight of enormous sacks in the afterlife as punish-
ment for their negligence.

I heard that a certain holy man, while he was in the choir, saw
a demon burdened as though with a very full sack. When he
commanded the demon to tell him what he was carrying, the
demon answered: "These are the misplaced syllables and
words and psalm verses, which those clergy in their morning
prayers have stolen from God; I keep these diligently for their
accusation." Therefore, keep watch carefully at the mystery of
the altar, so that indignation does not arise over the people.

———————————

However, certain people think empty thoughts and speak idle
words during sermons and in church, when they should be
paying attention to what is being said. When a certain holy
priest saw a demon stretching parchment with his teeth during
a time of great solemnity, he commanded the demon to tell

him why he was doing so. The demon responded: "I am writing down the idle words which are spoken in this church and because such words have multiplied today much more than usual because of the solemnity of the feast day, seeing that the sheet I brought with me will not suffice, I am trying to stretch the parchment with my teeth." Hearing this, the priest began to tell this story to the people and everyone who heard it began to feel sad and contrite. While they were feeling sad and penitent, the demon who had written down the words began to erase them until the sheet was blank. Therefore, you should with all diligence and devotion give your attention to the divine office and sound teaching and eat not the bitter morsel but rather the spiritual feast.

———————

A certain holy man saw a demon burdened as though with a full sack. When he commanded the demon to tell him what it was carrying, the demon answered, "I carry the syllables cut off from the readings and the verses of psalms which these clergy stole last night." And the holy man asked, "What is your name?" The demon responded: "I am called Tityvillus." This man composed a verse inspired by this answer: *Fragmina Psalmorum Tytyvillus colligit horum* ("Tityvillus gathers the fragments of those psalms . . .").

———————

At one time, when certain clerks in a certain secular church were singing with vigor, that is, noisily and without devotion, and raising their turbulent voices on high, a certain religious man who then happened to be present saw a certain demon standing higher up in the church and holding a long, voluminous sack in his left hand. With his right hand held out, he caught the voices of those singing and put them in his sack. When the service was over and these clerks congratulated each other, as though they had praised God vigorously and well, the man who had seen the vision said to them, "You have indeed sung well, but you have sung a sack full." They were confused and asked him why he had said this, so he explained his vision to them. An abbot of the Cistercian order, a man of the utmost authority, told this story to me.

Vocal prayer can be divided into many parts . . . The ninth kind is psalmody, with the singing of the psalms. This should be done attentively, distinctly, devoutly, correctly, and succinctly . . . Against those who sing the psalms inattentively and without devotion and indistinctly, or those who shorten the verses of psalms, gut them of their sense, omit words, forget or leave out letters, who do not sing intelligibly, but shout at one another like birds gathered in a flock, an exemplum of Master Jacob speaks to this, when he says that a devil carrying a full sack appeared to a certain holy man. Commanded to reveal what he carried, the demon said that he was coming from a certain church of secular canons, where he had gathered this sack filled with syllables and words cut out of the psalms, from which he would accuse them in judgment.

The same master said this about the same topic: I heard Brother Gaufridus de Blevez relating that in the diocese of Sens, when a certain priest had died and should have been buried, he was summoned back from death and rose up. Among other terrible things he was saying, he reported that he had met an innumerable multitude of priests and clerics suffering terribly and oppressed under the giant sacks they were carrying. And it was said to the one asking that they were carrying syllables and words and other parts of the psalms that they had failed to utter clearly, for which they suffered the most serious punishments.

SATAN'S FAMILY

Many legends circulated in the Middle Ages about members of Satan's family, who appeared infrequently in didactic literature written for preachers. Misogynist in character, descriptions of the loathsome nature of his mother, his wife, and his daughters were almost always allegorical. While his mother and wife were often depicted as nags and scolds, his daughters were personified mockeries of the seven cardinal virtues, who sowed discord at every station of human society.

(A) THE DEVIL'S MOTHER REMARKS ON HIS TAIL[1]

Satan and his mother were walking on the seashore. At that very hour it happened that many ships and sailors were put in jeopardy upon the sea and sank. Seeing this, the devil said: "Do you see, my mother?" And he added: "If I was there among them, men, who do not cease to defame me, would say that I was the one who had caused those boats to sink. Indeed, they call me the author of all maladies. It is lucky for me just now that you can serve as my witness that I was not there." His mother responded: "I know, my son, that you were not present there, but your tail most certainly was."

So it is with evil counselors when they are absent. They are thought to be innocent of what they have whispered to the detriment of others, when the deed that took effect through other channels proceeded from their counsel. But it is nonetheless clear to any wise person that their tail was present in that mischief.

Deceivers and flatterers have tails, because they always sow their venom in silence and in absence. Truthful people show their face because they speak the truth openly.

(B) SATAN'S WIFE AND DAUGHTERS[2]

It is said that the devil bore nine daughters with a wife very foul and lustful, who was as black as an extinguished coal owing to the burning of her depraved desires. She was rank due to infamy and sported swollen eyes due to pride, a long and misshapen nose due to the machinations and schemes of her sins, and large and floppy ears due to her curiosity. She listened eagerly not only to rumors of vanity, but also to words of iniquity and distraction. Her hands were contaminated by greediness and the grip of avarice. Her lips were gaping and her mouth fetid due to unclean and hostile speech. Her feet were twisted, like her unpredictable affect. Her breasts were pendulous, swollen, itching, and scab-ridden, one of which dispensed the poison of carnal desire to her whelps, while the other dispensed the wind of worldly vanity. Out of these daughters, the devil married eight of them to as many kinds of men: Simony to prelates and clerics; Hypocrisy to monks and those religious in name only; Rape to soldiers; Usury to townsmen; Fraud to merchants; Robbery to farmers, who steal the tithe sacred to God from the ministers of the churches; False Service to workers; and lastly Pride and Excess to women. The ninth daughter, Lust, wanted to marry no one, but instead, like a wicked prostitute, she offered herself to every kind of man, mingling with everyone, sparing no kind of man. Indeed, in the stench of her perfumes, men raced without caution to her brothel, like birds to a trap, mice to cheese, fish to a hook; it was difficult to escape her grasp once she had someone in her grip.

THE CRAVEN ANGELS

From the early Middle Ages onward, authors and poets whispered cryptic stories about the fate of the "craven angels." These were the angels who took no side in Satan's war against Heaven. While they did not participate in the Devil's conspiracy of sin, they also failed to declare their loyalty to God. As a result, they fell from Heaven with the ancient enemy and his minions, but their fate was open to question.

(A) WITH WINGS LIKE BELLS[1]

According to an eighth-century text known as the Voyage of Saint Brendan, *which recounted the seaborne journey of an Irish holy man and his brethren, these neutral angels wandered the world as incorporeal spirits, but on feast days and Sundays they took the form of birds and sang praises to God on a remote island.*

Moreover, when they had sailed near the island where they had been three days earlier, and came to its furthest end on the western side, they saw another island joined next to it, very grassy and wooded and full of flowers, with a small strait lying in between, and they began to seek a place to make land while sailing around the island. Then, making their way toward the southern shore of the island, they found a little river emptying into the sea, and there they landed their ship. When they had disembarked from the boat, Saint Brendan ordered them to drag the ship along the bank of the river with ropes, as far as they could. The river was just as wide as the width of the boat. The holy father remained sitting in the boat, and they pulled him along for a mile until they came to the source of the river. Saint Brendan then said, "Behold, our Lord Jesus Christ gave us this place to stay for Easter." And he added, "If we did not have any other supplies except this river, it would suffice, I believe, for our food and drink."

There was, moreover, a tree near the river's source with a circumference of incredible size, and no less wondrous in height, covered with very white birds. They covered it so much that they almost seemed to be its very leaves and branches. When the man of God saw them, he began to think to himself and ponder what this might be or what the cause of this had been, that so great a multitude of birds could be gathered in one place. And his grief over this was so great that he shed tears on bended knee and beseeched God, saying: "God, knower of the unknown and revealer of all that is hidden, you know my heart's distress. I beseech your majesty that through your great mercy you should see fit to reveal to me your secret, which I see now before my eyes. I do not presume to ask from my own merits or dignity, but from your immense clemency."

When he had said these things to himself and sat down again, behold, one of the birds flew from the tree toward the ship where the man of God was sitting, and its wings sounded like little bells. It alighted on the tip of the prow, stretched forth its wings like a sign of joy, and regarded the holy father with a peaceful expression. Immediately the man of God knew that God had heard his prayer, and he said to the bird, "If you are a messenger of God, tell me where these birds are from or for what reason they flock here?"

The bird said to him at once: "The great ruin of the ancient enemy brought us here, even though we did not participate in his conspiracy of sin. After our creation, Satan's fall with his minions resulted in our ruin as well. But our God is just and true. In his great judgment, he sent us to this place. We do not suffer punishment. Here we can see the presence of God, but he has separated us from the fellowship of those who remained loyal to him. We wander through different parts of the air and the firmament and the earth, just as other spirits who have been sent forth. But on holy days and Sundays we receive the bodies that you now see and we gather here and praise our creator. You and your brethren have spent one year on your journey, but six still remain. Where you celebrate Easter today, there you will celebrate it every year, and after that you will find what you have set in your heart, that is, the land of the saints' reward." When he had said these words, the bird took wing from the prow and flew back to the other birds.

(B) THEY CHOSE
THEIR OWN PERDITION[2]

By the early thirteenth century, the fate of the craven angels had changed for the worse. In his poem recounting the Arthurian legends, Wolfram von Eschenbach (ca. 1160/ 80–ca. 1220) portrayed these exiles from Heaven as the special guardians of the Gral (the Holy Grail), a stone with wondrous powers. In this account, a pagan seer named Flegetanis had foretold that God would forgive them for their disloyalty, but the truth came out by the story's end, when they were damned for their neutrality.

There was a heathen named Flegetanis who was highly renowned for his acquirements. This same *physicus* was descended from Solomon, begotten of Israelitish kin all the way down from ancient times till the Baptism became our shield against hellfire. He wrote of the marvels of the Gral . . . All humankind are affected by the revolutions of the planets. With his own eyes the heathen Flegetanis saw—and he spoke of it reverentially—hidden secrets in the constellations. He declared there was a thing called the Gral, whose name he read in the stars without more ado. "A troop left it on earth and then rose high above the stars, if their innocence drew them back again. Afterwards a Christian progeny bred to a pure life had the duty of keeping it. Those humans who are summoned to the Gral are ever worthy." Thus did Flegetanis write on this theme.

—————————

When Lucifer and the Trinity began to war with each other, those who did not take sides, worthy, noble angels, had to descend to earth to that Stone which is forever incorruptible. I do not know whether God forgave them or damned them in the end: if it was His due He took them back. Since that time the Stone has been in the care of those whom God appointed to it and to whom He sent his angel. This, sir, is how matters stand regarding the Gral.

—————————

"God has many mysteries," Trevrizent told Parzival. "Whoever sat at His councils or who has fathomed His power? Not all the Host of Angels will ever get to the bottom of it." . . . I lied as a means of distracting you from the Gral and how things stood concerning it. Let me atone for my error—I now owe you obedience, Nephew and my lord. You heard from me that the banished angels were at the Gral with God's full support till they should be received back into His Grace. But God is constant in such matters: He never ceases to war against those whom I named to you here as forgiven. Whoever desires to have reward from God must be in feud with those angels. For they are eternally damned and chose their own perdition.

(C) THAT NOISOME CHOIR[3]

Dante Alighieri (ca. 1265–1321) depicted the craven angels in the vestibule of Hell in his masterpiece The Divine Comedy (Divina Commedia). *Unlike their sympathetic portrayal in the Brendan legend, Dante described them as expelled from Heaven, yet unwelcome in Hell. Bereft of God and yet having no hope of death, they were doomed to spend eternity in envy of every other fate.*

"We have now come to the place, where I told you,
You will see the woeful people
Who have lost the good obtained by intellect."

And then he put his hand on mine and
With a smile that comforted me
He led me in among secret things.

There sighs and groans and plaintive wailing
Resounded through the starless air,
Which caused me to well up with tears.

Diverse tongues, horrible dialects,
Words of agony, accents of anger
And voices high and hoarse, and the sound of hands,

Made up a tumult that goes whirling on
Forever in that air forever black,
Just like sand, when the whirlwind blows.

My head with horror bound, I said,
"Master, what is this that I hear?
Who is this, so overcome by pain?"

He said to me, "This miserable condition
Afflicts the melancholy souls of those
Who lived without infamy or praise.

They are commingled with that noisome choir
Of angels, who were neither rebels nor
Faithful to God, but only for themselves.

The heavens expelled them, for they were not beautiful;
Nor did the depths of Hell receive them,
In this way depriving the damned of their glory."

And I, "Master, what is so grievous to them
That makes them lament so loudly?"
He answered, "I will tell you very briefly.

They have no hope of death;
And this blind life of theirs is so debased
That they envy every other fate.

The world allows them to have no glory;
Mercy and justice both despise them.
Let us not speak of them, but look and then pass by."

APES OF GOD

Demons in Early
Modern Europe

Satan and his minions came under increased scrutiny in early modern Europe (ca. 1400–1800). Some daring thinkers, like Nicole Oresme (ca. 1320/25–82), had already questioned the existence of demons altogether and attributed demonic activity more plausibly to natural causes than to fiendish agency. Others, like the Neoplatonist Marsilio Ficino (1433–99), revived the idea that human beings were born with their own personal demons, a notion made popular in antiquity by pagan philosophers like Plato and Apuleius (see pp. 42–47). These opinions were mere whispers, however, amid the chorus of voices expressing fear about the malice of demons and the lure of their power. As the survival of foreboding grimoires and spell books from this period suggests, students of occult philosophy practiced the dark arts to initiate contact with demons in an effort to increase their influence and worldly gain, but the costs were great. An overarching theme in depictions of Satan and his lieutenants at this time was the notion that their organization and activities were crude and derisive imitations of God's works. Writing in 1646, John Gaule concluded that "the Devil is God's ape, and one that fains to imitate him, though in contrary ways. And therefore, as God makes a covenant of grace with his, so doth the Devil with his a covenant of death."[1]

A COVENANT OF DEATH[1]

Just as God made covenants with his chosen people, so too did the Devil and his minions enter into legal agreements with human beings in order to lure them to their doom. These agreements usually involved people receiving some kind of material benefit in this life in exchange for renouncing the Christian faith and thereby jeopardizing their immortal souls. The earliest story about this kind of diabolical contract involved a Christian saint named Theophilus of Adana, who lived in the early sixth century. Told and retold over the course of the Middle Ages, this legend related how Theophilus made a deal with the Devil in order to restore himself to a church office, but he soon had second thoughts and was eventually freed from his contract by the Virgin Mary.

In Sicily in the year 537 there was a certain man, Theophilus by name, the deputy of a certain bishop, as Bishop Fulbert of Chartres says, who managed ecclesiastical affairs so prudently under his bishop that, when this bishop died, all of the people declared him worthy of the office. But this man was content being the deputy and preferred someone else to be ordained as bishop. At length, he was deposed from his office against his will by the new bishop and fell into such a great despair that he sought the counsel of a Jewish sorcerer to recover his sense of dignity. The sorcerer summoned the devil, who quickly answered the summons. At the demon's command, Theophilus denied Christ and his mother, renounced the Christian faith, and wrote out this denial and renunciation in his own blood and sealed what he had written with his ring and handed the sealed document over to the demon and yielded himself to its service. Therefore, on the next day, through the demon's machinations, Theophilus was received into the grace of the bishop and restored to the dignity of his former office.

At length, with a change of heart about what he had done, he lamented greatly and fled to the glorious Virgin with the full devotion of his mind in the hope that she might assist him. Soon the Virgin appeared to him in a vision, berated him for his impiety, ordered him to renounce the devil, and made him acknowledge Christ the son of God and all the teachings of Christianity. And thus she restored in this man both her grace and the grace of her son. As a token that he had been forgiven, she appeared to him a second time and returned to him the sealed document that he had given to the devil and placed it on his chest, so that he did not fear that he was still a servant of the devil, but rather rejoiced that he was made free by the Virgin. Once he had received this, Theophilus was overcome with joy. He related everything that had happened in the presence of the bishop and all of the people and with everyone marveling and praising the glorious Virgin, he fell asleep in peace three days later.

A FAUSTIAN BARGAIN[1]

The story of Theophilus of Adana served as the template for an early modern folk legend about a character named Faust. Based on a notorious German alchemist and magician named Johann Faust (ca. 1480–ca. 1541), this cautionary tale about the dangers of intellectual ambition became a popular theme in stage plays and popular literature throughout the seventeenth and eighteenth centuries, inspiring both Christopher Marlowe's play The Tragical History of the Life and Death of Doctor Faustus *(1604) and Johann Wolfgang von Goethe's closet drama* Faust *(1808). Having reached the limit of his learning, Faust entered into a contract with a demon named Mephistopheles to obtain the knowledge he craved. In return, he agreed to relinquish his soul to the demon upon his death. Like Theophilus before him, Faust composed and signed the contract in his own blood. Unlike the medieval saint, however, the early modern magician did not repent, sought no help from the Virgin Mary, and suffered the consequences for all eternity. The story was so well-known that the phrase "Faustian bargain" is still current as a way to express an agreement that involves abandoning one's moral principles in order to obtain knowledge or wealth.*

How Doctor Faustus began to practice in his devilish art, and how he conjured the Devil, making him to appear and meet him on the morrow at his own house.

You have heard before, that all Faustus' mind was set to study the arts of necromancy and conjuration, the pursuit of which he followed night and day. And taking for himself the wings of an eagle, he thought to fly over the whole world and to know the secrets of heaven and earth. For his speculation was so wonderful, being expert in using his *vocabula*, figures, characters, conjurations, and other ceremonial actions, that in all haste he put in practice to bring the Devil before him. And making his way to a thick wood near Wittenberg, called in the German tongue Spisser Waldt, that is, in English the Spissers Wood (as Faustus would often boast of it among his crew when he was happy), he came into the same wood towards evening at a crossroads, where he made with a wand a circle in the dust, and within that many more circles and characters. And thus he passed away the time, until it was nine or ten o'clock at night. Then began Doctor Faustus to call for Mephistopheles the spirit, and to charge him in the name of Beelzebub to appear there personally without any long stay. Then presently the Devil began so great a rumour in the wood, as if heaven and earth would have come together with wind, the trees bowing their tops to the ground, then fell the Devil to blare as if the whole wood had been full of lions, and suddenly about the circle ran the Devil as if a thousand wagons had been running together on paved stones. After this, at the four corners of the wood it thundered horribly, with such lightnings as if the whole world, to his seeming, had been on fire. Faustus all this while half amazed at the Devil's tarrying so long, and doubting whether it was best for him to abide any more such horrible conjurings, thought to leave his circle and depart, whereupon the Devil made him such music of all sorts, as if the nymphs themselves had been in place. Whereat Faustus was revived and stood stoutly in his circle surveying his plan, and began again to conjure the spirit Mephistopheles in the name of the prince of devils to appear in his likeness. Whereat suddenly over his head hung hovering in the air a mighty dragon. Then Faustus called again after his devilish manner, at which there was a monstrous cry in the wood, as if Hell had been opened, and all the tormented souls crying to God for mercy. Presently not three fathoms above his head fell a flame like lightning, and changed itself into a globe, yet Faustus feared it not, but did persuade himself that the Devil should give him his request before he would leave[2] . . . Faustus, vexed at the spirit's tarrying so long, used his charms with full purpose not to depart before he had his intent, and crying on Mephistopheles the spirit, when suddenly the globe opened and sprang up to the height of a man. So burning a time, in the end it converted to the shape of a fiery man. This pleasant beast ran about the circle a great while, and lastly appeared in the manner of a gray friar, asking Faustus what was his request. Faustus commanded that the next morning at twelve o'clock, he should appear to him at his house, but the Devil would in no way grant this request. Faustus began again to conjure him in the name of Beelzebub, that he should fulfill his request, whereupon the spirit agreed, and so they departed each one his way.

The conference of Doctor Faustus with the spirit Mephistopheles the morning following at his own house.

Doctor Faustus having commanded the spirit to be with him at his hour appointed came and appeared in his chamber, demanding of Faustus what his desire was. Then began Doctor Faustus anew with him to conjure him that he should be obedient unto him, and to answer him certain articles, and to fulfill them in all points:

1. That the spirit should serve him and be obedient unto him in all things that he asked of him from that hour until the hour of his death.

2. Furthermore, anything that he desired of him should be brought to him.

3. Also, that in all of Faustus' demands or interrogations, the spirit should tell him nothing but that which is true.

Hereupon the spirit answered and laid his case forth, that he had no such power himself, until he had first given his prince (that was ruler over him) to understand thereof, and to know if he could obtain so much of his lord: "Therefore, speak further that I may do thy whole desire to my prince. For it is not in my power to fulfill without his leave." "Show me the cause why." said Faustus. The spirit answered: "Faustus, thou shalt understand that with us it is even as well a kingdom, as with you on earth. Yea, we have our rulers and servants, as I myself am one, and we name our number the Legion. For although that Lucifer is thrust and fallen out of heaven through his pride and high mind, yet he hath notwithstanding a legion of devils at his commandment that we call the Eastern Princes, for his power is great and infinite. Also there is a host in the south, the north, and the west. And because Lucifer hath his kingdom under heaven, we must change and give ourselves unto men to serve them at their pleasure. It is also certain, we have never as yet opened unto any man the truth of our dwelling, neither of our ruling, neither what our power is, neither have we given any man any gift, or learned him anything, unless he promises to be ours."

Doctor Faustus upon this arose where he sat, and said, "I will have my request, and yet I will not be damned." The spirit answered, "Then shalt thou want thy desire, and yet art thou mine notwithstanding. If any man would detain thee it is in vain, for thine infidelity hath confounded thee."

Hereupon spoke Faustus: "Get thee hence from me, and take Saint Valentine's farewell and Crisam with thee, yet I conjure thee that thou return at evening, and bethink thyself on what I have asked thee, and ask thy prince's counsel therein."[3] Mephistopheles the spirit, thus answered, vanished away, leaving Faustus in his study, where he sat pondering with himself how he might obtain his request of the Devil without the loss of his soul. Yet fully he was resolved in himself, rather than to be deprived of his pleasure, to do whatsoever the spirit and his lord should decide upon.

The second time of the spirit's appearing to Faustus in his house, and of their parley.

Faustus continuing in his devilish thoughts, never leaving the place where the spirit left him (such was his fervent love to the Devil) as the night approached, this swift flying spirit appeared to Faustus, offering himself with all submission to his service, with full authority from his prince to do whatsoever he would request, if so be Faustus would promise to be his. "This answer I bring thee, and an answer must thou make by me again, yet will I hear what is thy desire, because thou hast sworn me to be here at this time." Doctor Faustus gave him this answer, though faintly (for his soul's sake), that his request was none other but to become a devil or at least a limb of him and that the spirit should agree unto these articles as follows:

1. That he might be a spirit in shape and quality.

2. That Mephistopheles should be his servant and at his command.

3. That Mephistopheles should bring him anything and do for him whatsoever.

4. That at all times he should be in his house, invisible to all men, except only to himself, and at his command to show himself.

5. Lastly, that Mephistopheles should at all times appear at his command, in what form or shape soever he would.

Upon these points the spirit answered Doctor Faustus that all this should be granted him and fulfilled and more if he would agree unto him upon certain articles as follows:

First, that Doctor Faustus should give himself to his Lord Lucifer, body and soul.

Secondly, for confirmation of the same, he should make a writing, written in his own blood.

Thirdly, that he would be an enemy to all Christian people.

Fourthly, that he would deny his Christian belief.

Fifthly, that he let not any man change his opinion, if so be any man should go about to dissuade or withdraw him from it.

Further, the spirit promised Faustus to give him certain years to live in health and pleasure, and when such years were expired, that then Faustus should be fetched away, and if he should hold these articles and conditions, that then he should have all whatsoever his heart would wish or desire, and that Faustus should quickly perceive himself to be a spirit in all manner of actions whatsoever. Hereupon Doctor Faustus' mind was so inflamed that he forgot his soul and promised Mephistopheles to hold all things as he had mentioned them. He thought that the Devil was not so black as they used to paint him nor Hell so hot as the people say.

The third parley between Doctor Faustus and Mephistopheles about a conclusion.

After Doctor Faustus had made his promise to the Devil, in the morning betimes he called the spirit before him and commanded him that he should always come to him like a friar, after the order of Saint Francis, with a bell in his hand like Saint Anthony, and to ring it once or twice before he appeared, so that he might know of his certain coming. Then Faustus demanded the spirit to tell him his name. The spirit answered: "My name is as thou sayest, Mephistopheles, and I am a prince, but servant to Lucifer, and all the circuit from north to south, I rule under him." Even at these words was this wicked wretch Faustus inflamed, to hear himself to have gotten so great a power to be his servant. He forgot the Lord his maker and Christ his redeemer and became an enemy unto all mankind, yea, worse than the giants whom the poets feign to climb the hills to make war with the gods. Not unlike that enemy of God and his Christ, who for his pride was cast into Hell, so likewise Faustus forgot that the high climbers catch the greatest falls, and that the sweetest meat requires the sourest sauce.

After a while, Faustus promised Mephistopheles to write and make his obligation with full assurance of the articles in the chapter before rehearsed. A pitiful case, Christian reader, for certainly this letter or obligation was found in his house after his most lamentable end with all the rest of his damnable practices used in his whole life. Therefore, I wish all Christians to take an example by this wicked Faustus, and to be comforted in Christ, contenting themselves with that vocation that it hath pleased God to call them, and not to esteem the vain delights of this life, as did this unhappy Faustus, in giving his soul to the Devil. And to confirm it more assuredly, he took a small penknife and pricked a vein in his left hand and for certainty thereupon was seen in his handwriting these words written, as if they had been written with blood: "O HOMO FUGE," whereat the spirit vanished, but Faustus continued in his damnable mind, and made his writing as followeth.[4]

How Doctor Faustus set his blood in a saucer on warm ashes and wrote as follows.

I, Johannes Faustus, Doctor, do openly acknowledge with mine own hand, to the greater force and strengthening of this letter, that since I began to study and speculate the course and order of the elements, I have not found through the gift that is given to me from above any such learning or wisdom that can bring me to my desires. And because I find that men are unable to instruct me any further in the matter, now have I, Doctor John Faustus, unto the hellish prince of the east and his messenger Mephistopheles given both body and soul, upon such condition that they shall learn me and fulfill my desire in all things as they have promised and vowed unto me, with due obedience unto me, according unto the articles mentioned between us.

Further, I agree and grant to them by these presents that at the end of twenty-four years next ensuing the date of this present letter, they being expired, and I in the meantime, during the said years be served of them at my will, they accomplishing my desires to the full in all points as we are agreed, that then I give them full power to do with me at their pleasure, to rule, to send, fetch, or carry me or mine, be it either body, soul, flesh, blood, or goods, into their habitation, wherever it is. And I defy God and his Christ, all the host of heaven, and all living creatures that bear the shape of God, yea all that lives; and again I say it, and it shall be so. And to the more strengthening of this writing, I have written it with mine own hand and blood, being in perfect memory, and upon it I subscribe to it with my name and title, calling all the infernal, middle, and supreme powers to witness of this my letter and subscription.

John Faustus, approved in the elements,
and the spiritual doctor

How Mephistopheles came for his writing, and in what manner he appeared, and the sights he showed him, and how he caused him to keep a copy of his own writing.

Doctor Faustus sitting pensive, having but only one boy with him, suddenly there appeared his spirit Mephistopheles in the likeness of a fiery man, from whom issued most horrible fiery flames, in so much that the boy was afraid, but being hardened by his master, he bade him stand still and he should have no harm. The spirit began to blare as in a singing manner. This pretty sport pleased Doctor Faustus well, but he would not call his spirit into his counting house until he had seen more. Anon was heard a rushing of armed men and trampling of horses. This ceasing, came a kennel of hounds and they chased a great deer in the hall, and there the deer was slain. Faustus took heart, came forth, and looked upon the deer, but presently before him there was a lion and a dragon fighting together, so fiercely that Faustus thought they would have brought down the house, but the dragon overcame the lion, and so they vanished.

After this came in a peacock with a peahen, the cock bristling his tail and turning to the female beat her and so vanished. Afterward followed a furious bull that with a full fierceness ran upon Faustus, but coming near him vanished away. Afterward followed a great old ape. This ape offered Faustus the hand, but he refused, so the ape ran out of the hall again. Then a mist fell upon the hall so that Faustus saw no light, but it lasted not, and so soon as it was gone, there lay before Faustus two great sacks, one full of gold, the other full of silver.

Lastly was heard by Faustus all manner of instruments of music . . . which so ravished his mind that he thought he had been in another world, forgot both body and soul, in so much that he was minded never to change his opinion concerning that which he had done. Then came Mephistopheles into the hall to Faustus, in apparel like a friar, to whom Faustus said: "Thou hast done me a wonderful pleasure in showing me this pastime. If thou continue as thou hast begun, thou shalt win my heart and soul, yea and have it." Mephistopheles answered: "This is nothing. I will please thee better, yet that thou mayest know my power and all, ask what thou wilt request of me, that shalt thou have, conditionally hold thy promise and give me thy handwriting." At which words, the wretch thrust forth his hand, saying: "Hold thee, there hast thou my promise." Mephistopheles took the writing and willing Faustus to make a copy of it, with that the perverse Faustus being resolute in his damnation, wrote a copy thereof, and gave the Devil the one, and kept in store the other. Thus the spirit and Faustus were agreed and dwelt together.

THOU PROFOUNDEST HELL
RECEIVE THY NEW
POSSESSOR

John Milton's towering poem Paradise Lost *(1667) opened with the eviction of Satan and his army of rebel angels from Heaven after their defeat in their insurrection against God. Although he had been cast down "to bottomless perdition," the Devil quickly rallied his demonic cohort to resume the war. Among Satan's lieutenants was a rogues' gallery of fiends bearing the names of Egyptian and Semitic gods familiar from the Hebrew scriptures, an echo of the medieval tradition that demons masqueraded as pagan deities to misdirect human worship from the one true God. One of the first tasks of the rebel angels was the construction of an infernal city called Pandemonium, a word coined by Milton, which meant "the place of all demons." There, in a vast audience chamber built in emulation of Heaven's halls, the lords of Hell plotted their next move.*

(A) THAT FOUL REVOLT[1]

Who first seduc'd them to that foul revolt?
Th' infernal Serpent; he it was, whose guile
Stird up with Envy and Revenge, deceiv'd
The Mother of Mankind, what time his Pride
Had cast him out from Heav'n, with all his Host
Of Rebel Angels, by whose aid aspiring
To set himself in Glory above his Peers,
He trusted to have equal'd the most High,

If he oppos'd; and with ambitious aim
Against the Throne and Monarchy of God
Rais'd impious War in Heav'n and Battel proud
With vain attempt. Him the Almighty Power
Hurld headlong flaming from th' Ethereal Skie
With hideous ruine and combustion down
To bottomless perdition, there to dwell
In Adamantine Chains and penal Fire,
Who durst defie th' Omnipotent to Arms.
Nine times the Space that measures Day and Night
To mortal men, he with his horrid crew
Lay vanquisht, rowling in the fiery Gulfe
Confounded though immortal: But his doom
Reserv'd him to more wrath; for now the thought
Both of lost happiness and lasting pain
Torments him; round he throws his baleful eyes
That witness'd huge affliction and dismay
Mixt with obdurate pride and stedfast hate: ·
At once as far as Angels kenn he views
The dismal Situation waste and wilde,
A Dungeon horrible, on all sides round
As one great Furnace flam'd, yet from those flames
No light, but rather darkness visible
Serv'd onely to discover sights of woe,
Regions of sorrow, doleful shades, where peace
And rest can never dwell, hope never comes
That comes to all; but torture without end
Still urges, and a fiery Deluge, fed
With ever-burning Sulphur unconsum'd:
Such place Eternal Justice had prepar'd
For those rebellious, here thir Prison ordain'd
In utter darkness, and thir portion set
As far remov'd from God and light of Heav'n
As from the Center thrice to th' utmost Pole.
O how unlike the place from whence they fell!
There the companions of his fall, o'rewhelm'd
With Floods and Whirlwinds of tempestuous fire,
He soon discerns, and weltring by his side

One next himself in power, and next in crime,
Long after known in Palestine, and nam'd
Beelzebub.[2] To whom th' Arch-Enemy,
And thence in Heav'n call'd Satan, with bold words
Breaking the horrid silence thus began.

(B) THE HORRID FRONT[3]

He call'd so loud, that all the hollow Deep
Of Hell resounded. "Princes, Potentates,
Warriers, the Flowr of Heav'n, once yours, now lost,
If such astonishment as this can sieze
Eternal spirits; or have ye chos'n this place
After the toyl of Battel to repose
Your wearied vertue, for the ease you find
To slumber here, as in the Vales of Heav'n?
Or in this abject posture have ye sworn
To adore the Conquerour? who now beholds
Cherube and Seraph rowling in the Flood
With scatter'd Arms and Ensigns, till anon
His swift pursuers from Heav'n Gates discern
Th' advantage, and descending tread us down
Thus drooping, or with linked Thunderbolts
Transfix us to the bottom of this Gulfe.
Awake, arise, or be for ever fall'n."
          They heard, and were abasht, and up they sprung
Upon the wing, as when men wont to watch
On duty, sleeping found by whom they dread,
Rouse and bestir themselves ere well awake.
Nor did they not perceave the evil plight
In which they were, or the fierce pains not feel;
Yet to thir Generals Voyce they soon obeyd
Innumerable. As when the potent Rod
Of Amrams Son[4] in Egypts evill day
Wav'd round the Coast, up call'd a pitchy cloud
Of Locusts, warping on the Eastern Wind,
That ore the Realm of impious Pharaoh hung

Like Night, and darken'd all the Land of Nile:
So numberless were those bad Angels seen
Hovering on wing under the Cope of Hell
'Twixt upper, nether, and surrounding Fires;
Till, as a signal giv'n, th' uplifted Spear
Of thir great Sultan waving to direct
Thir course, in even ballance down they light
On the firm brimstone, and fill all the Plain;
A multitude, like which the populous North
Pour'd never from her frozen loyns, to pass
Rhene or the Danaw, when her barbarous Sons
Came like a Deluge on the South, and spread
Beneath Gibralter to the Lybian sands.[5]
Forthwith from every Squadron and each Band
The Heads and Leaders thither hast where stood
Thir great Commander; Godlike shapes and forms
Excelling human, Princely Dignities,
And Powers that earst in Heaven sat on Thrones;
Though of thir Names in heav'nly Records now
Be no memorial blotted out and ras'd
By thir Rebellion, from the Books of Life.[6]
Nor had they yet among the Sons of Eve
Got them new Names, till wandring ore the Earth,
Through Gods high sufferance for the tryal of man,
By falsities and lyes the greatest part
Of Mankind they corrupted to forsake
God thir Creator, and th' invisible
Glory of him that made them, to transform
Oft to the Image of a Brute, adorn'd
With gay Religions full of Pomp and Gold,
And Devils to adore for Deities:
Then were they known to men by various Names,
And various Idols through the Heathen World.[7]
Say, Muse, thir Names then known, who first, who last,
Rous'd from the slumber, on that fiery Couch,
At thir great Emperors call, as next in worth
Came singly where he stood on the bare strand,
While the promiscuous croud stood yet aloof?

The chief were those who from the Pit of Hell
Roaming to seek thir prey on earth, durst fix
Thir Seats long after next the Seat of God,
Thir Altars by his Altar, Gods ador'd
Among the Nations round, and durst abide
Jehovah thundring out of Sion, thron'd
Between the Cherubim; yea, often plac'd
Within his Sanctuary it self thir Shrines,
Abominations; and with cursed things
His holy Rites, and solemn Feasts profan'd,
And with thir darkness durst affront his light.
First Moloch, horrid King besmear'd with blood
Of human sacrifice, and parents tears,
Though for the noyse of Drums and Timbrels loud
Thir childrens cries unheard, that past through fire
To his grim Idol.[8] Him the Ammonite
Worshipt in Rabba and her watry Plain,
In Argob and in Basan, to the stream
Of utmost Arnon. Nor content with such
Audacious neighbourhood, the wisest heart
Of Solomon he led by fraud to build
His Temple right against the Temple of God
On that opprobrious Hill, and made his Grove
The pleasant Vally of Hinnom, Tophet thence
And black Gehenna call'd, the Type of Hell.
Next Chemos, th' obscene dread of Moabs Sons,
From Aroar to Nebo, and the wild
Of Southmost Abarim; in Hesebon
And Horonaim, Seons Realm, beyond
The flowry Dale of Sibma clad with Vines,
And Eleale to th' Asphaltick Pool.[9]
Peor his other Name, when he entic'd
Israel in Sittim on thir march from Nile
To do him wanton rites, which cost them woe.
Yet thence his lustful Orgies he enlarg'd
Even to that Hill of scandal, by the Grove
Of Moloch homicide, lust hard by hate;
Till good Josiah drove them thence to Hell.

With these came they, who from the bordring flood
Of old Euphrates to the Brook that parts
Egypt from Syrian ground, had general Names
Of Baalim and Ashtaroth, those male,
These Feminine. For Spirits when they please
Can either Sex assume, or both; so soft
And uncompounded is thir Essence pure,
Not ti'd or manacl'd with joynt or limb,
Nor founded on the brittle strength of bones,
Like cumbrous flesh; but in what shape they choose
Dilated or condens't, bright or obscure,
Can execute thir aerie purposes,
And works of love or enmity fulfill.
For those the Race of Israel oft forsook
Thir living strength, and unfrequented left
His righteous Altar, bowing lowly down
To bestial Gods; for which thir heads as low
Bow'd down in Battel, sunk before the Spear
Of despicable foes. With these in troop
Came Astoreth, whom the Phoenicians call'd
Astarte, Queen of Heav'n, with crescent Horns;
To whose bright Image nightly by the Moon
Sidonian Virgins paid thir Vows and Songs,
In Sion also not unsung, where stood
Her Temple on th' offensive Mountain, built
By that uxorious King, whose heart though large,
Beguil'd by fair Idolatresses, fell
To Idols foul. Thammuz came next behind,
Whose annual wound in Lebanon allur'd
The Syrian Damsels to lament his fate
In amorous dittyes all a Summers day,
While smooth Adonis from his native Rock
Ran purple to the Sea, suppos'd with blood
Of Thammuz yearly wounded: the Love-tale
Infected Sions daughters with like heat,
Whose wanton passions in the sacred Porch
Ezekiel saw, when by the Vision led
His eye survay'd the dark Idolatries

Of alienated Judah.[10] Next came one
Who mourn'd in earnest, when the Captive Ark
Maim'd his brute Image, head and hands lopt off
In his own Temple, on the grunsel edge,
Where he fell flat, and sham'd his Worshipers:
Dagon his Name, Sea Monster, upward Man
And downward Fish: yet had his Temple high
Rear'd in Azotus, dreaded through the Coast
Of Palestine, in Gath and Ascalon
And Accaron and Gaza's frontier bounds.
Him follow'd Rimmon, whose delightful Seat
Was fair Damascus, on the fertil Banks
Of Abbana and Pharphar, lucid streams.
He also against the house of God was bold:
A Leper once he lost and gain'd a King,
Ahaz his sottish Conquerour, whom he drew
Gods Altar to disparage and displace
For one of Syrian mode, whereon to burn
His odious off'rings, and adore the Gods
Whom he had vanquisht. After these appear'd
A crew who under Names of old Renown,
Osiris, Isis, Orus and their Train
With monstrous shapes and sorceries abus'd
Fanatic Egypt and her Priests, to seek
Thir wandring Gods disguis'd in brutish forms
Rather then human. Nor did Israel scape
Th' infection when thir borrow'd Gold compos'd
The Calf in Oreb:[11] and the Rebel King
Doubl'd that sin in Bethel and in Dan,
Lik'ning his Maker to the Grazed Ox,[12]
Jehovah, who in one Night when he pass'd
From Egypt marching, equal'd with one stroke
Both her first born and all her bleating Gods.
Belial came last, then whom a Spirit more lewd
Fell not from Heaven, or more gross to love
Vice for it self: To him no Temple stood
Or Altar smoak'd; yet who more oft then hee
In Temples and at Altars, when the Priest

Turns Atheist, as did Ely's Sons, who fill'd
With lust and violence the house of God.
In Courts and Palaces he also Reigns
And in luxurious Cities, where the noyse
Of riot ascends above thir loftiest Towrs,
And injury and outrage: And when Night
Darkens the Streets, then wander forth the Sons
Of Belial, flown with insolence and wine.
Witness the Streets of Sodom, and that night
In Gibeah, when the hospitable door
Expos'd a Matron to avoid worse rape.
These were the prime in order and in might;
The rest were long to tell, though far renown'd.

———————————

All these and more came flocking; but with looks
Down cast and damp, yet such wherein appear'd
Obscure some glimps of joy, to have found thir chief
Not in despair, to have found themselves not lost
In loss it self; which on his count'nance cast
Like doubtful hue: but he his wonted pride
Soon recollecting, with high words, that bore
Semblance of worth, not substance, gently rais'd
Thir fainting courage, and dispel'd thir fears.
Then strait commands that at the warlike sound
Of Trumpets loud and Clarions be upreard
His mighty Standard; that proud honour claim'd
Azazel as his right, a Cherube tall:
Who forthwith from the glittering Staff unfurld
Th' Imperial Ensign, which full high advanc't
Shon like a Meteor streaming to the Wind
With Gemms and Golden lustre rich imblaz'd,
Seraphic arms and Trophies: all the while
Sonorous mettal blowing Martial sounds:
At which the universal Host upsent
A shout that tore Hells Concave, and beyond
Frighted the Reign of Chaos and old Night.
All in a moment through the gloom were seen

Ten thousand Banners rise into the Air
With Orient Colours waving: with them rose
A Forest huge of Spears: and thronging Helms
Appear'd, and serried shields in thick array
Of depth immeasurable: Anon they move
In perfect Phalanx to the Dorian mood
Of Flutes and soft Recorders; such as rais'd
To hight of noblest temper Hero's old
Arming to Battel, and in stead of rage
Deliberate valour breath'd, firm and unmov'd
With dread of death to flight or foul retreat,
Nor wanting power to mitigate and swage
With solemn touches, troubl'd thoughts, and chase
Anguish and doubt and fear and sorrow and pain
From mortal or immortal minds. Thus they
Breathing united force with fixed thought
Mov'd on in silence to soft Pipes that charm'd
Thir painful steps o're the burnt soyle; and now
Advanc't in view, they stand, a horrid Front
Of dreadful length and dazling Arms, in guise
Of Warriers old with order'd Spear and Shield,
Awaiting what command thir mighty Chief
Had to impose: He through the armed Files
Darts his experience't eye, and soon traverse
The whole Battalion views, thir order due,
Thir visages and stature as of Gods,
Thir number last he summs. And now his heart
Distends with pride, and hardning in his strength
Glories.

(C) PANDEMONIUM[13]

He now prepar'd
To speak; whereat thir doubl'd Ranks they bend
From wing to wing, and half enclose him round
With all his Peers: attention held them mute.
Thrice he assayd, and thrice in spight of scorn,

Tears such as Angels weep, burst forth: at last
Words interwove with sighs found out thir way.

He spake: and to confirm his words, out-flew
Millions of flaming swords, drawn from the thighs
Of mighty Cherubim; the sudden blaze
Far round illumin'd hell: highly they rag'd
Against the Highest, and fierce with grasped arms
Clash'd on thir sounding Shields the din of war,
Hurling defiance toward the vault of Heav'n.

There stood a Hill not far whose griesly top
Belch'd fire and rowling smoak; the rest entire
Shon with a glossie scurff, undoubted sign
That in his womb was hid metallic Ore,
The work of Sulphur. Thither wing'd with speed
A numerous Brigad hasten'd. As when Bands
Of Pioners with Spade and Pickax arm'd
Forerun the Royal Camp, to trench a Field,
Or cast a Rampart. Mammon led them on,
Mammon, the least erected Spirit that fell
From heav'n, for ev'n in heav'n his looks and thoughts
Were always downward bent, admiring more
The riches of Heav'ns pavement, trod'n Gold,
Then aught divine or holy else enjoy'd
In vision beatific: by him first
Men also, and by his suggestion taught,
Ransack'd the Center, and with impious hands
Rifl'd the bowels of thir mother Earth
For Treasures better hid. Soon had his crew
Op'nd into the Hill a spacious wound
And dig'd out ribs of Gold. Let none admire
That riches grow in Hell; that soyle may best
Deserve the precious bane. And here let those
Who boast in mortal things, and wond'ring tell
Of Babel, and the works of Memphian Kings
Learn how thir greatest Monuments of Fame,

And Strength and Art are easily out-done
By Spirits reprobate, and in an hour
What in an age they with incessant toyle
And hands innumerable scarce perform.
Nigh on the Plain in many cells prepar'd,
That underneath had veins of liquid fire
Sluc'd from the Lake, a second multitude
With wondrous Art found out the massie Ore,
Severing each kind, and scum'd the Bullion dross:
A third as soon had form'd within the ground
A various mould, and from the boyling cells
By strange conveyance fill'd each hollow nook,
As in an Organ from one blast of wind
To many a row of Pipes the sound-board breaths.
Anon out of the earth a Fabrick huge
Rose like an Exhalation, with the sound
Of Dulcet Symphonies and voices sweet,
Built like a Temple, where Pilasters round
Were set, and Doric pillars overlaid
With Golden Architrave; nor did there want
Cornice or Freeze, with bossy Sculptures grav'n,
The Roof was fretted Gold. Not Babilon,
Nor great Alcairo such magnificence
Equal'd in all thir glories, to inshrine
Belus or Serapis thir Gods, or seat
Thir Kings, when Ægypt with Assyria strove
In wealth and luxurie. Th' ascending pile
Stood fixt her stately highth, and strait the dores
Op'ning thir brazen foulds discover wide
Within, her ample spaces, o're the smooth
And level pavement: from the arched roof
Pendant by suttle Magic many a row
Of Starry Lamps and blazing Cressets fed
With Naphtha and Asphaltus yeilded light
As from a sky. The hasty multitude
Admiring enter'd, and the work some praise
And some the Architect: his hand was known
In Heav'n by many a Towred structure high,

Where Scepter'd Angels held thir residence,
And sat as Princes, whom the supreme King
Exalted to such power, and gave to rule,
Each in his Hierarchie, the Orders bright.
Nor was his name unheard or unador'd
In ancient Greece; and in Ausonian land
Men call'd him Mulciber; and how he fell
From Heav'n, they fabl'd, thrown by angry Jove
Sheer o're the Chrystal Battlements: from Morn
To Noon he fell, from Noon to dewy Eve,
A Summers day; and with the setting Sun
Dropt from the Zenith like a falling Star,
On Lemnos th' Ægean Ile: thus they relate,
Erring; for he with this rebellious rout
Fell long before; nor aught avail'd him now
To have built in Heav'n high Towrs; nor did he scape
By all his Engins, but was headlong sent
With his industrious crew to build in hell.
Mean while the winged Haralds by command
Of Sovran power, with awful Ceremony
And Trumpets sound throughout the Host proclaim
A solemn Councel forthwith to be held
At Pandæmonium, the high Capital
Of Satan and his Peers: thir summons call'd
From every Band and squared Regiment
By place or choice the worthiest; they anon
With hunderds and with thousands trooping came
Attended: all access was throng'd, the Gates
And Porches wide, but chief the spacious Hall
(Though like a cover'd field, where Champions bold
Wont ride in arm'd, and at the Soldans chair
Defi'd the best of Paynim chivalry
To mortal combat or carreer with Lance)
Thick swarm'd, both on the ground and in the air,
Brusht with the hiss of russling wings. As Bees
In spring time, when the Sun with Taurus rides,
Pour forth thir populous youth about the Hive
In clusters; they among fresh dews and flowers

Flie to and fro, or on the smoothed Plank,
The suburb of thir Straw-built Cittadel,
New rub'd with Baum, expatiate and confer
Thir State affairs. So thick the aerie crowd
Swarm'd and were straitn'd; till the Signal giv'n.
Behold a wonder! they but now who seemd
In bigness to surpass Earths Giant Sons
Now less then smallest Dwarfs, in narrow room
Throng numberless, like that Pigmean Race
Beyond the Indian Mount, or Faerie Elves,
Whose midnight Revels, by a Forrest side
Or Fountain some belated Peasant sees,
Or dreams he sees, while over-head the Moon
Sits Arbitress, and neerer to the Earth
Wheels her pale course, they on thir mirth and dance
Intent, with jocond Music charm his ear;
At once with joy and fear his heart rebounds.
Thus incorporeal Spirits to smallest forms
Reduc'd thir shapes immense, and were at large,
Though without number still amidst the Hall
Of that infernal Court. But far within
And in thir own dimensions like themselves
The great Seraphic Lords and Cherubim
In close recess and secret conclave sat
A thousand Demy-Gods on golden seats,
Frequent and full. After short silence then
And summons read, the great consult began.

SERPENT KINGS AND ANIMAL SPIRITS

Demons of the East

Long before the arrival of Hinduism, Judaism, Buddhism, Christianity, Islam, and the other great religions of world history, malevolent spirits made their homes in the untouched forests and undisturbed pools of the Eurasian steppe, the Indian subcontinent, and the Japanese archipelago. Hints of ancient prayers and fragments of amulets and other protective artifacts attest to the manifold fears that demons aroused in local peoples, who blamed them for the physical illnesses and spiritual maladies that afflicted humankind. While the theologies of the great religions attempted to impose order and meaning on these evil entities by finding places for them in the complex taxonomies of spiritual beings that inhabited their cosmologies, they were unsuccessful at eradicating the local and regional richness of demonic traditions that stretched along the Silk Road from Europe to eastern Asia. The dread of unseen malevolent forces was ubiquitous in eastern literature from the ancient period to the dawn of modernity, but the forms taken by these demons and their activities in the world were as varied and complex as the literary cultures in which stories about them flourished.

HYMNS AGAINST DEMONS
AND SORCERERS[1]

The fear of evil spirits and the human agents who bent them to their will with malevolent intent is as old as human history. Glimpses of it surface in the Rig Veda, *an ancient collection of Sanskrit hymns written in South Asia between 1500 and 1200 BCE. Directed to the storm god Indra and other deities, these chants called upon the protectors of goodness to "hurl down those who thrive on darkness," including sinister, shape-shifting demons known as rakshasas and their sorcerer masters, who could assume the forms of dogs and birds. The phrase "let the light blot out the fiends" referred to the power of dawn's first light to put to flight night-roaming spirits and their human handlers alike.*

Indra and Soma, burn the demon and crush him; bulls, hurl down those who thrive on darkness. Shatter those who lack good thoughts; scorch them, kill, drive out, cut down the devourers . . .

Indra and Soma, pierce the evil-doers and hurl them into the pit, the bottomless darkness, so that not a single one will come up from there again. Let this furious rage of yours overpower them . . .

Plot against them. Swooping down swiftly, kill the demons who hate us and would break us into bits. Indra and Soma, let nothing good happen to the evil-doer who has ever tried to injure me with his hatred . . .

Indra shattered the sorcerers who snatched away the oblation and waylaid him. Indra splits them as an axe splits a tree, bursting apart the demons as if they were clay pots.

Kill the owl-sorcerer, the owlet-sorcerer, the dog-sorcerer, the cuckoo-sorcerer, the eagle-sorcerer, the vulture-sorcerer. Indra, crush the demon to powder as if with a millstone.

Do not let the demon of the sorcerers get close to us. Let the light blot out the fiends who work in couples . . .

Indra, kill the male sorcerer and the female who deceives by her power of illusion. Let the idol-worshippers sink down with broken necks; let them never see the rising sun.

Look here, look there, Indra and Soma; stay awake! Hurl the weapon at the demons; hurl the thunderbolt at the sorcerers!

THE SERPENT-KING
ZAHHAK[1]

In medieval Persian mythology, the Devil (here called Eblis) infiltrated the court of the legendary King Zahhak and persuaded him to murder his father and thereby inherit his kingdom. According to Shahnameh *(The Book of Kings), an epic poem recounting the deeds of the Persian kings from antiquity to the seventh century, Eblis completed his corruption of Zahhak while disguised as his cook. His tainted touch turned the doomed monarch into a reptilian abomination with a monstrous appetite. No longer human, Zahhak ruled over the Persians for centuries, but his reign of terror inspired feats of heroism, including the daring escape of captives destined as fodder for the demonic despot.* Shahnameh *recounted that these survivors fled to the Iranian countryside and founded the Kurdish people.*

When Zahhak stretched out his hand and ate, he was astonished at the man's skill. He said to him, "You are a well-meaning man; consider what it is that you desire, and ask me for it." The cook said, "May you live forever, your majesty; my heart is filled with love for you, and my soul nourished only by your glances. I have one request to ask of the victorious king, even though I am quite unworthy of it, and this is that he will command me to kiss his shoulders and rub my eyes and face there." When Zahhak heard his words he had no notion of what the man was plotting and said, "I grant your request, and may your name be honored for it." Then he said that the cook should kiss his shoulders as if he were his bosom friend.

The demon kissed the king's shoulders, and disappeared forthwith; no man had ever seen such a wonder in all the world.

Two black snakes grew from Zahhak's shoulders. In his distress the king looked everywhere for a solution, and finally he simply cut them off. But they grew again on his shoulders like the limbs of a tree. Learned doctors gathered about him and one by one gave their opinions; they tried every kind of remedy, but were unable to cure the king of his affliction. Then Eblis himself appeared in the guise of a wise doctor and said to Zahhak, "These growths were fated to appear; leave the snakes where they are, they should not be cut back. You must prepare food for them, and placate them by feeding them; this is the only thing that you can do. Give them nothing but human brains to eat, and they should die from such food." And what was the evil demon's purpose in offering such advice, if not to empty the earth of mankind?

Zahhak reigned for a thousand years, and from end to end the world was his to command. The wise concealed themselves and their deeds, and the devil achieved their heart's desire. Virtue was despised and magic applauded, justice hid itself away while evil flourished; demons rejoiced in their wickedness, while goodness was spoken of only in secret.

Two innocent young women were dragged from Jamshid's house, trembling like the leaves of a willow tree; they were Jamshid's sisters, the crown among his womenfolk. One of these veiled women was Shahrnavaz, and her chaste sister was Arnavaz. Zahhak trained them in magic and taught them evil ways, since he himself knew nothing but evil—murder, rapine, and the burning of cities.

Each night two young men, either peasants or of noble stock, were brought to Zahhak's palace. There, in the hope of finding a cure for the king's malady, they were killed and their brains made into a meal for the snakes. At the same time, there were two noble, upright men who lived in his realm; one was named Armayel the Pious, and the other, Garmayel the Perceptive. Together they talked of the king's injustice and the evil manner in which he was nourished. One said, "We should go and present ourselves as cooks to the king, to see if we can save at least one of each pair who are killed to feed the snakes."

They learned how to prepare numerous dishes and were accepted as cooks in the king's kitchens. When the victims were dragged before the cooks, and the time came for their blood to be spilled, the two men looked at one another with eyes filled with tears and with rage in their hearts. Unable to do more, they saved one of the two from slaughter, substituting the brains of a sheep, which they mixed with the brains of the man they killed. And so they were able to rescue one of each pair, to whom they said, "Hide yourself away in the plains and mountains, far from the towns." In this way they saved thirty victims a month, and when there were two hundred of them the cooks secretly gave them goats and sheep, and showed them a deserted area where they could live. The Kurds, who never settle in towns, are descended from these men.

FATAL FOX-GIRLS AND
OTHER PERILS

In the early years of the Qing dynasty, a failed bureaucrat named Pu Songling (1640–1715) compiled a collection of stories with strange themes in his remote home province of Shandong. Strange Tales from a Chinese Studio *featured many kinds of indigenous Chinese spirits and their dealings with human beings. Chief among them were the fox-spirits (*hulijing*). Mercurial, sexually charged, and often dangerous, these were-vixens preyed upon young men and caused all manner of physical and emotional disorders. Other nameless demons haunted these pages as well. Some lurked on the outskirts of battlefields to devour the corpses of the fallen, while others infiltrated the bodies of their victims, who could hear their voices ringing inside their heads.*

(A) THE SPELL OF THE WERE-VIXEN[1]

Dong Xiasi was a young gentleman who lived in the western-most part of Qingzhou prefecture. One winter evening, he spread the bedding on his couch, lit a good fire in the brazier and was just trimming his lamp when a friend called by to haul him off for a drink. He bolted his door and off they went.

Among the guests at his friend's house was a physician well-versed in the arcane art of fortune-telling known as the Tai Su, or Primordial Method, performed by reading the pulse. The physician was demonstrating this skill of his for the benefit of all the guests present, and finally came to Dong and to another friend of his, by the name of Wang Jiusi.

"I have read many pulses in my time," he pronounced. "But

you two gentlemen have the strangest and most contradictory configurations I have ever encountered. One of you shows Long Life, side by side with contraindications of Premature Demise; the other one shows Prosperity, but with contraindications of Poverty. Strange indeed! And quite beyond my competence, I fear. Yours, sir," he said, turning to Dong, "is the more extreme of the two."

The two men were appalled, and requested some elucidation.

"I fear this has taken me to the very limit of my art. I simply can go no further. I can only beg you both to exercise the utmost caution."

At first they were greatly distressed by the learned physician's remarks. But then they reflected on the almost too-carefully worded ambivalence of his prognosis and decided not to pay it undue attention.

Dong returned home late that same night and was exceedingly surprised to find the door of his study standing ajar. He had drunk a great deal, and in his inebriated state he concluded that he must have forgotten to bolt the door earlier that evening. He had after all set off in rather a hurry. In he went and, without bothering to light the lamp, reached under the covers, to feel if there was any warmth left in the bed. His hand encountered the soft skin of a sleeping body, and he withdrew it in some trepidation. Hurriedly lighting the lamp, he beheld a young girl of extraordinary beauty lying there in his bed, and stood for a moment ecstatically contemplating her ethereal features. Then he began to caress her and fondle her body, allowing his hand to stray to her nether regions, where to his great alarm he encountered a long bushy tail. His attempt to effect a speedy escape was cut short by the girl, who was now wide awake and seized hold of him by the arm.

"Where are you going, sir?"

Dong stood there trembling in fear. "Madam Fairy," he pleaded with her, "I beseech you, have mercy!"

"What have you seen to make you so afraid of me?" said the girl, with a smile.

"It wasn't your face . . ." Dong stammered. "It was your tail."

She laughed. "What tail? You must have made some mistake."

She guided Dong's hand down beneath the covers again, drawing it across the firm, smooth flesh of her buttocks, and resting it gently on the tip of her backbone, which this time was indeed quite hairless to the touch.

"See!" she said, smiling more sweetly than ever. "You were just tipsy and letting your imagination run away with you. You really shouldn't say such unkind things."

Dong drank in her beauty with his eyes, by now totally spellbound and greatly regretting his initial misgivings— though he still found himself vaguely wondering what she was doing in his room and in his bed. She seemed to divine his thoughts.

"Don't you remember the girl next door, with the brown hair? It must be ten years now since my family moved away. I was not more than a child then, and you were just a little boy."

"Ah Suo!" cried Dong as the memory returned to him. "You mean the Zhous' little girl!"

"That's right."

"I do remember you! What a beautiful young lady you have become! But what are you doing here, in my bed?"

"For five long years I was wife to a simpleton. Both my parents-in-law passed away, and then my husband died, leaving me a widow and quite alone in the world. I thought of you, my childhood friend, and came here to seek you out. When I arrived it was already evening, and a moment later your friend called and invited you out, so I looked for a place where I could hide and wait for you to return. You were such a very long time, and I was beginning to shiver with cold, so I crept under your quilt to keep myself warm. You don't mind, do you?"

Ecstatically Dong stripped off his clothes and climbed under the quilt with her. His subsequent joy can well be imagined.

A month went by, and gradually Dong began to waste away. His family commented on his worsening condition, and expressed their concern, which he dismissed as groundless. But with time his features grew quite haggard and he himself began to take fright. He went to consult the same learned physician, who took his pulses again and declared, "You are clearly bewitched. My earlier prognosis of Premature Demise has been borne out. I fear there is no cure for you."

Dong burst into tears and refused to leave the physician, who performed acupuncture on his hand and moxibustion on his navel, and gave him certain herbal remedies to take.

"If anything untoward should cross your path, be sure to resist it with all your might."

Dong went away fearing for his life.

When he reached home, the girl greeted him with sweet smiles and wanted him in bed with her at once. He protested vehemently, "Leave me alone! Can't you see that I am at death's door!"

He turned his back on her.

"Do you really think you can still live?" she cried bitterly, shame and anger mingling in her voice.

That night, Dong took his medicine and slept alone, but the moment he closed his eyes in sleep, he dreamed he was making love to the girl again, and when he awoke he found that he had ejaculated in his bed. He grew more afraid than ever, and went in to sleep with his wife, who lit a lamp and kept close watch over him. Still the dreams continued, and yet every time he awoke the girl was nowhere to be seen. A few days later, he began to cough up large quantities of blood, and before long he was dead.

Now some while after this, Wang (the friend whose fortune had also been told on that fateful evening) was sitting in his own study one day when a young girl entered unannounced. He was immediately taken with her beauty, and made love to her without further ado. He asked her who she was and where she was from.

"I am a neighbour of your friend Dong, who was also a dear friend of mine," she replied. "Poor man! A fox cast a spell on him and he is with us no more! Foxes can cast powerful spells. Young gentlemen in particular, such as you and your friend, should guard against them."

Wang was deeply moved by her words and loved her all the more. As the days went by, he too began to waste away and his reason started to wander. One night, in a dream, Dong came and spoke to him: "Beware! Your lover is a fox. First she took my life, and now she wants yours. I have already laid charges against her before the courts of the Nether World, hoping to bring some comfort to my wounded spirit. On the night of the seventh day, you must burn some incense outside your room. On no account must you forget these words!"

Wang awoke and marvelled at his strange dream. He decided to speak to the girl.

"I am seriously ill," he said, "and it may soon be all up with me. It would be advisable for us never to make love again."

"Do not worry," she replied. "All is destiny. If you are destined for a long life, then no amount of love-making is going to kill you. And if you are destined to die, no amount of abstinence will save you."

She sat by him and toyed with him, smiling so sweetly the while that Wang was unable to restrain himself and soon found himself in her arms again. Every time they made love, he was filled with remorse. But he was incapable of resisting her advances.

The evening of the seventh day, he lit sticks of incense and stuck them in his door, but she pulled them out and threw them away. That same night, in a dream, Dong came to him again and reproached him for having failed to act on his advice. The next night, Wang secretly instructed his servants to wait until he was asleep and then to light the incense.

The girl was already in his bed.

"That incense again!" she cried, suddenly waking.

"What incense?" protested Wang, feigning ignorance.

She rose at once, and taking the sticks of incense, broke them into little pieces.

"Who told you to do this?" she said, as she returned to their room.

"My wife," lied Wang. "She is concerned at my illness, and believes that it can be exorcized."

The girl paced up and down, greatly perturbed.

One of the servants, meanwhile, seeing that the incense sticks had been extinguished, lit some more.

"Ah!" cried the girl. "Your aura of good luck is too strong for me. I shall have to tell you the truth. Yes, I did hurt your friend, and yes, then I came running after you next. I have done great wrong. I must go to the Nether World now and face your friend in the court of Yama. If you remember your love for me, I beg you, keep my body from harm."

With these words she climbed slowly from the bed and then promptly lay down and died. When he lit the lamp, he saw the body of a fox on the ground. Fearing it might come to life again, he instructed his servants to skin it and hang up the pelt.

His illness now entered a critical phase. One day, he saw a fox come loping towards him.

"I have been before the court of the Nether World," said the fox. "Judgement was given against your friend Dong, whose death was reckoned to have been the consequence of his own lust. But I was still found guilty of enchantment. They took away my Golden Elixir, the fruit of all my years of toil. They have sent me back to be reborn. Where is my body?"

"My servants knew no better and skinned it."

The fox was greatly distressed. "It is true that I drove many men to their death. I deserved to die long ago. But nonetheless, what a heartless man you are!"

She took her leave, sadly, bitterly.

Wang all but died of his illness. But after six months he was restored to health.

(B) THE DEMON DOG[2]

During the rebellion led by Yu Qi, men died in countless numbers, mown down like fields of hemp. At this time, a peasant by the name of Li Hualong was trying to find his way home through the hills when he came across a detachment of government troops on a night march. Afraid of being rounded up indiscriminately as a bandit, and seeing nowhere to hide, he lay down in a heap of decapitated corpses, pretending to be dead himself and staying there until long after the troops had passed.

Then suddenly he saw the corpses, for the most part headless and armless, stand up in serried ranks like trees in a forest. One among them, his head still dangling from his shoulders, gasped, "The wild dog is coming! We are done for!"

The others answered in a ragged chorus, "Done for! Done for!"

The next instant, they all tumbled down again and lay there in motionless silence. Li was about to rise to his feet (trembling with fear though he was), when he saw a creature coming towards him, with the head of an animal and the body of a man. As the "wild dog" came nearer, it bent down, sank its teeth into one after another of the heads and sucked out their brains. In terror, Li buried his own head under the nearest corpse. The monster tugged at Li's shoulder to get at his head, but Li burrowed down still further and succeeded for a while in staying out of its reach, until finally the monster pushed the corpse aside, thus exposing Li's head.

The terrified Li, groping around desperately on the ground beneath him, grabbed hold of a big stone the size of a bowl and clutched it tightly in his hand. As the creature bent down to bite into him, he heaved himself up and with a great cry smashed the stone into its mouth. The thing made an odd hooting noise like an owl and ran off clutching its face and spitting mouthfuls of blood on to the road. In the blood, Li discovered, when he looked more closely, two fangs, curved and tapering to a sharp point, each one over four inches long. He took them home with him to show his friends, none of whom had any idea what sort of a strange beast it might have been.

(C) THE EYE-DWELLERS[3]

In the city of Chang'an there lived a man by the name of Fang Dong, known as a gentleman of considerable accomplishments, while at the same time having a reputation as an unprincipled libertine. If ever a pretty woman caught his eye on the street, he would trail her and do his utmost to seduce her.

The day before the Qing Ming Festival, he happened to be out strolling in the countryside when he saw a small carriage pass by, with red curtains and embroidered blinds. It was followed by a train of servants and horses, including one particular maid on a pony, who struck Fang as being very good-looking. He went closer to get a better view of the girl on the pony and, as he did so, noticed through the slightly parted curtains of the carriage a young lady, about sixteen years old, gorgeously attired and of a beauty such as he had never witnessed in his life. He gazed at her dumbfounded, rooted to the spot, and then proceeded to keep up with the carriage for several miles, now walking slightly ahead, now trailing behind. Finally he heard the young lady command her maid to come to the side of her carriage.

"Let the blinds down, girl! Who does that wild young man think he is, the one who keeps ogling me in that insolent fashion!"

The maid let down the blinds and spoke angrily to Fang. "My lady is the bride of the seventh young lord of Hibiscus Town, and she is on her way to visit her parents. She is no village lass for the likes of you to gawp at!"

So saying, she took a pinch of dust from the ground by the carriage wheel and threw it in his face. Fang was momentarily blinded and could not even open his eyes. He rubbed them, and when finally he did succeed in opening them, carriage and horses, young lady and maid, had all vanished into thin air! He returned home in great perplexity of spirit, all the time aware of a continuing discomfort in his eyes. He asked a friend to lift up his eyelids and take a look inside, and the friend told him that there was a clearly visible film over each of his eyeballs. The next morning, the condition was still more pronounced and there was an unstoppable flow of tears from each eye. The film continued to thicken, and after a few days it was as thick as a copper coin. In addition, a spiral-shaped protuberance began growing from the right eye, which resisted any treatment.

Fang was now totally blind, and his condition filled him with despair and remorse. Hearing that a Buddhist scripture, known as The Sutra of Light, had the power to cure ailments such as his, he acquired a copy and found a person to teach it to him so that he could recite it by heart. For a certain period of time, his physical discomfort and mental perplexity continued unabated, but after a while he began to find a certain peace of mind. Morning and evening, he sat cross-legged chanting the sutra and counting the beads of his rosary, and after a year of this he eventually succeeded in attaining a state of genuine detachment and serenity.

Then one day, out of the blue, he heard a voice, quiet as a fly, coming from within his left eye. This is what it said: "It's pitch black in here! Unbearable!"

From his right eye came the reply, "Why don't we go out for a little stroll? It might help us shake off this gloom."

Then he felt a slight irritation in both nostrils, as if two little creatures were wriggling down his nose. After a while he felt the creatures return and make their way back up his nostrils and into his eye sockets again.

"I hadn't seen the garden for ages!" said one voice. "Aren't the Pearl Orchids looking withered!"

Now Fang had always been especially fond of orchids, and cultivated several varieties in his garden, which he had been in the habit of watering himself every day. But ever since losing his sight, he had lost all interest in them and had completely neglected them. Hearing this exchange, he promptly asked his wife why his orchids had been allowed to wither away. She in turn asked him how he even knew this to be the case, since he was blind, whereupon he told her about his strange experience. She went out into the garden, and sure enough, the flowers were quite dead. Greatly intrigued by what her husband had told her, she decided to hide herself in his room and keep watch. It was not long before she saw two little mannikins— neither of them any larger than a bean—emerge from his nose and fly buzzing out of the door. They were soon well out of sight, but were back again in next to no time, flying together up on to his face and in at his nostrils, like a pair of homing bees or ants.

They did the same thing two or three days running. Then Fang heard a voice speak from within his left eye.

"That tunnel is a dreadfully roundabout way of going in and out. Most inconvenient. We really should think of making ourselves a proper doorway."

"The wall on my side is very thick," replied the right eye. "It won't be easy."

"I'll try to make an opening on my side," said the left eye. "Then we can share my door."

Presently Fang thought he felt a scratching and a splitting in his left eye socket, and an instant later, he could see! He could see everything around him with absolute clarity. Beside himself with delight, he promptly informed his wife, who inspected his eyes afresh and found that in the left eye a minute aperture had appeared in the film, a hole no larger than a cracked peppercorn, through which gleamed the black globe of a pupil. By the next morning, the film in the left eye had disappeared altogether. But the strangest thing of all was that, on careful inspection, there were now two pupils visible in that eye, while the right eye was still obscured by its spiral-shaped growth. Apparently both of the two eye-mannikins, his talking pupils, had now taken up residence in the left eye. So although Fang was still blind in one eye, he could see better with his one good eye than he had ever done with two.

From that day forth, he was a great deal more circumspect in his behaviour, and acquired an impeccable reputation in the district.

(D) THE PAINTED SKIN[4]

A certain gentleman by the name of Wang, from the city of Tai-yuan, was out walking early one morning when a young woman passed him carrying a bundle, hurrying along on her own, though with considerable difficulty. He caught up with her, and saw at once that she was a girl of about sixteen, and very beautiful.

"What are you doing out here all alone at this early hour?" he asked, instantly smitten.

"Why do you bother to ask, since you are only a passer-by and can do nothing to ease my troubles?" was her reply.

"Tell me, what has caused this sorrow of yours? I will do anything I can to help you."

"My parents were greedy for money," she replied sadly, "and sold me as a concubine into a rich man's household. The master's wife was jealous of me, and she was always screaming at me and beating me, until in the end I could bear it no longer and decided to run away."

"Where are you going?"

"I am a fugitive. I have no place to go."

"My own humble abode is not far from here," said Wang. "I should be honoured if you were to accompany me there."

She seemed only too pleased at this suggestion and followed him home, Wang carrying her bundle for her. When they arrived, she observed that the house was empty.

"Do you have no family of your own?" she asked.

"This is my private study," he replied.

"It seems an excellent place to me," she said. "But I must ask you to keep my presence here a secret and not to breathe a word of it to anyone. My very life depends upon it."

He swore to this.

That night they slept together, and for several days he kept her hidden in his study without anyone knowing that she was there. Then he decided to confide in his wife, the lady Chen. She feared the consequences if the girl should turn out to have escaped from some influential family, and advised him to send her away. But he paid no heed to her advice.

A few days later, in the marketplace, Wang ran into a Taoist priest, who studied his face with grave concern. "What strange thing have you encountered?"

"Why, nothing!" replied Wang.

"Nothing? Your whole being is wrapped in an evil aura," insisted the Taoist. "I tell you, you are bewitched!"

Wang protested vehemently that he was speaking the truth.

"Bewitched!" muttered the Taoist, as he went on his way.

"Poor fool! Some men blind themselves to the truth even when death is staring them in the face!"

Something in the Taoist's strange words set Wang wondering, and he began to have serious misgivings about the young woman he had taken in. But he could not bring himself to believe that such a pretty young thing could have cast an evil spell on him. Instead he persuaded himself that the Taoist was making it all up, trying to put the wind up him in the hope of being retained for a costly rite of exorcism. And so he put the matter out of his mind and returned home.

He reached his study to find the outer door barred. He was unable to enter his own home. His suspicions now genuinely aroused, he clambered into the courtyard through a hole in the wall, only to find that the inner door was also closed. Creeping stealthily up to a window, he peeped through and saw the most hideous sight, a green-faced monster, a ghoul with great jagged teeth like a saw, leaning over a human pelt, the skin of an entire human body, spread on the bed—on *his* bed. The monster had a paintbrush in its hand and was in the process of touching up the skin in lifelike colour. When the painting was done, it threw down the brush, lifted up the skin, shook it out like a cloak and wrapped itself in it—whereupon it was instantly transformed into his pretty young "fugitive" friend.

Wang was absolutely terrified by what he had seen, and crept away on all fours. He went at once in search of the Taoist, but did not know where to find him. He looked for him everywhere and eventually found him out in the fields. Falling on his knees, he begged the priest to save him.

"I can drive her away from you," said the Taoist. "But I cannot bring myself to take her life. The poor creature must have suffered greatly and is clearly close to finding a substitute and thus ending her torment."

He gave Wang a fly-whisk and told him to hang it outside his bedroom door, instructing him to come and find him again in the Temple of the Green Emperor.

Wang returned home. This time he did not dare to go into his study, but slept with his wife, hanging the fly-whisk outside their bedroom. Late that night he heard a faint sound at the door, and not having the courage to look himself, he asked his wife to go. It was the "girl." She had come, but had halted on seeing the fly-whisk and was standing there grinding her teeth. Eventually she went away, only to return after a little while.

"That priest thought to scare me!" she cried. "I'll never give up! Not now, not when I am so close! Does he think that I'm going to spit it out, when I'm so near to swallowing it!"

She tore down the fly-whisk and ripped it to pieces, then broke down the door and burst into the bedroom. Climbing straight up on to the bed, she tore open Wang's chest, plucked out his heart and made off with it into the night. Wang's wife began screaming, and a maid came hurrying with a lamp, to find her master lying dead on the bed, his chest a bloody pulp, and her mistress sobbing in silent horror beside him, incapable of uttering a word.

The next morning, they sent Wang's younger brother off at once to find the Taoist.

"To think that I took pity on her!" cried the priest angrily. "Clearly that fiend will stop at nothing!"

He followed Wang's brother back to the house. By now, of course there was no trace of the "girl." The Taoist gazed around him. "Fortunately she is still close at hand."

He went on to ask, "Who lives in the house to the south?"

"That is my family compound," replied Wang's brother.

"That is where she is now," said the priest.

Wang's brother was appalled at the idea and could not bring himself to believe it.

"Has a stranger come to your house today?" asked the priest.

"How would I know?" replied the brother. "I went out first thing to the Temple of the Green Emperor to fetch you. I shall have to go home and ask."

Presently he returned to report that there had indeed been an old lady. "She called first thing this morning, saying she wanted to work for us. My wife kept her on, and she is still there."

"That's the very person we're looking for!" cried the Taoist.

He strode next door immediately with the brother, and took up a stance in the middle of the courtyard, brandishing his wooden sword.

"Come out, evil one!" he cried. "Give me back my fly-whisk!"

The old woman came hurtling out of the building, her face deathly pale, and made a frantic attempt to escape, but the Taoist pursued her and struck her down. As she fell to the ground the human pelt slipped from her, to reveal her as the vile fiend she really was, grovelling on the ground and grunting like a pig. The Taoist swung his wooden sword again and chopped off the monster's head, whereupon its body was transformed into a thick cloud of smoke hovering above the ground. The Taoist now took out a bottle-gourd, removed the stopper and placed it in the midst of the smoke. With a whooshing sound the smoke was sucked into the gourd, leaving no trace in the courtyard. He replaced the stopper and slipped the gourd back into his bag.

When they examined the pelt, it was complete in every human detail—the eyes, the hands and feet. The Taoist proceeded to roll it up like a scroll (it even made the same sound), placed it in his bag and set off . . .

THE ALLURE
OF THE INCUBUS

Demon Lovers
through the Ages

The legend of the seduction of human women by the rebel angels and the sinister character of their offspring, the Nephilim, resonated in the imagination of western authors for centuries. How could spiritual creatures composed of air intermingle with mortals to produce children? From late antiquity onward, Christian writers fused pagan tales about lustful agricultural gods with biblical and apocryphal traditions to fashion stories about seductive demons known as incubi. As Bishop Isidore of Seville (ca. 560–636) explained in his encyclopedic compendium of ancient learning called the Etymologies, *incubi took their name from the Latin verb* incumbere *("to lie upon"), a nod to their active role during intercourse. Demons also appeared in female form called succubi in order to seduce men. Early medieval authors did not place much stock in the reality of incubi and succubi, but after the turn of the first millennium they appeared more frequently in religious discourse. Preachers crafted moral lessons from rumors about their depredations, while theologians attributed the rise of witchcraft to their nefarious influence. Legends arose that powerful individuals, like the magician Merlin, had a fiendish heritage. Tenacious in their appeal to poets and songsmiths, the allure of the incubi has endured in folklore and popular songs down to the present day.*

THE AIR'S EMBRACE[1]

In his defense of the Christian faith in the wake of pagan criticism, Bishop Augustine of Hippo (354–430) left no stone unturned in his magisterial treatise Concerning the City of God Against the Pagans *(see pp. 42–47). The question of the capability of angels and other aerial spirits to interact with human women by touch clearly vexed him, however, because his primary authorities for religious truth—the Hebrew and Christian scriptures—were elusive on this issue. While Augustine had to concede that examples of physical contact between angels and humans were known from the Bible, most notably the story of the Nephilim (see pp. 5–6), he turned to pagan traditions to cast light on this dark corner of religious history. His equivocation on this issue gave Christian authors from the later Middle Ages license to pursue the topic further and thereby inflect it with their own concerns.*

In the third book of this work we mentioned in passing the question whether angels, being spirits, could have physical connection with women, and we left the answer unresolved.[2] Now Scripture says, "He makes spirits his angels," that is, those who are by nature spirits he makes into his angels, by imposing on them the duty of carrying messages.[3] For the Greek *angelos*, which becomes *angelus* in the Latin derivative, means *nuntius*, a "messenger," in the Latin language . . .

Nevertheless it is the testimony of Scripture (which tells us nothing but the truth) that angels appeared to men in bodies of such a kind that they could not only be seen but also touched.[4] Besides this, it is widely reported that Silvani and Pans, commonly called incubi, have often behaved improperly towards women, lusting after them and achieving intercourse with them.[5] These reports are confirmed by many people, either from their own experience or from the accounts of the experience of others, whose reliability there is no occasion to doubt. Then there is the story that certain demons, whom the Gauls call Dusii, constantly and successfully attempt this indecency. This is asserted by so many witnesses of such a character that it would seem an impertinence to deny it. Hence I would not venture a conclusive statement on the question whether some spirits with bodies of air (an element which even when set in motion by a fan is felt by the bodily sense of touch) can also experience this lust and so can mate, in whatever way it can, with women, who feel their embraces.

LASCIVIOUS SPIRITS[1]

Among the hundreds of moral lessons collected by Caesarius of Heisterbach (ca. 1180–1240) in his Dialogue on Miracles *was a cluster of stories about the dangers posed by incubi and succubi. Caesarius wrote in the aftermath of the Fourth Lateran Council (1215), which mandated that Christians take responsibility for their spiritual well-being by attending mass and confessing their sins at least once per year. It is thus no surprise to learn that confession was foremost among the remedies to rescue the men and women who had succumbed to the temptations offered by lustful demons.*

An example from *The Miracles of the Abbot Saint Bernard*, who drove away from a woman a demon incubus.

A woman in the region of Nantes had been tormented for six years with a voracious lust by a wanton demon to whom she had given her consent. That lascivious spirit had appeared to her in the guise of an especially handsome soldier and often misused her without being seen, while she was lying in the same bed as her husband. In the seventh year, terror seized her. When Saint Bernard, the abbot of Clairvaux, came to the aforesaid city, the wretched woman fell at his feet, confessed her horrible lust and the demon's disdain with many tears, and entreated the saint's help. Consoled by the saint and told what she had to do, the devil was no longer able to approach after she made confession, but nonetheless terrified her with words and threatened her most bitterly that after the abbot's departure he would resume her punishments, so that the one who had been her lover now became her cruelest oppressor. After she had reported this news to the saint, he came back on the following Sunday. In the company of two bishops, amidst burning candles, and with the support of all the faithful who were in the church, he anathematized the fornicating spirit, forbidding it by the authority of Christ to approach not only this woman, but any woman. When those sacramental lights were extinguished, the demon's every strength likewise went out. After making a general confession of her sins, the woman was freed completely from its influence. This happened in our own times.

Concerning the daughter of the priest Arnold, whom a demon corrupted.

A few years ago, in the parish of Saint Remigius in the city of Bonn there lived a certain priest, Arnold by name, who had a pretty daughter. He took the utmost care of her. Owing to her beauty, he was on his guard for her sake because of the threat of young men, and especially the canons of Bonn. As a result, whenever he left the house, he locked his daughter in the upper chamber. One day, the devil, appearing to her as a man, began to bend her mind toward love for him inwardly by silent suggestion and outwardly with flattering words. What more can I say? Won over and corrupted, the wretched girl afterward consented quite often to the demon to her own ruin. One day when the priest ascended to the upper chamber, he found his daughter moaning and crying, and he could barely compel her to reveal the cause of her sadness. She confessed to her father that she had been deluded and captured by a demon and therefore she had every reason to lament. Indeed, she had become so deranged and so divorced from her senses, both from sadness and from the demon's machinations, that she would collect worms from the ground, put them in her mouth, and chew them. Her grieving father sent her across the Rhine, hoping that the change of air would improve her condition and the river would provide an obstacle that would free her from the incubus demon. After she had departed, the demon appeared to the priest and addressed him with plain words, saying, "You bad priest, why have you deprived me of my wife? You have done this to your own harm." And then the demon struck him so hard on the chest that he vomited blood and three days later he was dead . . .

Novice: If demons are allowed to do such things, then women should especially be on their guard not to offer any opportunity to them nor to give them any hint of consent.

Monk: Not only should women be on their guard against them, but also men, because just as demons in the guise of men mock and corrupt women, as we have seen, so too in the guise of women, do they seduce and deceive men . . . I will also relate to you some other examples, by which you will see how men have been mocked by demons in the guise of women.

Concerning John, a scholar from Prüm, who is said to have slept with a demon.

There was a certain scholar of Prüm, John by name, a man with some learning, but shallow and deceitful. It is said concerning him and I heard it directly from the abbot of his monastery that a certain woman had promised to rendezvous with him one night. At the appointed time, she did not arrive, but a demon mounted the clerk's bed in her form and with a voice like hers. Believing the demon to be the woman who was well-known to him, he slept with it. Rising in the morning, when he urged the demon that he had mistaken for a woman to leave, it responded to him, "With whom do you think that you slept last night?" When he answered, "With such and such a woman," the demon replied, "Not with her, but with a devil." Upon hearing these words, John was shocked, and thus answered with a shocking word, which I am too modest to say, laughing at the devil, and caring not in the least concerning what had just happened . . .

Novice: If demons can mingle with human beings in assumed bodies, as these different examples show, I wonder if they can reproduce with women or conceive from men and give birth.

Monk: Concerning this question, I have no answer, but I repeat here what I have read in ancient histories.

Concerning the Huns and Merlin, and the truth about the humanity of the children of incubi.

When the race of the Goths migrated from Asia into Europe, as related in accounts of their histories, there were malformed women in their company, whom they cast out in fear that they might produce malformed children and thus deface the nobility of the Goths. Cast out from the camps, these women wandered into the forest, where incubus demons came upon them and produced with them sons and daughters. From these offspring proceeded the most stalwart race of the Huns. We read also that Merlin, the prophet of the Britons, was the son of an incubus demon and a holy woman. For the kings, who down to this day rule in Britain, which is now called England, are said to trace their descent from a phantom mother. Merlin was truly a reasonable man and a Christian, who foretold many future events, which are fulfilled as the days go by.

Novice: If human beings can only be conceived and born from the seed of both parents, how can they be called human beings, who draw the source of their flesh partly from a human and partly from a demon? Will someone rise at the Last Judgment who does not fully possess a genuine human nature?

Monk: I will relate to you what I have heard from a certain learned man pertaining to this very question. He says as follows: demons collect human semen that has been released contrary to nature, and from it they craft for themselves bodies in which they can be touched and seen by human beings, male bodies from the male seed and female bodies from the female seed. And so, the masters say that there is in fact a genuineness of human nature in those who are born from them and that they will rise at the Last Judgment truly as human beings.

DEMON SEED

Anxieties about the noxious influence of witches and their demonic agents reached their peak in the early modern period, when church authorities targeted thousands of people, predominantly older women, for interrogation and execution. The inquisitors kept detailed records of the testimony of convicted witches, which informed the handbooks that they composed to justify their industry in rooting them out. The creation of the printing press in the fifteenth century facilitated the circulation of these writings throughout northern Europe. Chief among them were Heinrich Kramer's The Hammer of Witches *(Malleus maleficarum), published in 1487, and Nicolas Rémy's* Demonolatry *(Daemonolatreiae libri tres), which appeared a century later in 1595. Informed by their authors' experiences as inquisitors, these manuals shared strategies for dealing with the threat of fiendish infiltration in European communities. Their insights and imaginings about the purpose and practice of sexual commerce between witches and their demon companions, especially their ruminations on the questions of how such commerce took place and whether it could produce offspring, revealed more about the preoccupations of the inquisitors than it did about the practice of witchcraft.*

(A) A POLLUTED PROGENY[1]

*How in modern time witches perform
the carnal act with incubus devils, and how they
are multiplied by this means.*

. . . But the theory that modern witches are tainted with this sort of diabolic filthiness is not substantiated only in our opinion, since the expert testimony of the witches themselves has made all these things credible; and that they do not now, as in times past, subject themselves unwillingly, but willingly embrace this most foul and miserable servitude. For how many women have we left to be punished by secular law in various dioceses, especially in Constance and the town of Ratisbon, who have been for many years addicted to these abominations, some from their twentieth and some from their twelfth or thirteenth year, and always with a total or partial abnegation of the Faith? All the inhabitants of those places are witnesses of it. For without reckoning those who secretly repented, and those who returned to the Faith, no less than forty-eight have been burned in five years. And there was no question of credulity in accepting their stories because they turned to free repentance; for they all agreed in this, namely, that they were bound to indulge in these lewd practices in order that the ranks of their perfidy might be increased . . .

Therefore, to return to the question whether witches had their origin in these abominations, we shall say that they originated from some pestilent mutual association with devils, as is clear from our first knowledge of them. But no one can affirm with certainty that they did not increase and multiply by means of these foul practices, although devils commit this deed for the sake not of pleasure but of corruption. And this appears to be the order of the process. A Succubus devil draws the semen from a wicked man; and if he is that man's own particular devil, and does not wish to make himself an Incubus to a witch, he passes that semen on to the devil deputed to a woman or witch; and this last, under some constellation that favors his purpose that the man or woman so born should be strong in the practice of witchcraft, becomes the Incubus to the witch.

(B) THE TOUCH OF AN ICILY COLD HAND[2]

Plutarch in his *Numa*, arguing against the beliefs of the Egyptians, says that it is absurd to believe that demons are captivated by human beauty and grace, and have intercourse with mankind for the sake of carnal pleasure.[3] For nature provides physical beauty as a stimulant to propagation, of which demons have no need, since they were created in the beginning in a certain fixed number. It must follow, then, that such intercourse is powerless to generate so wonderful a creation as man. For, in the first place, there must be a complementary correlation between the species; and this cannot exist between a demon and a man; so utterly opposite by nature are the mortal and the immortal, the corporeal and the incorporeal, the sentient and the insentient, or any two creatures which are even more opposite and contrary to each other. How such incompatibles can mingle and copulate together passes my understanding; and certainly I cannot believe that any perfect or complete issue can be brought to life by such a union. For there must always be some proportion between the active and the passive agent, and the extremes must meet in some common mean, if they are to produce any result.

Moreover, if like is born from like, how, I ask, can a living being spring from the union of such opposite and dissimilar natures? I know that you will say that when demons set themselves to this business, they assume some body which they endow with the powers, nature, and appearance of a living human form (for man is composed of spirit and body). Let it be granted to assume that they assume some body, for so far I am in agreement with you; but I think that body will be either the corpse of a dead man or else some concretion and condensation of vapors; for methinks that I say elsewhere that they usually adopt one of these two methods of manifesting themselves to us. But, I ask, can anything more absurd or incredible be said or imagined than that which is devoid of animal life can have any power or efficacy to impart life to another? For this process of procreation is governed by the laws of nature, according to which no semen can be fertile unless it comes from a living man. I am aware that Peter of Palude and Martin of Arles have said that when demons go about this work, they, as it were, milk the semen from the bodies of dead men, but this is as ridiculous as the proverbial dead donkey's fart.[4]

And if, as Saint Basil and many others have maintained, the demon's body is formed from a concretion of condensed vapors, still the business will go forward with no greater success, and such a body will be no more adapted to the work than that of which I have just spoken . . . [5]

It is a fact that all witches who give a demon free rein over their bodies (and this they all do when they enter his service, and it is as it were the first pledge of their pact with him) are completely in agreement in saying that, if the demon emits any semen, it is so cold that they recoil with horror on receiving it . . .

I need not here run through all the arguments which are usually adduced in support of this opinion, for the fact is proved by actual experience. Alexander ab Alexandro records that he knew a man who told him that the appearance of a friend who lately died (but it is probable that this was a spectral illusion of a demon) came to him, very pale and wasted, and tried to get into bed with him; and although he fought with him and prevented him from doing this, he yet succeeded in inserting one foot, which was so cold and rigid that no ice could be compared with it.[6] Cardan also tells a similar story of a friend of his who went to bed in a chamber which had formerly been notoriously haunted by demons, and felt the touch of an icily cold hand.[7] But to come nearer home, the confession of Ponsète of Essey, who was convicted of witchcraft at Montlhéry, agrees with what has been said above. She said that whenever she put her hand in her demon's bosom she felt it as hard and rigid as marble.

Averroës, Blessed Albertus Magnus, and several others add to the above two methods of procuring this monstrous procreation a third which is perhaps more credible and probable.[8] According to them, the demons inject as incubi the semen which they have previously received as succubi; and this view can reasonably be supported by the fact that this method differs from the natural and customary way of men only in respect of a very brief intermission in its accomplishment. This objection, moreover, they easily overcome by quoting the extraordinary skill of demons in preserving matters from their natural dissolution. But whether it be a man or a woman who is concerned, in either case the work of nature must be free, and there must be nothing to delay or impede it in the very least. If shame, fear, horror or some stronger feeling is present, all that comes from the loins is spent in vain and nature becomes sterile; and for this reason the very consummation of love and carnal warmth which it implies will act as a spur to the accomplishment of the venereal act. But all they who have spoken to us of their copulations with demons agree in saying that nothing colder or more unpleasant could be imagined or described. At Dalheim, Pétrone of Armentières declared that, as soon as he embraced his *Abrahel*, all his limbs at once grew stiff. Hennezel at Vergaville said that it was as if he had entered an ice-bound cavity, and then he left his *Schwartzburg* with the matter unaccomplished. (These were the names of their Succubae.) And all female witches maintain that the so-called genital organs of their demons are so huge and excessively rigid that they cannot be admitted without the greatest pain. Alexée Drigie reported that her demon's penis, even when only half in erection, was as long as some kitchen utensils which she pointed to as she spoke; and that there was neither testicles nor scrotum attached to it. Claude Fellet said that she had often felt it like a spindle swollen to an immense size so that it could not be contained by even the most capacious woman without great pain. This agrees with the complaint of Nicole Morèle that, after such miserable copulation, she always had to go straight to bed as if she had been tired out by some long and violent agitation. Didatia of Miremont also said that, although she had many years' experience of men, she was always so stretched by the huge, swollen member of her demon that the sheets were drenched in blood. And nearly all witches protest that it is wholly against their will that they are embraced by demons, but that it is useless for them to resist.

A WARNING FOR
MARRIED WOMEN[1]

First attested in 1657, this English ballad is a warning to wives about the perils of infidelity. According to tradition, a woman named Jane Reynolds became engaged to a sailor, but after his prolonged absence at sea and presumed death, she married a ship's carpenter instead, with whom she had a son. Seven years later, upon the sailor's unexpected return with a fleet of seven ships laden with treasure, Jane abandoned her family to sail away with her former lover, only to discover that he was in fact a demon, who ferried her to "the hill of Hell" as punishment for her unfaithfulness to her legitimate husband and son. This ballad acquired many variations as it spread from England to Scotland and eventually to North America, where it was especially popular in Appalachia.

"Where have you been, my long lost lover,
   This seven long years and more?"
"I've been seeking gold for thee, my love,
   And riches of great store.

Now I'm come for the vows you promised me,
   You promised me long ago."
"My former vows you must forgive,
   For I'm a wedded wife."

"I might have been married to a king's daughter,
   Far, far ayont the sea;
But I refused the crown of gold,
   And it's all for the love of thee."

"If you might have married a king's daughter,
   Yourself you have to blame;
For I'm married to a ship's-carpenter,
   And to him I have a son.

Have you any place to put me in,
   If I with you should gang?"
"I've seven brave ships upon the sea,
   All laden to the brim.

I'll build my love a bridge of steel,
   All for to help her o'er;
Likewise webs of silk down by her side,
   To keep my love from the cold."

She took her eldest son into her arms,
   And sweetly did him kiss.
"My blessing go with you, and your father too,
   For little does he know of this."

As they were walking up the street,
   Most beautiful for to behold,
He cast a glamour oer her face,
   And it shone like the brightest gold.

As they were walking along the sea-side,
   Where his gallant ship lay in,
So ready was the chair of gold
   To welcome this lady in.

They had not sailed a league, a league,
   A league but scarcely three,
Till altered grew his countenance,
   And raging grew the sea.

When they came to yon sea-side,
   She set her down to rest;

It's then she spied his cloven foot,
    Most bitterly she wept.

"O is it for gold that you do weep?
    Or is it for fear?
Or is it for the man you left behind
    When that you did come here?"

"It is not for gold that I do weep,
    O no, nor yet for fear;
But it is for the man I left behind
    When that I did come here.

O what a bright, bright hill is yon,
    That shines so clear to see?"
"O it is the hill of heaven," he said,
    "Where you shall never be."

"O what a black, dark hill is yon,
    That looks so dark to me?"
"O it is the hill of Hell," he said,
    "Where you and I shall be.

Would you wish to see the fishes swim
    In the bottom of the sea,
Or wish to see the leaves grow green
    On the banks of Italy?"

"I hope I'll never see the fishes swim
    On the bottom of the sea,
But I hope to see the leaves grow green
    On the banks of Italy."

He took her up to the topmast high,
    To see what she could see;
He sunk the ship in a flash of fire,
    To the bottom of the sea.

THE HUNTER BECOMES
THE HUNTED[1]

An eerie poem by the Scottish author Walter Scott (1771–1832), "Glenfinlas" recounted the legend of an ill-fated hunting trip that led to the horrific demise of a lustful Highland chieftain named Lord Ronald. The setting of the poem was a desolate valley called Glen Finglas, where Ronald and another chieftain called Moy tarried in a rustic cabin after several days of hunting. Lamenting the absence of "a fair woman's yielding kiss," Ronald left the cabin with his hunting dogs for a tryst with a local lady named Mary. Warned of danger by his gift of second sight, Moy remained behind. When a strange woman in green arrived at the cabin later that night, Moy's insight penetrated her disguise and he rebuffed her with prayer, for this maiden was in fact a predatory succubus. As the final stanzas of the poem made clear, in Ronald's pursuit of a female companion in that lonely glen, the hunter became the hunted.

> "E'en now, to meet me in yon dell,
>   My Mary's buskins brush the dew."—
> He spoke, nor bade the chief farewell
>   But call'd his dogs, and gay withdrew.
>
> Within an hour returned each hound;
>   In rushed the rousers of the deer;
> They howl'd in melancholy sound,
>   Then closely couch'd beside the Seer.

No Ronald yet; though midnight came,
    And sad were Moy's prophetic dreams,
As, bending o'er the dying flame,
    He fed the watch-fire's quivering gleams.

Sudden the hounds erect their ears,
    And sudden cease their moaning howl;
Close press'd to Moy, they mark their fears
    By shiv'ring limbs, and stifled growl.

Untouch'd, the harp began to ring,
    As softly, slowly, oped the door;
And shook, responsive, ev'ry string,
    As light a footstep press'd the floor.

And by the watch-fire's glimmering light,
    Close by the Minstrel's side was seen
An huntress maid, in beauty bright,
    All dropping wet her robes of green.

All dropping wet her garments seem;
    Chill'd was her cheek, her bosom bare,
As, bending o'er the dying gleam,
    She wrung the moisture from her hair.

With maiden blush she softly said,
    "O gentle huntsman, hast thou seen,
In deep Glenfinlas' moonlight glade,
    A lovely maid in vest of green:

"With her a chief in Highland pride;
    His shoulders bear the hunter's bow,
The mountain-dirk adorns his side,
    Far on the wind his tartans flow?"

"And who art thou? and who are they?"
    All ghastly gazing, Moy replied;

"And why, beneath the moon's pale ray,
          Dare ye thus roam Glenfinlas' side?"

"Where wild Loch-Katrine pours her tide,
          Blue, dark, and deep, round many an isle,
Our fathers' towers o'erhang her side
          The castle of the bold Glengyle.

"To chase the dun Glenfinlas deer,
          Our woodland course this morn we bore,
And haply met, while wandering here,
          The son of great Macgillianore.

"O aid me, then, to seek the pair
          Whom, loitering in the woods, I lost;
Alone, I dare not venture there,
          Where walks, they say, the shrieking ghost."

"Yes, many a shrieking ghost walks there;
          Then, first, my own sad vow to keep,
Here will I pour my midnight prayer,
          Which still must rise when mortals sleep."

"O first, for pity's gentle sake,
          Guide a lone wanderer on her way!
For I must cross the haunted brake,
          And reach my father's towers ere day."

"First, three times tell each Ave bead,
          And thrice a Pater-noster say;
Then kiss with me the holy reed;
          So shall we safely wend our way."

"O shame to knighthood, strange and foul!
          Go, doff the bonnet from thy brow,
And shroud thee in the monkish cowl,
          Which best befits thy sullen vow.

"Not so, by high Dunlathmon's fire,
          Thy heart was froze to love and joy,
When gaily rung thy raptured lyre,
          To wanton Morna's melting eye."

Wild stared the minstrel's eyes of flame,
          And high his sable locks arose,
And quick his color went and came,
          As fear and rage alternate rose.

"And thou! when by the blazing oak,
          I lay, to her and love resigned,
Say, rode ye on the eddying smoke,
          Or sail'd ye on the midnight wind!

"Not thine a race of mortal blood,
          Nor old Glengyle's pretended line;
Thy dame, the Lady of the Flood,
          Thy sire, the Monarch of the Mine."

He muttered thrice St. Oran's rhyme,
          And thrice St. Fillan's powerful prayer;
Then turned him to the eastern clime,
          And sternly shook his coal-black hair.

And, bending o'er his harp, he flung
          His wildest witch-notes on the wind;
And loud, and high, and strange, they rung.
          As many a magic change they find.

Tall wax'd the Spirit's altering form,
          Till to the roof her stature grew;
Then, mingling with the rising storm,
          With one wild yell away she flew.

Rain beats, hail rattles, whirlwinds tear;
          The slender but in fragments flew;

But not a lock of Moy's loose hair
      Was waved by wind, or wet by dew.

Wild mingling with the howling gale,
      Loud bursts of ghastly laughter rise;
High o'er the minstrel's head they sail,
      And die amid the northern skies.

The voice of thunder shook the wood,
      As ceased the more than mortal yell;
And, spattering foul, a shower of blood
      Upon the hissing firebrands fell.

Next, dropped from high a mangled arm;
      The fingers strain'd a half-drawn blade:
And last, the life-blood streaming warm,
      Torn from the trunk, a gasping head.

Oft o'er that head, in battling field,
      Streamed the proud crest of high Benmore,
That arm the broad claymore could wield,
      Which dyed the Teith with Saxon gore.

Wo to Moneira's sullen rills!
      Wo to Glenfinlas' dreary glen!
There never son of Albin's hills
      Shall draw the hunter's shaft agen!

E'en the tired pilgrim's burning feet
      At noon shall shun that shelt'ring den,
Lest, journeying in their rage, he meet
      The wayward Ladies of the Glen.

And we—behind the chieftain's shield,
      No more shall we in safety dwell;
None leads the people to the field—
      And we the loud lament must swell.

O hone a rie'! o hone a rie'!
  The pride of Albin's line is o'er!
And fall'n Glenartney's stateliest tree;
  We ne'er shall see Lord Ronald more!

CREEPING HORRORS

Malevolent Spirits in the Modern Imagination

The dawn of modernity did little to barricade human minds from the onslaught of the evil spiritual entities that had waged war against them since the advent of civilization. Indigenous cultures decimated by European colonialism bequeathed to their conquerors the lineaments of belief systems haunted by demons unknown and unnamed in the religions of the west. Desolate landscapes remained their primary ecosystem; the virulence of these diabolical entities increased the farther one encountered them from the outposts of human habitation. In the twentieth century, authors of weird fiction tapped into a rich inheritance of infernal imagery bequeathed by western traditions to craft for their readers hybrid horrors at once familiar and yet utterly alien.

FROZEN HEARTS

Indigenous peoples of North America nursed their own nightmares about malevolent spirits long before Europeans landed on their shores. Jesuit missionaries in New France were the first to put these stories into writing in the annual reports that they sent to their superiors in Rome. Active in modern Quebec, the Jesuit missionary Paul Le Jeune (1591–1664) provided the first description of the cannibal spirit known as the Wendigo, which drove starving people into a killing frenzy. The memoirs of nineteenth-century authors, like artist Paul Kane (1810–71) and the explorer Henry Youle Hind (1823–1908), testified to the tenacity of belief in the Wendigo among native peoples across the Canadian north. Other evil spirits haunted this landscape as well, including the giant flying heads of Iroquois lore, whose appearance heralded a death in the family.

(A) A CANNIBAL SPIRIT[1]

What caused us greater concern was the intelligence that met us upon entering the Lake, namely, that the men deputed by our Conductor for the purpose of summoning the Nations to the North Sea, and assigning them a rendezvous, where they were to await our coming, had met their death the previous Winter in a very strange manner. Those poor men (according to the report given us) were seized with an ailment unknown to us, but not very unusual among the people we were seeking. They are afflicted with neither lunacy, hypochondria, nor frenzy; but have a combination of all these species of disease, which affects their imaginations and causes them a more than

canine hunger. This makes them so ravenous for human flesh
that they pounce upon women, children, and even upon men,
like veritable werewolves, and devour them voraciously, without being able to appease or glut their appetite—ever seeking
fresh prey, and the more greedily the more they eat. This ailment attacked our deputies; and, as death is the sole remedy
among those simple people for checking such acts of murder,
they were slain in order to stay the course of their madness.
This news might well have arrested our journey if our belief in
it had been as strong as the assurance we received of its truth.
We did not, therefore, cease to pursue our way, pushing on
toward the end of the Lake, where empties the river that was
to afford us entrance into a country hitherto unknown to the
French.

(B) A HORRID REPAST[2]

We passed down the river "Macau," where there are some
beautiful rapids and falls. Here we fell in with the first Indians
we had met since leaving the Lake of the Thousand Islands;
they are called "Saulteaux," being a branch of the Ojibbeways,
whose language they speak with very slight variation. We
purchased from an Indian man and woman some dried stur-
geon. The female wore a rabbit-skin dress: they were, as I afterwards learned, considered to be cannibals, the Indian term
for which is *Weendigo*, or "One who eats Human Flesh."
There is a superstitious belief among Indians that the Weendigo cannot be killed by anything short of a silver bullet. I was
informed, on good authority, that a case had occurred here in
which a father and daughter had killed and eaten six of their
own family from absolute want. The story went on to state,
that they then camped at some distance off in the vicinity of an
old Indian woman, who happened to be alone in her lodge, her
relations having gone out hunting. Seeing the father and
daughter arrive unaccompanied by any other members of the
family, all of whom she knew, she began to suspect that some
foul play had taken place, and to feel apprehensive for her own

safety. By way of precaution, she resolved to make the entrance of her lodge very slippery, and as it was winter, and the frost severe, she poured water repeatedly over the ground as fast as it froze, until it was covered with a mass of smooth ice; and instead of going to bed, she remained sitting up in her lodge, watching with an axe in her hand. When near midnight, she heard steps advancing cautiously over the crackling snow, and looking through the crevices of the lodge, caught sight of the girl in the attitude of listening, as if to ascertain whether the inmate was sleeping; this the old woman feigned by snoring aloud. The welcome sound no sooner reached the ears of the wretched girl, than she rushed forward, but, slipping on the ice, fell down at the entrance of the lodge, whereupon the intended victim sprang upon the murderess and buried the axe in her brains: and not doubting that the villainous father was near at hand, she fled with all her speed to a distance, to escape his vengeance. In the meantime, the Weendigo father, who was impatiently watching for the expected signal to his horrid repast, crept up to the lodge, and called to his daughter; hearing no reply, he went on, and, in place of the dead body of the old woman, he saw his own daughter, and hunger overcoming every other feeling, he saved his own life by devouring her remains.

The *Weendigoes* are looked upon with superstitious dread and horror by all Indians, and any one known to have eaten human flesh is shunned by the rest; as it is supposed that, having once tasted it, they would do so again had they an opportunity. They are obliged, therefore, to make their lodges at some distance from the rest of the tribe, and the children are particularly kept out of their way . . .

(C) THE TRACKS OF A GIANT[3]

The Indian sat looking at the fire for many minutes. I did not want to interrupt his thoughts. After a while I filled his pipe, put a coal in it, and gave it to him. He took it, still looking at the fire. Perhaps he saw the spirit of his [recently deceased] cousin there, as Indians often say they do. He smoked for a long time. At length he spoke, looking at the body [of his cousin], and pointing to it, saying, "He said last winter that someone would die before the year was out."

I knew well enough that it was one of their superstitions that had troubled him, for he was a heathen not more than a year ago; and a man does not get rid of his heathen notions by being touched with a drop of Manitou water. So I said to him, "Did he see anything?"

"He came across tracks."

"Tracks?"

"A Wendigo," said the Indian.

"Have you ever seen one?" I asked him.

"I have seen tracks."

"Where?"

"On the St. Marguerite, the Mingan, the Manitou, the Oa-na-ma-ne. My cousin saw tracks on the Manitou last winter, and he said to me and to many of us, 'Something will happen.'"

"What were the tracks like?" I said to him.

"Wendigoes," he replied.

"Well, but how big were they?"

He looked at me and said nothing, nor would he speak on the subject again.

"These Montagnais think," continued Pierre, "that the Wendigoes are giant cannibals, twenty to thirty feet high. They think that they live on human flesh, and that many Indians who have gone hunting, and have never afterwards been heard of, have been devoured by Wendigoes. They are dreadfully superstitious in the woods . . ."

(D) THE FLYING HEAD[4]

There were many evil spirits and terrible monsters that hid in the mountain caves when the sun shone, but came out to vex and plague the red men when storms swept the earth or when there was darkness in the forest. Among them was a flying head which, when it rested upon the ground, was higher than the tallest man. It was covered with a thick coating of hair that shielded it from the stroke of arrows. The face was very dark and angry, filled with great wrinkles and horrid furrows. Long black wings came out of its sides, and when it rushed through the air mournful sounds assailed the ears of the frightened men and women. On its underside were two long, sharp claws, with which it tore its food and attacked its victims.

The Flying Head came most often to frighten the women and children. It came at night to the homes of the widows and orphans, and beat its angry wings upon the walls of their houses and uttered fearful cries in an unknown tongue. Then it went away, and in a few days, death followed and took one of the little family with him. The maiden to whom the Flying Head appeared never heard the words of a husband's wooing or the prattle of a papoose, for a pestilence came upon her and soon she sickened and died.

One night a widow sat alone in her cabin. From a little fire burning near the door, she frequently drew roasted acorns and ate them for her evening meal. She did not see the Flying Head grinning at her from the doorway, for her eyes were deep in the coals and her thoughts upon the scenes of happiness in which she dwelt before her husband and children had gone away to the long home.

The Flying Head stealthily reached forth one of its long claws and snatched some of the coals of fire and thrust them into its mouth—for it thought that these were what the woman was eating. With a howl of pain, it flew away, and the red men were never afterwards troubled by its visits.

A DARK HUNTSMAN
ON THE MOORS[1]

Desolate places always cause unease in lone travelers, es-
pecially after dark, when evil spirits are on the move in
search of prey. An upland area in Devon, England, known
as Dartmoor is rich in stories about the perils awaiting
anyone foolhardy enough to traverse the moors by night.
Pixies and ghosts wandered among the prehistoric stand-
ing stones that still litter the landscape like broken teeth,
but the most fearsome denizen of Dartmoor was a demonic
huntsman accompanied by a pack of spectral hounds. In a
story preserved by folklorist Sabine Baring-Gould (1834–
1924), a drunken moorman making his way on a stormy
night encountered this dark rider and petitioned him for a
share of his game, only to recoil in horror upon his return
home when lantern light revealed what he had received.

There existed formerly a belief on Dartmoor that it was hunted
over at night in storm by a black sportsman, with black fire-
breathing hounds, called the "Wish Hounds." They could be
heard in full cry, and occasionally the blast of the hunter's
horn on stormy nights.

One night a moorman was riding home from Widecombe.
There had been a fair there; he had made money, and had
taken something to keep out the cold, for the night promised
to be one of tempest. He started on his homeward way. The
moon shone out occasionally between the whirling masses of
thick vapor. The horse knew the way better perhaps than his
master. The rider had traversed the great ridge of Hameldon,
and was mounting a moor on which stands a circle of upright

stones—reputedly a Druid circle, and said to dance on Christmas Eve—when he heard a sound that startled him—a horn, and then past him swept without sound of footfall a pack of black dogs.

The moorman was not frightened—he had taken in too much Dutch courage for that—and when a minute after the black hunter came up, he shouted to him, "Hey huntsman, what sport? Give us some of your game."

"Take that," answered the hunter, and flung him something which the man caught and held in his arm. Then the mysterious rider passed on. An hour elapsed before the moorman reached his home. As he had jogged on, he had wondered what sort of game he had been given. It was too large for a hare, too small for a deer. Provokingly, not once since the encounter had the moon flashed forth. Now that he was at his door, he swung himself from his horse, and still carrying the game, shouted for a lantern.

The light was brought. With one hand the fellow took it, then raised it to throw a ray on that which he held in his arm— the game hunted and won by the Black Rider. It was his own baby, dead and cold.

A DEMON DRAWN
FROM LIFE[1]

The eerie stories of M. R. James (1862–1936), a professor of medieval manuscripts at King's College, Cambridge, often featured antiquarians in search of precious artifacts, only to discover that they held some kind of occult danger. In his short story entitled "Canon Alberic's Scrap-Book," an English scholar vacationing in France found the opportunity to examine an early modern scrapbook compiled from illuminated fragments cut out of rare and precious medieval manuscripts. At the end of the scrapbook, he discovered an unnerving drawing of King Solomon face-to-face with a hideous "demon of the night." After purchasing the manuscript, the scholar returned to his residence, only to discover to his horror that the demon depicted in the scrapbook had followed him home.

At once all Dennistoun's cherished dreams of finding priceless manuscripts in untrodden corners of France flashed up, to die down again the next moment. It was probably a stupid missal of Plantin's printing, about 1580.[2] Where was the likelihood that a place so near Toulouse would not have been ransacked long ago by collectors? However, it would be foolish not to go; he would reproach himself for ever after if he refused. So they set off. On the way the curious irresolution and sudden determination of the sacristan recurred to Dennistoun, and he wondered in a shame-faced way whether he was being decoyed into some purlieu to be made away with as a supposed rich Englishman. He contrived, therefore, to begin talking with his guide, and to drag in, in a rather clumsy fashion, the fact that he expected two friends to join him early the next morning. To his surprise, the announcement seemed to relieve the sacristan at once of some of the anxiety that oppressed him.

"That is well," he said quite brightly—"that is very well. Monsieur will travel in company with his friends; they will be always near him. It is a good thing to travel thus in company—sometimes."

The last word appeared to be added as an afterthought, and to bring with it a relapse into gloom for the poor little man.

They were soon at the house, which was one rather larger than its neighbors, stone-built, with a shield carved over the door, the shield of Alberic de Mauléon, a collateral descendant, Dennistoun tells me, of Bishop John de Mauléon. This Alberic was a Canon of Comminges from 1680 to 1701. The upper windows of the mansion were boarded up, and the whole place bore, as does the rest of Comminges, the aspect of decaying age.

Arrived on his doorstep, the sacristan paused a moment.

"Perhaps," he said, "perhaps, after all, monsieur has not the time?"

"Not at all—lots of time—nothing to do till to-morrow. Let us see what it is you have got." The door was opened at this point, and a face looked out, a face far younger than the sacristan's, but bearing something of the same distressing look: only here it seemed to be the mark, not so much of fear for personal safety as of acute anxiety on behalf of another. Plainly, the owner of the face was the sacristan's daughter; and, but for the expression I have described, she was a handsome girl enough. She brightened up considerably on seeing her father accompanied by an able-bodied stranger. A few remarks passed between father and daughter, of which Dennistoun only caught these words, said by the sacristan, "He was laughing in the church," words which were answered only by a look of terror from the girl.

But in another minute, they were in the sitting-room of the house, a small, high chamber with a stone floor, full of moving shadows cast by a wood-fire that flickered on a great hearth. Something of the character of an oratory was imparted to it by a tall crucifix, which reached almost to the ceiling on one side; the figure was painted of the natural colors, the cross was black. Under this stood a chest of some age and solidity, and when a lamp had been brought, and chairs set, the sacristan went to this chest, and produced therefrom, with growing excitement and nervousness, as Dennistoun thought, a large book, wrapped in a white cloth, on which cloth a cross was rudely embroidered in red thread. Even before the wrapping had been removed, Dennistoun began to be interested by the size and shape of the volume. "Too large for a missal," he thought, "and not the shape of an antiphoner; perhaps it may be something good, after all."[3] The next moment the book was open, and Dennistoun felt that he had at last lit upon something better than good. Before him lay a large folio, bound, perhaps, late in the seventeenth century, with the arms of Canon Alberic de Mauléon stamped in gold on the sides. There may have been a hundred and fifty leaves of paper in the book, and on almost every one of them was fastened a leaf from an illuminated manuscript. Such a collection Dennistoun had hardly dreamed of in his wildest moments. Here were ten leaves from a copy of Genesis, illustrated with pictures, which could not be later than 700 A.D. Further on was a complete set of pictures from a Psalter, of English execution, of the very finest kind that the thirteenth century could produce; and, perhaps best of all, there were twenty leaves of uncial writing in Latin, which, as a few words seen here and there told him at once, must belong to some very early unknown patristic treatise.[4] Could it possibly be a fragment of the copy of Papias "On the Words of Our Lord," which was known to have existed as late as the twelfth century at Nîmes?[5] In any case, his mind was made up; that book must return to Cambridge with him, even if he had to draw the whole of his balance from the bank and stay at St. Bertrand till the money came. He glanced up at the sacristan to see if his face yielded any hint that the book was for sale. The sacristan was pale, and his lips were working.

"If monsieur will turn on to the end," he said.

So monsieur turned on, meeting new treasures at every rise

of a leaf; and at the end of the book he came upon two sheets of paper, of much more recent date than anything he had yet seen, which puzzled him considerably. They must be contemporary, he decided, with the unprincipled Canon Alberic, who had doubtless plundered the Chapter library of St. Bertrand to form this priceless scrap-book. On the first of the paper sheets was a plan, carefully drawn and instantly recognizable by a person who knew the ground, of the south aisle and cloisters of St. Bertrand's. There were curious signs looking like planetary symbols, and a few Hebrew words in the corners; and in the north-west angle of the cloister was a cross drawn in gold paint. Below the plan were some lines of writing in Latin, which ran thus:

"Responsa 12^{mi} Dec. 1694. Interrogatum est: Inveniamne?
Responsum est: Invenies. Fiamne dives? Fies. Vivamne
invidendus? Vives. Moriarne in lecto meo? Ita." (Answers
of the 12th of December, 1694. It was asked: Shall I find it?
Answer: Thou shalt. Shall I become rich? Thou wilt. Shall
I live an object of envy? Thou wilt. Shall I die in my bed?
Thou wilt.)

"A good specimen of the treasure-hunter's record—quite reminds one of Mr. Minor-Canon Quatremain in *Old St. Paul's*," was Dennistoun's comment, and he turned the leaf.[6]

What he then saw impressed him, as he has often told me, more than he could have conceived any drawing or picture capable of impressing him. And, though the drawing he saw is no longer in existence, there is a photograph of it (which I possess) which fully bears out that statement. The picture in question was a sepia drawing at the end of the seventeenth century, representing, one would say at first sight, a Biblical scene; for the architecture (the picture represented an interior) and the figures had that semi-classical flavor about them which the artists of two hundred years ago thought appropriate to illustrations of the Bible. On the right was a king on his throne, the throne elevated on twelve steps, a canopy overhead, soldiers on either side—evidently King Solomon. He was bending forward with outstretched scepter, in attitude of command; his face expressed horror and disgust, yet there was in it also the mark of imperious command and confident power. The left half of the picture was the strangest, however. The interest plainly centered there. On the pavement before the throne were grouped four soldiers, surrounding a crouching figure which must be described in a moment. A fifth soldier lay dead on the pavement, his neck distorted, and his eyeballs starting from his head. The four surrounding guards were looking at the king. In their faces the sentiment of horror was intensified; they seemed, in fact, only restrained from flight by their implicit trust in their master. All this terror was plainly excited by the being that crouched in their midst. I entirely despair of conveying by any words the impression which this figure makes upon anyone who looks at it. I recollect once showing the photograph of the drawing to a lecturer on morphology—a person of, I was going to say, abnormally sane and unimaginative habits of mind. He absolutely refused to be alone for the rest of that evening, and he told me afterwards that for many nights he had not dared to put out his light before going to sleep. However, the main traits of the figure I can at least indicate. At first you saw only a mass of coarse matted black hair; presently it was seen that this covered a body of fearful thinness, almost a skeleton, but with the muscles standing out like wires. The hands were of a dusky pallor, covered, like the body, with long, coarse hairs, and hideously taloned. The eyes, touched in with a burning yellow, had intensely black pupils, and were fixed upon the throned king with a look of beast-like hate. Imagine one of the awful bird-catching spiders of South America translated into human form, and endowed with intelligence just less than human, and you will have some faint conception of the terror inspired by the appalling effigy. One remark is universally made by those to whom I have shown the picture: "It was drawn from life."

As soon as the first shock of his irresistible fright had subsided, Dennistoun stole a look at his hosts. The sacristan's hands were pressed upon his eyes; his daughter, looking up at the cross on the wall, was telling her beads feverishly.

At last the question was asked, "Is this book for sale?"

There was the same hesitation, the same plunge of determination, that he had noticed before, and then came the welcome answer, "If monsieur pleases."

"How much do you ask for it?"

"I will take two hundred and fifty francs."

This was confounding. Even a collector's conscience is sometimes stirred, and Dennistoun's conscience was tenderer than a collector's.

"My good man!" he said again and again, "your book is worth far more than two hundred and fifty francs, I assure you—far more."

But the answer did not vary: "I will take two hundred and fifty francs, not more."

There was really no possibility of refusing such a chance. The money was paid, the receipt signed, a glass of wine drunk over the transaction, and then the sacristan seemed to become a new man. He stood upright, he ceased to throw those suspicious glances behind him, he actually laughed or tried to laugh. Dennistoun rose to go.

"I shall have the honor of accompanying monsieur to his hotel?" said the sacristan.

"Oh no, thanks! It isn't a hundred yards. I know the way perfectly, and there is a moon."

The offer was pressed three or four times, and refused as often.

"Then, monsieur will summon me if—if he finds occasion; he will keep the middle of the road, the sides are so rough."

"Certainly, certainly," said Dennistoun, who was impatient to examine his prize by himself; and he stepped out into the passage with his book under his arm.

Here he was met by the daughter; she, it appeared, was anxious to do a little business on her own account; perhaps, like Gehazi, to "take somewhat" from the foreigner whom her father had spared.

"A silver crucifix and chain for the neck; monsieur would perhaps be good enough to accept it?"

Well, really, Dennistoun hadn't much use for these things. What did mademoiselle want for it?

"Nothing—nothing in the world. Monsieur is more than welcome to it."

The tone in which this and much more was said was unmistakably genuine, so that Dennistoun was reduced to profuse thanks, and submitted to have the chain put round his neck. It really seemed as if he had rendered the father and daughter some service which they hardly knew how to repay. As he set off with his book, they stood at the door looking after him, and they were still looking when he waved them a last goodnight from the steps of the Chapeau Rouge.

Dinner was over, and Dennistoun was in his bedroom, shut up alone with his acquisition. The landlady had manifested a particular interest in him since he had told her that he had paid a visit to the sacristan and bought an old book from him. He thought, too, that he had heard a hurried dialogue between her and the said sacristan in the passage outside the *salle à manger*; some words to the effect that "Pierre and Bertrand would be sleeping in the house" had closed the conversation.

At this time a growing feeling of discomfort had been creeping over him—nervous reaction, perhaps, after the delight of his discovery. Whatever it was, it resulted in a conviction that there was someone behind him, and that he was far more comfortable with his back to the wall. All this, of course, weighed light in the balance as against the obvious value of the collection he had acquired. And now, as I said, he was alone in his bedroom, taking stock of Canon Alberic's treasures, in which every moment revealed something more charming.

"Bless Canon Alberic!" said Dennistoun, who had an inveterate habit of talking to himself. "I wonder where he is now? Dear me! I wish that landlady would learn to laugh in a more cheering manner; it makes one feel as if there was someone dead in the house. Half a pipe more, did you say? I think perhaps you are right. I wonder what that crucifix is that the young woman insisted on giving me? Last century, I suppose. Yes, probably. It is rather a nuisance of a thing to have round one's neck—just too heavy. Most likely her father has been wearing it for years. I think I might give it a cleanup before I put it away."

He had taken the crucifix off, and laid it on the table, when his attention was caught by an object lying on the red cloth just by his left elbow. Two or three ideas of what it might be flitted through his brain with their own incalculable quickness.

"A pen-wiper? No, no such thing in the house. A rat? No, too black. A large spider? I trust to goodness not—no. Good God! A hand like the hand in that picture!"

In another infinitesimal flash he had taken it in. Pale, dusky skin, covering nothing but bones and tendons of appalling strength; coarse black hairs, longer than ever grew on a human hand; nails rising from the ends of the fingers and curving sharply down and forward, gray, horny and wrinkled.

He flew out of his chair with deadly, inconceivable terror clutching at his heart. The shape, whose left hand rested on the table, was rising to a standing posture behind his seat, its right hand crooked above his scalp. There was black and tattered drapery about it; the coarse hair covered it as in the drawing. The lower jaw was thin—what can I call it?— shallow, like a beast's; teeth showed behind the black lips; there was no nose; the eyes, of a fiery yellow, against which the pupils showed black and intense, and the exulting hate and thirst to destroy life which shone there, were the most horrifying feature in the whole vision. There was intelligence of a kind in them—intelligence beyond that of a beast, below that of a man.

The feelings which this horror stirred in Dennistoun were the most intense physical fear and the most profound mental loathing. What did he do? What could he do? He has never been quite certain what words he said, but he knows that he spoke, that he grasped blindly at the silver crucifix, that he was conscious of a movement towards him on the part of the demon, and that he screamed with the voice of an animal in hideous pain.

Pierre and Bertrand, the two sturdy little serving-men, who rushed in, saw nothing, but felt themselves thrust aside by something that passed out between them, and found Dennistoun in a swoon. They sat up with him that night, and his two friends were at St. Bertrand by nine o'clock next morning. He himself, though still shaken and nervous, was almost himself by that time, and his story found credence with them, though not until they had seen the drawing and talked with the sacristan.

Almost at dawn the little man had come to the inn on some pretense, and had listened with the deepest interest to the story retailed by the landlady. He showed no surprise.

"It is he—it is he! I have seen him myself," was his only comment; and to all questionings but one reply was vouchsafed: "Deux fois je l'ai vu; mille fois je l'ai senti."[7] He would tell them nothing of the provenance of the book, nor any details of his experiences. "I shall soon sleep, and my rest will be sweet. Why should you trouble me?" he said.

We shall never know what he or Canon Alberic de Mauléon suffered. At the back of that fateful drawing were some lines of writing which may be supposed to throw light on the situation:

Contradictio Salomonis cum demonio nocturno.
Albericus de Mauleone delineavit.
V. Deus in adiutorium. Ps. Qui habitat.
Sancte Bertrande, demoniorum effugator, intercede pro me miserrimo.
Primum uidi nocte 12^{mi} Dec 1694: uidebo mox ultimum.
Peccaui et passus sum, plura adhuc passurus. Dec. 29, 1701.

The dispute of Solomon with a demon of the night.
Drawn by Alberic de Mauléon.
Versicle. O Lord, make haste to help me. *Psalm.* Whoso dwelleth (xci.)[8]
Saint Bertrand, who puttest devils to flight, pray for me most unhappy.
I saw it first on the night of Dec. 12, 1694; soon I shall see it for the last time.
I have sinned and suffered, and have more to suffer yet. Dec. 29, 1701.

I have never quite understood what was Dennistoun's view of the events I have narrated. He quoted to me once a text from Ecclesiasticus: "Some spirits there be that are created for vengeance, and in their fury lay on sore strokes."[9] On another occasion he said: "Isaiah was a very sensible man; doesn't he say something about night monsters living in the ruins of Babylon? These things are rather beyond us at present."[10]

ALL I WANT'S MY TAILYPO[1]

The story of the Tailypo, a furry fiend native to Appalachia, has been well-known in the American South since the early twentieth century. A version of the story first appeared in print in Uncle Remus Returns *(1918), one of a collection of volumes of African American folktales compiled by Joel Chandler Harris (1848–1908). In this story, a hungry hermit and his three dogs encountered an elusive creature in their lonely cabin and cut off its tail. After the hermit ate it and retired to bed, the vengeful varmint returned three times that night and demanded the return of its tail. The beast's ability to talk and its "big fiery eyes" betrayed its demonic origin.*

Once upon a time, way down in the big woods of Tennessee, there lived a man all by himself. His house didn't have but one room in it, and that room was his parlor, his sitting room, his bedroom, his dining room, and his kitchen, too. At one end of the room was a great, big, open fireplace, and that's where the man cooked and ate his supper. One night after he had cooked and ate his supper, there crept in through the cracks of the logs the most curious creature that you ever did see, and it had a great, big, long tail.

Just as soon as that man saw that varmint, he reached for his hatchet and with one stroke, he cut that thing's tail off. The critter crept out through the cracks of the logs and ran away, and the man, like a fool, took and cooked that tail—he did!—and ate it. Then he went to bed and after a while, he went to sleep.

He hadn't been asleep very long, when he woke up and heard

something climbing up the side of his cabin. It sounded just like a cat, and he could hear it *scratch, scratch, scratch*, and by and by, he heard it say, "Tailypo, tailypo; all I want's my tailypo."

Now this here man had three dogs: one was called Uno, and one was called Ino, and the other one was called Cumptico-Calico. And when he heard that thing, he called his dogs, *huh! huh! huh!* And those dogs came boiling up from under the floor and they chased that thing way down in the big woods. And the man went back to bed and went to sleep.

Well, way long in the middle of the night, he woke up and he heard something right above his cabin door, trying to get in. He listened, and he could hear it *scratch, scratch, scratch*, and then he heard it say, "Tailypo, tailypo; all I want's my tailypo." And he shot up in bed and called his dogs, *huh! huh! huh!* And those dogs came busting around the corner of the house and they caught up with that thing at the gate and they just tore the whole fence down trying to get at it. And that time, they chased it way down into the big swamp. And the man went back to bed again and went to sleep.

Way long toward morning he woke up, and he heard something down in the big swamp. He listened and he heard it say, "Tailypo, tailypo; all I want's my tailypo." And he shot up in bed and called his dogs, *huh! huh! huh!* And you know that time, those dogs didn't come. That thing had carried them way off down in the big swamp and killed them or lost them. And the man went back to bed and went to sleep again.

Well, just before daylight, he woke up and he heard something in his room, and it sounded like a cat, climbing up the covers at the foot of his bed. He listened and he could hear it *scratch, scratch, scratch*, and he looked over the foot of his bed and he saw two little pointed ears, and in a minute, he saw two big, round, fiery eyes looking at him. He wanted to call his dogs, but he was too scared to holler. That thing kept creeping up until by and by it was right on top of that man, and then it said in a low voice: "Tailypo, tailypo; all I want's my tailypo." And all at once that man found his voice and he said, "I ain't got your tailypo." And that thing said, "Yes, you have." And it jumped on that man and scratched him all to pieces. And some folks say that he got his tailypo.

Now there isn't anything left of that man's cabin way down in the big woods of Tennessee, except for the chimney, and folks that live in the big valley say that when the moon shines bright and the wind blows down the valley, you can hear something say, "Tailypo," and then die away in the distance.

NIGHT-GAUNTS[1]

Little known in his lifetime, Howard Phillips Lovecraft (1890–1937) is widely considered to be the most influential author of modern American weird fiction. He published almost exclusively in pulp magazines like Weird Tales, *which specialized in fantasy and horror literature. Lovecraft pioneered the genre of cosmic horror, in which his protagonists risked madness as they discovered secret knowledge that betrayed the insignificance of human existence. In the late 1920s, he composed a series of thirty-six sonnets called "Fungi from Yuggoth." Drawing inspiration from the dream poems of Lord Dunsany (1878–1957), many of these sonnets described nocturnal visions of an alternate and thoroughly alien reality. While Lovecraft's writings rarely touched on Christian themes, his description of the "night-gaunts" in the eponymous sonnet from this series was strongly reminiscent of depictions of demons in the Christian tradition.*

Out of what crypt they crawl, I cannot tell,
But every night I see the rubbery things;
Black, horned, and slender, with membranous wings,
And tails that bear the bifid barb of hell.
They come in legions on the north wind's swell,
With obscene clutch that titillates and stings,
Snatching me off on monstrous voyagings
To grey worlds hidden deep in nightmare's well.
Over the jagged peaks of Thok they sweep,
Heedless of all the cries I try to make,
And down the nether pits to that foul lake
Where the puffed shoggoths splash in doubtful sleep.
But oh! if only they would make some sound,
Or wear a face where faces should be found!

Notes

THE MYSTERY OF THE NEPHILIM

1. Translated by Scott G. Bruce from the Latin Vulgate version of Genesis 6:1–8.

THE PRISON OF THE FALLEN

1. Enoch 6–11, trans. R. H. Charles, in *The Apocrypha and Pseudepigrapha of the Old Testament in English*, 2 vols. (Oxford: Oxford University Press, 1913), vol. 2, pp. 191–99 (modified).
2. Jared was a Jewish patriarch of the sixth generation after Adam and Eve and the father of Enoch. Mount Hermon is the highest point of the mountain range that separates modern Syria and Lebanon.
3. The list is incomplete. One name has been lost in the manuscript transmission.
4. A cubit was a unit of measurement based on the distance between a grown man's fingertips and elbow (about eighteen inches), so these giants were thought to be thousands of feet tall.
5. The name Duda'el means "cauldron of God" in Hebrew. Its location is unknown.
6. In the text that follows, Enoch's visions are sometimes fragmentary and garbled because they have been preserved out of order in the manuscript tradition.
7. The Dan River is a northern tributary of the Jordan River. It was named after the city of Dan, the northernmost settlement of ancient Israel located in the shadow of the mountains separating modern Israel and Lebanon.

8. The exact location of Lesya'el is unknown. Sanser is another name for Mount Hermon.

9. In ancient Judaism, cherubim are angelic creatures who served God in Heaven.

AGAINST THE GIANTS

1. Jubilees 4:15–25, 5:1–11, 7:19–28, and 10:1–13, trans. R. H. Charles, in *The Apocrypha and Pseudepigrapha of the Old Testament in English*, 2 vols. (Oxford: Oxford University Press, 1913), vol. 2, pp. 18–20, 24, and 27–28 (modified).

2. This is a play on words in Hebrew, as the root of the name Jared derives from the word for "descend."

3. This passage refers to the visions collected in the Book of Enoch. See the previous entry in this chapter.

A REMEDY AGAINST DEMONIC ATTACKS

1. Translated by Scott G. Bruce from Josephus, *De bello Judaico libri septem* 7.6.3, ed. Edward Caldwell, 2 vols. (Oxford: E Typographeo Academico, 1837), vol. 2, p. 371.

INTIMATE ADVERSARIES

1. Translated by Scott G. Bruce from the Latin Vulgate version of the Gospel of Matthew 4:1–11.

2. Translated by Scott G. Bruce from the Latin Vulgate version of the Gospel of Mark 5:1–20.

3. Translated by Scott G. Bruce from the Latin Vulgate version of the Acts of the Apostles 16:16–19.

IN THE GUISE OF GODS

1. Justin Martyr, 2 *Apologia* 5, trans. Philip Schaff, in *Ante-Nicene Fathers, Volume 1* (New York: Christian Literature, 1885), p. 190 (modified).

THEIR WORK IS THE RUIN OF HUMANKIND

1. Tertullian, *De spectaculis* 25–26, trans. Alexander Roberts and James Donaldson, in *Ante-Nicene Fathers, Volume 3* (New York: Charles Scribner's Sons, 1918), pp. 89–90 (modified).
2. Tertullian, *Apologeticus* 22, trans. Alexander Roberts and James Donaldson, in *Ante-Nicene Fathers, Volume 3* (New York: Charles Scribner's Sons, 1918), pp. 36–37 (modified).

ORIGEN'S FOLLY

1. Jerome, *Epistola* 124, trans. W. H. Fremantle, G. Lewis, and W. G. Martley, in *Nicene and Post-Nicene Fathers, Second Series, Volume 6* (New York: Christian Literature, 1893), pp. 238–44 (modified).
2. Epicurus (341–271 BCE) and other ancient atomist philosophers believed in the plurality of worlds.

DELIVERED FROM FILTHY TYRANNY

1. Augustine, *Concerning the City of God Against the Pagans* 8.14, 16–17, 22, and 9.13, trans. Henry Bettenson (New York: Penguin Books, 1972), pp. 318–19, 321–23, 330, and 360.

THE ANGELS OF TARTARUS

1. Translated by Scott G. Bruce in *The Penguin Book of Hell* (New York: Penguin Books, 2018), pp. 37–44.

THE FALL OF SIMON MAGUS

1. Jacobus de Voragine, *The Golden Legend: Selections*, trans. Christopher Stace (New York: Penguin Books, 1998), pp. 149–51.
2. For the earliest version of this confrontation, as told in the second-century Acts of Peter, see *The Book of Magic: From Antiquity to the Enlightenment*, ed. Brian Copenhaver (New York: Penguin Books, 2015), pp. 219–21.

FROM SAGE TO MAGE

1. Translated by Scott G. Bruce from the Latin Vulgate version of 1 Kings 4:29–34.
2. Josephus, *Antiquities of the Jews* 8.2.5, trans. William Whiston, in *The Works of Josephus* (Hartford, CT: S. S. Scranton, 1905), pp. 248–49 (modified).
3. Vespasian was emperor of Rome from 69 to 79 CE.

ENSLAVED BY SOLOMON'S RING

1. Translated by D. C. Duling in *The Old Testament Pseudepigrapha, Volume 1: Apocalyptic Literature and Testaments*, ed. James H. Charlesworth (London: Doubleday, 1983), pp. 960–87.
2. In premodern folklore, demons and other malevolent spirits have an aversion to iron.
3. Storax is a fragrant balsam from the bark of a tree related to witch hazel commonly used as incense in the ancient world.
4. *Elo-i* means "my God" in Aramaic, perhaps a reference to Jesus's utterance on the cross (Mark 15:34 and Matthew 27:46).
5. Probably a reference to 1 Kings 2:25, Solomon's execution of Adonijah.
6. A clear reference to the demon who identifies himself by the same name in Mark 5:1–13. See pp. 32–33, above.
7. A clear allusion to the crucifixion of Jesus.
8. On the queen's visit to Solomon, see 1 Kings 10:1–13.
9. Psalm 118:22.
10. On these events, see Exodus 4–14.

THE DESERT, A BATTLEFIELD

1. Athanasius, *Vita Antonii* 5, 8, 9–10, 22–23, 35, and 53, trans. Carolinne White, in *Early Christian Lives* (New York: Penguin Books, 1998), pp. 11–12, 14–16, 23–24, 30–31, and 41.

TAMING A HELL-BEAST

1. Jerome, *Vita Hilarii* 23, trans. Carolinne White, in *Early Christian Lives* (New York: Penguin Books, 1998), p. 101.

FRENZIED POSSESSIONS

1. Sulpicius Severus, *Vita Martini* 17, trans. Carolinne White, in *Early Christian Lives* (New York: Penguin Books, 1998), pp. 149–51.

THE ANCIENT GODS ARE FRAUDS

1. Martin of Braga, *De correctione rusticorum*, trans. Brian Copenhaver, in *The Book of Magic: From Antiquity to the Enlightenment* (New York: Penguin Books, 2015), pp. 248–50.

LURKING ON THE THRESHOLD

1. Gregory the Great, *Dialogorum libri quattuor* 1.4, trans. Philip Woodward, in *The Dialogues of Gregory the Great* (London: Philip Lee Warner, 1911), pp. 17–18 (modified).
2. Gregory the Great, *Dialogorum libri quattuor* 3.7, trans. Woodward, pp. 113–16 (modified).

INHABITANTS OF HELL

1. Translated by Scott G. Bruce in *The Penguin Book of the Undead: Fifteen Hundred Years of Supernatural Encounters* (New York: Penguin Books, 2016), pp. 81–84.

ENTRUSTED TO TORMENT YOU

1. Translated by W. Tanner Smoot and Scott G. Bruce from Felix, *Vita sancti Guthlaci* 31–34, ed. Bertram Colgrave, in *Felix's Life of Saint Guthlac* (Cambridge: Cambridge University Press, 1956), pp. 101–11.

2. Compare Psalm 15:8.
3. Psalm 84:7.

QURANIC DEMONOLOGY

1. *The Koran* 34.12–14, 46.29–33, and 72.1–13, trans. N. J. Da-
   wood (New York: Penguin Books, 2015), pp. 428, 505, and 571.

A SHORT HISTORY OF THE JINN

1. *Epistles of the Brethren of Purity* 22.8, trans. Lenn E. Good-
   man and Richard McGregor, in *The Case of the Animals versus
   Man Before the King of the Jinn* (Oxford: Oxford University
   Press, 2009), pp. 131–33 and 42.
2. Idrīs is the Arabic name of the biblical prophet Enoch, who foretold the fall of the rebel angels. See pp. 7–17, above.
3. A mangonel is a kind of catapult.
4. See Qur'an 34:10–14.
5. Bilqīs is the Arabic name for the Queen of Sheba, who visited
   Solomon and bestowed many gifts upon him. See 1 Kings 10:1–
   13 and Qur'an 27:15–45.
6. Compare Qur'an 27:38–40.
7. See Qur'an 72:8–9.
8. Qur'an 72:10.
9. Qur'an 72:1–2.

PRISONS OF THE JINN

1. *The Arabian Nights: Tales of 1001 Nights*, trans. Malcolm C.
   Lyons, 3 vols. (London: Penguin Classics, 2008), vol. 3, pp. 746–56.
2. *The Arabian Nights*, trans. Lyons, vol. 1, pp. 21–24 and 35–36.
3. Qur'an 17:36.
4. *The Arabian Nights*, trans. Lyons, vol. 2, pp. 527–30.

MONKS CONTEMPLATE THE NATURE OF DEMONS

1. Translated by Richard P. H. Greenfield from Michael Psellos [?],
   Concerning Demons, ed. Paul Gautier, in "Le *De daemonibus*

du Pseudo-Psellos," *Revue des études byzantines* 38 (1980): 105–94, at pp. 163–77.

2. The source of the maxim attributed to Antigonos is unknown.

3. The quotation is from Homer, *Iliad* 3.35.

4. On the demon Onoskelis, who appeared to King Solomon as a beautiful woman with the legs of a mule, see pp. 66–67, above.

SAINTS IN PURSUIT OF THE GELLOU

1. Translated by Richard P. H. Greenfield from the anonymous *Life and Conduct of the Saints of Christ Sysinnios and Sysinnodoros, the Brothers of Saint Meletene*, ed. Richard P. H. Greenfield, in "Saint Sisinnios, the Archangel Michael and the Female Demon Gylou: The Typology of the Greek Literary Stories," *Byzantina* 15 (1989): 83–142, at pp. 86–89.

2. Laurentios is a fictional king.

3. The meaning of this cryptic phrase is unclear.

4. See Luke 1:37, quoting Genesis 14:18.

5. In this case, the phylactery is the protective amulet with writing on it that keeps the demon at bay. This story is intended to provide a backstory to and convincing explanation for the effectiveness of written amulets containing the names of Gellou.

6. Translated by Richard P. H. Greenfield from the anonymous *Conjuration of the Archangel against Spirits to be said for a House and over the Sick*, ed. F. Pradel, in *Griechische und südtialienische Gebete, Beschwörungen und Rezepte des Mittelalters* (Giesen: A. Töpelmann, 1907), pp. 275–76.

THE LADY OF THE MOUNTAIN

1. Translated by Richard P. H. Greenfield from the anonymous *Concerning the Beautiful Lady of the Mountains*, ed. Armand Delatte, in *Anecdota Atheniensia, Tome 1: Textes grecs inédits relatifs à l'histoire des religions* (Paris: Édouard Champion, 1927), p. 600.

2. These magical words have no apparent meaning.

LEGENDS OF THE CHILD-EATER

1. John Cuthbert Lawson, *Modern Greek Folklore and Ancient Greek Religion: A Study in Survivals* (Cambridge: Cambridge University Press, 1910), pp. 70–71 and 177–79 (slightly modified).

2. On Leo Allatios's 1645 treatise *On the Beliefs of Some Greeks Today* (*De Graecorum hodie quorundam opinationibus*) and traditions about the Gellou preserved therein, see Karen Hartnup, *"On the Beliefs of the Greeks": Leo Allatios and Popular Orthodoxy* (Leiden: Brill, 2004), pp. 85–172.

A MALICE FORETOLD IN SCRIPTURE

1. Translated by Scott G. Bruce from Caesarius of Heisterbach, *Dialogus miraculorum* 5.1, ed. Joseph Strange, 2 vols. (Cologne: H. Lempertz, 1851), vol. 1, pp. 274–76.

2. Isaiah 14:12.

3. Luke 10:18.

4. Job 1:6.

5. Psalm 109:6.

6. Habakkuk 3:5.

7. Apocalypse 12:7.

8. Ezekiel 28:12–13.

9. Ephesians 2:2.

10. Psalm 74:23.

11. John 8:41 and 44.

12. Job 40:23.

13. 1 Peter 5:8–9.

14. Matthew 25:41.

TUNDALE'S TORMENTORS

1. Translated by Scott G. Bruce in *The Penguin Book of Hell* (New York: Penguin Classics, 2018), pp. 96–101.

2. Compare Matthew 7:13.

DUNSTAN'S TONGS

1. Translated by W. Tanner Smoot and Scott G. Bruce from Osbern of Canterbury, *Vita sancti Dunstani* 14, ed. William Stubbs, in *Memorials of Dunstan, Archbishop of Canterbury* (London: Longman, 1874), pp. 84–85.
2. Mark 9:28.

FROM HOLY HOUND TO DEVIL DOG

1. Translated by Scott G. Bruce from Stephen of Bourbon, *Tractatus de diversis materiis praedicabilibus* 370, ed. A. Lecoy de la Marche, in *Anecdotes historiques, légendes et apologues tirés du recueil inédit d'Étienne de Bourbon, dominicain du XIIIe siècle* (Paris: Librairie Renouard, 1877), pp. 325–28.

PREYING ON THE LAITY

1. Translated by Scott G. Bruce from Caesarius of Heisterbach, *Dialogus miraculorum* 5.2, 5.4, and 5.7, ed. Joseph Strange, 2 vols. (Cologne: H. Lempertz, 1851), vol. 1, pp. 276–78, 279–81, and 287.

THE PSALM-SKIPPER DEMON

1. These five vignettes about the demon Tityvillus have been translated by Scott G. Bruce from the following sources: (*a*) Jacques de Vitry, *Exempla ex sermonibus vulgaribus* 19, ed. Thomas Frederick Crane, in *The Exempla, or Illustrative Stories from the Sermones Vulgares of Jacques de Vitry* (London: Folk-Lore Society, 1890), p. 6; (*b*) Jacques de Vitry, *Exempla ex sermonibus vulgaribus* 239, ed. Crane, in *The Exempla*, p. 100; (*c*) *A Selection of Latin Stories from Manuscripts of the Thirteenth and Fourteenth Centuries*, ed. Thomas Wright (London: Percy Society, 1842), p. 44; (*d*) Caesarius of Heisterbach, *Dialogus miraculorum* 4.9, ed. Joseph Strange, 2 vols. (Cologne: H. Lempertz, 1851), vol. 1, pp. 181; and (*e*) Stephen of Bourbon, *Tractatus de diversis materiis praedicabilibus* 212, ed. A. Lecoy de la Marche, in

Anecdotes historiques, légendes et apologues tirés du recueil inédit d'Étienne de Bourbon, dominicain du XIIIe siècle (Paris: Librairie Renouard, 1877), pp. 184–85.

SATAN'S FAMILY

1. Translated by Scott G. Bruce from *Narrationes aliquot fabulosae* 30, ed. David R. Winter, in *The Llanthony Stories* (Toronto: Pontifical Institute of Mediaeval Studies, 2021), pp. 104–5.
2. Translated by Scott G. Bruce from Jacques de Vitry, *Exempla ex sermonibus vulgaribus* 243, ed. Thomas Frederick Crane, in *The Exempla, or Illustrative Stories from the Sermones Vulgares of Jacques de Vitry* (London: Folk-Lore Society, 1890) p. 102.

THE CRAVEN ANGELS

1. Translated by Benjamin A. Bertrand and Scott G. Bruce from *Navigatio sancti Brendani* 11, ed. Carl Selmer, *Navigatio Sancti Brendani Abbatis from the Early Latin Manuscripts* (Notre Dame, IN: University of Notre Dame Press, 1959), pp. 22–25.
2. Wolfram von Eschenbach, *Parzival* 9 and 16, trans. A. T. Hatto (New York: Penguin Classics, 1980), pp. 232, 240, and 395.
3. Translated by Scott G. Bruce in *The Penguin Book of Hell* (New York: Penguin Classics, 2018), pp. 141–43 (*Inferno*, Canto 3, lines 16–51).

APES OF GOD

1. John Gaule, *Select Cases of Conscience Touching Witches and Witchcrafts* (London: W. Wilson, 1646), pp. 68–69.

A COVENANT OF DEATH

1. Translated by Scott G. Bruce from Jacobus de Voragine, *Legenda Aurea* 131, ed. T. Graesse, in *Jacobi a Voragine, Legenda Aurea*, 2nd ed. (Leipzig: Libraria Arnoldiana, 1881), pp. 593–94.

A FAUSTIAN BARGAIN

1. *The History of the Damnable Life and Deserved Death of Doctor John Faustus 1592*, ed. William Rose (London: George Routledge and Sons, 1925), pp. 67–79.
2. A fathom is six feet in length.
3. "Crisam" is an English rendering of the Greek word *chrisma*, the oil used for anointing.
4. The Latin phrase "O homo, fuge!" means "Flee, O man!"

THOU PROFOUNDEST HELL
RECEIVE THY NEW POSSESSOR

1. John Milton, *Paradise Lost: A Poem in Twelve Books*, 2nd ed. (London: S. Simmons, 1674), pp. 3–5 (Book 1, lines 33–83).
2. Matthew 10:25; Mark 3:22; and Luke 11:15.
3. Milton, *Paradise Lost*, pp. 11–19 (Book 1, lines 314–507 and 522–73).
4. Amram's son was Moses. For what follows, see Exodus 10:12–15.
5. A reference to the barbarian peoples who invaded the Roman Empire in the early fifth century.
6. Compare Revelation 20:11–15.
7. A reference to fallen angels taking the names of pagan gods. See pp. 108–10, above.
8. Moloch was a Canaanite god associated with child sacrifice.
9. Chemosh was a Moabite diety. See 1 Kings 11:7.
10. Ezekiel 8:14.
11. Exodus 32:1–20.
12. The rebel king is Jeroboam. See 1 Kings 12:28–30.
13. Milton, *Paradise Lost*, pp. 20 and 22–26 (Book 1, lines 615–21 and 663–799).

HYMNS AGAINST DEMONS AND SORCERERS

1. *The Rig Veda* 7.102, trans. Wendy Doniger (New York: Penguin Books, 2004), pp. 293 and 295.

THE SERPENT-KING ZAHHAK

1. Abolqasem Ferdowsi, *Shahnameh: The Persian Book of Kings*, trans. Dick Davis (New York: Penguin Books, 2016), pp. 11 and 13–14.

FATAL FOX-GIRLS AND OTHER PERILS

1. Pu Songling, *Strange Tales from a Chinese Studio*, trans. John Minford (New York: Penguin Books, 2006), pp. 143 and 145–49.
2. Pu Songling, *Strange Tales*, trans. Minford, pp. 95 and 97.
3. Pu Songling, *Strange Tales*, trans. Minford, pp. 18 and 20–22.
4. Pu Songling, *Strange Tales*, trans. Minford, pp. 126–27 and 129–30.

THE AIR'S EMBRACE

1. Augustine, *Concerning the City of God Against the Pagans* 15.23, trans. Henry Bettenson (New York: Penguin Books, 1972), pp. 637–38.
2. Augustine, *Concerning the City of God* 3.5, trans. Bettenson, pp. 92–93.
3. Psalm 104:4.
4. See, for example, Genesis 10:1–22 and Judges 6:12–22.
5. Silvanus was an agricultural deity, while Pan was a pastoral god identified with the Roman Faunus.

LASCIVIOUS SPIRITS

1. Translated by Scott G. Bruce from Caesarius of Heisterbach, *Dialogus miraculorum* 3.7–12, ed. Joseph Strange, 2 vols. (Cologne: H. Lempertz, 1851), vol. 1, pp. 120–24.

DEMON SEED

1. Heinrich Kraemer, *Malleus maleficarum*, Part II, Qn. 1, Ch. 4, trans. Montague Summers (London: John Rodker, 1928), pp. 109–14.
2. Nicolas Rémy, *Demonolatry* 1.6, trans. E. A. Ashwin (London: John Rodker, 1930), pp. 11–14.
3. Plutarch (ca. 46–ca. 120 CE) composed many biographies of notable Greeks and Romans, including an account of the life of Numa, the legendary second king of Rome.
4. Peter Paludanus (ca. 1275–1342) was a thirteenth-century prelate who served as the Latin Patriarch of Jerusalem, while Martin of Arles (ca. 1451–1521) was a canon and archdeacon who wrote against witches active in the Pyrenees.
5. Basil of Caesarea (330–78) was an influential theologian who was well-known in the western tradition for his teachings about Christian asceticism.
6. Alessandro Alessandri (1461–1523) was an Italian lawyer and humanist.
7. Most likely Gerolamo Cardano (1501–76), a prolific Renaissance scientist.
8. Averroës (1126–98) was a medieval Muslim philosopher active in Spain, while Albertus Magnus (ca. 1200–1280) was a learned Dominican friar in Germany.

A WARNING FOR MARRIED WOMEN

1. *The English and Scottish Popular Ballads, Part VIII*, ed. Francis James Child (Boston: Houghton, Mifflin, 1882), pp. 366–67 (no. 243E: The Daemon Lover).

THE HUNTER BECOMES THE HUNTED

1. Walter Scott, "Glenfinlas," in *The Poetical Works of Sir Walter Scott* (Boston: Phillips, Sampson, 1850), pp. 516–20.

FROZEN HEARTS

1. *The Jesuit Relations and Allied Documents: Travels and Explorations of the Jesuit Missionaries in New France 1610–1791, Volume XLVI (Lower Canada, Ottawas, Canadian Interior, 1659–1661)*, ed. Reuben Gold Thwaites (Cleveland: Burrows Brothers, 1899), pp. 264–65.
2. Paul Kane, *Wanderings of an Artist among the Indians of North America* (London: Longman, Brown, Green, Longmans, and Roberts, 1859), pp. 58–60.
3. Henry Youle Hind, *Explorations in the Interior of the Labrador Peninsula*, 2 vols. (London: Longman, Green, Longman, Roberts, and Green, 1863), vol. 1, pp. 58–59.
4. William W. Canfield, *The Legends of the Iroquois Told by "The Cornplanter"* (New York: A. Wessels, 1902), pp. 125–26.

A DARK HUNTSMAN ON THE MOORS

1. Sabine Baring-Gould, *A Book of the West, Volume 1: Devon* (London: Methuen, 1899), pp. 183–84.

A DEMON DRAWN FROM LIFE

1. M. R. James, "Canon Alberic's Scrap-Book," in *Ghost-Stories of an Antiquary* (London: Edward Arnold, 1905), pp. 3–28, at pp. 10–28.
2. A missal is a common book that contains the services for the Christian mass over the course of a year.
3. An antiphoner is another common liturgical book that contains the chants known as antiphons sung by the choir during the church service.
4. Uncial is a kind of Latin script employed by scribes between the fourth and eighth centuries.
5. Papias (ca. 60–ca. 130 CE) was an obscure early Christian bishop, whose writings are known to us only through quotations by later authors.
6. *Old St. Paul's: A Tale of the Plague and the Fire* was the name of a novel written by William Harrison Ainsworth, which was

serialized in 1841. It included a chapter in which a seventeenth-century canon claims to have used astrological calculations to discover treasure hidden beneath St. Paul's Cathedral.

7. This French phrase translates as "Twice I have seen him; a thousand times have I felt his presence."

8. Psalm 91.

9. Ecclesiasticus 39:28.

10. Isaiah 34:14.

ALL I WANT'S MY TAILYPO

1. Adapted and rendered into modern English by Scott G. Bruce from the oral account of Mr. Richard Wyche (1867–1930) printed in John Harrington Cox, "Negro Tales from West Virginia," *Journal of American Folklore* 47 (1934): 341–57, at 341–42.

NIGHT-GAUNTS

1. H. P. Lovecraft, "Night-Gaunts," *Weird Tales* (December 1939), p. 59.

Credits

Index

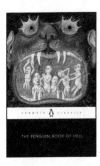

THE PENGUIN BOOK OF MERMAIDS

Edited by Cristina Bacchilega and Marie Alohalani Brown

Among the oldest and most popular mythical beings, merfolk have captured the imagination long before Ariel sold her voice to a sea witch in *The Little Mermaid*. *The Penguin Book of Mermaids* is a treasury of tales showing us how public perceptions of this popular mythical hybrid illuminate issues of spirituality, ecology, and sexuality.

THE PENGUIN BOOK OF EXORCISMS

Edited by Joseph P. Laycock

Levitation. Speaking in tongues. A hateful, glowing stare. The signs of spirit possession have been documented for thousands of years and across religions and cultures. *The Penguin Book of Exorcisms* brings together the most astonishing accounts. Fifty-seven percent of Americans profess to believe in demonic possession; after reading this book, you may too.